Josep Maria de Sagarra

PRIVATE LIFE

Translated from Catalan by Mary Ann Newman

archipelago books

Copyright © Josep Maria de Sagarra, 1932
Originally published as *Vida Privada* by Llibreria Catalònia, 1932, Barcelona
English translation copyright © Mary Ann Newman, 2015
First Archipelago Books edition, 2015

Library of Congress Cataloging-in-Publication Data
Sagarra, Josep Maria de, 1894-1961.
[Vida privada. English]
Private life : a novel / Josep Maria de Sagarra ; translated from
Catalan by Mary Ann Newman. -- First Archipelago Books edition
pages cm
ISBN 978-0-914671-26-8 (paperback)
I. Title.
PC3941.S3V513 2015
849'.9352--dc23
2015019288

Archipelago Books
232 Third Street, Suite A111
Brooklyn, NY 11215
www.archipelagobooks.org

Distributed by Penguin Random House
www.penguinrandomhouse.com

cover art by Ramon Casas i Carbó courtesy of the Museu de Montserrat

This publication was made possible with support from the Institut Ramon Llull,
Lannan Foundation, the New York State Council on the Arts, a state agency, and
the New York City Department of Cultural Affairs.

PRINTED IN THE UNITED STATES OF AMERICA

PRIVATE LIFE

A NOVEL

Part I

HIS EYELIDS OPENED with an almost imperceptible click, as if they had been sealed shut by earlier contact with tears and smoke, or by the irritated secretions that come from reading too long under a dim light.

As his pupils struggled to make something out, he rubbed his eyelashes. He flicked at them rapidly, using the pinky finger of his right hand much like a comb. All he could see was a vague panorama of limp, watery shadows, the kind of scene a man blinded by daylight might perceive on entering an aquarium. Against this murky background, a long vaporous blade the color of crushed oranges on the piers came increasingly into focus. It was a beam of light stealing through the slats of the shutters only to sour in the dense atmosphere of the room.

It must have been about four-thirty in the afternoon. Frederic de Lloberola, the man with the aching eyelids, had awakened on his own. No one had called him, no sounds had startled him. His nerves had had their fill of sleep. They had sapped to the dregs a colorless, absurd dream, the kind that leaves hardly a trace of its plot when you awaken. The kind you have when nothing is going on in your life.

Frederic spent no more than eight seconds surfacing into reality.

On the worn tile floor lay items of his clothing, embarrassed at their own disorder, entangled with chiffon stockings and a woman's deflated and, frankly dirty, cotton knit nightgown.

All four chairs were piled with her things. The little vanity was weighted down with miniature bottles, powder cases, tweezers and scissors, and the open armoire resembled a funeral procession. The dresses and coats on the hangers, lively with bright colors and appliqués, brought to mind a series of too-thin carnival princesses who had been decapitated and pierced through the trachea with a hook. Atop the armoire rested empty dust-coated hatboxes, keeping company with a stuffed dog. The dog had been entrusted to an inept taxidermist who had stuffed it deplorably, leaving all the stitches visible between the hairs on its moth-eaten belly. His mistress had adorned the dog's neck with an old-fashioned garter from which three minuscule roses peeped out, like three drops of blood.

Frederic began to notice the smells in the close chamber. One single odor, of spent tobacco, dominated like a bitter medicine.

The trapped smoke impregnated the sheets and Frederic's skin, mingling with traces of a store-bought cologne and all the vapors produced in the abandon of two bodies, which the night maliciously stores up to proffer mercilessly when the storm has passed and sleep has placed a wall of incomprehension between a somnolence of expectant contacts and a livid, skeptical, and unaroused awakening.

To combat the assault of the odors outside and the bad taste inside his mouth, Frederic stretched out his arm and picked up his cigarette lighter and a Camel from the night table. Only two draws were necessary; the experiment with a fresh cigarette was fruitless.

Frederic ran his fingers over the pink fabric of the pillow that lay beside his own, a slightly damp fabric impregnated with smelly oils. His fingers lingered over the fabric, reposing dumbly, his fingernails scratching out a faint sound on the relief of the embroidered initials: R...T...R...T...Ah, yes, Rosa Trènor. His lips said the name softly, repeating it mechanically...A little grease, a little dampness remained behind on her pillow, along with the hollow of her head. But anything she might have left behind of her dreams had already died a cold death. Frozen, perhaps poisoned, by the smoke and breath of this man, Frederic, alone in bed since she had closed the door, sleeping his brutal, inconsiderate, insatiable sleep, turbulent with hydrochloric acid.

Frederic looked at the clock in fear. In this type of situation, verifying the exact time always provokes a certain panic; one needs a start to face reality. And, yes, it was four-thirty in the afternoon.

Frederic wondered why he had let himself go, why he had allowed this surrender. What had happened was understandable. Frederic had been biding his time for fifteen years. Ever since his breakup with Rosa, he had watched the woman's evolution from afar with disdain and apparent coldness. Their breakup had been obligatory at the time of his marriage; the truth be told, he had maintained his relationship with the woman out of vanity. It was not that Rosa was so terribly common, as Frederic's friends thought. But he saw nothing more in her than intimacy with a woman with whom he had a certain history and who could not be classified in the same category as other kept women.

What Frederic appreciated in Rosa was her "class"; he had never appreciated all the woman's personal characteristics while their bond lasted, before his marriage. Even worse, with absolute insensitivity he had carried on affairs as ephemeral as suited his needs with other women, ladies of the trade. Never in his experience of love, whether the woman in question was Rosa or one of the others, had he perceived the slightest difference among them, or anything that might lend a touch of lyricism to the basic physiology of the act.

Perhaps the very vanity that led Frederic to maintain his scandalous friendship with Rosa Trènor contained a certain taste for anarchy, a feeling of rebellion against the conventions of his own class, even if such a feeling was baseless, because Frederic, like all the Lloberolas, was weak and cowardly, and his youth had been absolutely lacking in imagination.

If Frederic had taken an anonymous woman of unsuitable extraction for his lover, he would have been no different from any other Lloberola. Perhaps the only opportunity life had offered him to be a bit original was to become the lover of Rosa Trènor, a woman who had been on a first-name basis with his own cousins, who might even have prepared for first communion with them or slept in the bed next to them at boarding school.

We have already said that in the period preceding his marriage Frederic's experiences of love had not gone beyond the most elementary physiology. In the intimacy of love, Frederic was the kind of man who didn't show the least concern for the female element involved. A woman, for him, was just an inevitable accessory to the complete satisfaction of his instincts. Exceedingly selfish and lacking in the habit of reflection, incapable of the slightest critical thought, and never having observed the need to compare his own sensations with those of others, the truth is that, though he had had dealings with and had come to know quite a number of women, Frederic, in fact, did not have the slightest understanding of what a woman was.

With marriage, though, things changed completely. The very thing he didn't have the intuition to divine, and would never have taken the trouble to discover, began to come into being as his married life progressed and little by little took shape in Frederic's consciousness. As a single woman, Maria Carreres had been exciting. Frederic became accustomed to her love, in those moments of tender and tearful rapture that are the domain of garden-variety egotists. With all his banality and moral inconsistency, Frederic had a vague idea of what it was to be a gentleman, and even a few genuine, perhaps atavistic, gentlemanly instincts. So, his gentlemanly façade accepted by everyone, Frederic reached the state of matrimony.

From the very first, though, Maria Carreres showed a detachment, perhaps even a revulsion, toward those moments of shadow and contact in which the nervous and angelic battle of the instincts, of shame and the beast, is fought. Frederic had struck a bad sexual bargain. Maria Carreres had one of those indifferent and inhospitable physiologies that react with the chill of a cemetery and provoke virile dissatisfaction. Frederic bore his disappointment with dignity. He let days and months go by, hoping for a possible solution to his conjugal drama. But after their first son was born, the situation took a turn for the worse. It was then that Frederic realized that women's sexuality was a more heterogeneous item than he had imagined. Finding himself tied to a person insufficient to his needs, to whom he had intended to offer absolute fidelity, little by little he began to find the idea of such fidelity odious. Frederic took to chancing afternoon adventures that could not compromise him or complicate his life in any way.

Frederic found himself again through these adventures; he found the lost taste for love, as he understood it. And these small evasions brought him vague reminiscences – occasionally precise memories – of what had been his greatest happiness in erotic affairs, his relations with Rosa Trènor.

Six years into his marriage, Rosa had become an obsession for him, but if indeed Frederic was a man of extremely malleable conscience, he was also spineless. He was afraid of his wife, afraid of her name, afraid of her father's white moustaches, and even afraid of the last button on her father's shirt that dug into the flesh on his neck. The thought of initiating the slightest negotiation with his former girlfriend produced an understandable alarm in him, because Rosa Trènor, even supposing she would have anything to do with Frederic, would not be one of those inconsequential afternoon trysts. Frederic feared, correctly, that taking up with her again would be his perdition. What's more, the years had also gone by for Rosa Trènor. Most likely the woman he had known would have undergone pronounced evolutions in the tenuous ramifications of her nervous system, and the fragrance of Rosa Trènor's heart would be for him like the disconcerting perfume of a boat that has sailed over many seas, picking up the contradictory resonances of all the ports where it has berthed.

Frederic spent fifteen years mulling over these questions. What gullies must Frederic Lloberola's soul have fathomed to arrive at the spent air of that chamber, facing the glass eyes of a desiccated dog with a garter around its neck?

FOR MONTHS NOW Frederic and Rosa Trènor had been eyeing each other at the bar of the Hotel Colón. Penetrating the discipline she imposed with mascara, he had perceived a gaze that was neither indifferent nor ill-disposed. Seen from a distance, her make-up applied with severity, his former lover's skin still had its effect. Frederic knew from his friends that Rosa's situation was dire. She had lost any trace of regular patronage, and only her arts – praised by many who had had dealings with her – and the imperative of the air a woman who has been very beautiful never entirely loses, allowed Rosa Trènor, pushing forty, to risk still playing the role of a lady in the theater of love, retaining her dignity under the benign deference of the half-light.

The habitués and professionals of the demimonde knew Rosa Trènor by heart, and her presence or the memory of it elicited merciless commentaries. Still, from time to time, at her table, in the wee hours of the night or, if you will, in the first hours of the dawn, some gentleman of good intentions, fortified with a relative enthusiasm, would approach the florists of the most effervescent cabarets to choose and purchase, without haggling, the best bouquet of camellias for Rosa Trènor. One of those men who drink in moderation and do not entirely lose all respect at the sight of painted lips. Those admirable gentlemen, generally the object of ridicule in the view of rowdy and raucous youth, who have the distinction of considering that a woman is never, not even in her saddest condition, a beast inferior to a man, who can be brutalized as if she had no soul.

One of Frederic's most loyal friends, Robert Xuclà, whom everyone knew as Bobby Xuclà – and this pretentious and somewhat gigoloesque name of Bobby was somewhat laughable as applied to a middle-aged bachelor with thinning hair, short of leg and large of girth, in whom all the most inoffensive and homely Barcelona essences came together – was the kind soul who acted as the intermediary between Frederic and Rosa Trènor.

In part because of her brilliant past, and a kind of cynical and offhanded way of behaving, proper to the aristocracy, but even more because of her taste for reading and penchant for argument, Rosa's prestige as a superior woman was acknowledged among the vaporous clan of kept women who could flaunt their diamonds and even dump a five-star gent with relative impunity. One of these vamps was Mado, Bobby's erstwhile girlfriend. Not that Bobby had the exclusive; Mado was a girl whose hospitality was luscious, inconstant, ephemeral, and as absolutely lacking in intelligence as a branch of lilac. Fidelity, for Mado, was just as impossible as wearing garters attached to a girdle. Whenever she had tried to put on such garters she had had to give up in the attempt, because they made her feel faint. This is why Mado was constantly pulling up her stockings, a peculiarity that lent her a rather lewd charm, of the kind seen in ports and sailors' taverns.

Though Mado devoted every evening to humiliating Bobby, he was an understanding fellow, and even as he entered his girlfriend's apartment, he would often wear the polite and somewhat beleaguered air of a man who is afraid he's not welcome.

Mado's little apartment was the place Rosa Trènor favored whenever she felt the irresistible desire to exercise her spiritual ascendancy. Even though Mado loved to deflate, denigrate, and tell horrible stories about Rosa Trènor, she held her in great esteem. More than once the kindness and good heart of Mado or some other girl had got Rosa out of a jam, and whenever she had received a favor from one of those young women, Rosa Trènor would put on such dignified airs and affect such grande dame simpers that no one could ever have doubted that it was precisely Rosa Trènor who had done the favor and was enjoying her own generosity.

Through Mado and Bobby, Frederic was gathering ideas about Rosa Trènor's soft spots. Once Bobby had half-dragged him over to Rosa's table, but Frederic had resisted. Under no circumstances did he want this event to take place in public. One of the characteristics of Frederic's insignificance was that he thought of himself as a sort of central character on whom all eyes converged.

Other times Bobby had tried to bring them face to face, because Frederic was dying of anticipation, but the circumstances had not quite been ripe.

News had been reaching Bobby about Frederic's irregular situation and his family disasters, but even though their friendship was longstanding, he behaved with the utmost discretion in this regard. Despite the confidence Bobby had always inspired in him, and unwilling, in the way of the Lloberolas, to surrender his lordly airs, Frederic had never said so much as half a word to his friend about what he called "unpleasant" things.

Frederic could tell Bobby about some despicable thing he had done, or reveal an intimate detail about his wife, with the crudity, vulgarity, or ferocity of a feudal lord; he could go on at length with the most boorish remarks about certain things of a physiological nature pertaining to his own person. But never, among all the sad confidences he had entrusted to Bobby, had Frederic told him that his father had mortgaged such-and-such a property or that he himself had been obliged to pawn his wife's jewels.

And, once Frederic had made up his mind, when the circumstances were ripe for the encounter with Rosa Trènor, he had also hidden the "unpleasant" cause, the immediate and determining factor of his decision, from Bobby. Even though it was, in fact, an extremely unexceptional event. In the preceding years the economic disarray of Frederic and his wife had reached scandalous proportions. Everyone was aware of the situation both Frederic and his father faced. Everyone knew that the Lloberolas had had to sell off a great deal, and curtail their expenses. But Frederic was not about to relinquish his histrionic streak; he had covered things up any way he could, and at the point where this story begins, he was facing the threat of a loan about to come due. It was a personal credit extended to him without an underwriter. Frederic could not make the payment. There had been talk of an extension, but this would not be possible without his father's guarantee. Naturally, Frederic was incapable of disavowing his signature or risking the consequences of non-payment. But horrible as these things seemed to him, the interview with his father filled him with even greater dread. The amount in question was considerable enough to produce scenes Frederic had no stomach for.

Worries about money had been the dyspepsia of his entire life, but at that point they had become acute. Frederic had been holding on for a long time; for the first time the possibility arose of not holding on, nor wanting to hold on, nor making the slightest effort to hold on.

It didn't faze Frederic to spin out of control, to plunge into the mud with one foot now that he was mired in the mud with the other, to combine economic disgrace with a daring, glaring fling, or to resolve with weepy, theatrical cynicism what a genuine person would resolve with humility.

The circumstances were ripe. Frederic wanted twenty-four hours of oblivion, or twenty-four hours to hide his head in the sand like an ostrich. One day far from his family and from the overdue promissory note.

It was for all these reasons that Frederic asked Bobby to go with him to Mado's house, where he was sure to run into Rosa Trènor.

And the day after that decision, stretched out between the sheets, mechanically interrogating the stuffed dog with his gaze and once again lightly running his fingernails over the initials on the pillow, he started reconstructing the scenes of the previous night.

———·——·——

AT HALF PAST ELEVEN, he and Bobby were on their way up the stairs. Mado herself opened the door; she was wearing colonial blue and silver striped pajamas. The satin pajama fabric strained over her breasts, which resembled two boxes of bonbons of the kind you would have seen at the turn of the century on top of the piano of a family of modest means. Frederic took much more notice of Mado's pectoral ploy than of the explosive kiss the young woman planted on Bobby's lips, forcing up his nostrils the dregs of smoke that clung to her gums. Frederic ran the nail of Mado's pinky finger over his lips, and with an almost musical peal of laughter she pushed the two men into the dining room.

Mado's living room contained the expectation produced by sudden twists of fate; gambling dilated the eyes, producing stinging and natural tears, and causing mascara to be forgotten. Tics, cold stomachs, or cold feet, and a displacement of the jaw and nasal creases disturbed the equilibrium of the features. In such a place, when things were going badly for someone, an atavistic simian air left its bold imprint on the faces there.

Among the players was Reina, a very young girl with platinum hair, her back exposed to below her kidneys, revealing a stretch of bloodless whitish muscles molded into the casing of a more vegetal and decorative skin.

Reina was Mado's best friend, and there were those who attributed certain predilections to them, because Reina treated the young men who surrounded her as if she always had a fissure ready through which the eel of her soul could make its escape.

When it came time to play cards, Reina's concentration breached the limits of the most elementary manners: she allowed no jokes, her extremely forced smile revealed teeth with an excessive secretion of saliva, produced by her state of nerves, not unlike that of a group of hyenas that have convened upon the cemetery. More superstitious than the others, when Reina was dealt a card, before looking at it she would press down on it with her index finger until it hurt, leaving behind the slight imprint of her nail. Suspicious minds attributed this to a wish to mark the cards, but this was an entirely false accusation, because Reina had no intention of cheating when she did this. It was a superstitious quirk that she combined compulsively with lifting her chin and staring off into the distance. At moments like this Reina's eyes took on the alluring artificial brilliance of fake gemstones. As Frederic walked into the dining room, propelled by Mado's laughter, the first thing his eyes fell upon was that stare. Frederic, who was acquainted with Mado and the other girls in the game, felt repelled by those eyes, which appeared to him as a new and hostile thing. His first reaction was to fall back, not to continue forward toward the encounter with Rosa Trènor. Reina's involuntary gaze, which bore no ill will toward Frederic, had cooled the temperature of his audacity, and Frederic had felt like a coward again; but before he could formulate any kind of decision, Rosa Trènor's small, plump hand was covering Frederic's lips, and he felt bound by the warm, dry silk of that hand.

In Mado's living room, Rosa abstained from any complicated toilette; she was wearing a simple dress topped by a cherry-colored sweater; the same clothes she would have worn at home, on a winter's night, with a migraine or the vague beginnings of a cold. Her lack of concern for clothing was considered a characteristic of good taste; when the time came to say good-bye, Rosa enveloped her flesh and the worn clothing that covered it in a great beaver coat, a bit moth-eaten and the worse for wear, with the tender good humor of a person who was going off to rest with no intention of giving anyone cause for alarm.

When Rosa paid this kind of visit to the girls, she carried with her an enormous snakeskin bag, which she opened with the unctuous sigh of a philanthropist of popular lore ready to hand out bread and cheese to a band of raggedy children. In point of fact, Rosa didn't hand out anything she carried in the bag; she would rummage around inside and extract skeins of multicolored wool and a sweater she had just started. Mixed in with that bit of feminine handiwork, Rosa had books, papers, notebooks, a little bottle of peppermint, the keys to her house, and an entire battery of rouges, mirrors, compacts, and combs. Rosa Trènor's bag was one of her most personal belongings. She talked about "her" bag in the same way that a hairdresser with fantasies talks about "his" hair-growing elixir.

When Rosa started weaving her web, she would tantalize her admirers with hints and meaningful glances. She would attribute a lie she had just read in a trashy novel to some fashionable fellow – someone from "her world" as she put it – far-removed from the present company of kept women and famous for his wife's fur coats and infidelities. Rosa had a special gift for twisting gossip and for making tacky, trashy comments without altering her tone of voice or the monotonous movement of her lips. Sometimes her conversation meandered onto paths of tenderness and morality, and she affected dismay at something some honorable gentlemen had told her about a lady of the finest reputation.

Rosa's natural grace consisted of a sort of careless, authentic Barcelona flair that she, the daughter of a notary, born in the old city center, had not entirely managed to lose despite the bastardization of her contacts and the coming apart of her life.

When the time came to shuffle the cards, Rosa left off pontificating and set to trying her luck, in the flaccid, voracious way of a leech sucking blood from bruised flesh. On those occasions, Rosa would produce a discreet amount of money and lay her bet with the yellowish grimace characteristic of people with kidney problems. In general, Rosa didn't lose much, but when she did, her sweater turned a deeper red, by contrast, because all the rouge on Rosa's cheeks was not enough to veil her pallor.

When gambling, the disinterested feelings those bosom friends affected towards one another turned into a miserly and ferocious conduct known only in the world of insects.

The presence of men neutralized the corrosive tension of the game. Which didn't mean that some of them, like the insignificant and tubercular Baró de Foixà, did not apply an intricate technique to their wagering, or were not intransigent and unwilling to entertain any kind of irony when their money was at stake. The Baró de Foixà was very wealthy and more than once he had settled a baccarat debt by appropriating a diamond or taking a mink coat to the pawnshop himself, taking no notice of the ladies' tears or the coarse comments of the gentlemen regarding his sanctimonious regard for the letter of the law. There were those who recalled that the baron had once lost the favors of a girl he was head over heels in love with, because of his insistence on collecting an insignificant gambling debt from her.

Rosa Trènor greeted Frederic with a smile of indifference, not looking up from her cards, as if they had been chatting no more than a half hour before. Anyone familiar with Rosa would not have seen anything unusual in her attitude, knowing as they did how she liked to appear eccentric and disconcert her audience.

Even though Rosa had a vague notion of the precarious situation of her ex-lover, she still hoped that Frederic might once again turn out to be a solution. Rosa believed that though Frederic's fortune was not, by a long shot, what it used to be, he could still not be mistaken by any means for a pauper, and his sexuality, a bit weaker and more disenchanted with age, might manifest itself with a drop of sickly tenderness, which Rosa could use to her advantage. Frederic's possibilities would be more generous, he would abandon himself with fewer conditions and, knowing him as she did, Rosa would be able to administer his sentimentalism more profitably than a more tender and inexperienced body could.

In those days Rosa's head was ruled by her stomach. In the theater of love she would waste no time on the build-up, heading straight for the "bedroom scene." And here, though Rosa could not wield the weapons she had had at eighteen, she had perfected a technique of turning on and off the switch of pathos, which made her a dangerous woman for a certain type of man. Out of both vanity and the instinct for survival Rosa most definitely subscribed to the rustic aphorism, "The old hen makes the best soup."

The game of baccarat went on without a hitch with Frederic and Bobby's contributions; the bets got heftier amidst the electrical vibration of jaws and eye sockets. The women ended up winning, as always, except for Mado, who thought it wasn't right for the hostess to win all the time, and paid off her losses from Bobby's wallet. Besides the beverages, Mado offered her friends a bit of caviar sprinkled on salted crackers, which everyone accepted except Rosa Trènor. With her pretensions to being an old-fashioned grand dame, Rosa thought caviar was awful; she betook herself to the kitchen to prepare some toast rubbed with tomato pulp, which she tore into voraciously with an intentionally unsophisticated abandon.

When the time came to retire, Bobby winked at Frederic, and Rosa Trènor showed no desire to envelop herself in her beaver coat.

Mado said she was a little dizzy, and Reina offered to stay and sleep with her. Understanding as always, Bobby bade his lady friend farewell with the usual explosive kisses, and the group headed down the stairs, muffling their laughter so as not to scandalize the neighbors. The group was Bobby, Marta, Gisèle, the Baró de Foixà, Ernest Montagut and Pep Arnau, the youngest son of the Comte de Tabartet, a boy as fat and innocent as a pig, who never got beyond the door of his lady friends' domiciles.

Rosa Trènor had said that she would stay another half hour or so to finish teaching Mado the stitch for her sweater, and everyone found it perfectly natural that Frederic should take the stopper out of a crystal bottle and serve himself a respectable dose of cognac without saying goodbye to anyone.

Then Mado and Reina went into Mado's bedroom, not before Mado had told Rosa Trènor, "Make yourselves at home, don't mind us." On a divan upholstered with silk the color of a turtle dove's breast, before the half-drunk glasses, the scattered cards, and the occasional inert grain of caviar that had leapt to its death on the tablecloth out of repugnance at dying between Bobby's teeth, Rosa Trènor and Frederic de Lloberola initiated their dialogue.

After a few exploratory words from Frederic, consisting only of polite remarks and a few inoffensive *double-entendres* to see how she would react and to try to gain the upper hand, Rosa Trènor, in a vague and apparently cold way, started talking in the blasé tone of "her milieu."

"Yes, frankly, it was a bit of a surprise…"

Later, in response to an unfortunate question from Frederic,

"Rancor? No, I feel no rancor towards you…"

Silence, a great sigh from Rosa, a fluttering of eyelashes and a natural smile:

"But, now that we've said our hellos and we're friends again…You know what I think? I think you should go home…As for me…"

Frederic began to harbor the terrible suspicion that Rosa Trènor was being sincere. He tried another tack:

"That's the best thing we could do."

Fearing this was too strong, though, he added:

"But stop, enough pretending. I wanted to talk with you because I need you…"

At that point Rosa let out a raucous and offensive peal of laughter. Frederic flinched, but he had no choice but to swallow it. Once Rosa stopped laughing, her voice became sweeter:

"You need me, Frederic? Now you realize it?…After…how long has it been?"

Never a good actor, Frederic went for this question like a ton of bricks, and Rosa coquettishly covered his mouth before he could answer:

"No, no! Don't tell me how long…; it's rude to talk about age. But, still, it's been a while, eh? So I guess it's true that…you really do need me…"

With a maternal air, Rosa knit her brow in mock pity. Smiling, Frederic said:

"Do I look…so bad to you?"

Rosa ran her fingers over his shirt and the knot in his tie and straightened his thinning hair. Like a caged rabbit, Frederic let her do it, and Rosa took a good look at him, cocking her head like a photographer:

"No, you don't look bad to me at all. But you can be sure I wouldn't stand for a tie like the one you're wearing...And now that I think of it, I need you, too, but not for what you think...I need to talk with you about Eugènia D. Yes, yes, your wife's cousin; you must have heard about it..."

Frederic opened his eyes wide in ignorance. Rosa thought it would be good to stretch the situation out and went back to her foul talk again:

"The other night at the Grill it was all people were talking about. Now, the worst gossips were a couple of drunken urchins like Mado and Kity – who's running around with that fool, Bonsoms, the eye doctor – wenches whose hands still smell of dishwater."

It occurred to Frederic, who found the affectation of brazen speech in a woman to be offensive, that one way out would be to pretend that Rosa's vocabulary was appealing to him:

"Rosa, you're incredible. When I hear you talk...I just can't believe..."

"What is it you can't believe?"

"You make me feel younger by the minute!"

"Oh! I've changed a great deal since we've been out of touch. I've become more 'refined'...But don't you dare make fun of me!

Tell me, what have you heard about Eugènia D…? Is it true about the diamond?"

Frederic realized, with some annoyance, that his praise had not had the effect he was hoping for, so, dropping the pretense, he said brusquely:

"That's none of my business. I don't keep track of my wife's relatives. As you can imagine, I haven't come here to talk about my family."

Rosa was radiant. Her conversation was annoying Frederic. She went on without batting an eye:

"Oh, aren't you the babe in arms. Even a dope like Bobby who never catches on to anything knows all about it, and it turns out you…Well, you needn't worry. I don't give a hoot, I just mentioned it to pass the time. When push comes to shove, you know very well I won't be a penny richer or poorer if one of your cousins is giving her jewels away to some piece of trash from the Bataclan music hall."

Rosa's chatter about his cousin and the call girl from the Bataclan was of the most indecent and uncharitable kind; Frederic was getting nervous. Rosa didn't let up and, with a condescension that suggested that the interested party was in fact Frederic, she added:

"What's more, if you must know…That's exactly what I said yesterday to those little snipes: as long as they leave me out of it… Because as you well know, I've never enjoyed this kind of rubbish…"

Rosa Trènor knew through Bobby and other friends of Frederic's that Eugènia D. was his wife's dearest friend, and that, beyond their blood relationship, there was a genuine closeness and affection. She was certain that Frederic would find these conjectures – absolutely false, in point of fact – about some supposed depravity on the part of Eugènia D. offensive. Realizing he had no other recourse, and simply to have something to say about Rosa Trènor's remark regarding "this kind of rubbish," Frederic responded in a completely idiotic tone:

"How old-fashioned you are!"

He might just as well have said, "How rude you are!" or "What a piece of work you are!" Rosa Trènor pretended not to have caught Frederic's tone, and quickly responded:

"Indeed I am! That's what I always tell these young guttersnipes. We did things differently in my house…A man, oh yes! With a man, the sky's the limit. But only if he's well-mannered, a "gentleman." Don't you think I'd have diamonds just like Mado if I weren't so choosy, if I took up with the first young buck who showed up at the Excelsior?"

Even though at the moment Frederic was starting to feel a sort of peculiar pleasure at being drawn into Rosa Trènor's low, wretched domain, he couldn't suppress a skeptical laugh.

"All right, go ahead and laugh," Rosa said. "I don't mean, of course, that the first guy you run into will come bearing diamonds. But one thing leads to another, and if you have no scruples, before you know it you find a couple hanging from your earlobes. And mine have been in hock for years now."

Sensing that the sauce was starting to thicken nicely, Rosa took the conversation down a different, slightly more undulating and benevolent, path:

"But I'm being tiresome. Yes, I am, don't deny it, I'm boring you to tears…Isn't it funny…It feels as if it were only yesterday that we were talking…I don't know, what can I say…this all seems so natural…As if we were just as close as before…"

And then she brought the first notes of the aria down to earth with a sneeze, and an anecdote about perfume:

"I have a cold, you know…? Have to keep my handkerchief close by at all times…"

Rosa ran her handkerchief under Frederic's nose, and, closing his eyes, he relaxed a moment as he inhaled the fragrance, while he searched for a way to broach the big subject.

"So you like this perfume…Oh yes, as you will soon see, I haven't lost my good taste. Mado and Reina smell exactly the same: an unremitting horror from Guerlain that they consider the height of chic. Sara brought them a sample bottle. Four hundred francs, not counting what they had to pay the customs agents at Portbou. I'm surprised I didn't pass out today. Lucky for me my nose is stuffy…But, my darling, what a sleepy face! You mind me, grab your hat and go home. I want to look in on those silly girls. They won't mind. It's perfectly safe. They're probably reading some dirty book; Reina, that is, because Mado doesn't know how to read. Bobby lent them a picture book, a filthy thing…Now, you mind me, go home and sleep; what will your wife say…? You married men have to behave…"

Frederic looked up and burned Rosa's eyes with an acid smile. She added, in an afterthought:

"Though with me…after all…"

Frederic was starting to worry, but her last words, her "Though with me…after all…", gave him license to press on, and Frederic said:

"Now, see here, Rosa, don't you realize what an exciting woman you are? You're the most delightful, intelligent…"

And here Frederic let out a grotesque, inarticulate moan, something akin to the whining of a dog, because Rosa had placed her hand upon his mouth to keep him from adding more adjectives. Stubbornly, her hand still on his mouth, Frederic tried to continue, and when he was convinced it was no use, he bit gently into the soft flesh of her palm, grabbed her hand violently, and covered it with kisses. Rosa didn't stop him. Both of them were breathing heavily. Rosa improvised a couple of tears:

"But no, dear boy, no; don't you see that my mascara will run! Can't you see the tears in my eyes?…What is this! What is happening? You, too?…Are you really crying, Frederic?"

Frederic confessed as if in a cut-rate melodrama ("I was a dog with you, a dog!"). He confessed as if in an Italian opera ("How could I tolerate such slander!"). Frederic evoked scenes from his past with Rosa, moments of intimacy, he stumbled over his words, he blushed, because those moments included ludicrous or indecent details, which, naturally, he omitted; but omitting them punctured the effect of the phrase a little, and it came out flat. At the end of his confession, Frederic himself was taken aback at his own words: "What we meant to each other, what we had together, has been the only truth in my life…"

Frederic's speech had the effect of a musical interlude. After hearing Frederic out, Rosa abandoned her crass talk, and adopted the attitude of an abandoned Niobe, bedecking herself in the folds of the most solemn tunic. Rosa played her grand role with an eye to Frederic's emotional range, to marvelous effect. With a dancer's grace the abandoned Niobe lifted the solemn folds of her tunic, and Frederic found Rosa Trènor's calf, warm beneath her chiffon stocking, in his hands. Rosa had been – and still was – famous for having perfect legs. The fruition of those legs had been one of Frederic's most legitimate sources of pride, and in that critical moment it was her legs that contained the most positive evocative power of the past, with all the consequences of a fierce arousal.

Frederic felt that words were of no use and, while still respecting the border that separates man from gorilla, he attempted to achieve a definitive outcome on top of that silk divan, the color of a turtle dove's breast; but modestly, yet still strongly insinuating, Rosa objected:

"No, Frederic, not here…"

"Why not?"

"Because…"

Convinced that everything was going perfectly, Rosa stood up all at once, enveloped herself in the beaver coat, and said:

"Let's go, they must be asleep by now…Little darlings!…"

Frederic obeyed Rosa Trènor without a word, and they started down the stairs of Mado's house on Carrer de Muntaner. The street was the color of milk and ash. Frederic started to hail a cab; Rosa hinted:

"No need for a cab. It's just a few steps away…"

Frederic felt all the sadness and cold of the dawning day run down his spine. He no longer had the heart to continue living out his chapter in the Rosa Trènor novel. When they reached the door to her house, Rosa opened her famous bag, turned the key in the lock twice, and took Frederic by the hand. At that point the Frederic of the family worries and the loan about to come due briefly confronted the Lloberola gentleman. He had just heard the screech the wheel of an early morning trolley car makes against the rail the moment it brakes. That little screech that sets your teeth on edge echoed too mechanically in Frederic's chest cavity, in a painful, yet liberating, way. Frederic felt as if the festering in his heart were being scraped clean. Frederic had had enough of Rosa Trènor. But his pride – perhaps simply the Lloberola weakness and cowardice – wouldn't let him abandon her. Every convention, every comfort drove him homeward; but the true gentleman – or at least this was the justification Frederic came up with – must reject convention and comfort and follow the path of duty. And his duty at that moment was to go to bed with Rosa Trènor. Rosa, the grand dame, knew how to read a gentleman perfectly. After a look from Frederic, Rosa shrugged her shoulders, smiled – the smile of an eighteen-year-old – and began climbing the stairs arm in arm with Frederic.

The friction of the beaver coat against his suit jacket felt to Frederic like that of a real live beaver, as feral and repugnant as such an animal could be.

Upstairs in the apartment nothing mattered any more to Frederic. The dialogue went on in bed, and Frederic made mechanical promises; projects took shape amid a strange and painful desire to sleep.

Rosa Trènor set the alarm clock for eleven a.m., when she must get up without fail. She had to see her dressmaker. Frederic fell asleep with Rosa Trènor's mouth stuck to his teeth with the viscosity of a crushed flower, or of viscera. What kind of flower? Frederic wasn't sure because it was all vague and monstrous, it was all already taking place in the atmosphere of dreams...

LYING BETWEEN the sheets, Frederic had just mentally identified and reproduced these scenes. He concluded that it had all been a terrible mistake.

As for Rosa Trènor's bedroom, he was making note of the uncomfortable architecture, the airlessness and disorder of the chairs and the armoire. Frederic felt like a man charity has rescued from a shipwreck, who wakes up in someone else's home whose inhabitants have coarser habits and a harsher and shabbier way of life than he.

Despite her airs, Rosa Trènor was a woman who had been worn down by privation, and by the need to spend the night with men she had known for a half an hour. Like other kept women of her kind, she had no sense of privacy. Just as she entered into all kinds of physical intimacies with the skin of strangers, she found it natural that the stranger should have the same intimacy with everything that was hers: her bed, her furniture, her stuffed dog… And she thought the stranger would find it perfectly natural to wake up in a chamber in which his hanging clothing would necessarily feel ashamed and out of place.

And, fifteen years later, and unfamiliar with Rosa Trènor's apartment, Frederic was that stranger, that shipwrecked soul lying between her sheets, taking stock of a setting that both cowed and repelled him.

Under the impression that her novel, *Frederic: Part II,* was in the bag, Rosa had decided to treat Frederic with a conjugal candor, with the lightheartedness and nonchalance of a woman whose husband has just come back from a long journey during which she has been unfaithful and affects a tender and unaffected informality in order to avert suspicion. This was why Rosa had got dressed and unceremoniously left Frederic snoring, like the lord of the manor, convinced that this was the best way for Frederic to become reacquainted with her "essence." But Frederic was simply overwhelmed by the lordship of that apartment. He couldn't wait to get out of there, yet at the same time an absolute corporeal sluggishness kept him pinned to the sheets, at that unspeakable hour of four-thirty in the afternoon. Still incapable of making a decision, his hands ran over the damp warmth of his undershirt adorned with the trophy of a few of Rosa Trènor's tears, tinged with the mascara she had not quite finished removing from her lashes in the last-minute rush.

If the foreground of Frederic's moral landscape – his night with Rosa Trènor – had had a more exciting hue and a more pleasing volume, perhaps the background would not have gone so dark so quickly. Just as a migraine develops at the temples – following the characteristic signs of such an attack – and one begins to note the actual pain in a weak, insinuating, and treacherous way, in Frederic's moral landscape Rosa's image was fading, giving way – with almost the same physical pain as a migraine – to one clear image of a promissory note and to another of Frederic's father. The foreground had changed completely. It was no longer a bygone chapter of a half-failed novel, but a future anguish of a pressing urgency and a reality that left no room for doubt.

Frederic had to make a supreme effort; the twenty-four hours had elapsed. At the foot of the bed a pair of reproachful socks lay in wait. Frederic began to get dressed with the disgust of having to put on those socks, which had not exactly come fresh from the armoire. Frederic walked straight to the bathroom, but it was of no avail and, besides, there was no more time. He didn't even know how to turn on the water heater. In the bathtub two fingers of dirty water flirted with a sponge that floated there like a soaking intestine. That small, cramped bathroom, with the red rubber douche hanging on the wall and the expressionless curves of the sanitary devices, had an air that was both criminal and pornographic all at once. Frederic washed up superficially and was furious to discover that all the towels were used and stained with either lipstick or mascara. Frederic decided that Rosa Trènor was a dreadful, neglectful person. Doing up his tie, he felt a sense of humiliation when he caught sight of the wretched smudges on his sweaty collar. It was humiliating not to be able to change his collar. Nevertheless, he tied his tie with a kind of casual coquetry. His ill-shaven cheeks were another source of humiliation. To hide the darkness of his skin he tried some of Rosa's dusting powder but soon he was scrubbing his face in rage with a terry cloth towel until he left his skin raw, because the powder was of no use. He stared long and hard at his reflection in the mirror. Frederic's face looked deplorable, but his puerile vanity was compensated by the sight of his tall, full form, with no offensive obesity, and the slight receding of his jaw, which he considered a sign of spent or even slightly degenerate aristocracy. He rubbed at the two small, shiny, symmetrical black triangles that served as his moustache.

Frederic realized there wasn't a soul in Rosa Trènor's apartment. Everything had been left to its own devices. One of those women who see to the cleaning of a string of rental apartments had probably come in to tidy up and timidly left for fear of waking him. Or maybe Rosa had left word that no one should disturb him. Frederic looked into the kitchen and saw a cup with the dregs of a coffee with milk and sugar. The ingredients had separated, and a scrawny cat – which must have jumped in through the open window, because it was hard to imagine that Rosa would keep such an unprepossessing specimen – was licking the inside of the cup. When it saw Frederic it started to meow with a sour and resigned rhythm.

The sadness of the apartment was poisonous, and Frederic felt a deep pity for Rosa Trènor, who had to put up a front, who had to cloak herself in the veils of pretension, suffering the brutality of one man or another, all for the upkeep of a miserable olio of perfume and pink sheets. Frederic had some understanding of those humiliations and pretenses; but nothing in his bitter reality was so strained and funereal as that cup in the kitchen, wobbling and weakly protesting, like a frightened animal bleating, as it endured the lashing of the cat's tongue.

———·——·———

THE STORY OF THE Lloberolas was one of many family histories that come to a distasteful and impoverished end, without even a reaction to lend it some tragic nobility or, at very least, a scandalous or picturesque vivacity. Don Tomàs de Lloberola i Serradell, the head of the family, had seen all the family's former grandeur melt in his hands until he had become a poor, gray, defenseless man in a massive, unimportant, practically anonymous residence, amid the uniform geometry of Barcelona apartment buildings.

Heir to what, to all appearances, was a grand inheritance but which had already been depleted by the monarchist Carlist Wars of the 19th century and by his father's follies. Mortgaged to the hilt and obliged to pay interminable spouse's shares, legacies, and pensions to the other dependents, when he was twenty-eight years old Don Tomàs found himself owning a big old mansion on Carrer de Sant Pere més Baix. He had a university degree that was of no use to him, a fat, fussy wife who was also of no use to him, and a perfect ignorance of everything that matters if one is to fight tooth and nail to turn situations to one's advantage and, if nothing more, to save one's own skin from the ferocious attacks or caresses of one's fellow men.

What Don Tomàs de Lloberola did have to keep him going, in compensation, was a consciousness of his own magical superiority, which flowed directly and legitimately from thirty generations who had never so much as lifted a blade of straw from the ground. The only weapon Don Tomàs de Lloberola could brandish in his defense was his pride of family, without a shred of irony, and without a drop of cunning.

The Lloberolas belonged to the kind of lineage, still in ascendancy at the end of the 19th century, whose profound ignorance of time and space carried within it the termite that would turn it into a harmless ghost: families attached to a not-so-old tradition that formed part of that petty rural aristocracy that acquired its noble titles in the seventeenth and eighteenth centuries from the kings of Spain, by occupying some more or less flashy bureaucratic commission in the colonies, obtaining a kinship with more creditable and illustrious names through the grace or disgrace of marriage, and contributing a notable contingent of second and third sons and daughters to convents, the secular clergy, and the military service. Their only contact with their rural roots was maintained through attorneys and administrators, even though, in fact, during the expansion of Barcelona they had built their big old mansions – many of which have now vanished – in the most venerable, ripe, and crusty neighborhoods, those most steeped in the enterprising spirit of medieval trade guilds and the petty bourgeoisie.

Contact with the land, for families like the Lloberolas, was strictly an affair of the belly. Their property allowed them to cling to the reminiscence of their lost dominions, of which nothing remained but the title to the terrace farms and a house equipped with a the most basic comforts. There they could spend the summer months, or shoot, from time to time, a few rounds of buckshot into some hare's back. Like so many families of their kind, the only thing the Lloberolas loved about the rural landowners who had engendered them was the revenue they received, always skimmed and filtered by the craftiness of caretakers and administrators. They hadn't so much as set foot on many of their properties, nor had they tried to improve them. Without batting an eye, and to the detriment of the land, they would occasionally order a forest to be brutally cut down to satisfy some urgent need, nearly always the result of vanity or lack of foresight.

But anything having to do with a sort of spiritual affection for the land and, at very least, enough industriousness and cleverness to perceive its value and make the most of it, anything that might signify an intelligent and moral contact with a small parcel of the world that was theirs, and that often represented a great treasure, didn't enter into the reckoning of these families. They looked upon the caretakers and terrace farmers with offensive paternalism, accepting their fawning, and the roast chickens and salads they provided for mid-afternoon picnics, as they would the obligatory affection of a dog. What they did not take into account was that – once the magical prestige of the landowner had been destroyed in our country – those caretakers were their enemies, who more often than not ended up taking over the properties and throwing them out. And if the caretakers didn't do it, there was never any lack of spiders spinning a web of usury for aristocratic foibles. They would offer a low appraisal to take over a rundown property, and turn it into a first-rate homestead.

Along with this estrangement from the land, dating from the early 19th century, came a Castilianization of the greater part of the Catalan petty aristocracy. They became parasites, who turned their backs completely on the real traditions and all the essential local sentiments that were awakening little by little at the time in our country. The civil wars of the period contributed to the economic and moral suicide of many of these families. And when the wars died down, one could say that the political passion that leads one to risk even his own skin died down as well, and all that remained was a fading anachronistic ferocity, the consequence of discord produced by the wars themselves. Hence, for many of these gentlemen, politics was nothing but the spirit of the lowest form of *caciquisme*, local machine politics exercised through cronyism and ties to Madrid and the Court. Sometimes, this would serve a utilitarian purpose, perhaps the concession of a highway that would benefit a property; other times it was for nothing more than to satisfy the delusional heart of an insignificant character, who would willingly dismantle his inheritance for a seat in the Senate.

Religious sentiment cleaved to the backs of this aristocracy in the form of the most ineffectual clericalism. Owing to their blood ties with the Church, through a profusion of relatives in the clergy, be they parish priests, canons, or even bishops, the machinery of religion in these families proceeded with perfect rhythm. Each family had its own parish or church where they could put on airs at a specific Mass. They were members of the parish board, the benevolent societies, or the merely religious associations that occupied preferred places in solemn processions, wearing uniforms of extinct grandeur and bearing candles with more blessings than any ordinary candle. Each family had its own specific number of religious orders to patronize, and in the salons of those cold, damp houses whose pomp fell somewhere between sepulchral and carnavalesque, infinite pairs of nuns wearing the most heterogeneous wimples and scapularies warmed the brocade chairs.

Often the only way for one of these aristocrats to highlight his own figure with a color that might stand out against the surrounding gray was a solemn religious event, at which he might be positioned by the side of a bishop, his military coat emblazoned with stripes and his three-cornered hat trimmed with noticeably moth-eaten feathers.

These religious mechanics took the form of a sort of penitent's parade that discharged its offices in those grand houses from the vestibules to the most intimate recesses of the bedroom. Those dark bedrooms held great canopied beds, in the vicinity of which the bathrooms and sanitary apparatuses had been replaced by all manner of colorful images in pathetic robes standing in glass cages, by the side of holy water fonts or hulking black armoires crowned with escutcheons and filled with never-worn undergarments whose lace trim had yellowed with sadness.

Outward morality was so fastidious in these families that often it was considered scandalous merely to drop the name of a famous actress or dancer, or intelligent author, or the title of a novel. During visits to the lady of the house no lips would ever mention a topic of conversation that might be considered even remotely free, and dialogues centered exclusively on religion, illness, the children's upbringing, or questions regarding servants or property. And in a very vague way, from a very peculiar angle, politics might be commented upon.

Moral rigidity, strictly external, was no impediment to the secret practice in the heart of the most prim and proper families of the basest imaginable sexual practices, cases of vile degeneration. A respectable white-bearded gentleman, the bearer of candles and canopies in processions, might be inverted with all that such a thing entails, or a sadist might be keeping his tastes under the most cowardly wraps with the complicity of the most sordid people.

AT A TIME WHEN the amorous life of our city was not yet as big and brazen as it is today, some of those aristocrats relieved their sexual inclinations in airless, plebeian surroundings. It wasn't at all unusual for their excitement to be focused on the stockings of a cook or the fleshy opulence of a hired wet nurse. The aristocrat who gave a diamond necklace to a dancer from the Liceu Opera, or who bedecked a seamstress in a hat trimmed with cloth camellias and the wings of an exotic bird, was considered lacking in moral fiber, a man who brought public offense to his class.

The most outstanding characteristic of houses like that of the Lloberolas was a life of isolation, spent in relations with only a very limited number of families, who attributed to one another all the moral and social value the Catalans could muster. Anyone who did not pay social visits in an open carriage with a coat of arms on the door – even if it was dilapidated – was considered inferior. Likewise any lady who did not dispose of damp and lugubrious salons with sofas upholstered in pearly silk (but with arthritic swollen legs) for her conversations with canons, generals, or seamstresses – often the only counsel available to the lady of the house.

A whole new life was emerging in Barcelona, where pirates, espadrille-makers and fugitives from the factory were becoming great industrialists, where thrifty shopkeepers who counted their pennies found themselves with enough capital to devote to new construction and the expansion of the city. Meanwhile, this unimaginative aristocracy, without a shred of initiative, was becoming deflated, impoverished, and utterly annihilated. A few members of this class of families modernized, made arrangements with those among the industrialists they might once have called common, and the occasional, shall we say, morganatic, marriage turned out to be good business for certain families. Others had the good fortune of a felicitous investment or were favored by very particular circumstances. Others, like the Lloberolas, had no choice but complete annulment, because the decadence they harbored in their blood no longer had the strength to react.

DON TOMÀS DE LLOBEROLA lived in an apartment that occupied a whole floor on Carrer de Mallorca. It was furnished in an incongruous and unappealing way with the last remnants of his time of glory. The occasional dresser or mirror that held pride of place in the history of their former house played the empty, chipped role of a relic in that space. Leocàdia, la Senyora de Lloberola, couldn't abide seeing mercenary hands touch that furniture, so every morning, when she got home from Mass, she would set to dusting them and caressing them tenderly, as if stroking the cheeks of a paralytic old grandmother who in better days had been a holy terror.

The situation of the Lloberolas was almost invisible; if it weren't for Frederic, who retained some contact with the upper crust – where naturally a nebulous, irregular, or precarious position is no impediment to retaining such contacts – one could say that, with the exception of their closest relatives, the Lloberolas saw almost no one, were not invited anywhere, and were never seen at any notable gatherings. Many of those who knew Frederic had never heard a word about his family, and they accepted him like any other parvenu. Leocàdia, limited by her husband's bronchitis, and more and more scandalized by people who just laughed and squandered, acclimated her old age to a sad, pious, and housebound life.

Even though Leocàdia had never been beautiful, and an early obesity had robbed her, even when she was single, of that special excitement men used to find in bustles and leg-of-mutton sleeves, she was still a lady of refinement, delicate and docile. Leocàdia married Tomàs de Lloberola without a whit of passion, but entirely convinced that there could be no other man for her than her husband. Between her innocence and the unremitting moral norms she had bred in the bone, she accepted the bit of recreation afforded her by intimacy with a heavy, graceless, and monotonous man with the tender resignation of Sarah in the bed of Abraham. Still, always full of compunction, she would drone on in the ears of her spiritual directors with the rustling of a pious owl, resistant to pacification. The only thing that mollified her was the persuasive counsel of a prestigious priest, who told her that in holy matrimony the woman must be amenable and have a bit of patience. In time, Leocàdia found it all very natural, and even came to feel genuine love for Don Tomàs. By dint of the sort of mimicry that can be seen in some animal species and some married couples, Leocàdia began to lose her own initial refinement and her family colors, to reabsorb in her soul and display in all their variations the most banal qualities of the personality of the Lloberola patriarch.

Leocàdia adopted Don Tomàs's family vanity. In this regard she was an old-fashioned lady, the kind who shrink and fade away in the presence of their lords and masters, never showing them up or expressing a contrary opinion. It was only with regard to her husband's great economic disasters and absurd spending sprees that Leocàdia might timidly protest, advise, or insinuate, with that conservative and practical spirit women generally possess. Still, she was never energetic about it, but always phlegmatic, in keeping with her phlegmatic constitution, and she never managed to avert a single catastrophe.

Believing, in error, that he was at the top of his game, Don Tomàs de Lloberola continued, with an evident lack of intelligence, to make terrible business decisions. Later, in consequence, he would have to take out a loan at a usurious rate, or a second mortgage that squeezed them to the bone. Leocàdia never opened her mouth, crying in secret and chalking up to bad fortune what was nothing more than the consistent ineptitude of her husband.

Despite having served two or three times as President of the Association of Catholics, and on the board of the Committee for Social Defense, which was one of the most bovine and cloying ways of being reactionary, Don Tomàs had passed up no opportunity to be unfaithful to his wife, and the loveseats of the Liceu Opera House served more than once as a cover for certain adventures that the Senyor de Lloberola preferred to keep to himself. The always innocent Leocàdia, believing in the good faith of her husband, had fallen prey on one or two occasions to the torment of suspicion, at which point instead of crying out to the four winds, she preferred to keep her counsel and offer up her devotions to Don Tomàs's guardian angel.

The hardest blow for Leocàdia was the sale of the family manor, which came about not because it would bring in a great amount of money, but because maintenance of the property occasioned a series of unsustainable expenses. Up to that point, she and her husband had been able to keep up appearances before their acquaintances. The word was that the Lloberolas were in a bit of a jam, but no one suspected that a family with so much history and such an important inheritance could fall apart so suddenly. Their renunciation of past splendors came to light gradually. If Don Tomàs, on realizing his situation, had simply stopped short, unsentimentally cut back, and put his cards on the table for the world to see, perhaps he could have saved a great deal more than he did, and perhaps the Lloberolas could have continued to play a relatively brilliant role. But his stubborn vanity, the centuries-long heritage of the family, and a willful insistence on pretending to have more that they had meant that his transactions and patchwork solutions were always negotiated more or less under the table, in the worst of conditions, and sometimes the Senyor de Lloberola – who saw himself as a real shark – ended up simply being fleeced.

The first cry of alarm announcing to Barcelona society the toppling fortunes of the Lloberolas – a special kind of protestation, containing inflections of laughter muted with phony compassion, like that of a flock of crows the scruffiest and most gossipy of which has happened upon a dead cow – went up on the feast day of Saint Hortènsia. On that day many of the ladies who went to visit the widow Hortènsia Portell saw the Gobelins tapestry that had famously presided over the green room of the Lloberolas hanging in her salon. That tapestry, one of the most magnificent of those possessed by the old families of Barcelona, was so well-known in society, and so familiar, not only to the eyes of the ladies, but even to the neighborhood shopkeepers and mechanics, who had never laid eyes on it, that when they wanted to identify the Lloberolas they would say, "that family with the tapestry." Hence the general surprise produced in Hortènsia Portell's salon could not have been more acidic and smeared with gossip. The question was on everyone's lips, mixed in with theatrical variations on "Well, I never." Hortènsia, both ashamed and amused, said, "Yes…the poor Lloberolas…you could see it coming for some time now. I got a good price for it because, as you can imagine, I am not in a position to own such a thing. But I didn't want to let it slip away. Better for it to stay here. If not, who knows where it might have ended up!" Later, in a more intimate setting, and in a lower voice, Hortènsia would drop the tearful tones and pick up the kitchen shears that could rip out the innards of a hake without a hint of compassion.

Back then Hortènsia Portell was still a fresh and radiant widow. Blond, plump, with a lorgnette and too much make-up – elegant ladies were not yet using make-up in those days – she attracted a blend of authentic aristocracy, social climbers, artists, and men of letters. Hortènsia was known for being a free thinker, though she was both very proper and very chaste. Some of the ladies – Leocàdia among them – found her affected, common, and brazen. If indeed they didn't dare give her the cold shoulder in public, in no event would they ever have invited her to their homes or deigned to set foot in hers. Hortènsia considered those ladies to be "démodé" and called them "old biddies," and she made fun of their fussiness and their lack of style. Still, the truth be told, their snubs hurt her feelings, and it could be said that in the purchase of the Lloberola tapestry there was as much *amour-propre* and spirit of revenge as artistic enthusiasm.

The "shock" of the tapestry dissolved into fifty-thousand spoon-fuls of nightly soup in the apartments of Barcelona until the shock of other sizeable sales came along, and the final thunderclap when the Lloberolas abandoned their house.

Don Tomàs's tactic was to hide his head under his wing like an ostrich, and Leocàdia naturally followed suit, as we said before. Out of consideration, people accepted the grandiose and defensive behavior of el Senyor de Lloberola, who continued to speak of his glories in the same tone of voice as before. If at some point he made a fool of himself at the betting table he frequented in the Cercle del Liceu, the regulars pretended not to notice, and el Senyor de Lloberola would clear his throat with his usual leonine roar, convinced that no one had noticed a thing.

His two sons, Frederic and Guillem, and his daughter, Josefina, were Don Tomàs's torment. Married off to the young Marquès de Forcadell, Josefina had escaped the conflagration and, even though she truly loved her mother, and shared her phlegmatic, dull, and acquiescent nature, her married state and the atmosphere of comfort that filled her lungs made her selfishly set foot as rarely as possible in the apartment on Carrer de Mallorca. Don Tomàs, who never bit his tongue and was an unrepentant and tempestuous *pater familias* with his children, loosed his harshest fulminations upon Josefina's ample blubber, considerably sweetened by massage. He spoke of her ingratitude, lack of consideration, frivolous habits, and lack of respect, in the thorny crimson tones a good prophet might use. Josefina would weep and protest, and Leocàdia would play the role of Sarah by the side of her penniless Abraham. All she got out of it, though, was a scolding from Senyor Lloberola that sent mother and daughter fleeing in a damp veil of tears. When she got home, Josefina would tell her husband the tale, playing the part of the victim. The young Marquès de Forcadell would then declare that his father-in-law was a beast and didn't deserve all the deference they showed him.

Frederic, whom we met in Rosa Trènor's bed, was the *hereu*, the heir and firstborn. He was the spitting image of his father, and he had all the family flaws. Yet he didn't have Don Tomàs's theatricality or tremolo, and hence, he didn't have his charm. Because, in spite of it all, Don Tomàs had a certain charm. Since the one had been molded with the defects of the other, Frederic and his father couldn't stand each other. When Don Tomàs had to name a person in whom every moral calamity converged, the first name he came up with was Frederic; when his son had to conjure up the beast of the Apocalypse, he thought inevitably of his father. In early youth, Frederic had tried to study many things, but he was successful at none. His head full of the airs of the *hereu* to a fine household, he ended up tossing his books to the wind and deciding to live off the fat of the land. Despite the outrage and reprimands of Don Tomàs, Frederic – who at the time was convinced of the solidity of the family fortune – got his way. Partially in secret and partially in open rebellion, he prevailed over his father's feeble objections. In his heart of hearts, his father relished having such a brilliant, modern son, with such fine taste in clothes and coveted by no few mothers. The match with Maria Carreres was not entirely satisfactory to Don Tomàs, who aspired to a daughter-in-law from the household of a duke of Madrid. Maria Carreres came from a distinguished bourgeois family, which naturally could not measure up to the shields and traditions of the Lloberolas, but she had a good dowry and seemed like an excellent young woman.

When the time came for his son to marry, Don Tomàs was feeling the pangs of insolvency. The sale of the famous tapestry coincided with the birth of his granddaughter Maria Lluïsa. From that time on, relations between Frederic and Don Tomàs became more and more grim. All Frederic wanted was to save himself. He started a business, got rapped on the knuckles with two or three bad deals, and buried his wife's dowry on a particularly bad transaction. The Carreres and Lloberola families had a falling-out. Maria Carreres, inexpert and melodramatic, was the Iphigenia of the situation. Frederic hid his discomfort by coughing, though with less of a roar than his father at the card table of the Cercle del Liceu. With no money to throw around, Frederic felt like a cat with a can tied to its tail. Accustomed to spending heedlessly, it was a terrible blow to him to accept a post at the Banc Vitalici, a position that was unrewarding and ill-paying because the firstborn son of the Lloberolas could barely read or write. When Don Tomàs sold the house, the older and younger couples went their separate ways. Having happened upon a decent lawyer, the elder Lloberolas were able to save a sum of some importance on which to live. Don Tomàs was able to pass his son a monthly pension, since his daughter-in-law's dowry was now nonexistent and the salary from the Banc Vitalici was a pittance. Among the properties Don Tomàs had managed to salvage was the Lloberola estate on the outskirts of Moià. He wouldn't have given up this estate for anything in the world. To do so would have made him feel as if the imponderable liquid of his nebulous feudal ancestry were being sucked from his veins.

Even though Frederic rejected the stuffy ceremony and traditional airs of his father, and wanted to be a carefree, modern man, he still took pride in his name, his coat of arms, and his estate, which was known as the Lloberola castle. He would take his friends, including the ever-present Bobby, to hunt there as often as he could, even though they never killed so much as a pitiful heron.

Don Tomàs's other son, Guillem, lived with his parents. There was an age difference of twelve or thirteen years between the two brothers, because Leocàdia was one of those unfortunate mothers who, bending with brutish submission to the insatiable task of procreation, had been cruelly compensated by a fate that conceded her only three children. All the rest were either sacrificed to miscarriages or sickly creatures who ended up in the cemetery before they had use of reason.

Don Tomàs de Lloberola was starting to feel over the hill, and had turned into a toothless lion unawares. His ailments had brought him close to Leocàdia. You might say that when his children were not around, his limp despotism was transformed into a more human and comprehending attitude. He and Leocàdia had done all they could. They had slept side by side for so many nights, they knew each others' snores and guttural sounds so thoroughly, that from time to time, in those moments of liquid sadness old people are given to, moments empty of passion and ambition, Don Tomàs would take refuge in the winter fruit of Leocàdia's skin, as if attempting to breathe a bit of joy into his sapped nerves.

Sometimes when the two of them found themselves at table, and Don Tomàs found the oil on the cauliflower a bit rancid or maybe he had choked on a lump in his semolina soup, he would start to spit out words of bile against his elder son or his daughter. Leocàdia would observe the volcanic explosion of her husband's teeth and the artificial cloud of smoke formed by the scarce and untamed bristles of his moustache, speckled with semolina. As the wick of his anger burned down, Leocàdia's pupils, veiled by an otherworldly web, would scrub the pepper from Don Tomàs's tongue and he would finish up with a little cough and bend his head over his plate. After a moment of silence, husband and wife would look at each other in embarrassment, and the bead of a tear would shimmer in the corner of their eyes.

It was then that Don Tomàs realized that of all the fruits he had harvested in this world of vanities, all he had left was that little handful of flesh and bones, that white head, those eyes and those wandering teeth. Don Tomàs realized that, for him, love, friendship, sexual joy, and his most vibrant expectations had all come down to the smile of a whitish lady who could barely draw an easy breath, by the name of Leocàdia…

Leocàdia! That overblown, romantic, inexpressive flower, as full of virtues as an aged *ratafia* liqueur, whom he had met at a storied ball held in Barcelona to celebrate the first marriage of Alphonse XII. In those days Leocàdia wore a suffocating corset and a pink satin dress with a bustle and a ruffled train, and amidst the combination of stitches and backstitches and the chastity of her chemise breathed the flesh of Leocàdia's bosom, made of bland white camellias, lacking in fragrance or promise, restrained by her extremely discreet neckline and a great ribbon of sky blue velvet, as tight as a dog's collar. Leocàdia was escorted by her father, the old Senyor de Cisterer, blind in one eye from a bullet fired by the liberals, taut and plump as a bass viol and having the same deep, hoarse, and solemn resonances as a bass viol. Old Cisterer introduced his youngest daughter, who dared not lift her eyes from the ground, and when the time came to meet the Lloberola heir, who was in those days resplendent, wealthy, and unattainable, a discreet tremor ran over her camellia bosoms in a lyrical and devoted way, as if they were obeying the gentle gust produced by the wing of a dove.

In the moments of arid vision that followed his distaste at the adulterated cooking oil or the lump in the semolina, Don Tomàs de Lloberola, his eyes half-closed, was fond of discovering, in the failed pretensions of his inner landscape, the Leocàdia of the rose-colored dress clinging to the rigid sleeve of old Cisterer, beneath the innumerable glass chandeliers with their thousand yellow tongues of gas instinctively following the rhythm of the rigaudon. The music of that dance was in some way reminiscent of a military parade, and it gave el Senyor de Lloberola satisfaction to follow the complicated steps of the rigaudon, because it seemed to him that they evoked a tactical *je-ne-sais-quoi*. That silly music lacking in spirit or passion, infused with the most colorless mechanical frenzy, filled his heart with the trembling of his adolescent hours, the Carlists in the mountains, the barricades and fanfares of the brass bands (that might just as soon accompany a bishop as a thief being led to the garrotte) or the poor cripples dressed up in grotesque costumes for Carnaval who were paraded past the Lloberola mansion, where he would go out on the balcony and throw them a few xavos, the coins that had been used to pay the indemnization for the African war. Over the tablecloth of the dining alcove Don Tomàs relived that earlier Leocàdia and that earlier Barcelona, in which he still meant something. For Don Tomàs everything had changed. To console himself over his current misery he would repeat continually: "In my day it was not so...", "I am from another world..." His Leocàdia was also from another world; the young woman with the bustle clinging to the arm of old Cisterer was a poor, insignificant old lady, whom no one respected or held in consideration, who would be given no special treatment in a clothing store. Only at the door of a church in the old neighborhood, when Leocàdia would go back for some particular devotional rite, would she come across a woman as anachronical as she herself, who had been begging for alms there for years. When Leocàdia bent down over her alms plate and dropped a five cèntim coin into it, the poor woman would look at her with glacial and obsequious eyes and effortlessly utter:

"May God be with you, Senyora Marquesa."

———·———

AS FREDERIC LISTENED to the weak, rhythmic tinkling of a coffee cup subjected to the pressure of a phosphorescent cat's tongue in Rosa Trènor's kitchen, some curious scenes were unfolding in Dorotea Palau's dress shop.

Dorotea had once been Senyora de Lloberola's family seamstress. Leocàdia would have her to her house two afternoons a week. Following the tradition of the ladies of old who preferred, whenever possible, for their clothing to be fabricated at home, Leocàdia invested a great deal of her time in the sewing of underwear for her husband and children, among other things of a more decorative nature. In those days Dorotea was a quiet and retiring girl, with a romantic oval-shaped face, and eyes between green and gray, without sparkle, like the wings of those quiet insects that blend into the leaves of plants. Dorotea turned out to be an excellent worker; she was always in the company of a young man she claimed was her brother, who must have been a couple of years older than she. Everyone was convinced of Dorotea's modesty and good faith until, one day, without anyone's ever knowing the reason why, Dorotea stopped serving in the Lloberola house, as a result of which Don Tomàs and Leocàdia wore long faces for a week. Later on, as it appears, it came to be known that Dorotea was the protegée of an important gentleman who spent seasons in Paris, and she had married a French hairdresser. Others said she hadn't married, but had had a child; still others that Dorotea was dead. But all of this is old news, and most likely a pack of lies.

Twenty years after leaving the service of the Lloberolas, Dorotea Palau was a single woman over forty, rich, generous with others, and the head of her own fashion house, which was patronized by very well-known ladies from the finest set. That afternoon, a man who couldn't quite seem to decide whether or not to press the doorbell stood before Dorotea's door. On the door was a plaque that proclaimed "Palau-Couture" to anyone who could read. It was a young man whom no one would have guessed to be more than twenty-three or twenty-four years old, though he must have been past thirty. Dressed in the style of the young men of the day concerned with being in vogue, his garments were clearly refashioned hand-me-downs. Biting down on a dying cigar that was unraveling like an old broom, the young man squeezed his eyes shut and pulled the brim of his hat down over his nose. After contemplating the plaque, he shrugged his shoulders and rang the bell with the puerile force and ill will of a boy crushing an ant's belly.

IN THE FOYER, Dorotea greeted the young man with a profusion of smiles, and then, to break the silence, she said, in a maternal voice:

"It's not even five in the afternoon! You certainly have come early today!"

"I was tired of walking around, Dorotea, and as you know we have a bit of business beforehand. I am like a great actor; I need a good bit of time to apply my makeup."

"Please don't talk so loud, for the love of God! I have more than twenty-five girls working in the front workshop and two ladies waiting in the dressing room!"

"Oh, Dorotea, always putting on airs!"

"Not airs, my boy; this is work. And in the midst of my workday to have to look after these things that, naturally, are not to our liking, neither yours nor mine…."

"You need not worry your head about me, Dorotea!"

"But, you must understand, she is my best client."

"Indeed, and I can certainly say she is my best client, as well."

"Well, aren't you the cheeky one!"

"Be that as it may, Dorotea, I don't think I can spend all day here in this foyer."

"Yes, fine, go on in. I'll be with you shortly."

"Is there anything in the dining room, Dorotea? Because I'm a bit hungry."

"Go right ahead, you needn't stand on ceremony."

The young man stood on tiptoe, as if by doing so he could breathe in more easily the feminine air that emanated from the workshop. He turned his back on Dorotea and went down the corridor to the dark, deserted dining room of the house. He turned on the light and starting rummaging around on the sideboard. Throwing away the cigar that tasted more or less like a crematorium, he stretched out on the divan that Dorotea used for her naps, and started in on an improvised sandwich.

When he was down to the last crumb, and just as he was wiping a bit of grease from the fat of the cured ham off his fingers and onto the dining room curtains, Dorotea came in:

"Time to get started?"

"Just a moment, I'm not sure everything is ready."

"No need for such a fuss, Dorotea."

"Oh, that's easy for you to say. They are very elegant people."

"You have a strange idea of elegance, Dorotea."

"What do you mean? I don't pass judgment on personal tastes… But come along, come along…"

Dorotea led her visitor into a bedroom off the dining room. It was her own room.

Family portraits, an oil engraving of Our Lady of Sorrows, a mahogany bed covered by a great pumpkin-colored comforter, and on top of the comforter a package of clothing wrapped in a kerchief. Dorotea inspected the package.

"Yes, I think everything is here."

The young man sat down on a low chair and began to undo his tie and take off his clothing piece by piece, replacing it with the dirty, torn and pitiful clothing Dorotea had put in the package on the comforter.

"What most riles me, Dorotea, is that you make me put on this Frégoli the impostor act."

"If you like, you can come just as you are! No, I haven't quite lost my mind yet. They think that you…just imagine…if they suspected you were…"

"Uh-huh, sure, any day now we'll slip up on something, and that will be a show worth selling tickets to."

"God forbid!"

"Go ahead and look shocked. I can just see myself running into him coming out of the Club Eqüestre on my brother's arm…"

"Don't you believe it. Do you think for a minute he would recognize you? Don't you realize they are both under the illusion..."

"What do you think of this underwear, Dorotea? Patched up all over. Mamà makes me put them back in the drawer because of this sudden obsession they have with saving money. I never wear them except on these solemn occasions..."

"I hear her health is very fragile."

"Yes, she hardly ever leaves the house...And what about the shirt? Do I also have to change my shirt?"

"What do you think! Don't you realize your shirt is made of silk?"

"Papà certainly complains enough about it. But, Dorotea, do you really want me to wear this disgusting thing? My Lord, where do you find all these rags? No, no, I am not going to wear that! I'd be afraid of catching..."

"The clothes are disinfected, I swear it. Oh, and the medallion and gold chain, give them here..."

"If my mother wouldn't die of sorrow, I would tell you to keep the medallion. One day at the beach club I almost threw it into the water."

"Don't play the heretic with me."

"Dorotea, I think you're going to have to find someone else... because, really, how long can this go on?"

"What are you saying! That's all I need right now. It's not easy to find someone..."

"...someone as shameless as I, am I right? Well, I don't like to see myself all decked out like this. I think I look like a guy about to go out and hunt for cigarette butts and, frankly, even though Papà has gone and blown all our dough, we haven't sunk that low."

"Look here, do you think you can get away with those smooth cheeks? Didn't I tell you to come with at least one day's beard?"

"I forgot, what can I say? Yes, I do look a little too cute; it's not easy for a kid from a good family to hide it."

"Maybe a little dark blue eye shadow…"

" Not a bad idea! This mascara will do wonders…"

"No, that's too much. Wait, let me do it; this will give you a sort of natural grime…"

"Thanks a lot, Dorotea."

"No offense intended."

"And you needn't be such a perfectionist, Dorotea; nowadays everyone knows that even ditch diggers bathe and wear cologne when they have a date with a lady from the aristocracy. Hygiene has become commonplace…It won't be such a novelty if they find me a bit too clean."

"Oh my God, Mrs. Planell must be cursing my name – I've had her in the fitting room for an hour and a half!"

"Who is this Planell woman?

"Don't you know her? She's Don Enric Planell's wife, a beautiful, bright young woman. Oh, you would like her, all right."

"Come on, now, don't make things any harder. Listen, the doorbell."

"I don't think they can be here, yet, but she's always so keen to…"

"I swear to you, Dorotea…if it weren't for the fact that…Well, no, I'm not going to tell you, you're too much of a gossip."

"Ingrate!"

"No, what I mean is, I'm fed up with all this."

"Be patient my son...three hundred pessetes are three hundred pessetes. Come back here now...to the 'scene of the crime'...and for the love of God, don't make as much noise as you did last time. You can hear everything in an apartment like this."

The "scene of the crime" was a room that had been converted into a luxurious bedroom, with a glossy, perfumed, and illicit air, imitating a kind of pomp that is no longer in fashion in homes with good taste, but is very common in certain high-ticket Parisian bordellos, frequented by the scions of South American families. Dorotea Palau had pretty precise knowledge of such places, even if no direct experience.

In the bedroom, the young man from a good family dressed as a ditch digger was left to wait, perusing the suggestive iconography on the walls with a cynical chuckle and flicking his pocket lighter on and off, while at the door Dorotea greeted a lady and gentleman of honorable appearance with affected amiability, leading them into one of the fitting rooms. Even though the moment of pleasantries had been extremely brief and the couple had already vanished behind a curtain, the lady could not avoid being spotted by Claudina C., who had been torturing Isabel, the chief apprentice of the house, for two hours. Having finished up her business there, she grabbed Dorotea by the arm in high dudgeon and said to her, one foot inside the door and one on the landing outside:

"That Conxa can't seem to go anywhere without that pansy of a husband."

Not wishing to take sides, Dorotea responded:

"They are an exemplary couple; he expresses his opinion on everything; la Baronessa doesn't so much as baste a stitch without consulting him. They are madly in love, and bear in mind that he is no spring chicken."

"Go on, woman, go on! The man is a dolt. He should be ashamed of himself. I assure you that if my husband came to me with this kind of nonsense…! I just don't know what to think."

"For the love of God, Donya Claudina, you're being very mean! Quite a few ladies come here in the company of their husbands."

"You're talking about a different kind of 'lady,' now…But you have work to do, and I'm in the way…Everything must be ready the day after tomorrow, eh? I'll be furious if it isn't."

"Rest assured, Donya Claudina."

"Ah! And Isabel showed me that other matter. If you can't bring it down, just cancel the order."

"But we can't, Donya Claudina. You know that was a special price for you only."

"Always the same story. We've known each other too long for this, Dorotea."

"For the love of God, Donya Claudina…"

"I'll think about it."

"At your service, Donya Claudina."

Dorotea closed the door and stepped into the fitting room where the honorable couple awaited her.

"Have I kept you waiting? Please forgive me."

"Is the room quite safe? No one will be able to hear us? There are so many girls here, and they can be such tattlers."

"El senyor Baró can put his mind to rest."

"Let's get on with it, Dorotea. Is it the same one as the last time?"

"Yes, the same one. But with the leave of el senyor Baró, it can't be done for less than a thousand pessetes."

"This is unthinkable, Dorotea. Dealing as you are with a client of my wife's category..."

"La Baronessa will understand perfectly. Look at the risk I'm exposing myself to..."

"You mean the risk we are all exposing ourselves to, surely."

"Oh, no, sir. It can't be done for less than a thousand pessetes. As el senyor Baró knows, I am under no obligation. What's more, you have requested something that is quite dear and hard to find. I assure you that if the Baró and Baronessa didn't have these qualms, another kind of person could be found, let's say of a more decent class, more well-bred, a fine young man, in a word; and then the price would be more reasonable."

"But Dorotea!"

"You must understand, there are many possibilities. But who could trust a person like that, a so-called fine young man? What I am offering you is foolproof. He can't possibly compromise anyone, and what's more, he's authentic, the genuine article. This is the truth:

it's hard to find someone like this. You can't imagine the repugnance one must face, the transactions one must engage in. All of this with kid gloves, for fear someone might have suspicions. What would the clients and even my staff think if they saw a character like that come in my door? I would do anything for the Baronessa, but for God's sake, you must understand my position!"

"All right, Dorotea, not another word. A thousand pessetes."

"Believe me, I would prefer not to earn this money. It burns my fingers, senyor Baró. If it were not for the esteem in which I hold you…"

"Enough, enough, let's get on with it, Dorotea."

"Just a moment. I am going to make sure everything is in order, and that the passage to the dining room is 'free,' so we won't run into…You know…"

"Yes, yes, we know, Dorotea."

The couple, now all by themselves in the fitting room, seemed stunned. The man's features looked boiled, as if sucked in by an inexplicable inner fever. His cheeks had a grayish pallor and his eyes the soft dull stare of a dead hare. They didn't dare look at each other or say a word, but their lips trembled with the rhythm of a mechanical toy.

In ethnographic museums you can often find those shrunken heads produced by Ecuadorean savages, in which the features appear to have been reduced by a strange force pulling from the center of the cranium, pressing and compressing the external muscles, sucking away the volume of flesh, until only a minimal, but horrifically expressive, amount remains. And there in Dorotea's fitting room, his head and her head reminded you of those repugnant little heads, because there, too, it seemed as though there were a force pulling and shrinking their faces, making them more expressive. Surely what was reducing and impoverishing their features, minimizing their flesh, and injecting into them the sharp expression of a specter was the moral suppuration forged by their desire.

Her extraordinary beauty and extraordinary elegance vanished. Morality has its own aesthetic, and aesthetic catastrophes are implacable.

When Dorotea returned, the baron and the baronessa stood up, and both of them snapped to. With great effort – an effort perhaps akin to self-esteem – they swapped the grayish pallor on their faces for a more normal skin color. Dorotea ushered them to the "scene of the crime," and softly closed the door.

If someone had caught Dorotea's smile at the moment she closed the door, he would have been hard put to say whether it was the smile of an experienced mother-in-law leading the newlyweds to their bed-chamber after the wedding dinner, or the smile of an imperial executioner who would sew a man into a sack with a rooster, a serpent, and a monkey.

An hour and a half later, the young man disguised as a ditch digger had taken off his costume and was soaping up his face and neck in Dorotea's bathroom. Two steps away, Dorotea observed the young man's bare arms and the soapy water that flowed off his cheeks with no little admiration, as she might contemplate Sinbad the Sailor at the moment he rose to the water's surface still full of the mystery of an underwater cove. Because the service Dorotea had just provided was not exclusively out of love of lucre. In the woman's penchant for gossip a series of elements well beyond the ordinary converged. Dorotea was a devotee, perhaps even a collector, of clinical cases. In her inner depths she must be harboring some unsuspected monster, and one of the consequences of that monster was probably the scene that had just taken place in that house of fashion. Dorotea was aware that these specialities and attentions to her clients could be the source of headaches that would truly compromise her, and it was precisely that little frisson of risk and danger that added spice to her original role as a go-between. Some claimed that Dorotea had rented an apartment for the resolution of certain peculiar transactions; this had never entirely been proven, but it was evident that by using her fashion house during regular business hours for that kind of secret, abnormal task, Dorotea gave her own twisted sexuality, or if you prefer, her perversion, an undulating vivacity that could shift from the pearly drape of a length of silk to the pornographic imagery of the "scene of the crime," or from the vulgar rumor-mongering of a Donya Claudina – before whom Dorotea groveled and scraped with sadistic humiliation – to the conversation with a young man from a good family about to commit the imprudence of leaving a gold medallion hanging around his neck. This is why Dorotea, on seeing the bare arms and soapy hands of the young man, would have liked to have a needle in the pupils of her eyes able to penetrate the mystery. She wanted to hear the whole story, including the most unspeakable parts.

So, a bit breathless with this desire, but pretending that nothing was amiss, Dorotea asked one question after another to which the young man responded with evasions and monosyllables, his voice muffled by the Turkish towel with which he was scrubbing his face.

"Listen, Dorotea, all of this is a professional secret. I...I don't want to...your three hundred pessetes don't give you the right to anything more."

"But what about him...? "

"He is a pig, Dorotea, a...it doesn't seem possible...No, really, I swear! Never again. The last time he was more inhibited...but today..."

"How odd. Such a formal gentleman; such a nice man..."

"They didn't get a good look at my face, because between the darkness of the room and that trick you suggested with the pillow... And not a single word...There must not have been a bit of noise today."

"If you could only have seen them at the door when they left: a couple of angels, perfect angels."

"Never again, Dorotea! Just find a beggar! It's too disgusting! I have a pretty strong stomach...and for three hundred pessetes one can put one's stomach to the test, but this is too much."

"Oh, I almost forgot to return your medallion."

In the foyer, the young man from a good family, restored to his natural personality, had run into a bright, coarse, and very elegantly dressed young woman on the arm of a gray and proper man, the kind who can never conceal their jealousy. When the young woman saw the false ditch digger she blushed and said, just to have something to say:

"Hello! What are you doing here?"

The false ditch digger smiled and let them pass.

As they went down the stairs, the gray and proper man who couldn't conceal his jealousy asked his companion:

"Who is that guy?"

"Don't you know him? That's Guillem de Lloberola, a boy from a very high society family without a penny to their name, they say. Ah, and if you must know, he's a perfectly pleasant young man who runs around with a group of fellows who write poems and risqué verses…"

"What do you care about poetry? You're just a dizzy dame. You know I don't like you running around with riff-raff."

"Oh, come on. No need to be so touchy."

———·———

GUILLEM, THE LATE FRUIT OF Don Tomàs and Leocàdia, had developed a tactic completely different from that of his brother Frederic. Some would say that the young man took after his mother's side of the family. Tales were told about old Cisterer, and about Leocàdia's brothers – unctuous characters, with incredible escapades. They had a character that was both charming and shrewd, and an egotism disguised as refined solicitude. It seems they had found their echo in Guillem's ability to stay on both sides of the fence in any family situation.

Guillem had started life at a point when it was no longer possible to conceal the Lloberolas' economic cataclysm. Guillem's education, so different from Frederic's, had met with a feeble and depleted Don Tomàs de Lloberola, a father who in appearance deployed an honor guard of fire and brimstone, but in fact was easily distracted and handily deceived. In contrast with Frederic, Guillem had never suffered his father's regimen of surveillance, never been spied on every Friday, as if by a detective, to ensure that he had actually taken communion if he said he had. Inspections of his private drawers and the books in his bedroom had been neglected, or perhaps the energy required to carry them out had flagged. When he got home mid-supper on a winter's night, the paternal interrogation was cursory and in a tone left sort of hanging in the air. Guillem was able to achieve perfection in the art of lying and hiding the truth, the art most easily displayed by children with their parents. As a consequence of his self-important, foolish, and chivalric character – his authentically Lloberola character – Frederic often rebelled openly and provoked stupid conflicts. In the meantime, Guillem, opportunely lowering his gaze, stifling a comment, or murmuring a well-timed "Yes, Papà," or "Forgive me, Papà," with a velvety, feminine inflection, averted many conflicts and concealed certain kinds of things of which Don Tomàs lived in utter ignorance. Had he so much as suspected them, it would have been at least enough for his younger son to have suffered some damage to a rib.

Guillem had studied law, just to study something. He took two or three civil service examinations, to no avail, first of all, because he was so apathetic and distracted he had never studied for them, and second of all, because he had had no interest in passing them. Guillem had a horror, now more than ever, of any kind of discipline, anything that obligated him to get up at a particular time or take orders from anyone. He preferred the penury of being the son of a useless family, with pretensions to being a misunderstood man of letters, and feeding himself in whatever parasitic way he could, to having a bit of order and economic independence. Guillem was past thirty-one, yet he practiced the absolute lack of responsibility of the youngest of the household, who can always squeeze a *duro* from someone's pocket, with the excuse that they're still just boys and will always be just boys and never have to concern themselves with the things adults concern themselves with.

The Lloberola way of being, and the conditions in which their ruin had come about – conditions of vanity and disarray – were just the ticket to fostering the kind of juvenile mentality Guillem displayed, and just the ticket for a young man like him to find himself more and more lacking in moral sense as time went on. Guillem had absolutely no respect for his father; Don Tomàs's presence was observed by his son through a magnifying glass of denatured ferocity. Despite the apparent hatred and incompatibility of character that separated him from Don Tomàs, Frederic still had a core of respect and consideration for the old man, while Guillem could have feigned the tenderest of tears as he watched his father's death throes, and still been cold as marble inside. Between Don Tomàs and Guillem yawned an abyss of years. All the excellent qualities his father proclaimed for his epoch merely disgusted Guillem. He saw his father as a poor deluded man who had brought him into the world by accident, in his dotage, when his capacity to engender was half-exhausted. He felt that Don Tomàs had done nothing for him. He had not taken an interest in him and had not loved him. In simple obedience to a grotesque and clerical criterion of education, he had deprived Guillem of things he wanted just because. He had imposed religious and moral duties on him that Guillem had never carried out in good faith, which had only served to cultivate his hypocrisy.

Guillem never stopped to think that, despite all the defects Don Tomàs might have, the good man truly loved him, had spent sleepless nights on his account, had suffered anxiety for him, had even done truly outrageous things for him. Guillem didn't even want to suspect what that old man would be capable of to save him. And it wasn't that Guillem was a criminal, but simply that he hadn't yet had occasion to meditate a bit on the dramatic situation of parents and children. Guillem lived his life apart, concerned with things that had no point of contact with those of his father. Guillem inhabited an atmosphere that was amoral, weak and selfish and, even though he would never dare admit it, lacking in dignity. Guillem might be a much more intelligent and refined person than Frederic, but his understanding always missed the mark when it came to his father. Inclined to the easy life, he was offended by Don Tomàs's miserliness, his refusal to give money when requested, and his sermons in response to every bill from the shirt maker or any expense that Lloberola found useless or wicked.

Nothing worthwhile came of that young man. Don Tomàs had undeniably stopped worrying on his account, and his every whim was tolerated. Don Tomàs said to him: "You'll wise up one of these days, because if you're counting on the family..." But Guillem never wised up.

Or if he did, it was more often than not in a despicable way because, when he needed some cash, he didn't waste time on scruples. Of the traditional family ineptitude he had inherited the decadence: an absolute collapse of the will in the face of catastrophe that reached levels of baseness he considered part of the merit and grace of his aristocratic cynicism.

Outside the house, Guillem had another personality entirely. In his dealings with certain men and women, he was considered a brilliant and charming young man, who displayed a combination of nerve and elegance. No one knew better than Guillem how to accept a banknote from a lady's hand with a smile that managed to be both noble and Franciscan at once, the smile of a good *jongleur* in the circus ring following a particularly difficult act.

Guillem's circle of friends ran the gamut from the most select and unconventional people to the kind of individual with whom he could close a deal with a wink of the eye from twenty meters away.

Guillem's world was completely different from Frederic's. This had allowed him to have a good relationship with his brother, and even to take advantage of a few breaks that wouldn't have been possible in a community of acquaintances.

Leocàdia looked upon Guillem with the delicate and tender eyes of a mother, inflamed at once with both pride and ignorance. She felt that all the things that enchanted her about her son – his cheeks, his youthful and somewhat feminine profile, his obsessively manicured hands – had nothing to do with her, even though she had brought him into this world. Nor did they have anything to do with what she would have liked this final exuberant fruit of her maturity to be.

When Leocàdia kissed him, it was a breathless kiss of admiration, respect, foreboding, and the kind of animal tenderness we feel for something we ourselves have created, even if it is monstrous, even if it fills us with fear.

———·———·———

IT MUST HAVE BEEN around six in the afternoon when Frederic started up the stairs of the house on Carrer de Mallorca. It had been a good month since he last set foot in there. The less he and his father saw of each other, the better. Maria, Frederic's wife, took the children there every so often, so their grandparents could have a look at them. No one derived any pleasure from these purely perfunctory visits. Ever since their parents' falling-out things continued to worsen, and the daughter-in-law, as inept as she was wronged, was subjected to nothing but bitter words. Don Tomàs, in his skull cap and scarf, just rounded off the unpleasant panorama of her husband's presence, as Maria saw the complement to intimacy with Frederic in that decrepit, fussy, and reactionary man. In contrast to Leocàdia, Maria was never able by any means to adapt to the mentality of the Lloberolas.

Frederic would hear from Maria about the fluctuations of Don Tomàs's rheumatism and the situation of Leocàdia's canaries. But what led the heir and firstborn to his parents' house that afternoon was a topic of greater importance, a mission he could not delegate to his wife. The odd thing is, even as the most critical moments of his adventure with Rosa Trènor transpired, the figure of his ex-lover began fading from his sight, while the interview with his father and the obligation of the promissory note came closer to his heart. Yet now that the interview was imminent, separated by only fifty-seven marble steps, he could not pry the sight of Rosa Trènor's kitchen, the spectral cat, and the bathtub with its inch or two of dirty water from his imagination. Distracted by these sad images, Frederic didn't notice that the door was opening, a door adorned with an image of the Sacred Heart that read *I will reign*. A sweet voice, a rivulet of water trickling through the grass of the most luminous fields of his childhood, reached his ear, and he heard these words from his mother's mouth:

"Thank God, Frederic! What a sight for sore eyes!"

Frederic kissed Leocàdia on the cheek, and with a theatrical and affected flourish, as if there had been a death in the house, he asked:

"How is Papà?"

Leocàdia's response fell somewhere between a sigh and a frown:

"He's in his office. He had a very bad night, he's a bit fatigued. For God's sake, my son, please don't get him started again…your poor father…"

"But, Mamà…"

Frederic ran his hand delicately under Leocàdia's wrinkled chin, and that tenuous filial massage seemed to reassure Senyora Lloberola, who without another word patted her son on the back and led him down the hallway toward his father's room.

Don Tomàs spent the whole day secreted away in that place he called his office. The word "office" was most definitely excessive, a product of Don Tomàs's predilection for exaggeration. In Barcelona's old mansions, even if the head of the household had never written so much as a single line or counseled a single person, there was always a room designated as the office. The only things that took place there were meetings with an administrator, or signings of rental receipts, or the reading of some journal that spoke of miracles or the parable of the fishes. In his apartment on Carrer de Mallorca, Don Tomàs had wanted to preserve his office, even though by that time anything having to do with his properties, or with receiving or making payments, had been reduced to a minimum. Don Tomàs used his office to dunk the dry day-old biscuits known as *secalls*, to take naps, to cough his chronic habitual cough, and, once every fortnight, to write a few lines of his memoirs. From time to time, the *masover* who administered the only property he still owned, or a relative, or some sad priest who had served the Lloberolas as a seminarian, or one of those poor devils without a penny to his name who go from house to house telling tales of illness, would give Don Tomàs's office the appearance of something that was not quite entirely a coffin.

They lived in a standard neighborhood, whose houses were designed with no imagination and according to geometric principle in such a way that a vertical line traced from the roof to the storefronts would run through five frying pans with their corresponding omelets, or five married couples making love, or five cooks singing the same tango. What Don Tomàs wanted to bring to life in his office was that very personal and slightly wacky decorative mishmash you would find in the old mansions, in which generations of sedimentation had produced clashing styles and stockpiles of absurd pieces. Some of the pieces of furniture in Don Tomàs's office came from his grandfather, some from his great-grandfather, some he had bought himself, and others had been inherited from a cousin who went off to the Philippines or an aunt whose taste leaned toward aberrations like seashells and stuffed birds. All of this was crammed into a too-small room that twisted like a contortionist to make space for the little paintings, the holy pictures, the documents signed by the king, or the family portraits. And it still had to struggle to make space for the bust of a pope to breathe or for a view of the mountains of Montserrat made of fingernails, rabbit hair, and beetle shells to peep out – this last the work of a slightly crazy Lloberola uncle. Don Tomàs's furniture was all made of the most accredited mahoganies and jacarandas, with tiles and incrustations, but it was tubercular and worm-eaten, with a patina of tears and disappointments, bloated by the rhetorical wind of two hundred years of Lloberolas. The effect caused by the jumble in that room in the apartment on Carrer de Mallorca was one of overstuffed incongruity.

In the big old house on Carrer de Sant Pere més Baix, all that planed and polished wood engrafted with metals and nacre, gleaming with exotic varnishes and gums, affecting potbellied protuberances or Gothic spires, had a reason to exist and a reason to take up space because the big old house was just like that furniture, and the walls and the decorations supported each other and gave each other meaning. A meaning that was a bit absurd, as we have already noted, but with its elements of grandeur. In that apartment on Carrer de Mallorca, the only thing left was the absurdity, exaggerated even more by the meager space and the agglomeration of the pieces. To the eyes of an outsider who didn't know what it was all about, every piece of Don Tomàs's historic furniture, every memory loudly clinging to every stick of wood, would resemble a wretched gang who had taken refuge from a fire in the first convenient place they had found. You couldn't tell if they were crying, begging, or brazenly showing off their cracks and worm holes because they knew perfectly well that they were done for.

Presiding over the bric-à-brac of tradition hung a painting yellowed with linseed oil that portrayed Don Tomàs de Lloberola i de Fortuny, the Marquès de Sitjar i de Vallromana, stiff inside the uniform of the Order of the Knights of Saragossa. The painter had captured his physiognomy on his deathbed, and though he had done all he could, the portrait came out with the *Dies Irae* already grazing his lips. Fortunately he had daubed his galloons with silver and his lapels with an impulsive red, and he had lingered over the curls of the gray forelock and turned the sideburns hiding the dead flab of his cheeks into furling escaroles.

The jowls of the Marquès de Sitjar rested uncomfortably on a high, rigid military collar, so stiff you could slice bread with it. It appears that the marquis had only donned this asphyxiating item of clothing on two occasions: the day he was married and the day he was carried to the cemetery.

Beneath that portrait, in a ceremonial friars-chair, sat the grandson of the Marquès de Sitjar, Don Tomàs de Lloberola i Serradell. The grandfather's braided uniform had given way to the grandson's colorless, shapeless suit jacket with the odd stain. Don Tomàs's shirt collar was unbuttoned, and he had sort of swaddled himself in a silk scarf of a hardy and indeterminate shade. He still had all his whitish hair, which he hid under a scholar's cap. Over his moustache, streaked in salt and pepper, advanced the prow of an enormous red nose with cratered skin and aggressive nostrils. It was the nose of a peasant from the time of the *remences*, the late medieval uprising of the indentured servants. Don Tomàs's milky blue eyes defended themselves behind gold eyeglasses, and his long monastic cheeks and receding chin sank with a bit of coquetry into the cool fabric of the scarf that swathed his neck, as if dipping into a silken bath. Don Tomàs was a tall, swollen, apoplectic man, slow to react, whose movements were sluggish and whose breathing was fatigued. An indefatigable cougher, he cleared his throat out of mere habit, because in point of fact, there was nothing there to clear.

Frederic's visit surprised him in the midst of one of those earth-shaking coughing fits. Wiping his mouth with a handkerchief, Don Tomàs peered over his glasses, wrinkled his brow, made a face and then quickly bowed his head, looking askance at his son with an expectant and wary expression. Frederic walked over to his father's desk, and Don Tomàs extended his hand, which Frederic kissed not with effusion but rather with some repugnance.

"Hello, my boy! One might think you had all been brought up in an orphanage. You don't seem to recall that you have a father, or that your father has been ill, and very ill at that…"

"But, Papà, I didn't know anything about it. Mamà just told me right now."

"Oh, you didn't know. You didn't know. Must we tell you everything? Your wife was here just the day before yesterday. Didn't she have the sense to tell you? That's right, poor old granddad…Everyone likes to kick a man when he's down. Father has a headache? It will go away! And your sainted mother, putting up with it all. You only have a thought for us on the day of your monthly allowance. No better than a servant, a man with no love of hearth and home, just waiting around to come into what little you all haven't already spent on me. Oh, Lord, if I could only…"

"Papà, please, for the love of God, don't get started. Then you wonder why we don't come to see you."

Frederic had said that because he just couldn't take it anymore, but he realized he had got off on the wrong foot and tried to make a fresh start.

"If you only knew what headaches and worries Maria and I have to face. While you, in all honesty, only complain about unimportant things. I don't know what has you in such a foul humor. I can assure you, you are looking quite fine, magnificent, in fact. Indeed, my first glimpse of you made me very happy."

"How would you know if I am looking or feeling well? Do you think you can play games with me? Don't I know best how I'm feeling? It's only natural; old people and sick people are a bother. But let's not get into that. I know very well that gratitude cannot be forced, much less the gratitude of one's own children…"

"Papà, please, I have children, too. And believe me, I repeat, I have a lot of headaches that you…Right this moment, if you only knew… I came over here expressly to tell you, to confess to you…"

"To confess to me? What could you have to confess to me! What have you done now, eh? What have you done? Frederic, my son, you're too old for this. Do you understand? Too old! And I would rather not know…"

"Papà, believe me. I feel more alone than you. I have no one. My wife…"

"Your wife, hmm, your wife. There's a ninny for you."

"She is the way she is. She is not to blame…"

"All right, son, get on with it, tell me what's bothering you…But be mindful, child, be mindful! If you want to see me dead…If you've had enough of your old father…"

"Please don't talk that way, Papà. It's just not right. Do you think I'm made of stone?"

"No, you're not made of stone. But when it comes to headaches, you certainly have given me your share…"

"Are you starting again?"

"No, no, go on. Go ahead and tell me: what is on your mind?"

"I am very sorry to have to confess this to you, as you can imagine. But there is no other way. The problem is a promissory note…"

"A promissory note? Another wretched promissory note?"

"Yes, just that. A note I accepted, which comes due the day after tomorrow. I have tried to get an extension but the creditor will not agree to it unless I have another signature, do you see? He wants a guarantor."

"A signature. From whom?"

"Imagine how it pains me to have to say this, to have to bother you with this, especially now, when you are not feeling well. But they have me under the gun. I could go to prison…It is just a question of the signature. I will pay it down the road; I will have the money. I swear to you there isn't the slightest danger."

"There will be no swearing, do you hear me? I don't know what has happened to you young people. You speak without the least bit of respect…"

"Papà, forgive me. But I beg you in the name of what you most love. I am trapped. I am being squeezed. If you could just be my guarantor…"

"And what credit do I have? Who am I, poor devil? You are asking me to underwrite a debt? This is too much, believe, me, too much. I can't do it, do you understand? I can't…"

"But, Papà, I assure you there is absolutely no danger…"

"And what is the amount of this note?"

"Nothing out of the ordinary…"

"How much?"

"Fifty thousand pessetes…"

"Fifty thousand pessetes? Have you gone mad? My son, what is to become of you? What is to become of us all? No, Frederic, no. This is all my fault, oh yes, all my fault…"

"But, Papà, I will have the money. This has just come at a bad time…"

"What about your father-in-law?"

"My father-in-law is of no use to me. I don't have the heart to ask my father-in-law for anything. Can you imagine…"

"So, naturally, the whipping boy will have to be your poor old father. Isn't it enough to have done everything you've already done? You're not going to stop until I am even poorer than I am now, destitute, begging alms. Is that what you want? That's what all of you are after! Fifty thousand pessetes! Let's imagine the note comes due again, and once again you cannot pay. What, then? What will be left of our household?"

"Papà, there will be plenty left! Fifty thousand pessetes is a trifle! I'm telling you again, there is absolutely no danger…"

"No, no, no, and no again. The time has come to turn off the faucet, do you understand? It is pointless to go on: I will not sign the note. Go find one of those rich friends of yours, find anyone, but under no circumstances will I do it."

"What can I say, Papà? Frankly, I think your attitude is a bit… unfair."

"Unfair! Unfair, you say? Unfair! Are you not ashamed of yourself, at your age, with three children of your own, to have come to be such a good-for-nothing, a degenerate…"

"Papà, please, you can't go on like…"

"Can't go on? Am I wrong, by any chance? Is this what brings you to visit your ailing father? Is this what reminds you of your poor mother? This nonsense will be the death of me. Haven't you done enough? You've been doing this all your life. You will never change, never, it's no use, never!"

"That's enough, Papà, enough! Enough sermons! I've come to ask for your help, not your sermons. I've heard enough sermons…"

"You don't want sermons, eh? Well, you'll just have to put up with them. Because I am your father, and I have every right. Do you hear me? They don't want to hear sermons! What nerve. Spoiled, pompous little brats. Believe me, I would never, but never, have dared to address my father in the tone in which you address me. I know, times change. Today there is absolutely no respect for age. The elderly, let them die. Parents, poor things, don't count at all. Shame on you! We sacrifice in every way for them, we satisfy all their desires, we give them everything they want and then they dare to raise their voices. Don't dare say a word, for they're made of sugar – they might melt! They take offense! Their father offends them! I tell you, I would rather die than see such things, that's a fact. I would rather die. Yes, may our Lord Savior deliver me soon, I'm not meant to…I'm not meant…"

"Believe, me, Papà, you do not understand. You deserve every respect, but frankly you must take a bit more stock of things. You don't understand, and when you get this way…"

"When I get what way! I declare! What way? You are so shameless as to come and ask for fifty thousand pessetes because, truth be told, this note is just a bit of nonsense; when the day comes they will be at my throat and to avoid a trial I'll have no recourse but to pay, you understand, pay and pay again. For forty years I've done nothing but pay, and I am an old man who cannot earn a living, and I have no more money! Much less for your degenerate vices!"

"Papà, for the love of God, I beg you! You know, I have a slow fuse, but…"

"A slow fuse! What you have is debauchery! Between the allowance I give you, your earnings from the bank, and the remains of your wife's dowry, you should be living like royalty! Fifty thousand pessetes! You useless idler! Do you think I don't know that you spend your days and nights gambling at the Eqüestre, and other things I prefer not to know because my ears would burn with shame. My father taught me that I should die before yielding to such frailties. And I say frailties out of kindness, do you hear? A Christian, a Catholic, a gentleman, a decent man, a family man would not…"

"Enough, Papà! Enough!"

"Enough! That's not the half of it! You are a bad son. Do you hear what I say? A bad son! Look, look here, this is your great-grandfather. Do you know who this man was? He was a man of conscience. You know the story of Uncle Manuel, don't you? You don't? Well, Uncle

Manuel committed a heinous act, the kind pious persons refrain from mentioning, and my grandfather, the gentleman you see here in this portrait, who was his father, chose never to forgive him. He didn't even forgive him on his deathbed. He condemned him! Do you hear me? He damned him to hell. Uncle Manuel spent his whole life with the sting of his father's malediction in his heart. What do you think of that! And Grandfather was a saint, an upstanding man, of the kind that are no more in Barcelona. No more. Do you understand me? So now, listen closely: what do you want? What do you expect of me? Do you want to be the Uncle Manuel of our family, do you want to be the family disgrace? Do you want your father to condemn you?"

"Enough, Papà. I've had enough of this nonsense. I could care less if you condemn me, do whatever you like. You don't want to give me a hand? That's just fine! This endless stream of sermons is just mean-spiritedness, the fear of losing fifty thousand pessetes. Very well, sir, very well. You and your saints, and your airs, and your good conscience. When all is said and done, what have you ever done? You lost your fortune in the most ridiculous way! Have you ever so much as bent down to lift a blade of straw from the ground? Have you ever done anything worthwhile? What kind of education and what kind of example have you provided for us? Maybe I am a no-good idler. Whose fault is that? And let's not get started on debauchery and piety! You have done everything everyone else does, you have not denied yourself a thing. Don't start in on how virtuous you are as an excuse not to give me your signature. We both know perfectly well what Mamà has gone through with your affairs."

"Ah, you wicked child! Wicked! My children! Can these be my children…? You are killing me. Just kill me now…I can't go on!"

Don Tomàs de Lloberola was seized by a terrible congestion. He tried to cough, but he choked. In a word, he was suffocating. Convulsed, he gripped the wooden arms of the chair, and when he could finally catch his breath, he released a sob that could not have been more shattering and intense. Frightened at his father's appearance, Frederic tried to approach him, but Don Tomàs brushed him away violently.

"Don't touch me…you want to kill me…let me be…Leocàdia, Leocàdia, I'm dying…they're trying to kill me…!"

Accustomed to these scenes, Leocàdia walked in at a resigned and practical pace, didn't so much as say a word, and stood by her husband's side. He took her hands and, sobbing as he spoke, almost suffocating, he said:

"Mamà…poor Mamà…Now you see it. These are our children… This is what you've brought into this world…poor Mamà…!"

Leocàdia cast Frederic a dry and timid glance of reproach, of pity, even of understanding, and still without opening her mouth, helped the enormous Don Tomàs get up. Hobbling and crying out, "Ai…! Ai…! Leocàdia, I'm dying…! Mamà, I'm dying…!", he vanished into his bedroom. Frederic stood flabbergasted in the middle of the room. Chewing on his lips, he said under his breath: "What a farce…! What a farce…!" as he listened to his father moaning from the bed in which Leocàdia had helped him lie down.

A few minutes later – Frederic could not have said how many – Leocàdia appeared.

"My son! Can't you see what a state he is in?"

"But, Mamà, there is nothing wrong with him!"

"There is something wrong. You don't see him as I do! He's asking for Dr. Claramunt, he wants to see Dr. Claramunt above all else. He wants to make his confession."

"Mamà, this is absurd. It's ridiculous! People will say we've gone mad."

"This is how it goes, you know that. It's the only thing that calms him down."

"Right now?"

"Yes, my dear son, I'm asking you this favor. Do it for me, my son…for your poor mother."

"For the love of God, Mamà, let's not get all worked up."

"Please do me this favor. Go and fetch Dr. Claramunt – you'll find him at home. Tell him what's going on. Dr. Claramunt knows him well."

"All right, Mamà, all right. But, frankly, this is too much…"

"Right away, my son. Don't be too long."

For many years now, there had been two indispensable figures for the Lloberolas: one was Dr. Josep Claramunt, the spiritual confessor of the cathedral. The other was Don Ignasi Serramalera i Puntí, who was a medical doctor, a full professor at the University, an academic, a director and member of the board of several hospitals, and the Lloberola family doctor. These two persons, when spoken of by a Lloberola, received dual consideration. In the first place, the consideration due to a magical and sublime eminence. In the second place, the kind of consideration, selfish and condescending in equal measure, that traditional families develop for an object, an animal, or a person who belongs to them, whom they have the exclusive enjoyment of, whose excellences are known only to them, and whom they can squeeze to the bone. When Don Tomàs spoke of the family doctor or the family priest, he did so with the conviction with which he would speak of a medicine to which he owed his life. For Don Tomàs there was no better doctor than Dr. Serramalera, nor any wiser, more prudent and more virtuous priest than Mossèn Claramunt. If anyone dared to touch a hair on the head of one of these two men, Don Tomàs would fly into a rage. Needless to say, the immunity, the prestige, and the superstition they enjoyed was comparable only to the effect produced by a witch doctor with animal blood in the heart of the most pagan tribe of Africa. Anything one of these two individuals so much as hinted at was considered an article of faith. They were the definitive arbiters of both the temporal and the eternal health of the family.

When some distant relative died, Don Tomàs would say: "They got what they deserved, for being stubborn. They didn't want Dr. Serramalera to visit them and naturally they have a doctor who's not up to the task…"

But those two eminences were two poor old men of crushing ineptitude and ordinariness. All their value proceeded from the

Lloberolas, who had either made them or imposed them on others. The pride of the Lloberolas lay in the fact that both their doctor and their priest were like those linen underpants that Don Tomàs's mother used to cut out and sew: solid, invulnerable underpants, insured against splitting and laundering. It was because they wore this kind of underpants that the Lloberolas held themselves to be superior to the rest of the Barcelona gentry. Mossèn Claramunt had been in residence with the Lloberolas since his years as a seminarian, and the old Marquès de Sitjar had paid for Dr. Serramalera's studies. What's more, since both one and the other had breathed the air of the old mansion on Carrer Sant Pere més Baix, they held the key to the Lloberola foibles. They could read their minds. They would contradict them when a contradiction was what the patient's subconscious demanded. Often they would not show up for a requested visit because what the Lloberolas desired for their peace of mind was precisely for the doctor to pay no heed to the supposed illness and neglect to pass by.

Even a person as entirely simple and lacking in imagination as Don Tomàs can offer a psychologist willing to lose a few hours the most novel of wrinkles and the most mysterious of hollows. And a man who knows all those wrinkles and hollows by heart can achieve the most complete domination of the person under study. What Dr. Serramalera or Mossèn Claramunt had not come by through keen perception or psychological skill, they had acquired through practice, routine, and years of contact with the furniture, the dust, and the vanity of the Lloberolas.

For Don Tomàs and for Leocàdia these men had yet another virtue, perhaps the most important one; but this virtue was appreciated unconsciously, because Don Tomàs and Leocàdia never realized it was there: of all the people who had had dealings with the Lloberolas, the doctor and the priest were the only ones who continued treating them in their decline exactly as they had in their days of splendor. The same respectful and familiar smile Mossèn Claramunt had worn in the salons of the old house as Don Tomàs held forth on how his stable was the best in Barcelona, he wore on entering the little dining alcove of the apartment on Carrer de Mallorca, as Don Tomàs gnawed on a hazelnut with a tear trapped in each eye. On the reverend's lips, the marquis was just as much a Senyor now as before, and even though, as we said, he was not conscious of it, for Don Tomàs this was tantamount to maintaining an illusion. It meant he could extract from the priest's sanctimonious pupils the delicate gleam of a white lie that lengthened his life.

After a series of detours that poured drops of hot wax on his heart, in a state of compressed rage and desperate impotence, Frederic managed to get Mossèn Claramunt into a taxi. Not two hours had passed since his obsession with the stuffed dog with the garter around its neck in Rosa Trènor's bedroom. Though the comparison was not entirely fair, that monstrous and ill-stitched object appeared to him again, on finding himself in the taxi next to the priest. Doctor Claramunt seemed not wholly human to him, like an ill-stitched creature. To the Lloberola scion those cheeks – over which the father confessor scraped a straight razor every morning, as if on tiptoe, as if it were a metallic virgin stepping timidly over the stumps of a holy field – looked like the stuffed viscera from a museum of anatomy that a perverse biologist had powdered over and wound up. The cheeks of the father confessor quivered nervously, as what little remnant of facial muscle supporting his flabby and pendulous skin jerked up and down. The priest's lips stretched tightly and his pointy chin thrust forward or shrank back against his Adam's apple, as if he had such a painful inflammation of the gums that he could not avoid this grotesque maneuver.

Frederic discovered that one can have the same clinical sensation, the same desire to escape when facing a respectable confessor or a bathtub with two inches of dirty water and a floating sponge.

In the taxi, Doctor Claramunt was talking to himself. Frederic had given him a vague idea of what was going on. His eyes glued to the nape of the driver's neck, the priest was emitting a string of very empty, slightly honey-coated words:

"*Bueno, bueno, bueno*," he said in Spanish. "So, el Senyor Marquès. *Bueno, bueno, bueno*," – now he switched from Spanish to Catalan, "Of course, of course, of course! Yes, yes, yes, naturally. I understand, I understand. *Bueno, bueno, bueno...*" "An argument, at his age, eh? An aggravation? *Bueno, bueno...*His heart, of course, his heart! *Bueno, bueno, bueno...*Yes, of course, he is feeling anxiety. All the Lloberolas suffer from anxiety. *Bueno, bueno, bueno...*"

The father confessor rubbed his hands together, as if detecting the smell of the cards and the partners for a game of tuti, a courtly precursor to bridge. The gesture betrayed a touch of the pure, dispassionate concupiscence that is the province of theologians.

Frederic's untimely visit to the father confessor had actually put him out. He was a methodical man with a strict routine and, indeed, if it had not been at the behest of Don Tomàs, the priest would never have left the house at the very moment he devoted to his prayers and to the classification of his herbariums. Because, in fact, Claramunt was a reputed botanist. He had begun his studies of plants because they were not unlike his idea of chastity, and what he had started in some sense out of morality and lyricism ended up turning into a proper scientific vocation.

When they reached the apartment on Carrer de Mallorca, after a brief word with Leocàdia, Dr. Clarament went into the patient's room, and Frederic went into the dining room, to smoke a Camel and swear under his breath.

He did not swear alone for long, though, because Guillem had just rung the bell. When he heard that Don Tomàs was doing poorly and the father confessor was in house, he headed straight for the spiral of smoke curling out from under the lamp in the center of the dining room. Elbows on the table, his head hidden between his hands, Frederic was letting the minutes tick by, without even enough drive to take a puff of the Camel that was burning out on its own. When he heard his brother's footsteps, he lifted his gaze and looked at him with utter indifference. Guillem took three hundred pesseta bills out of his pocket and examined them in silence. Smiling the forced smile one adopts on leaving the dentist after he has extracted a molar, Frederic said to Guillem:

"You seem to be flush?"

"Yes, a little business, very minor, nothing much at all, three bills. Blue bills, the pale blue of the month of Mary. I don't know why they tint money such an innocent shade of blue. Look, King Philip II – what a face, huh? Don't you think Papà bears some resemblance to Philip II in the portraits of him as a youth? He has the same mouth and protruding chin, and eyes that always seem to be watching a Corpus procession. If Papà had been Philip II he would already have had me killed, just like the Infant Don Carles. Speaking of which, I hear he's not well, and Mossèn Claramunt is in there humoring him."

"We had an argument, yes. Let's say I'm responsible."

"I don't know when you're going to learn how to deal with Papà. Don't you see there's no point in arguing? We will never be able to get along with him."

"I assure you, if it weren't out of pure necessity, I wouldn't say as much as half a word to our father."

"You take the wrong approach. The two of you don't get along because you're as alike as two raindrops. You are just like Papà…a little bit more modern, at best."

"Look, Guillem, I don't want to hear this cr…"

"Watch your words, brother dear. If Mamà should hear you…"

"Guillem, I tell you I'm in no mood, eh?"

"All right. What's the matter?"

"It's none of your business. It's not as if you could do anything about it."

"You never know, my dear brother. I take it you argued about money?"

"Look, Papà has a way about him that's just not right. I asked him to co-sign a promissory note. There is absolutely no danger to him, for now, at least. A year from now is another thing. And he flew into a rage!"

"It's entirely natural. I don't know how you dare propose such a thing to him."

"I'm not joking, you know."

"Neither am I!"

"You must understand, even if you're just a kid, that there are moments of gravity in life, and I…"

"What do you mean?"

"I mean that if he doesn't want to sign, he is perfectly within his rights. But for him to say by way of justification that I am this or that, and to threaten me with damnation…"

"Just a bunch of words. Does any of this matter to you?"

"Well, even if he is my father, he has no right to say such things. And I didn't bite my tongue either. I gave him an earful. I've had enough of all his virtue and saintliness and…"

"For God's sake, Frederic, stop shouting. And enough of this offensive rubbish. You have no sense of diplomacy, my boy. One more episode like this and he's a goner, and then it will be even worse. Ludicrous as he is, there are still a lot of things that don't collapse because he's around – don't you realize that?"

"You know what, I just don't care anymore. Let it all go to rot!"

"Listen, how much is this note for?"

"Fifty thousand pessetes."

"And do you know anyone who would still lend you fifty thousand pessetes?"

"Don't be an idiot! Of course I can find someone. I can get an extension, they just want Papà's signature."

"And who is this very…cautious person?"

"You don't know him. He's one of my card partners at the Eqüestre."

"And his name cannot be revealed?"

"Oh, yes, sure. It's Antoni Mates, the cotton dealer…"

"Antoni Mates? Oh, this is just too rich! Ha, Antoni Mates."

"What are you talking about, Frederic, you're too young to know him. What's with all this silly laughter? He's a friend of mine, you know, a perfect gentleman."

"Antoni Mates! The one who bought his title – el Baró de… what was it?"

"Yes, yes, El Baró de Falset."

"And you spend your time with pigs like him?"

"I am telling you, he is a perfectly respectable person, who did me a great favor. I abused his generosity, and now the man naturally wants some security."

"All right, Frederic, all right. Congratulations on the friendships you keep."

"Listen, Guillem, do you realize you're being a jerk?"

"I do. But, look, let's speak frankly now, man to man."

"Don't get all uppity on me now."

"Frederic, I assume you do not have fifty thousand pessetes."

"Of course I don't."

"Nor will you have them a year from now."

"That's very likely."

"And Papà wants nothing to do with it."

"Nothing at all."

"And there is no one you can go to with your sob story."

"No one."

"So now what?"

"I don't know."

"Will Antoni Mates swallow the debt?

"How naive can you be?"

"You're the one who's naive, thinking he's such a gentleman and such a good friend. Now let's imagine Antoni Mates wants the debt to be paid, and this takes precedence over your friendship and your bridge table. Do you think Antoni Mates is capable of such a thing?"

"Not only do I think he's capable of it, I'm certain that's exactly what will happen."

"And your great friendship…?

"Well, friends, maybe we're not friends…when there's money at stake, there's no such thing as friendship. In any case, Antoni Mates is under no obligation to me. He must have been in a generous mood. Maybe he had had a little too much whiskey. Lately our relations have changed a bit…"

"Listen, Frederic. Do you want to get this note you signed back? Do you?"

"Guillem, unless I pay, I don't see any way for the note to come back to me."

"You're being obtuse. If it were a question of paying so much as a penny I wouldn't have asked the question."

"Do you mean I should steal it?"

"Steal? What an inelegant word."

"Then I don't get it."

"Your 'good friend' owes me a sort of favor that could obligate him to a an act of absolute generosity. Do you understand now?"

"Listen, I like to play clean."

"Will Antoni Mates play clean if you don't pay up?"

"I don't know, but he will play legal."

"And to hell with you?"

"All right, that's enough. If you want to play games, you can play with someone else."

"I'm not playing games. I want to save your skin, don't you get it? If you want to play the gentleman, you can pay your debt to Antoni Mates, if you feel so inclined, when you are able. But for now, allow me to speak in our self-interest. I am just as much your father's son as you are, I carry the same 'illustrious' name as you, and, understand me, Frederic, I will also suffer the ill effects of your 'irregularities' if the Lloberola name is left at the mercy of the first Antoni Mates who comes along."

"What do you mean?"

"I mean that it is in my interest for you not to pay off this note and for Antoni Mates to send it to you as if he were sending you a box of cigars. I do this not only for you, but for me, as well, and for Papà, and for my own personal business dealings."

"Go on, Guillem, you must be kidding. I assure you Antoni Mates will not be so generous. It's impossible, I tell you. Impossible."

"What do you bet?"

"A thousand pessetes."

"All right. On one condition. If I lose, I pay nothing, because I don't have a thousand pessetes. But if I win, you will pay me."

"That is a ridiculous condition, but I accept. Listen to me, let's stop talking nonsense, because I don't believe in miracles…or in your little games…"

As the brothers went on like this, Doctor Claramunt let his voice be heard from the corridor:

"*Bueno, bueno, bueno,* now that he is reconciled with the Lord God, el Senyor Marquès has found some peace of mind. *Bueno, bueno, bueno,* yes, a bit of peace. It was nothing, really nothing, nothing at all…Anxiety, a bit of aggravation. A shame, a shame, that such pious families… *Bueno, bueno, bueno,*" he trailed off in Spanish.

Frederic escorted the good father out and Guillem slipped off unobtrusively to his bedroom, so as to avoid Father Claramunt's tiresome theology.

When the name Antoni Mates fell upon Guillem's ear, he felt a voluptuous and utterly depraved fingernail softly trace the surface of his medulla. Guillem had hid this inexcusable sensation from his brother with a glacial and almost imperceptible smile. Guillem had combined this sensorial gangue, which not everyone can feel, even if he wants to, with a tender, noble, almost childlike sentiment. Because Guillem was not precisely a bad person in the strict sense of the word. He was just a weak, amoral, and selfish person, a man lacking in dignity. A product of the family degeneration, hapless, in a way, capable at certain moments of affection and pure sentiment, and above all capable of that biological bond that exists between two fruits of the same tree.

It is not uncommon for two brothers to be indifferent to each other, or to dislike or even hate each other. Fratricides are relatively frequent events. But all this is no obstacle to the existence of a very special sentiment that is only registered in fraternal relations. This is the sentiment that leads one brother to help another, and in a moment of danger even to give preference to his brother over everything else. We know of families in which two brothers do nothing but insult each other, between whom the physical and moral differences could not possibly be stronger, and in which each aims his life toward a different or even opposite path. But in a moment of true danger – true dangers almost always involving the physical or economic health of a person, because in the face of such dangers, emotional health takes second place – these brothers come together, and they do what they would not do for anyone else. What's more, the sacrifice made for a brother doesn't bear the weight of a sacrifice made for a friend, because it is seen as something natural, biological, a fateful obligation they share with each other. In these moments of danger a family apparently dispersed by circumstance contracts to become a defensive, homogeneous mass. The memory of the maternal entrails that created a series of apparently distinct individuals becomes imperative and turns into a solid cord that binds the hearts of brothers in mutual aid.

We have known families that, even after the most inhuman quarrels, have erased their differences and their distance and their pride in the face of death, a difficult operation, or economic disaster. Thus brother could stand by brother, in such a way and with such expression as perhaps to be the only integrally disinterested and loving sentiment in the world. Because, as we have said, brotherhood does not obey the will, or affection, or any other kind of sentimental fancy. No, it is a purely biological product that falls into the category of the instinct for preservation that all human beings share.

Guillem certainly didn't have any feelings for his brother. He kept his distance from him, just as he kept his distance from his parents. In ordinary circumstances, they were two brothers united by indifference. But when he heard the name Antoni Mates, Guillem saw the chance to save his brother. It is possible that in his circle there might be some fellow for whom Guillem felt great affection, but it is also possible that if this fellow found himself in a similar situation, Guillem would not have come up with such a rapid, imperative, biological plan to save him. And since in this world good feelings are so often entwined with awful feelings, besides seeing a way to save

Frederic, Guillem also saw a chance to do some mischief. The kind of mischief that would require unbelievable sangfroid to pull off. It was a despicable *chantage*. Naturally, the object of this extortion was by no means immaculate, at least not in Guillem's eyes. But even so, the act the young man was prepared to carry out was certainly repugnant and, depending on the circumstances, perhaps even risky.

As he evolved in the world, Guillem had turned out to be an inoffensive and cowardly person, like all the Lloberolas. His dissipation had occurred by degrees, in the kind of effortless decline that allows the moral sense to disappear gradually and painlessly, with no active resistance. Guillem considered himself an ordinary man within the unprincipled gray mass of society that sustained him. He had never yet struck a bold and violent blow, hewn to perfection, with artistic flair and a coherent narrative and mise-en-scène. Now, the occasion had arisen, and it did so precisely as a way to save Frederic. Naturally, Frederic didn't suspect a thing, nor would he ever know what had gone on. And the secrecy and mystery in the transaction that Guillem believed would assure his success only added pleasure and piquancy to the wickedness of his plan.

Shut up in his bedroom, Guillem meditated. He plotted a precise and delicate strategy. The vanity and satisfaction Guillem would feel when he saw his brother's face in the instant in which he gave him a "gift" of fifty thousand pessetes would be transcendental. The lies Antoni Mates would have to tell and the lies he himself would have to tell in order to justify it all left him breathless with joy.

As he thought and plotted, Guillem realized it was nine o'clock and he was late for dinner at the Cafè-Restaurant Suizo on the Plaça Reial, known to everyone in Barcelona as the "Suís." Furthermore, he had not yet found the time to go in and see his father. Timidly, he opened the door to Don Tomàs's room and found him sitting up in bed, swaddled in an enormous frayed woolen shawl, eating his usual semolina soup, happy as a clam.

"What do I hear, Papà, are you not feeling well?"

"No, indeed I am not. And I think you might have…"

"Papà, I just this minute got home, and I'm having supper out."

"You just arrived and you're leaving again? What about your poor mother? Will she have to dine alone?"

"They're expecting me…"

"Go on, go on. Just keep this up, my sons, keep this up, and you'll see what happens. Oh yes, you'll see…"

"If I had known, but I am really expected. It would be terribly impolite at this point…"

"Yes, yes! I said yes! Do as you wish, boy, as you wish!"

"Good night, Papà."

And Don Tomàs de Lloberola and Serradell, swaddled in his tatty woolen shawl, in which he looked like a beggar at a Sant Vincent de Paul conference, slurped his semolina soup in his great-grandfather's bed, a grand bed of mahogany and gold metal from the time of the Reign of Terror. It had come from Paris in a stagecoach, like those gentlewomen who fled the guillotine only to end up in the old Fonda of the Four Nations alongside some Italian fan dancer, destined for the bed of the Captain General or the President of the Barcelona Justice Tribunal.

———·———·———

ONE MIGHT HAVE thought Guillem was fleeing the family soup, Swiss chard, and omelet repast for a revelry of skirts, *sauce anglaise* and depravity, but the supper Guillem was bound for was as conventional and honest as they come. The truth is the young man was having dinner at the Suís with a married couple. The fact that he seemed destined to consort with married couples did not mean that the collaboration always had to be unpalatable. In this case, the husband was a young lawyer, a lifelong friend of Guillem's, by the name of Agustí Casals. Agustí Casals was of humble extraction. His father, an exemplary working man, had reared a good brood of children, sent them all to school, and given each one a start in life. Agustí's wife was an intelligent young woman who, though she was no beauty, had personality and charm. Agustí Casals earned a comfortable living and had a large apartment furnished with taste and grace. His books were well chosen, he had a horror of appearing extravagant, and his intelligence, and even natural modesty, precluded so much as a whisker of snobbery. Agustí Casals, with his varnish of ordinariness, was in fact a rather spiritual and broadminded young man, especially when you took into account that life had dealt him a difficult hand, that his field of vision had always been limited by work, courtship and family, and that his knowledge of the world had not been influenced by colorful affairs or voyages or complicated sentimental relations. When it came to women, in fact, he knew only one, because his bachelor indiscretions hadn't allowed him so much as time for reflection. Agustí Casals made an effort to be well-read and up on things as he made his way. But all in all he had a fresh-faced innocence that he didn't attempt to hide and wasn't ashamed to admit. In some aspects of life his criteria were primary and narrow-minded, and with the brutal optimism of a healthy man with no dependencies, Agustí Canals would impose his opinion by laughing, shouting, or getting red in the face and cursing like a longshoreman.

Agustí Casals knew perfectly well who Guillem de Lloberola was. He had known him since they were children, and the friendship of this boy had seemed to him like the friendship of an ambassador from a completely unknown land, who had come to bare his soul in a new environment.

The world of the Lloberolas and the world of Agustí Casals's family were at opposite poles. Agustí Casals was the child of the democratic shopkeeper's class ruled by savings: the saving of space, the saving of time, the saving of money, and the saving of clothing. The apartment he had been born in had no personality. His education, the kitchen in his house, his shoes – purchased ready-made, like the ready-made shirts he had worn – absolutely everything had been as lacking in personality as a ten cèntim coin. Agustí Casals had frequented the variety shows on the Paral·lel, the amusement park at the top of the Tibidabo, the picnics at Les Planes, the beaches at Banys Sant Sebastià, the cafès on the Rambla, and the commonest brothels, in the most anonymous way, just like thousands of students and apprentices and hired hands by the name of Casals, like him, who had no pride of family nor even much of an idea of who their grandfather had been. This was why, beyond being a flesh-and-blood boy like himself, in the person of Guillem de Lloberola, Agustí Casals saw the representative of another race. And since Guillem was a talkative, brilliant and friendly guy, Agustí Casals (and once they were married, his wife, even more), derived great enjoyment from hearing Guillem's stories about the grandeurs and disasters of his family, his childhood memories from the house on Carrer de Sant Pere més Baix, his picturesque perspective on his relatives, and the interminable tales Guillem had picked up from his father about the 19th century aristocracy of Barcelona and the Carlist Wars fought over the return of the Bourbon monarchy. Agustí Casals listened to his friend's stories with genuine tenderness, because even though his blood had no connection to that antique bric-à-brac, when as a student he had ventured into the old neighborhoods, more than once he would stop before the courtyard of a house bearing an illustrious name. He felt a delicate admiration for this select and useless world that nowadays has failed so miserably, and of which Don Tomàs de Lloberola was a particular example.

Agustí Casal's wife was a healthy young woman, satisfied with and utterly enamored of her husband. Though she herself had a somewhat dizzy and spontaneous way of talking, she enjoyed Guillem's conversation. He would tell stories about some of the most well-known ladies of the brilliant leisure class, whom Agustí Casal's wife never dreamed of mixing with, though within her own discreet position she was a refined young woman with an unaffected natural quality, who could have fit in anywhere. Guillem was aware of this soft spot of hers, and he would make things up and exaggerate, sometimes in good fun, sometimes spurred on by his own literary pretensions. Without ever betraying himself, or transmitting too much passion, he managed even to relay certain things of which he had professional experience.

From time to time, Agustí Casals enjoyed inviting his friend to dinner at the Suís because this restaurant imbued with the palm trees and noble architecture of the Plaça Reial (known nowadays as the Plaça de Francesc Macià) retained some of the essence of the final throes of the Barcelona he wanted to discover in the weak and amoral person of Guillem de Lloberola. The Cafè Suís, nowadays a bit run-down, despite the pre-war renovations, used to retain, and still retains, a touch of the air of the tony old cafès and restaurants. It retained the prestige of a good chef and servers who appeared not to have heard of communism. Agustí Casals liked to eat well; the taste for fine cuisine was something he had discovered recently, and when he found himself before an excellent dish he felt a bit of the shivering emotion of a parvenu.

Fine cuisine was part of his sentimental and somewhat literary attachment and devotion to the Barcelona of yore. Thanks to Guillem de Lloberola he knew that the Cafè Suís had seen parades of good gourmets enamored of opulent French women wearing agonizing corsets and picture hats with birds of paradise, trailing endless boas made of ostrich feathers dyed indigo blue. And in the winter the same women had hidden their tiny diamond-encrusted hands inside cylindrical beaver muffs.

Agustí Casals was sorry that the restaurant, either because of the crisis, or perhaps the changing fashion, had seen the migration of its old clientele of flamboyant playboys and Olympian nymphets. At suppertime, with his wife and Guillem, the Suís had the peaceful air of a convent. At the other tables sat the occasional foreigner, who had heard of the restaurant's reputation before coming to Barcelona, or the regulars, gentlemen who were faithful right down to their tables. But, all in all, it had the air of a Monday night.

After dinner, time stretched on and the conversation got lively, with the natural excitement produced by drinks, coffee, and smoke. It was the sort of oasis of happiness that comes of the digestion of a good filet mignon accompanied by a genuine cognac. The two friends had brought up a topic that made Senyora Casals simper and pretend to fuss, though that didn't keep her from offering her two cents every so often, in a sort of affected, yet inoffensive way.

They must have been halfway through the topic and halfway through the cigar; Agustí Casals was speaking with his characteristic vitality, the aplomb of a man with no complications.

"What can I say, Lloberola? I find this all a bit comical. The thing is, in Barcelona people like to grandstand, but it's all just hot air. You can't convince me that such things actually go on among these people you call 'the aristocracy.' Frankly, there is no aristocracy here. It all has the shriveled air of a highfalutin middle class. Just imagine that I decided to behave like a marquis. It would be quite silly, no?"

"No, Agustí, no, don't get carried away. These stories have nothing to do with the aristocracy. You're right, it's all just middle class, bourgeoisie with new money, if you wish, with a lingering whiff of lint and machine oil that could make your eyes tear. What I was saying has nothing to do with any kind of refinement or decadence. It just exists. It exists here as it does everywhere. Sometimes it's the most insignificant and gray of men, or the most apparently ordinary and decent married couple."

"What can I say…what can I say…. You run around in a world of tarts and idlers, and, well, you see things that aren't there. This is what's in vogue now. After a war, people will do anything to wallow in the low life and try to seem interesting. The sort of respect people used to show one another is gone. You know that better than anyone. We've all become a little bit more shameless. Right now we're talking in front of my wife about things I am certain my mother never heard of in all her life. This is not distinction, or anything of the kind. This is just pure nonsense."

"Who said anything about distinction? This is a fact, a flaw, a sickness of our times…"

"No, no, I'll have none of that. Foolish fantasy, literature for the blasé, like you. "

"Dear, you're getting all riled up! Lower your voices, both of you! That man with the bandage on his cheek thinks you're arguing and he hasn't taken his eyes off you." (Naturally, it was Agustí Casals's wife who said this.)

"Mind your own business, do you hear? We'll speak as loud as we like. What we say is no one else's affair, and after working all day long, I can certainly be allowed to shout a little. All right? So, Lloberola, to get back to what we were talking about, this is more a literary obsession than anything else. Proust and Gide are in fashion these days, along with that foolishness about Freud that Dr. Marañón is publishing in Madrid. You've all read Proust, and you want to discover mysterious bonds and unnatural societies everywhere. I agree that these things exist in Barcelona just as they do everywhere else, and that there are as many degenerates here as you like. These people live in broad daylight, it's written on their faces, they are part of a perfectly demarcated world. But these married couples, these strange combinations, these respectable and respected people..."

"Well, yes, in fact, all of this exists."

"Why do only some people know about it? Why, above all, does only a certain type of person talk about it? No, my friend, no. Anyone can be tarred by a story like this. Anyone who has been the butt of gossip can...But where is the proof? Have you ever seen such a thing? Do you have positive evidence?"

"Casals, there's just no reasoning with you. Listen. Don't you have a nose?"

"A nose, why?"

"To sniff things out, to connect the dots, to reach conclusions..."

"As you can imagine, I have better things to do. I have other kinds of dots to connect. In my world, if you do no evil, you think no evil."

"You see, you see, what a dope you are? Do you see why there's just no reasoning with you?"

"You know, Lloberola is right. He knows more about these things than you. He knows these people…" (This, too, was Senyora Casals.)

"Did you hear that, from my wife? Always against the husband! What do you know about what Lloberola knows? You would be better off keeping quiet and pretending not to listen…"

"I can't imagine why…"

"That's neither here nor there, we're talking about something else. I'm telling you this, Casals, because I know you're interested, because you have a bit of the soul of a novelist, and what I've heard about this couple is a truly horrifying thing."

"So who is this couple?"

"Look, as you can imagine, the person who tipped me off is someone with an interest in the affair and he didn't mention any names. Some people think I'm a blabbermouth. But he swore they were very well-known…"

"All right, but get to the point, what's the story? Because you still haven't been very clear…"

"For God's sake, Casals! You want me to tell you all the details? You know that your wife is here…"

"I assure you I understood perfectly what was going on." (Once again Senyora Casals was speaking, laughing, but blushing a bit.)

"Well, I haven't understood perfectly. That is, I can't get it through my head…it seems too preposterous…You said…what did you say?"

"You want me to repeat it? It's the wife, the husband, and…let's say, a hired man…Not a friend, you understand. Someone who earns a fee."

"Yes, yes…I get it…"

"Well, the husband…the husband plays a role…let's say he's passive with regard to the wife…and active (if you can call that active, because it's a little complicated), with regard to the other…And the other and the wife…you get it…"

"Yes, yes, of course, I get it."

"But the strange thing is that, to do this, the man needs for the wife to be there…and the wife…"

"The wife needs for the husband to be there…"

"That's right! What do you think?"

"I think it's perfectly disgusting. And you say the wife is a beautiful woman…"

"Beautiful…! Well…, that's what they told me. And the strangest part is that this gentleman has no other outlet than this. I mean, he doesn't go off on his own, not at all. He's not one of these ordinary perverts, you understand? Unless his 'legitimate' wife is present, nothing happens…"

"And what about when he and his wife are alone?"

"Nothing, nothing at all."

"But this is monstrous!"

"Monstrous, indeed. Who could deny it."

"What I don't understand is that there could be a person who can provide such details, who knows things firsthand, who could know, for example, that there is nothing going on between him and his wife…"

"Look, Casals, I'm telling you exactly what they told me; I didn't see it myself, as you can imagine."

"And the guy who agrees to play this third-rate little game?"

"It seems there are more than a few guys like that in Barcelona…"

"But you have to have a lot of nerve…"

"That's it exactly. I would say you needed unimaginable nerve."

———·——·——

FREDERIC WAS CERTAIN his brother was a nobody. "What kind of relations could Guillem have with Antoni Mates? Hah! I don't think they've even met…! If I could find a way to get it over on that Jew…. Because, ultimately, what could actually happen to me? So what if I don't pay? Will they put me in prison? Would my father go so far as to allow his name to be dragged through the courts? And, even if he is a son of a b…, if I don't pay, Antoni Mates won't have the guts to sue me." This is what was going through Frederic's mind, this is what he was muttering to himself, after he dropped Mossèn Claramunt off. The scene with his father didn't matter to him at all. It wasn't the first, and it wouldn't be the last: "Father always overacts. He's just a poor old fool." Perhaps as a distraction, Frederic started thinking about the role the priest had played in the whole affair. Frederic had derived a negative, arbitrary opinion of priests from observing their behavior in the family enclave. Frederic's anticlericalism was cowardly and shameful, like everything else about him. He would never dare confess to his mother that he had not been a practicing Catholic for many years. Curiously, he would never even have confessed it to his wife. With his children Frederic always affected a great respect for things religious, and, in the days when they lived in the big house on Carrer de Sant Pere més Baix, he had not been averse to bearing the canopy in Corpus processions wearing the uniform of a Knight of the Mestrança. Later on, he would joke about it with his friends, and say whatever entered his mind, but a strange sort of fear had kept him from ever touching a rib of beef on a Friday during Lent. After the failure of his latest business, he had become a bit more brazen with his conscience, even to the extent of formulating ideas that would have terrified him years before. He was so furious and so cornered that his impotence drove him to take out his rage on the nose and cheeks of Mossèn Claramunt. That decrepit charlatan, whom he had been putting up with ever since he had the use of reason, seemed to him to be the vilest of farceurs. He imagined the scene of the goodly priest hearing his father's confession. "How hilarious! My father calling for this crank to soothe his conscience, for fear of going to hell. And what should he be confessing for? For having dragged us all to ruin, for having been the most egotistical of men. For having threatened to condemn me to hell. To hell! What was the poor man thinking? Does he think I'm going to lose a moment's sleep over his malediction? He doesn't want to co-sign a promissory note, so he calls for his priest! He doesn't want to help his son, so he requires the church canon! And he's afraid to die! He's a fool, a hypocrite! What does he need the money for? Whom should the few bills he has left be for, if not for me? And that idiot priest must be sitting down to dinner now, thinking he's done something grand. He went to hear el Senyor Marquès's confession. No, but this one is cleverer than my father; he knows exactly what he's doing…And they will both sleep peacefully because they have complied with the law of God. As if God didn't have better things to do than watch over these miserable failures. Meanwhile, his son can drop dead. That's what religion means to them…"

It is very possible that Frederic's idea of religion was even more flawed than his father's, because Frederic's line of reasoning was that of a frustrated illiterate, an egotist who isn't getting his way, a weak, vain man with no convictions, who would have eaten his father and all his timeworn religious prejudices alive. And yet, when he was in the mood, he would affirm that true aristocrats like himself were a superior race, and he would sing the praises of his family, even being so puerile as to describe his coat of arms to someone who couldn't give a hoot about coats of arms, and who could clearly appreciate that Frederic de Lloberola was just as ordinary, undistinguished, and insignificant a being as any grocer or tram conductor. Frederic had promised Rosa Trènor that they would meet up before dinner, but he was not at all in the mood to see the woman. It is strange to see the effect twenty-four hours can have on inconsistent men who think themselves extraordinary but are in fact just about able to get by, and no more. Frederic's brain was in a quixotic lather. At every step reality was revealing his mediocrity and his failure but, if nothing more, the blood of the Lloberolas was good for fabricating illusions. The day before Frederic had envisioned himself in a novel of scandalous and flamboyant rebellion. It is not that in the intimacy of his marriage Frederic should not have had his reasons for desiring something more. But an ordinary man will do whatever crazy thing comes along, out of pleasure or necessity, without the slightest interference from any concept of chivalrous duty. Frederic believed that even in the wildest or basest things – what people call "bad deeds" – chivalric duty ought to intervene. For him, this duty consisted of seeking out the woman who had been his lover fifteen years earlier, because in this way the plot took on a romantic perfume that disinfected it of the undistinguished whiff of the plebeian in an overdue promissory note. The day before, the memory of Rosa Trènor's sexual prowess had seemed absolutely incandescent; his disgust with his legitimate spouse had also become infinitely more acute. Paradoxical as it may seem – and with a poor devil like Frederic everything can seem paradoxical – what required the intervention of "chivalric duty," the quixotic lather that warped his brain, was precisely the possibility of a rebellious and novelesque situation of that kind. Supposing that Rosa Trènor were actually worth it, a man with his feet more firmly planted on the ground might possibly have chosen a more pleasant and opportune moment, one less charged with worries and overdue notes – for the affair, or the reconciliation. To Frederic this would have seemed ill-bred. The more prosaic and obtuse people are, the more they are consumed with the need to shroud their acts in pathetic and literary braggadocio. In certain situations it is the gossipy concierge who is best able to find the most overblown and melodramatic language. In many ways, Frederic de Lloberola had the mentality of a concierge.

Though a romantic situation can rise very suddenly, it can just as suddenly deflate, and turn into a tame cowardice that advances on foot, no longer dreaming of legendary steeds. This is what was happening to Frederic. Rosa Trènor had been a disappointment, though perhaps not an absolute disappointment. Frederic would go back to her, and she would let Frederic come back, but things would proceed without enthusiasm. The novel had been foiled by the night itself, the conversations with Don Tomàs and his brother, and finally the vision of Mossèn Claramunt. Frederic had filtered the anxiety of the promissory note through the eyes of Rosa Trènor. Later, he could hardly see Rosa Trènor at all, while the very real vision of the fifty-thousand pesseta note, perhaps because it was coming closer, was also the more cynical, placid and resigned one. And in the midst of it all there was still the question of whether his brother Guillem could work a miracle. Naturally, he didn't believe he could; it was like the hope one placed in winning the grand prize in a raffle. You struggle against it, as the most gratuitous and absurd of hopes, but even so you think: "Well, someone has to win it; who knows? Anything is possible." And, naturally, the illusion persists.

So after Frederic de Lloberola dropped Mossèn Claramunt off, he decided to go home instead of going to see Rosa Trènor. Frederic's house was an apartment on Carrer de Bailèn. The staircase smelled of chicken wings, garbage cans, and the cheap local cigarillos known as *caliquenyos*. It was an odor peculiar to some apartment houses in the Barcelona Eixample, which everyone puts up with and whose source no one can determine. Residents are subjected to it five or six times a day, and they complain to the concierge, who complains to the manager, but no one does anything about it. And alongside the natural whiff of the house there is a whiff of whining, ill humor, rancor, and feeble protest. Sometimes the smell comes from the laundry room; sometimes from the apartment of a German man who deals in drugs or specialized straps, and the smell coming from the German man's apartment mingles with a repugnant codfish boiling in the concierge's house. At that point, the chemical reaction in the entryway is reminiscent of the beard of the knights who traveled to the Holy Land or the nightgown of the paramour of an ancient king of Castile. Occasionally the smell proceeds from the souls of the ladies on the first floor, which are completely dead, and give off an odor of dead soul that not even carrion crows would have anything to do with.

Frederic's apartment had an air of neglect. When the time comes to cut back, people accustomed to spending freely and living with a certain pomp adopt a kind of elegiac disregard that softens their bones and extends to all the details surrounding them. It drapes itself over the furniture and over the cooks' hairdos. You can detect it in the chipped glassware, in the dining room chandelier missing two bulbs that no one bothers to replace, in the sad figurine that has lost a hand, and in the rug that is losing its pile and revealing its veins and bald spots. In the most intimate spaces, the bedrooms and the bathroom, this negligence exposes the cavities in their teeth and their dirty undershirts. The water heater never quite works, the water never flows properly, the towels are always damp. When someone is ill, and a stranger has to come into the bedroom, the lady of the house agonizes over how to conceal the details, the flaws in the room, the peeling wallpaper, or the chair with the broken seat. In the small salon of the house, a bit of proper decorum is maintained, and care is taken to keep everything in order so that the ladies who come to visit can rest their eyes on a serene view as they take their tea, and not feel an uneasiness that would be just as bleak as the shame of their hosts.

In Frederic's house, this feeling of neglect was even sadder because the furniture was in bad taste but of good quality, and too large for the apartment. Frederic had crammed the foyer with shields and coats of arms and even the occasional fake suit of armor. The same was true of the dining room and the salon: grotesque, incongruous and overbearing heraldic insignias shared the space with awful picture cards and paintings purchased who knows where at ridiculous prices, hung without a particle of discernment.

Maria, Frederic's wife, was a person without initiative, whiny, bitter, and peevish, who little by little had also taken on the dusty sluggishness of Frederic's family. Maria lived outside her time. She had adopted all the modifications introduced into the lady's toilette after World War I: she patronized good hair stylists, manicurists and masseuses. But she followed their regimens in an unenergetic way, never getting any fresh air, never taking into account that in order for the work of the beauty salons to be effective it requires the constant collaboration of the client. The day after she had her nails polished, her hands already looked unkempt. When she tried applying makeup, it only made things worse, as she had no instinct for it. She had lost the desire to be attractive, to be interesting, to breathe a smidgen of charm into the air around her. Maria's friends affirmed that this was not a recent thing, that she had always been this way; moreover they said she was dirty. Maria's bad taste was evident because she was incapable of putting together a serviceable outfit. Sometimes she would ruin an elegant evening dress by wearing misshapen old shoes whose leather or silk was worn from use. Like all slovenly people, Maria spent money absurdly. She was hopeless at saving or at the art of making do. Over the years she had been seized by a strange piousness, characterized not by religious fervor or faithful observance, but rather by the sneering and general disapproval born of self-righteousness and moralism.

Maria had pretty hair and nice skin; despite her children, who were now getting big – her daughter had just turned fourteen – she conserved her slim waist and didn't need girdles or orthopedic wiles to prop up her somewhat abundant but still fresh body. With a different temperament Maria could have been a first-rate woman, but it seemed as if she were bent on killing any positive effects, on limiting herself to being a person without the least bit of sex appeal.

Having thrown in her lot with a family that had not known how to hold on to its wealth, and had exhausted her dowry as well, Maria started rolling out her instinct for unabashed complaint and unmotivated sniveling. While Frederic didn't want it said that he was ruined, and childishly clinging to the Lloberola airs, he continued to talk in the thousands of thousands like a grand gentleman, Maria did quite the opposite. When a friend praised the fine points of an overcoat, a refrigerator, a dog, or a device for piercing an egg for drinking, Maria would start with the ohs and ahs and roll her eyes back in her head. After this she would put on a sad face and shrug her shoulders, always with the same comment: "Lucky you! None of these things for poor me. With all our household expenses, just imagine! We have to save! Even now we're getting along with just one maid. When you've had the problems we've had…" If Maria's name came up, the ladies would always say, "Poor Maria." This ostentation of poverty reached irritatingly grotesque proportions. If she went to visit friends who were close enough to receive her in the dining room as they ate, she would comment on every course: "What beautiful asparagus! Of course, you can enjoy such a delicacy. It's been a long time since we've seen asparagus like these in my house. The way prices have risen!" These comments made the friends who were eating the asparagus want to say: "Here, Maria, be quiet and have some asparagus." Naturally, this didn't usually happen, but it made her friends feel bad, and they would end up getting no enjoyment out of the asparagus. When she was invited to a party she was dying to attend, she would snivel, just to play hard to get: "Impossible! X and Y will be there, and I don't have a dress. I would have to wear my black georgette again, and they've seen me in it three times."

This behavior reached funereal heights in the family circle. Her lack of skill at avoiding avoidable things, her sadistic delight in continually pointing out the mended patches and placing the blame on her husband – never with violence, but with the slack demeanor of a beaten-down cat – and a mewling singsong full of bitterness and apparent resignation made her an odious woman. If the compensation of tender and passionate interludes, of something visceral and alive, had existed, perhaps a man could have found her relatively tolerable. But she was cold in intimacy, with a rigid and imperceptible sensuality, full of vengeful sighs of aversion.

The only person she got along with was her mother. Senyora Carreres, flush with money and diamonds, seemed to dissolve with voluptuosity when she contemplated the precarious situation of her daughter and son-in-law. She felt a sort of joyous middle class bad blood on seeing how the Lloberolas had squandered their fortune, right down to her daughter's dowry. When Maria married, Senyora Carreres had learned that the Lloberolas found the Carreres family undistinguished and had wrinkled their noses at the match. Years later, Maria's mother felt as if she were bathing in rose water on seeing herself so full of life, so well-fed and well-positioned, just as Frederic de Lloberola had had to lower himself, and beg clemency, often for ludicrous sums. Senyora Carreres cultivated her daughter's tearful incontinence, inflaming her against her husband's family, and creating an unbearably tense situation. It had been years since the in-laws had seen each other, and Frederic tolerated his wife's parents out of pure necessity. Instead of keeping a bit of distance so as not to call attention to their contrasting fortunes, Senyora Carreres spent the entire day at her daughter's side, saying "My poor dear! What misfortunes we must bear, dear God!" And she wasn't good for a cent. Sometimes when Frederic got home he would find the two of them sitting in a corner of the dining room. When he came in they barely said a word to him. Maria would bow her head, and Senyora Carreres would glare at him with eyes that appeared to want to cry. She would move her head with the cadence of a disappointed cow, like the ones that secretly lived in the heart of the densest and most impoverished neighborhoods of Barcelona. Frederic would take in the viscous gleam of those ruminant eyes and then, pretending not to have noticed a thing, begin to tell them tales of grandeur or bits of piquant gossip that he knew his mother-in-law would find offensive. Senyora Carreres would adopt an increasingly acidic, passive, and abused attitude, scratching her cheeks with her little doll's nails. And Frederic would finally take off, wishing he were one of those despotic medieval Lloberolas who could have had the pleasure of sealing the two of them behind a wall, alive.

WHEN FREDERIC HAD dropped the priest off and decided to go home, he realized it had been twenty-four hours since he had last set foot there. Even though relations with his wife had attained a glacial chill, he had had to come up with a story and invent a trip with Bobby in order to spend the night away. He thought about seeing his children again, along with the same tablecloth and the same oil and vinegar cruets and perhaps even the same anemones from two days before. They would now be in a state of withered decomposition, because his wife was so neglectful that it wouldn't be at all strange if she had not seen to changing the flowers.

Returning once again to the promissory note, and to Antoni Mates, Frederic went so far as to think that if things looked really bad he would have no choice but to flee. Then the melodramatic side of Frederic's nature began to see that night as the possible prelude to a tale of emigration. Twenty-four hours earlier, his wife, his entire family, had seemed intolerable to him; Rosa Trènor had been his liberation. After dropping off the priest, he had breathed in the bouquet of his family from afar with a nose of bathos. Just a moment before, like some barroom thug, Frederic had given his father a tongue lashing that left him limp as a doll. Then, erratic and weak, he had come to entertain the idea that it was all his own fault. The fifty thousand pessetes had not all gone to covering up urgent debts. Frederic knew full well that twenty thousand of those pessetes had been spent on an affair that had momentarily obsessed him, but had turned out to be a disappointment, like all the others. And that was just around that time that his wife had been whining because she couldn't buy a coat that cost only four thousand pessetes, and Frederic ignored her and had the gall to say that she must be out of her mind, and the coat was out of the question. Maria never knew a thing, and still didn't know a thing, about the damned promissory note because Frederic had done everything possible to keep it from her, trusting as he did that things would work out favorably in the end, and Antoni Mates would agree to renew the loan on the same conditions.

Selfish as a spoiled child, Frederic always found a way to justify himself and to play the victim. Still, he also had his moments of wretched *mea culpas*, as exaggerated and contemptible as his moments of conceit. In just twenty-four hours the change had been radical, and the closer he got to his house, the more desperate and purple the idea became of emigrating, abandoning his family, and sullying forever more his illustrious family name.

A moment ago he was saying, "Hah! Even though Antoni Mates is a son of a b…, he wouldn't dare bring a case against me." He would take a position of resigned cynicism, adopting an attitude of having seen it all. Later, without rhyme or reason, something he had seen on display in a shop window, or a simple incident on the street, would bring about a change of heart. The reactions of a man like Frederic can have the most absurd causes. He didn't know if he should confess everything to his wife or if he should let fall, in some vague way, the idea of a troubling situation and a possible trip. Or if he should do it coldly, as if in passing, or strike a more declamatory air, his gestures combining desperation and repentance. How he behaved would depend on the mood his wife was in, the dinner she served, the vinegar cruets, or the wilted anemones.

When Frederic walked in the food was on the table. Maria barely commented on the false trip, showing an absolute indifference to anything that concerned him. In the presence of his children Frederic couldn't say a word. As he crossly swallowed his soup, he dropped his melodramatic projects and his intention to confess. "With a wife like this, what's a man to do," Frederic thought, as Maria scolded Lluís, their youngest son, for no reason. "Let him be, Maria, let him be, don't be on his back all the time," said Frederic. Then Maria, losing control and paying no attention to the children, launched into one of those aggrieved monologues that Frederic listened to without a word. Maria completely lost her appetite with her crying, and dinner came to a disastrous end.

Frederic thought, "What a wretched life." He opened the newspaper and pretended to read. The truth was he didn't see a thing. He felt a desire to flee the house, not only because of the promissory note, or the danger he was in, but for everything. He wanted to flee without explanation. Once again he had become the victim. Once again Rosa Trènor turned into a glamorous odalisque. Once again his father's image appeared before him with all the flaws that cruelty, repugnance, and incomprehension can expose. Bobby would probably be at the Eqüestre; his other friends would be there, as they were every night. The only thing he feared was having to see Antoni Mates's face. But, what the devil, the note wasn't due for two more days, and a lot can happen in two days. Just a moment ago he had been thinking of going to America; after dinner, this solution seemed ridiculous. Maybe Bobby, maybe it would be more practical to do what his Lloberola pride had never allowed him to do, to test Bobby's friendship…who knows…

After dinner, Frederic didn't say so much as a word to his wife. He changed from head to toe and fled from his family, feeling the same disgust and pity he had felt in Rosa Trènor's kitchen, with the scrawny cat's tongue licking the dirty coffee cup…

—·—·—

CONXA PUJOL'S GRANDFATHER, *l'avi Pujol*, had earned a lot of money in Cuba in the days of the slave trade. His family were sailmakers from Sant Pol de Mar, respectable, dignified people. Conxa Pujol's grandfather had given up the sails and the ovens and joined a trading company, with a few *duros* he managed to steal from someone, a pipe, three jerseys, a knife, and a pistol.

In no time, l'avi Pujol was a well-known figure in the factories on the Guinean coast and the ports of the Antilles. He was a man of good fortune. Later he would convert the business of coffee-colored skin into the business of actual coffee, and he held government office in the colonies. When he was a bag of worn-out bones with a biblical beard, he turned up in Barcelona, carrying a sweet young mulatta piggyback, and built himself a house of stone on the Rambla de Santa Mònica. The mulatta blossomed in the rocking chairs of the house on the Rambla like a languorous, undulating dahlia, under a buttery silk peignoir that exhaled all the overseas perfume of her skin.

L'avi Pujol died of gall bladder cancer, leaving behind a sickly, squirrelly boy who in time would get into all sorts of mischief. He ended up an extremely rich and respectable gentleman, the manager of a famous shipping agency.

Conxa Pujol was the daughter of that gentleman and a certain Sofia Guanyabens, who proceeded from the dreariest middle class. She died in childbirth. Conxa Pujol had been a dark, magnificent creature, with imponderably dewy skin, and the phosphorescent eyes of a tropical beast. Everyone in the family said that Conxa took after her grandmother, the sweet young mulatta old Pujol had carried home piggyback. Conxa had the aura of a lazy pearl, but not without her moments of malaise. In Sant Pol de Mar, where her father had expanded the old family home and provided every comfort, Conxa spent the summers of her adolescence amid vaporous nights full of shooting stars and vanilla perfume. In that house, el Senyor Pujol kept souvenirs of the old family trade and of the grandfather's navigation, business, and customs. Conxa Pujol's hours of leisure within the white walls of the summer house were made up of dreams of sailing ships, Puerto Rican prints, black men in red-striped white cotton pants whose sweat was whisked away with bullwhips, and birds that flew in loop-the-loops, as if their bellies were full of rum. An entire rhythm of water and rumba, a whole sensual world of madrepore and coral reefs.

Conxa Pujol leafed through books with incredible engravings, navigation diaries, letters, and family portraits. On the beach she would toast her skin with the patience of a slave. She would find a place tucked away between sharp dry canes so no one would see her, where she could lie nearly nude on the sand and watch as her perfectly proportioned breasts took on the sweet amber glow of the fruit of the palm tree.

Bogged down in the opulence of his business, Conxa Pujol's father only half-remembered her. Conxa's only censor in her adolescence was Madame Pasquier, an ugly, depraved Frenchwoman from Toulon with a penchant for the literary.

Madame Pasquier allowed Conxa to do whatever foolish thing crossed her mind, and she encouraged her in the development of modish affectations. Conxa felt no attraction at all to boys of her own stripe, but when she saw the young fishermen pulling their boats along behind pairs of oxen or setting out in the evening for sardine trawls or night fishing, her phosphorescent eyes cast off doleful cinders. Conxa had the heart of a hysterical medusa. She would have liked for those burly, brutish, and inoffensive young men to dive naked into the sea, knives clenched between their teeth, and bring her back a slimy, fascinating sea monster. Conxa would have aspired to other things, too, and one of those brutish and inoffensive boys captured those aspirations perfectly, flashing his extremely white teeth at her one day when "the young lady from Can Pujol" wandered perilously close to those undershirts enhanced with sweat and salt. Conxa gave in to her own private democratic impulses, and an evil tongue assured that one night among the boats she had been seen arching her back like a grouper out of water, beneath the unrefined attentions of a young man who was known among the sailors as "Plug Ugly."

But none of these things had been verified. In Sant Pol they circulated with some acidity, but by the time they reached Barcelona they were completely watered down.

Even so, el Senyor Pujol came to realize that marriage was as necessary for his daughter as their daily bread. Enigmatic Conxa, with the tropical insouciance she had inherited from her grandmother, didn't protest at all when Antoni Mates, a man twenty years her senior, but a peerless match in both economic and social terms, asked for her hand. Nor when the marriage took place, with insulting and baroque pomp, in the Basilica of Our Lady of Mercy, known popularly as La Mercè.

Once married, Conxa – who was still what one might call a child – took up her place at the forefront of the women of Barcelona with the greatest success in attracting yearning glances and sighs. La Senyora Mates produced an effect of original and disconcerting elegance that only she could carry off. Other women tried to imitate her, but they could never find the right balance, nor did they possess Conxa's skin, that exotic and irreplaceable accessory that could achieve whatever Conxa wished to achieve.

When the most sought-after stylists wanted to fob off some overpriced hat on a customer, they would claim it was a model that la Senyora Mates had chosen, and put aside, for one of those reasons stylists could always come up with. This happened everywhere: "We're making one just like it for la Senyora Mates," "La Senyora Mates has just ordered three." "La Senyora Mates is on her way in to try it on."

It goes without saying that Conxa had been besieged by the crème de la crème of lady-killers, living as she did in the midst of a corps of sweet panthers who saw no incompatibility between the sacrament of matrimony and the existence of a gigolo, or even of a gentleman who at some point might pick up some little tab. But despite the approaches of some and the fabrications of others, no one had gotten anywhere with her. This was odd, because it would have seemed natural that a woman who had been the stuff of legend when she was single might have continued to be the source of stories once married to a man who wasn't exactly a head-turner. Sad as it may have been for some, the Mates's seemed united, as if by some anatomical mystery, like Siamese twins. There was not a woman in Barcelona who spoke more glowingly of her husband or affected more constancy to the vows she had taken, and, moreover, behaved accordingly. Conxa had given up golf because her husband's occupations didn't allow him to accompany her. She had given up a great many things, and she put up with being criticized for it and taken for a fool by the other married ladies.

Conxa's attitude was all the more rare in the world she lived in and all that much more opposed to the modern conception of "elegance" when you took into account that her marriage had produced no children, and the maternal tasks that justify so many things could not be adduced in her defense. What no few mature men, devotees of the current market value of adultery, asked themselves was this: "What the devil does a woman like her see in a wet blanket like Mates?"

That "wet blanket," the Baró de Falset by the grace of the Dictator – because the Mates clan came from Falset, and he had paid to build some schools in the town, and invited General Primo de Rivera to the inauguration – had a history that didn't go beyond mediocrity. Antoni Mates was the son of a rag merchant and of a woman who had butchered hens in the Born Market. The ragman had been a member of the inner circle of Planas i Casals, a famous local boss, and the fact that he had paid for the construction of two convents in the exclusive Bonanova district without any ill effects upon his fortune, is a perfectly natural thing, which everyone in Barcelona takes in stride. Antoni Mates was a cotton merchant of the highest order. His father had sent him to England for a few years and, despite his unpromising physical complexion for sport, it was said that he had been a good hockey player. In Barcelona, before the war, he had acquired some notoriety for his bright red bowler hat and for a little black horse he would spur on full speed down the Passeig de Gràcia.

Once married, Antoni Mates left horses and bowler hats behind, and turned into a sweet, dull, reactionary, and extremely religious man. His ragman's fangs only came out at the office and at the meetings of the infinite boards on which he served. Lacking in political convictions and entirely skeptical about life, he had lain down like a dog before Primo de Rivera's military Directory. Occasionally, of an afternoon, he would go to the Eqüestre to play bridge, and when he was thirsty he would order a Johnny Walker. These were the only two vaguely British things he still clung to. In contrast, if, on the occasional Sunday he accompanied his wife to the golf course, he would stretch out, bored to tears, and listen to the birds sing.

As he did every morning, the Baró de Falset had risen at eight-thirty. While he was still in the bathtub, oblivious to the spectacle of a body that would not have stood up well in a nudist camp, the servant knocked on the door.

"Senyor Baró, there is a young man here who says he must see you."

"I don't receive anyone at this time of day."

"He says that it is quite urgent. He says it is of great interest to el Senyor Baró…"

"What is this young man's name?"

"Guillem de Lloberola."

"Guillem de Lloberola? Oh, yes! All right. See him into the parlor; ask him to be kind enough to wait."

Twenty minutes later, Antoni Mates and Guillem de Lloberola were exchanging the usual pleasantries. When he heard Guillem's voice, Antoni Mates had a moment of panic, of horrible panic, which he disguised as best he could. The young man's voice had reminded him of another voice. Oh, yes, Antoni Mates was familiar with that voice, or another that was practically identical. He remembered having heard it recently, in a feverish, or drunken, or dream-like state, in a moment of sweat, of nervous contortion…an inexcusable moment. But, of course, that was impossible. It was mere chance, one of those idiotic and utterly illogical resemblances that crop up in life. The young man's air, his physique, also gave the Baró de Falset an uneasy feeling, but he couldn't pin down the memory. There had been so little light, he had been so beyond himself…No, the cotton merchant had fallen victim to a gratuitous attack of panic. It was impossible, absolutely impossible. Guillem de Lloberola…Guillem de Lloberola…He was perfectly familiar with the name, and the boy's clothing and demeanor reassured him. All these thoughts had run through his head in under three seconds. The moment of panic had passed.

"I do not have the pleasure of having met el Senyor Baró personally, but I believe you are a very good friend of my brother's."

"One of my very best friends, indeed. Don't you ever go to the Eqüestre? Are you not a bridge player?"

"No, no, sir, I'm not."

"Well, I don't want to give you the wrong idea, I don't play very often. It is quite a waste of time, and I have a great deal of work! I would be delighted to while away the hours as your brother does. But we working men, you understand...So, tell me, what is it that brings you here? How can I be of assistance?"

"It is precisely about a question affecting my brother that I have come to see you. And it doesn't only affect my brother, but also my poor father. Father is in very delicate health, and any unpleasantness could kill him. Just yesterday he gave us an awful scare. My brother Frederic is a bit frivolous, as you are probably aware..."

"Oh, not at all! A delightful, elegant man, your brother is; a first-rate companion, first-rate..."

"Well, on the social scene he can be very pleasant...and even elegant; you are very kind and have an undemanding concept of elegance...Well, Senyor Baró, I realize that I am robbing you of your precious time. What I have to say is extremely distasteful to me; I find myself in the obligation, not so much for him, but for my poor father..."

"Please, speak, whatever is in my hands..."

"I believe you have in your power a promissory note you extended to my brother..."

"Excuse me, my dear sir; just the day before yesterday we discussed this question of the note, that is, he discussed it.... This is a question between your brother and me.... Frankly, it is hard for me to understand how you have become involved in this affair...Or how your brother has..., well..., has brought you into it..."

"Forgive me, Senyor Baró. As I have already said, my brother is of very little concern to me. If I have come to see you it is on account of my poor father..."

"All right, young man, all right; tell me what it is you want..."

"I simply want you not to demand my father's signature; I don't want my father to know that Frederic...Understand me: my father's situation is rather critical...Relations between my father and Frederic are quite strained..."

"You are very young, my dear sir; you are a child, and perhaps you are not aware of the significance of some things...I did your brother a favor; I trusted him and two other persons I considered good friends. What your brother has done with me is something, how should I put it...not entirely decent. Your brother has cheated me. I could take him to court, do you understand? I don't know what explanation your brother has given you, but the truth is that his behavior is an abuse of confidence. Naturally, you can object that the amount is not astronomical, and that my position and my home do not depend on the fifty thousand pessetes that your brother owes me. But you must also understand that I am under no obligation to allow myself to be swindled. I am aware of your family situation. I know perfectly well that the grandeur and pomp your brother has the nerve – forgive me –

to go on about are a sham. But I also know that your father can answer for the fifty thousand pessetes – which are mine, after all – without risking death."

"But couldn't another person be found to answer for the debt, someone other than my father?"

"Of course, as long as it is someone who offers me some guarantee. But this is up to your brother. As you can imagine, it is not up to me to provide him a guarantor on a silver platter! That will be the day, my friend! You bloodline "aristocrats" (because, you must know and understand, your brother always brings up his blue blood) are a bit too blasé or distracted…What can I say, I'm sure you follow me."

"But if my brother can't find this person…"

"Well, of course, because no one trusts your brother. He's charming enough, full of jokes, with lots of friends when the time comes to buy champagne. But when things get difficult, my friend, people… how can I put it…prefer someone with his feet on the ground…"

"Well, then, let's get our feet on the ground, Senyor Baró. I mean, let me get my feet on the ground…"

"I want nothing more than that, my son! Nothing more!"

"Senyor Baró, I am under the impression that you give a great deal of weight to material credit. What about…moral credit?"

"Naturally, to moral credit. Above all, to moral credit. It is for this moral credit that I was willing to lend your brother those funds, in the belief that I was dealing with a gentleman, and not – forgive me, I realize the word is a bit strong – with a swindler."

"Precisely, Senyor Baró. With a swindler, you couldn't be more correct. Well, not exactly correct, because my brother has not yet swindled you out of anything, and as you understand, my father would never allow such a thing. He would beg for alms before he would allow it to be said that one of us…"

"I am certain of it! I have never for a moment doubted your father's honor!"

"Excellent, Senyor Baró. 'Moral credit!' 'Honor!' These are precisely the cards I am missing…"

"Missing, what do you mean? I don't follow you."

"I'll tell you what I mean. The cards I'm missing to play a hand that, I must confess – and you, as a bridge player, will understand this perfectly – is quite a hard nut to crack. Senyor Baró, I imagine you hold your moral credit, your honor, your immaculate and invulnerable situation in the world of money and in the world of decent people, in even higher esteem than your fortune. You have looked into my father's situation; I, too, have taken the liberty of looking a bit into your situation. And I congratulate you, Senyor Baró: it is an enviable situation. You are scrupulously conscientious, your relationships smack of solid honesty and capital. Your clients…that pin from the Parish Perseverance League on your lapel…"

"Excuse me, I don't understand what this is all about. I don't understand and what's more, I warn you, I am getting irritated…"

"That is perfectly natural, Senyor Baró. But it is necessary for me to make these affirmations so that we can come to an agreement. As you well know, in Barcelona, in a world more or less left to its own devices, a world that lives day to day and without many scruples, and which, moreover, doesn't have anything to lose, certain...things, certain... perversions, haven't the slightest importance. But in your world, in the world of prejudices and 'moral credit,' in the world of holding on to clients by dint of breast-beating and paying for chapels and schools, there are certain types of scandals that can do one real harm...A sort of scandal that, understand me, may lead the victim to an often desperate and almost always fatal solution. Because there are some things that people don't understand...or don't want to understand... People are so hypocritical, so cruel, with those who fall from favor! And, when this fallen person is a gentleman with a great deal to lose, well, just imagine...!"

"I find your line of reasoning quite remarkable. I'm sure I don't know what scandals you are referring to, but, well, I can only imagine. But truly, my friend, I am at a loss as to what this has to do with the fifty thousand pessetes your brother owes me."

"Just be patient, Senyor Baró, and answer me this question. If you're willing to answer it, that is..."

"Well, it depends what we're talking about."

"It is very simple: what would happen to you, if you were to find yourself tied up in a scandal, in one of those shameful scandals, do you get my drift? Indeed, what if you were the protagonist?"

"Listen to me, young Lloberola. This question of yours is utterly preposterous. Whom do you think you are speaking with? Your question has no more effect on me than if you asked what would happen if I had four noses instead of one!"

"I do not find the comparison to be sound. I find it a bit exaggerated. Indeed, Senyor Baró, I think you are a formidable optimist! All right, then, if you do not wish to answer my question, don't answer it. I will ask you another, much more direct, question: What were you doing yesterday at six in the afternoon in the house of Dorotea Palau, the dressmaker?"

From the start of the second half of this dialogue, Antoni Mates had been anticipating a catastrophe. His initial flash of panic had been replicated with two or three of Guillem's words. As the young man continued to talk, the Baró de Falset felt like one of those philanthropic souls who lie down on an operating table to offer their blood for a transfusion. Little by little, the baron was growing weaker. By the time the direct question arrived, the loss of moral calories had reached the magnitude of a collapse.

The baron was materially frozen. At the base of each hair on his head he felt a cruel sting, as if one of those parasites that inhabit the scalps of filthy ragamuffins had taken up strategic residence at the roots of his own hair. And at one precise moment each and every one of those parasites, obeying an imaginary bugle call, had sunk its monstrous pincers into the skin of el Senyor Baró.

Three seconds were all it took for the blood to return to his brain and for him to come up with a response. A response he offered up without much faith and with very little hope of success.

"Listen, young man, I don't feel obligated to answer your question, but I need not hide anything I do. At six o'clock yesterday afternoon, at the home of the dressmaker you mentioned, I was accompanying my wife as she was fitted for a few outfits. Naturally, it may seem ridiculous to you that I should accompany my wife to the dressmaker's, because young people, I mean young people nowadays, often do not understand the attentions that persons like myself consider worthy of dispensing. But as I see it…"

Clearly this grotesque comment on the part of Antoni Mates, this groveling to justify something as simple as accompanying his wife, was simply pathological. In point of fact, the baron barely knew what he was saying, he tripped over his tongue, he muddled about stupidly, because, though he was no genius, neither was he an idiot. Guillem spent a moment of cruel voluptuosity listening to these "theories" on attentiveness, understanding, or lack of understanding, but, since Guillem was also standing on shifting sands and felt a little frantic himself, he cut the baron's comments short with these words:

"Senyor Baró, please. Enough theatrics. I asked you what you were doing at six o'clock in the afternoon. There is no need for you to tell me. I know as well as you, or perhaps even better, what you were doing. It would not be elegant to go into detail. You and I are both perfectly aware."

Now the baron was like one of those boxers felled in the ring, who hear the count of five, six, seven, eight…, who are aware of everything, who want to make an effort to get up, but whose legs are glued to the mat.

"Are you taken aback, Senyor Baró, at my speaking with such confidence? There are only two people who could know what you were doing yesterday at six o'clock in the afternoon, is that not true?

La Senyora Baronessa and an…other, a…, well, it doesn't matter, call him what you will. And I am very surprised, Senyor Baró, that you have not yet realized that that 'other' was I."

If Antoni Mates had been a normal man, a man physiologically like the majority of men, perhaps he would have reacted like an orangutan, going for the jugular of that cynical creature, attempting to strangle him, trying to do something – something a man would do. Instead, a suppuration of sad misery escaped from his closed lips, and with his eyes on the ground, his cheeks livid, like an absolute idiot, like a martyr disposed to be beaten, the Baró de Falset could not say a word. Perhaps within a few seconds he would have found a way to articulate words, but for the moment it was no use. Guillem, who was perfectly aware of what was going on, and who was enjoying how well the scene was going, took a pistol from his pocket.

"Senyor Baró, I admit that what I am doing here is an unspeakable fraud. And I offer you a solution because it can come to an immediate end, if you so desire. All you have to do is shoot; the pistol is at your disposal. At such a short distance, even if your hand trembles, the shot will almost certainly be on target. But think what you expose yourself to. It would be difficult, you understand, to justify a murder in this salon, at this time of day, in these circumstances. I don't recommend suicide; it would be grotesque. What's more, to commit suicide requires a measure of valor. Until now, only I know about 'this.' Your wife knows about it, too, and Dorotea Palau knows (but naturally not in full detail). It is in your interest, and in mine as well, but much more in yours, that no one else should be privy to 'this.' The procedure is very simple: the promissory note for fifty thousand pessetes, which you extended to my brother, should immediately be transferred into this satchel."

Antoni Mates had found a way to articulate words. Not a particularly clever way, because in fact he was beaten. Even if the man blackmailing him had possessed all the facts needed to compromise him, if it had been any other than the very person who had "collaborated" in the secret liaison at the dressmaker's house, he would have felt in possession of at least a scrap of dignity. But the fact that it was that very person produced such an intense shame in him, such an unbearable collapse, that everything Antoni Mates did manage to say must be considered of great merit, because his natural impulse was to abandon himself to guttural moaning, and to wailing like a wild beast. Strange as it may seem, Antoni Mates had never, never, considered this possibility; it had seemed inconceivable to him that such a thing could happen. And this way of seeing it is perfectly normal for a man of Antoni Mates's stripe. Any person who has a shameful flaw that essentially obligates him to behave differently from others is the victim of a certain innocence, because his desire outweighs everything else, and he cannot measure the consequences. When someone provides him a way to satisfy his abnormality, no matter how few guarantees are offered, he madly pursues its satisfaction, despite the insufficiency of the guarantees. And herein lies the innocence of these deviants. It consists in their believing in the good faith of others, in the good faith, above all, of the accomplice, and in hoping against hope that the thing will remain hidden. And sometimes this takes place in imprudent circumstances, in circumstances in which it is impossible for the secret to be kept. But the poor deviant doesn't see it. Sad to say, he gives in; he will run any risk, like a child incapable of foreseeing danger. And when he realizes that the secret is no secret, when he realizes there could be a scandal, and in the enormity of the scandal, the poor deviant, if his name is Baró de Falset, becomes demoralized, and loses all control, all his masculine integrity. In the case of Antoni Mates, the type of amusements to which he had surrendered himself aggravated the situation. He had debased himself, he had debased his wife, he had engaged in an indefensible conjugal monstrosity. Antoni Mates was aware of it all; he saw all the consequences of the extortion clearly. A strong person, a real scoundrel, could have confronted the consequences, would have found thousands of ways out. He could have forged ahead and neutralize the perfect swine who had lent himself to such a vile ceremony for three hundred pessetes. But a pirate is needed for such occasions, and Antoni Mates only revealed his ragman's fangs at the meetings of the board. In a contest such as this the only teeth he showed were weak and womanish.

"I see. You want the fifty thousand pesseta note? That's what you want, you say. And what if I say I don't care to give it to you? Then what? You can spread the rumor, you have a thousand ways of spreading whatever rumor you like about me. Who will believe you?"

"Everyone."

That "everyone," those three grave monotone syllables, spoken with the solemnity of a death knell, had been intoned by Guillem with such conviction that Antoni Mates truly saw that "everyone" would believe it, that "everyone" knew. Before his eyes paraded the equivocal expressions, the telling smiles, the whisperings. He saw himself infected with a special leprosy, as if his clothing gave off a smell that could not be disguised. Even so – and completely irrationally – he came up with these audacious words:

"So what?"

"You know best."

"But where is the proof, where is it...?"

"What greater proof than my own confession, than my own debasement? When a man lowers himself so far as to be able to tell the tale I can tell about both you and me, they will have no choice but to believe him. Do you understand? No choice."

Naturally, Guillem said this because he was sure that he would win the bluff and there would be no need for him to tell the tale. Moreover, if the need arose, he could find a way to tell it without going into certain details.

"You..., well, clearly you...what can I say...You are a..."

"Say no more, Senyor Baró. It would behoove us to treat this whole affair as if it were a business deal; to go into explanations would be too unpleasant. I am offering you an absolute guarantee. You have my word. To be frank, I think you're getting off quite cheaply at fifty thousand pessetes."

"I have been known to be...Well..., how do I know what I am capable of, poor devil...But you, and your cynicism..."

"Senyor Baró, your words..."

"What about...Dorotea Palau...? What assurances do I have?"

"No need for concern. Dorotea Palau has behaved with the most absolute good faith. The best thing, believe me – I'm saying this for your own good – the best thing is for you to do nothing, and to register no complaints. Dorotea Palau should never hear about this scene. Otherwise the scandal would be unavoidable!"

"Suppose I do give you the note. How do I justify this act of 'generosity' in your brother's eyes?"

"It's very simple. I'll take care of it. Ah, and I warn you: my brother is fool enough not to accept this gesture from you. He has a lot of 'pride,' my brother does."

"And so…?"

"And so, I suggest that you keep granting him extensions on the note, and my brother will keep accepting them, ad infinitum, but without need of an underwriter…Do you understand me? No underwriter. And, what's more, I assume you will be good enough not to charge him interest…"

"But how can I trust you? You…"

"Naturally, you would be an idiot if you trusted me entirely, but for the time being I think I can be trusted."

"What do you mean, for the time being?"

"I mean that I sort of have you at my mercy…"

"We'll see about that…"

"Silence is the best strategy. Don't lose your composure, Senyor Baró. Silence will be best, believe me…"

"Do you want the note right away?"

"If you will be so kind."

Antoni Mates got to his feet. He had a pitiful air and gait. Three minutes later, he was back with the notorious promissory note. Guillem placed it in his satchel.

"Senyor Baró, before noon you will have a draft of the letter you are to write my brother this very day. Don't get upset; it is a letter you will be able to sign in good conscience…"

Without responding, Antoni Mates saw Guillem to the door.

"Don't you want to shake my hand…, Senyor Baró?"

"Enough cynicism. Just leave."

———·——·——

ON THE SAME DAY Guillem visited the Baró de Falset, Frederic received a letter that stunned him. The letter was from the baron himself; he called him "dear friend," he used the familiar "tu" and he closed it with, "A handshake from your good friend." The content of the letter was enough to make him feel faint. Had Guillem truly managed to work a miracle? Frederic didn't know what to think. Among other things, the letter read "A person I imagined was related to you, but whom I didn't have the pleasure of knowing as your brother, came to speak with me about your situation and that of your family. I am sorry you weren't more sincere with me, and didn't convey to me the difficulty you were having in getting your esteemed father to underwrite the note. If you had been more frank, we could have found a better way to work things out, that is, we would have arranged things in your best interest. But this is where we find ourselves now:

your brother and I had a very important affair to settle between us, having to do with my business. In exchange for some very special services, for which I can never express enough gratitude, I am in your brother's debt, both personally and for a considerable amount. He has informed me that you are not very close, and that neither you nor your esteemed father was aware of the business relationship between your brother and me. Hence, in a display of altruism and unselfishness that you, his brother, who knows him well, can comprehend better than I, he has asked me to give him the promissory note you accepted, which if my memory serves comes due tomorrow or the day after, to wipe out part of my debt to him. He swears that his intention was to give you a surprise and avert an unpleasantness for your father, and that he will give you the note and you will make your own arrangements from there on in. He has intimated, moreover, that he owes you a few large favors, and having learned only lately of your compromised situation, the circumstances were ideal for him to show you this kindness. As I consider this perfectly natural, I have given him the note and, as he requested, I am writing you this letter."

As Frederic went on reading, he didn't understand a thing. "Consider this *perfectly natural*"? Frederic thought, "Perfectly natural...? I find it entirely mysterious and bizarre. What kind of dealings could Guillem have with this fool? Was Guillem actually capable of earning money, of collaborating in a serious enterprise, of doing something worthwhile? Indeed, was this letter from Antoni Mates the genuine article? It would be incredible if the whole thing were some prank of Guillem's." Frederic kept going back and rereading the letter. Below the signature, the Baró de Falset had added these words: "I will be forever and deeply grateful if you tear up and burn this letter." "What is that all about? What does it mean?" Frederic thought. "Why should I burn the letter? After all, nothing he says here could compromise anyone."

The request that he "burn the letter" was a liberty Antoni Mates had taken; he had added it when he copied over the draft that Guillem had sent him. The baron, despite bearing the weight of a great despondency, believed that he was being prudent in asking Frederic to "burn the letter."

Frederic's perplexity knew no limits. The day before, after dropping Mossèn Claramunt off, when he thought about Antoni Mates, he would say to himself, "If I could only find the way to put one over on this Jew," and the following day, "that Jew" had written him the strangest and most absurd letter he could ever have imagined. Frederic's cowardice and distrust conjured up another idea in his mind: "But why did he give him the note? I mean, since this morning my brother is in possession of a promissory note that was extended to me…What does my brother want with this note? That rascal could have the nerve to pull a fast one on me!" In his state of excitation and amazement, Frederic didn't remember that he and his brother had made a thousand-pesseta wager – a wager Frederic had considered to be a joke. He didn't remember that Guillem had promised he would get the note back for him. His caviling didn't last very long, because Guillem had calculated the time, trusting absolutely in the state of docile devastation in which he had left Antoni Mates. And just as Frederic had begun to get nervous, Guillem rang his doorbell. The following dialogue rapidly transpired between the two brothers:

"Guillem, what is this all about?"

"It means I won the bet. Here's the promissory note."

"But what sort of business do you have with Antoni Mates?"

"That's none of your affair. Tear up the note and you no longer owe anyone a cent. What I mean is, you don't owe fifty thousand pessetes to el Senyor Baró de Falset."

Having taken the note Guillem handed him, with a Lloberola air of wounded pride:

"But you understand I cannot accept this…"

"What is it you cannot accept? Let's see: Antoni Mates, to 'pay me' for some services he owes me for, transfers a credit he has against you to me. And, instead of cashing in on the credit myself, I release you, I make a gift to you of the dough. What exactly is it that you can't accept? Having such a 'generous' brother?"

"What can I say, I find the whole thing incredibly strange. I would like to know what kind of services he might have to pay you for…"

"Listen, Frederic. I'm thirty-one years old, you know? I mean I am well past being of age, and you have no right to meddle in my affairs. I don't ask you what you're up to, or what you eat, or whether you win or lose at cards, or whether you go to your mother-in-law for money…"

"All right. But now I owe you fifty thousand pessetes. That much is clear."

"Maybe...But you needn't worry your head about repaying me... I won't issue you any more promissory notes, not me...And it seems to me that, rather than adopt this professorial tone, you might think about thanking me. All things considered, I think I've freed you from a more than considerable predicament..."

Frederic de Lloberola was not at all convinced. What kind of mystery could there be here? Was his brother capable of some extremely peculiar form of larceny? He knew Guillem; he knew he was an inoffensive philanderer, a good kid, at heart, incapable of anything dishonorable, or anything that had anything to do with the penal code. But why did neither Antoni Mates in his letter nor Guillem right here and now offer a clear explanation?

Even so, Frederic saw his salvation. The document was authentic. Antoni Mates's letter was, too. His distress of the last few months was dissolving; the shady dramas were fading from his mind; and his savior was his brother Guillem. He gave in to his native cowardice, to his parasitic and self-centered way of behaving in the face of all life's challenges. Once Frederic had the promissory note in his hand, once he had Antoni Mates's letter in his hand, justifying the events, however mysteriously, but justifying them in the end, he decided not to delve any deeper. Pretending to find the whole thing "perfectly natural," like the Baró de Falset himself, he took Guillem by the arm and said:

"I don't get it, Guillem. I feel as if I were dreaming. I feel as if I had won the lottery, yes, something like that. Guillem, I swear, I will remember this favor you have done me all my life..."

"I'm telling you, it's nothing. Do you have the letter?"

"Yes, it's right here…"

Guillem read the letter meticulously. He verified that the Baró de Falset had behaved like a gentleman, but when he got to the end, he wrinkled his nose. "What does he mean, burn the letter?" Guillem thought. And then a wicked idea occurred to him. Guillem thought he had been an idiot to go to so much trouble just to do his brother a favor. Naturally he needn't desist from exploiting the baron. But the letter to Frederic would simplify things a great deal. In the event Guillem attempted a new attack it would avert his having to have too shamefully "personal" a role in the extortion. Guillem thought, "This filthy pig must really be lost, he must truly not know what's happening to him, because no one in his right mind would have made the mistake of signing a letter like this and then go on to suggest that it should be burned." As these things went through his mind, Guillem looked at his brother and grumbled:

"Fine, Frederic, you're very grateful, that's all well and good. But what about our wager?"

"What do you mean?"

"The thousand pessetes you owe me…from yesterday's wager. Now that I think of it, though, you don't have to pay me the thousand pessetes. Give me the letter from Antoni Mates, and we'll call it even."

"Impossible. You can't keep the letter."

"What do you mean?"

"Guillem, you see what he says, here, at the end…"

"I will be forever and deeply grateful if you tear up and burn this letter." Uh-huh. And so?"

"And so it is my duty to burn the letter…"

"That is quite debatable. He says he will be deeply grateful, nothing more. He will be grateful, but he doesn't demand it."

"Guillem, I think it's very clear. Moreover, what do you want it for?"

"I don't know, it amuses me."

"Guillem, this whole affair is very strange…"

"Are you going to start that again? What an ass! Look, I'm keeping the letter and that's that. The worst that can happen is that he will not be 'forever and deeply grateful.'"

Guillem kept the letter, and Frederic didn't insist. He had no doubt that he was an accomplice in a very murky affair. His brother appeared before him in a disconcerting light. Frederic didn't say another word and shrugged. As we have already said, the Lloberolas are a weak and cowardly clan.

———·——

THE XUCLÀS WERE descended from Jews. Bobby's ancestors had goat's hair beards and thin, dirty, mercantile fingernails, and lived in the Barcelona neighborhood that nowadays is still known as the *Call*, the ghetto. But even in the 18th century these Barcelonans were already considered honorable and somewhat ennobled people, and they infused blood of the highest quality into their matrimonial alliances. Bobby's father had been one of the most elegant roués of Barcelona. Still, instead of squandering his inheritance, he had derived great profit from the last ties to the colonies. He was on good terms with the Comillases, the Arnúses, and the Gironas, and with all the other households that in those days held the purse strings of commerce. He was also a shrewd and diligent man, a man of the world with an eye for the fine print. As a result, he held a solid and extremely brilliant position in society, which continued only to expand and to grow in prestige. In old Xuclà's personality, the banker, the voracious shark, varnished with a generous flexibility, stood side by side with the gallant ladies' man. The art of the elder Xuclà lay in knowing how to have his cake and eat it, in such a way that his adventures and scandals never put his business at risk, and could be seen by his friends with amusement, and sometimes even with admiration.

His widow was considered by some to have been a victim. "Poor Pilar," was the plaint, because all her wealth and elegance could not compensate for her husband's having shown up every month with a new acquisition extracted from the demi-monde, whom he would materially smother in pearls. Nor did they compensate for the famous banker's long sojourns in Vienna during which, under the cover of business, he sowed the wild oats of his temperament between a gypsy violin and a rose of Bulgaria.

Old Xuclà had imbibed the entire epoch of the waltz and the square sideburn. This is why when he was in Paris his heart yearned for Vienna, because the women there were taller, whiter, blonder, more animal, with easier laughter and a more primal sexuality. Above all, they had a more docile and lyrical flesh, accustomed as they were to being brutalized by the shiny despotism of military officers and the hands of country bumpkins.

In truth, "poor Pilar" couldn't have cared less about all this. She had never loved her husband, and it was far more pleasant to have at her side a pompous, spiritual philanderer who lavished all manner of attentions upon her, than to be saddled with a reactionary Tomàs de Lloberola, brimming with uncomprehending egoism, who, between processions and intonations of the Tre Sanctus would have given her a horrible life.

Pilar de Romaní i Miralles was the youngest daughter of the Comtes de Sallent. She had rejected her family's proposal that she marry a young man from Madrid, a nephew of the Duques de Medinaceli, because, besides being Castilian, the man was dull and had green teeth. After rejecting three or four more proposals, she leaned, against her parents' preferences, toward Xuclà, the banker. He was a bit past his prime, but he had a perfect command of the use of gardenias and of double-entendres. For Pilar – who at the time was the prettiest and most elegant young woman in Barcelona – this preference for a man of Semitic extraction was the sign of a special temperament at odds with the tenor of her family. Like their cousins, the Lloberolas, the Comtes de Sallent made much of the tawdry vanity of their blue blood. What they wanted in a son-in-law was a rheumatic subject with the heart of a rabbit who would offer no risks and be faithful to tradition. If the title they picked up was from Castile or Aragon, all the better – no matter if there was a touch of syphilis along the way. In contrast, Pilar was an unconventional young woman, with a delicate anarchic streak, and by one of those biological miracles that can never be explained, the daughter of the Comtes de Sallent had turned out to have personality. That personality was a throwback to the Barcelona that preceded the Universal Exhibition of 1888, sensitive to the fragrance of colonial breezes, factory greases, the efficiency of cotton spinners and the broad populist humor of Serafí Pitarra. As a girl, she had been roundly castigated by her mother for her insistence on speaking Catalan, which was the language of the cook, the coachman who cared for the household's horses, and the poets who gathered at the Cafè Suís.

Pilar had a democratic mentality and, without her realizing it, her heart took part in the air of rebirth that was becoming more and more accentuated in Barcelona.

When she married Xuclà the banker, her personality became more refined; bit by bit, it was honed. In her, a traditional and popular Barcelonism was united with natural elegance and perfect beauty. Pilar was the least affected, most natural lady one could ever hope to meet. The somber timidity of the black armoires, the doleful chiffarobes, the lady's bustles, the lack of hygiene, and the cone-shaped *cucurulles* worn by penitents in Holy Week processions could be summed up, in a word, as the provincialism that would convert the Catalan aristocracy of the turn of the century into a sort of shabby and reactionary extension of restoration Madrid. Against all this Pilar offered up, unabashed, a seamstress's little snub nose and the kind of laughter you might hear among the carts of the greengrocers and the red breeches in the soldiers' garrisons.

Once they were married, a state of polite coolness did not take long in manifesting itself in the marriage. Xuclà the banker was quite satisfied with his wife, because she was intelligent, she was decorative, and she was the most dazzling person in Barcelona. But Xuclà the banker had other kinds of tastes, and his polygamous temperament led him on the chase for fresh quarry. Pilar surrounded herself with a motley circle and showed utter scorn for her parent's circle of relations. Out of obligation, she would take up her position in the front seats at the grand parades, and her place there was never in question. Yet her sense of humor and her offhanded way of speaking scandalized certain segments of the circle of the Comtes de Sallent, and word began to get around that Pilar had a wandering eye. Another segment of the aristocratic sphere maintained, through thick and thin, that Pilar's behavior was beyond reproach. This was the plaintive segment that wept for "poor Pilar" and accused her husband of being perfectly vile.

As always, there was truth and untruth on both sides of the question. Among her detractors, some crusty and unbearable marquesa would claim that Pilar Xuclà was worse than a *cocotte*, that a dozen lovers were too few for her and that her husband was within his sacred right to seek distraction elsewhere. This was a great exaggeration. Pilar didn't share the compunctions of the other grandes dames. She had had actresses over to her house on Carrer Ample, and in particular she had been quite friendly with a ballerina who had danced for two seasons at the Liceu and was famous for being brazen and for having blackmailed a prince from the house of Orleans. The day this dancer performed before a select audience at one of Pilar's salons, a panic not dissimilar to a run on the stock market rippled through many

Barcelona families. The scandal was sublime. There are those who remember it even today. So as not to have to break off relations with their daughter once and for all, the Comtes de Sallent pretended not to have heard a word about it. To avoid comment they spent four months away from Barcelona.

Pilar stood her ground. Three of the most prominent ladies of the day assembled to discuss whether they should continue receiving her in their homes. It is said that this conference – according to people who remember this, as well – broke all records in terms of feminine ferocity. The attempt by the three ladies was a fiasco. Pilar was too pretty and too brilliant. And her husband had too much money and was too enmeshed in the interests of many of her detractors. All la Senyora Xuclà had to do was don a floor-length ermine coat to distract the ladies' tongues away from the pecadilloes of the lady who wore it.

Of all the improprieties attributed to Pilar, the only one that might have had some substance involved Sebastià Ripoll, the artist. This painter, a friend and disciple of Martí Alsina, died a miserable death in Paris in the days when artists of means like Ramon Casas and Santiago Rusiñol were striking out to discover Montmarte. In Pilar's youth, though, he had possessed the most exciting black beard in Barcelona. Sebastià Ripoll was no bohemian, but the son of a manufacturer, and a friend to opulent chorus girls and idle fellows with artistic leanings. He had a place at certain privileged tables and a chair in the *penyes* of the men's clubs, bull sessions at which the topics of the day were discussed.

Sebastià Ripoll was an easygoing and agreeable painter, of a piece with the bourgeois tastes of the moment. He painted *Pierrots*, indigents and odalisques. He also painted portraits by commission, in which he dissolved flesh into caramel and redingotes into squid's ink, applying a theatrical grace between the lips and the eyes that even today is not entirely obnoxious on one wall or another.

Aside from his paintbrushes and his juvenile erotic vanity, Sebastià Ripoll was a delicate bon vivant. Pilar selected him from among all her friends to be the artistic dictator of her home. The banker gave him cigars worthy of breaking out on the high holidays, and Ripoll the painter declared that the most velvety coffee of Barcelona could be had on Carrer Ample, where there was a lady who could be tenderly spiritual, with manners redolent of pepper and cinnamon, while not looking down on authentic homegrown garlic.

Pilar and Sebastià Ripoll enacted a novella in which it cannot be asserted that bedrooms, quilts and physiology played an exclusive role. The banker was unperturbed by the novella. A broadminded independence reigned in their marriage and he continued to treat the painter with generous liberality. And when he went abroad, he didn't lose a moment's sleep knowing that as his best friends sipped on an *orxata* or sniffed a carnation, they would be categorically affirming that his wife was cuckolding him.

As Xuclà the banker had inherited from his ancestors a good Hebrew complexion, regarding virile honor he had very clear and intelligent ideas. Pilar agreed with her husband's ideas, but she made sure not to abuse them. Not out of any respect for the capricious kid-gloved satyr she was married to, but because Pilar, a good daughter of the nineteenth century, still believed that a lady with any self-respect didn't go around losing her corset in any old corner, like a butcher woman coming down from an Ash Wednesday tryst on Montjuïc.

A portrait by Ripoll the painter of the Pilar of those days has been preserved in the home of D., the collector. Even if you observe the canvas with a hint of skepticism, abstracting the element of personal passion on the part of the black-bearded man, you cannot help but take in all the perfume of an extinct Barcelona that touches the heart of those who appreciate such things. In the painting, Pilar is standing with the smiling immobility of a Juno. Her neckline reveals bare arms and a rather generous triangle of flesh under her neck. Her skirt, made of mulberry satin, has a very long ruffled train and clings gently to her hips and thighs. She is wearing gloves the color of polished white bone that reach to above her elbow, and she holds a silk mask between two fingers of her right hand. A set of silver dominoes and a great bouquet of camellias bursting from a striped paper cone rest upon a strategically-placed sofa.

Ripoll's ambition had sucked so deeply into her face that blood would have surged to the most academic lips. Her nose, chiseled slightly upward, seems still to be breathing in the sweat and fragrances of a masked ball. Her eyes reveal nothing but the great discretion hidden in her irises, green as the impenetrable gray green of the flounder's slimy skin. And her hair, part gold, part ash, has something of a storm and something of the moss on a stone, a sort of geological romanticism reminiscent of the verses of Verdaguer's *Atlantis*.

But the Pilar Romaní of the portrait precedes by many years the initial events of the story we are writing. When Bobby escorted Frederic to Mado's house, the widow Xuclà was a matron well into her seventies; she and Bobby, the only child she had with the Semite banker, still lived in her house on Carrer Ample.

In her dotage, the widow Xuclà had been seized by the intransigence of social caste regarding the growing materialism and loss of control of Barcelona society. This genuine lady, who had caused such scandal as a young woman with her democratic and slightly uncouth attitudes, brandished the very same rigidity of which she had been the victim in her day against the loosening of principles that affected the beauties of the present day. When they told her Senyoreta X had taken as a gigolo a store clerk whose only merit was to have built up his biceps a bit at the Club Nàutic, or that Senyora R. had mortified her husband by word and deed before a gathering of young men at the golf club, and that yet another lady had taken a taxi to a *meublé* on the Diagonal, or that the Baronessa de T., in the midst of her divorce proceedings, had made an appearance at a cabaret only attended by prostitutes and the occasional inexperienced married couple from the provinces, Pilar Romaní was filled with indignation. Not in the tone a lady of Leocàdia's temperament might have used, but in that of an old fox who has seen it all, but who still demands a bit of etiquette and a bit of dignity even in unavowable affairs. Though Pilar Romaní had been broadminded and paid little heed to the morality of her times, there were some lines she had been very careful not to cross. She had been careful to drape even her vices or caprices in a romantic gauze, revealing only a delicate silhouette of poetry and distinction. Even though she and Ripoll had caused tongues to wag, still the painter had been no vulgar passion, and Pilar Romaní had taken care to embroider the letters of a sentimental, mentholated novel on their relationship. When she spoke of these outrageous young women, the widow Xuclà would use her own very picturesque and somewhat crude way of speaking, which in time had turned rather bitter. Sometimes a phrase uttered by Pilar would subsequently be reported in a half dozen places, commented upon, laughed at by the men and sharpened to a fine point, whereupon inevitably it would reach the ears of the woman in question. Behind Pilar Romaní's back, her humor was considered the "tantrums of a doddering old witch," but no one dared say such a thing to her face.

In time, the widow Xuclà suspended her get-togethers and visits and called on fewer and fewer homes. Among the very few exceptions was the home of Hortènsia Portell. If Hortènsia threw a party, Pilar Romaní's presence was assured. She would enter with the air of a queen, and all the ladies yielded to her. They would needle her to get her talking. Some days she would be gloomy and reserved, and would pretend to be deaf for conversations that went too far. Other days she would be in a friskier mood, and she would nibble away in the sharp and dainty way of a ferret. The widow Xuclà's clothing was always a bit old-fashioned, in shades perhaps too light and bright for a lady of her age. She was tall and strong; no one could have guessed her age. She was a magnificent specimen, and her wrinkled and shrunken features still resisted old age to reveal the traces of a great beauty.

The widow Xuclà would attend Hortènsia Portell's salon, above all, out of a particular liking for that plump, fashion-conscious woman, and because in Hortènsia's circle of vulgar elegance she could still find the occasional intelligent man. He would be a sad, skeptical character without pretensions with whom she might enjoy a long conversation about Catalan affairs and hear a few things that might have a bit of spirit and spark. Pilar Romaní no longer learned of anything on her own account. She read no newspapers, nor any new books. She lived off her memories. All art and literature had come to a stop for her before the War in Cuba, when she would invite the people of sensibility of the day to her house on Carrer Ample. Pilar Romaní was of the opinion that the best things had come and gone, that the literati wrote so that no one would understand them, that modern art – her idea of modern art was more quirky than she herself – was insufferable, and that painters were bent on making life ugly and deforming the grace of things.

She would criticize some young women's lack of taste, their unattractiveness, their absolute ignorance, their precarious ambition, their lack of personality and resulting willingness to be swept away entirely by what was au courant and fashionable. She would criticize the cowardly morality of some, and the inexcusable lack of modesty of others, and what most disgusted her was the snobbish enslavement to the latest thing and to American fashion. She bemoaned the loss of character and the mongrelization that had swept Barcelona. The big fashion houses and the automobile had leveled everything out. Pilar Romaní couldn't countenance the fact that, simply because she possessed a magnificent Hispano-Suiza automobile, a woman who had come from who knows where was invited to dinner and supper at the homes of the daughters of the same old aristocratic dowagers who years before had hung her out to dry.

The widow Xuclà had a penchant for going off on her own. Many mornings she would go out with her chauffeur and barrel down the highway until she found a nice place where, with the help of her eyeglasses, she might work on a sweater for the daughter of the concierge or for some member of her household staff. The widow Xuclà took an enormous interest in people of more humble condition. She liked to talk with the workingmen and the servants, and in the summer she would spend long hours with the people who tended her land. She was lavish, and generous to a fault, and a tear or two was enough to take her for all she was worth.

Her true friends were few and far between. She was close to another lady of her time, a distant relative, the Marquesa de Descatllar. She was more acid-tongued and more class-bound than Pilar Romaní, and she was absolutely outrageous. The marquesa had been separated from her husband for many years, and in her case it was absolutely true that she had no relations at all with anyone. Pilar Romaní always defended her in her circle, maintaining that she was a true lady and had been very unfortunate. The marquesa had a dark complexion and hard, virile features. She went around with narrowed eyes as if everything disgusted or infuriated her. No matter what turn fashion took, she always wore a bunch of dyed black bird-of-paradise feathers hanging over her forehead. They looked as if they had been plucked from the headdress of a cannibal leader. Stories were told of shameful contact between the marquesa and brutish subjects of the lowest extraction. In the afternoon she would often go to the Paral·lel with her chauffeur and her manservant to see bawdy shows or revues with a great deal of naked flesh on display. She would generally sit half-hidden in a box seat on the mezzanine. Pilar Romaní would occasionally accompany her on these theatrical excursions. They had a particular liking for Catalan vaudeville, with beds and underwear onstage.

From a distance, the marquesa had a magical effect. In the days when only two-horse carriages traveled up and down the Passeig de Gràcia, the marquesa, dark and solitary in her open sedan, contrasted with the pale cream, pea green or turquoise blue mistresses under their monumental hats, complemented by a dog who might have been stolen from a Van Dyck canvas.

At the height of summer, the Marquesa de Descatllar and Pilar Romaní always went abroad together. Some years they would go to Marienbad, but later, as they got older, they found the trip too long. Then they wouldn't get any farther than the baths at Luchon, or they would drop in for a few days at Biarritz.

On the beach, the two ladies made fun of the female fashions and customs, of the lack of breasts and the diminishing hips. They thought the craze for turning the skin into an artifact resembling a cocoa bean or a jacaranda wood desk was absurd. From the terrace, the two ladies would spend hours and hours under the shelter of a garish, antiquated umbrella and, with the aid of their opera glasses, they would destroy the fabric of the flashiest beach pajamas and what little flesh they covered up. A blink of the marquesa's eyes was as implacable as a hair clipper.

Occasionally, they would become entranced with the maillot and the curly nape of some sporty, boorish and optimistic young man, and they would savor him from afar, with deliberation. They would digest him slowly and carefully, like serpents, with all the bitterness and impotence of depraved old women.

Another friend of the widow Xuclà's was Lola Dussay, who was the polar opposite of the marquesa.

Lola Dussay was older than Pilar, but not by much. She lived on Carrer de Montcada, in a three-hundred-year-old house that was starting to collapse. The ground floor, the stables, and the courtyard,had been rented to an individual who kept a drug warehouse there. Lola lived on the *principal*, the main floor of her large noble home, which was enormous for her and the two maids and one manservant who attended her. Lola was single, religious, and prim and proper, but she shared with the widow Xuclà a taste for tradition and popular culture. Lola didn't have so much as a particle of intelligence; she was loud, fussy, and rude, all things she compensated for with an enormous heart and an absolute selflessness. Every spring Lola would throw a party at her house. She only abandoned this custom four years before she died. Her guests were old stock, faded and reactionary. They were married couples who lived in their own world and young men with medallions around their necks, heraldic coats of arms on the rings between the hairs on their fingers and genuine imbecility diluted throughout their bodies who came to fish for fiancées. Lola was as simpleminded as an octopus, and at these parties some, it seems, had taken advantage of her innocence in the dark, damp, and interminable corridors of her house on Carrer de Montcada, as the chandeliers trembled in the salons, excited by the upheaval of a polka.

Lola spent her days and nights caring for the ill, visiting midwives and expressing condolences. Her main passion was cooking, and her greatest joy was the killing of the pig. Lola had hair white as snow, an enormous belly, and cheeks that were red and taut from the heavy food she prepared. She would spend long hours in the kitchen, sweating and overheated, preparing sauces and tending to roasts. Among her best friends was Don Felicià Pujó, just as much an old bachelor as she was a spinster. Don Felicià Pujó was President of the Brothers of Peace and Charity. He was cold, gentle, and delicate in the extreme. There were those who took for granted that Lola Dussay and Don Felicià Pujó were secretly married. What is beyond all doubt is that Lola expected Don Felicià Pujó to partake of her culinary marvels. Sometimes at midday, when Don Felicià got home from sitting in the sun, he would find Lola Dussay's manservant in his foyer with the following mission:

"Donya Lola sent me, *senyoret*, because today the pig's feet have turned out first-rate and she would like the master to come and try them."

Don Felicià Pujó, who was dyspeptic, would sadly shrug his shoulders, put on his mid-crown top hat, pick up the cane he always carried with an ivory dog's head for a handle, and set out for Carrer de Montcada to dine on pig's feet. Later, at home, no cannula or thyme infusion would suffice to calm his irritable bowels.

Despite Lola Dussay's religious devotion, she liked to use blue language. This was not out of malice, but stupidity, as often she didn't understand the double-entendres, and she repeated everything she heard, whether it made sense or not.

Pilar Romaní appreciated her cooking talents and her frivolous, picturesque, and singular way of living her life.

The house on Carrer Ample was decorated according to the banker Xuclà's taste, with the counsel of persons like Ripoll the painter, whom Pilar considered to be peerless. The house had all the heavy, gold-leaf pomp of the turn of the century. Bobby had made a few more modern contributions, but only in moderation so as not to hurt the widow's feelings.

Bobby loved his mother a great deal, though days and days could go by without their exchanging a word. Much more intelligent than most of the people in his milieu, Bobby was subdued, and rather shy. He was in the habit of never contradicting anyone and never arguing with anyone, more out of apathy than anything else. He was skeptical and tolerant; he almost never laughed, but neither did he get angry. He had inherited from his mother a natural and unaffected elegance, and a pure essence of Barcelona that transcended time and space, or literature and politics. Bobby wasn't au courant, nor did he want to be. He tended to express very vague and noncommital opinions. Perhaps the clearest vestige in Bobby of his family's

Jewish heritage was a somewhat reptilian flexibility that allowed him to put on a smile that was neither hot nor cold, a smile that was sort of who-gives-a-damn, yet not at all offensive, in the face of the things that usually spark men's passions. It was more a product of indolence or of a delicate egoism born of not wanting to be get worked up about anything.

Bobby understood his mother's way of life, and he respected it in every way. He had a very high opinion of his father; he understood his dynamism and his infidelities, and he saw fit to apply prudent and conservative principles to his enjoyment of the fortune his father had left them.

Bobby was the ideal lover. His continual contact with women was neither out of vanity nor because he was a man of passion. Bobby was often bored, and he found women amusing. With women, moreover, he could avoid having to talk: he could let them do the talking. He enjoyed their world of little squabbles and henpecking, and above all he liked to breathe in the superfluous warmth that flows from blood to pearls and from pearls to gossip.

This is why Bobby felt equally at ease in the world of trollops, young married ladies, or at Hortènsia Portell's table in a comfortable tea parlor. He was the kind of man who needed nothing more than a comfortable chair and a pair of lips prepared to sip and talk of their own volition.

The widow Xuclà wanted her son to marry. Bobby never contradicted his mother when her sermons took this tack. He would let her go on, while he scratched his moustache as if to say he had all the time in the world.

The widow Xuclà had no love lost for the men of the Lloberola clan. She thought Frederic was a useless ne'er-do-well. Old Don Tomàs reminded her of a mummy festooned with rosaries and hypocrisy. Nevertheless, she felt a real affection for Leocàdia. And, despite Leocàdia's being so different from Pilar, leading a life of patience, devotion and spiritual retreat, not a month would go by without her visiting the widow on Carrer Ample. Conversation between these two old ladies was a little painful. Pilar didn't have the slightest interest in the things that interested Leocàdia. Though there were long interludes of silence, neither of them would give up these visits, and whenever Pilar spoke of Leocàdia, she praised her to the heavens. Narrow-minded Leocàdia, in the days when Pilar's reputation was in danger, was among those who always spoke of "poor Pilar." If Frederic ever mentioned the widow Xuclà's fancies and frivolities to his mother, Leocàdia would respond, even a bit forcefully, "You know I don't like it when you speak like this about one of the people I hold in highest esteem. What's more, I'm certain it is all untrue."

When the bottom fell out for the Lloberolas, and they stopped seeing practically anyone, the widow Xuclà took special care to be kind to Leocàdia and to visit her more often.

Don Tomàs was grateful for the widow Xuclà's attitude, because she was the daughter of the Comtes de Sallent, because their grandparents were cousins, and because on the Romaní coat of arms there was a branch of rosemary, a dog and a half-moon. These things were very important to Don Tomàs.

—·—·—

FREDERIC HAD GONE looking for Bobby at the Club Eqüestre the very night of his father's calamity and the scene with the mossèn, but Bobby was still at supper at the Liceu Opera House, as he was every night. Frederic telephoned him and he came right away.

Frederic felt trapped and had no inkling that things would be resolved so favorably for him the following day.

Bobby was expecting him to relay some particular about Rosa Trènor, or give some account of how the reconciliation had gone. Frederic had to make a tremendous effort to impress upon Bobby that the issue was money. Bobby's expression became distant. Frederic realized this, but he persisted. When Bobby realized how much was involved, he retreated further, and said he couldn't take any immediate action without consulting his mother. Frederic knew this response was just an excuse. He knew Bobby could dispose of that much money and a great deal more without any prior consultation. Frederic was consumed with a distinct hatred for his friend. He saw how the blood of the conservative Jew flowed beneath those cheeks, generally considered the least judgmental and most generous cheeks in Barcelona. Frederic used an expression that Bobby found a bit rude, which led to five tense minutes between the two friends. Seeing that nothing good would come of that approach, Frederic surrendered his

Lloberola pride and supercilious attitude, and tried to speak with his heart in his hand. Perhaps he revealed a bit too much weakness, and even groveled a bit, but Bobby didn't budge.

At heart, Bobby had no real liking for Frederic. He had tolerated him all his life, out of an aversion to discord. He had listened in disgust, always with a pleasant smile, to all Frederic's stories of grandeur. Bobby pretended to have a great friendship with Frederic precisely because of the antipathy his mother professed for all the Lloberola men. For Bobby, who truly loved Pilar Romaní, this defiance regarding Frederic was one of those silly punctilios that sometimes crop up between two people who love each other.

But now, what Frederic was asking of Bobby was very unpleasant. It was a nuisance for a man as passive, self-centered and indolent as Bobby Xuclà. As he watched Frederic grovel and go into excessive detail about his family's privations, on the inside he was feeling avenged for all the tedious heraldic lectures, grand adventures, and useless irritating rhetoric that Frederic had foisted on him, oblivious to how annoying he was. Bobby concentrated his entire being behind his little blond moustache and his dead blue gaze. He listened to Frederic with relish, and Frederic barreled ahead, trying to make an impression on him, to touch his heart. If Frederic had been more astute, perhaps he would have realized he was on false ground. Perhaps he would have understood what Bobby's blond moustache and dead gaze were saying.

When Frederic had finally hung out all his dirty, mended laundry, Bobby, colder than ever, but with some sense of satisfaction, pronounced a few words, the same few words he had put him off with before. He had taken a stand, and even if Frederic's children had appeared chopped to pieces at his feet, he wouldn't have gone back on it. Offering Frederic no assurance, Bobby said he would speak with his mother and give him a definitive answer the following day.

When he was alone, Frederic was full of shame and desperation at his weakness, at having made such a confession to a Jew. But necessity was stronger. He would have been capable of approaching Pilar Romaní himself, or, as he referred to her in his running monologues of entrapment, "Tia Pilar, that rotten b...."

The next day things had changed, as if by miracle. We already know how Guillem got the letter, and how Frederic was freed of his commitment to the Baró de Falset. Once Frederic was sure of his salvation, he went over to Bobby's house to spit all his scorn in his face.

In the meantime, Bobby had spoken with Pilar of the Lloberola situation. In his cool manner and his monotonous and apathetic voice, he told his mother about the scene with Frederic in such a way that the widow Xuclà wasn't certain if he was happy or sad about his situation. Pilar advised Bobby to help Frederic, not because "that nincompoop deserves it, nor because it will change anything, because there will be nothing left of the Lloberolas. But do it for Leocàdia, who is so unfortunate, and has always been such a good friend to me."

As we have said, Bobby venerated the widow Xuclà, and he found in his mother's way of speaking the elegant and unspoiled mercy of a grande dame. He decided to underwrite the promissory note or, if necessary, to hand Frederic a check for fifty thousand pessetes, and put a stop to the whole thing, without setting any conditions for its restitution.

But the mercy of the grande dame had not been transformed into the mercy of the gentleman in Bobby. Bobby felt like humiliating his friend a bit, to impress on him the favor he was doing him. If Frederic had been a different kind of man, Bobby would have behaved in a cool, indifferent and even elegant way. But twenty-five years of intolerable condescension and vanity on Frederic's part had peppered Bobby's tongue.

When the two friends found themselves face to face, the Lloberola heir, huffing and puffing, smiling, a bit heated, wore the supercilious look of a man who has just discovered America and spies a mouse gnawing at his heels. Slowly he spat these words out onto Bobby's blond moustache and dead gaze:

"I've come to tell you that you needn't put yourself out. I am grateful for your generosity but you needn't speak with your mother. Fortunately, I don't need to ask favors of anyone. I have resolved the issue of the promissory note. I am only sorry to have taken up your time and to have spoken of disagreeable things…with a person who…"

Bobby was deepy outraged. His dead gaze took on a special life, as if a wasp had stung him in the eye. His pupil felt engorged with blood and rage, like a mongoose in the presence of a cobra. Bobby was furious, because the scene in which he would humiliate Frederic, and make him pay for twenty-five years of condescension, had come to naught. Bobby would have given half his fortune to make Frederic eat the fifty thousand pessetes like a dog.

But this burst of cholera took its time in reaching Bobby's tongue, and he intimated in his usual tone of voice (fully prepared to substitute whatever tone of voice was necessary):

"I couldn't be more pleased…, but I assure you – if you wish, I will show it to you – that I had a check for fifty thousand pessetes signed and made out to you…"

"Thank you, my friend, thank you. That is very generous of you, I won't be needing it…"

"Listen, Frederic, I find your tone of disdain offensive. Anyone would think I had done you wrong. You came and regaled me with a string of misfortunes that I couldn't care less about, do you understand? Not at all. And I was prepared to be generous with you…"

"Generous!"

Frederic let loose with a peal of laughter worthy of Rigoletto, and Bobby couldn't take it any more. He let it all come out, he rained insults on him, calling him ridiculous, grotesque, an ass, not just him, but his father and his whole family. And a joyful Frederic replied at an even higher pitch, dizzy at the opportunity to offend that person to whom he had always felt so superior, whom he had always considered an also-ran. Now, seeing short, pudgy Bobby with his blond moustache, confronting him, tall and stately, a Lloberola from head to foot, he lost control. Amid the coarse invective, he included a reference to the widow Xuclà. "What did you say about my mother?" shrieked Bobby, his voice rising to a squeal, which made Frederic observe him with even greater disdain. Naturally, Frederic thought he was within his rights to say what he wished about her, and he said it all in the most stupid, unthinking and gratuitous way he knew how.

Bobby dug his fingernails into Frederic's face. The only reason Frederic didn't thrash him was that he was in his house, and among gentlemen it is not customary to thrash the master of the house when paying a visit.

On the most idiotic account, for practically no reason at all, these two apparently inseparable friends quarreled, and never spoke to each other again for the rest of their lives.

That night Bobby didn't dine at the Liceu. He stayed home and kept his mother company. Bobby accepted the widow Xuclà's way of thinking. He found her youthful indiscretions to be very human and considered the whole thing fine and dandy, because Bobby was a skeptic and his morality was rotten to the core. But that night, in reaction to the insults Frederic had dared to hurl at the widow Xuclà, he saw his mother as a saint. Above all, he valued more than ever her mercy and her elegance. She was a true lady. In the folds of her lips, her slightly pronounced chin, her wrinkles, her tired eyes, and the white hair of her decrepit majesty, still tall and smiling, he found the full essence of that aristocratic and mercantile Barcelona, popular, proud, and a bit childish, all traces of which were fading.

And Bobby was right. The widow Xuclà represented all those things, and more. Even more than a man, an old woman who has lived a full life retains the imprint of the past and the sensible permanence of memory. Women have more passive nerve receptors, and more receptive souls, so they do not consume themselves nor do they expend all their energy in action as men do. Women are both more covetous and more foresightful. Between the folds of their wrinkled skin, they have the good faith to collect dreams, to gather up adventures, and to preserve there what cannot be seen and can only be sensed: the perfume of history.

—·—·—

EL BARÓ DE FALSET didn't say so much as a word to his wife about how Guillem was blackmailing him. He spent two months in agony. The day after he sent the letter to Frederic, he realized how stupid he had been to write it. Guillem hadn't approached him, but he feared a new attack at any moment. Two months later, an event occurred that caused a commotion among many Barcelona ladies. It bore all the features of a crime of passion, and eased the baron's terrible anxieties a bit. The event in question was the murder of Dorotea Palau, the dressmaker.

Dorotea was found with a dagger through her heart in a well-known *meublé*. She was in the company of a French individual whom all the circumstances seemed to incriminate, despite his protesting that he had had nothing to do with the crime. The court found him guilty.

Yet the alleged murderer was entirely innocent. For the reader to have some idea of how things came about, we will have to delve a little deeper into the private life of the Baró and Baronessa de Falset and their chauffeur, and follow certain paths that until now had been secret and unknown.

The first few years of marriage between Antoni Mates and his wife had apparently been quite normal. Conxa's husband did not satisfy her in the least, and her own "personal" adventures in that first period of marriage, which we will have occasion to go into at other points in this story, were suspected by no one.

Antoni Mates made a tremendous effort to overcome something he didn't dare confess even to himself, something he had hoped was long behind him. But he was powerless before his, shall we say, malady. As its effects inflamed his blood, Conxa became colder and more wooden, so much so that at times Antoni Mates felt he was sleeping with a dead body.

As we have said, Conxa had a very special and piquant beauty. Antoni Mates was madly in love with her, but it was a strange sort of love mixed with admiration that didn't procure him satisfaction, nor was it capable of slaking the other thirst that consumed him.

Neither of them dared confess to the other how cold and empty their encounters were. A pathological sadness, deaf and dumb, crept into the marriage. They kept it out of the public eye by enacting the most delightful of honeymoons.

One afternoon the couple set out on an little trip, intending to spend a couple of days in a town on the coast. Antoni Mates had a new chauffeur; he had been in their service for just two weeks. He was a sporty young man who looked like a ladykiller. He had a youthful grace, and was pleasant and attentive. By nightfall the couple and their chauffeur reached the town where they would be staying. The inn was clean and quite comfortable, and practically empty because the summer season had not yet begun. At dinnertime, it was as if the time they had spent together, each keeping his and her respective secrets, had had an effect upon their nerves, as if instinct, or the beast, had revealed what the power of reason had denied. Conxa and her husband both looked simultaneously at the chauffeur, who was sitting three tables away, focusing on his plate of chops and not daring to look at his masters. The gaze of husband and wife must have been very particular and not very subtle because, later, when they realized what they were doing, and when their own eyes met, they both blushed, trembling and disconcerted. But that lasted only a couple of seconds because Conxa, with a great sigh, looked at her husband again with a smile. And her husband smiled back, as a flash of liberation flared in his eyes. Antoni Mates saw clearly that Conxa understood him, and accepted what he would never have dared to confess, just as he accepted her thoughts, in turn. Without so much as a word or the briefest remark, with just that redness of cheek, that discomposure, those sighs and that shimmer in their eyes, they came to a perfect understanding and mutual endorsement. The depravity of each was completely different from that of the other, but it tended toward one same objective, one same desire, that would be enjoyed in different ways.

Conxa mentally put the final touches on the idea. It didn't alarm her in the slightest. She found it eccentric and quite chic. And since she found her husband disgusting, this could not be any worse.

She had read novels that told of similar permutations; in Paris, in the great world of the disabused, such practices were an everyday thing. The fact is, if "that" was what her husband was, and she had already suspected it – in fact, she had been certain of it, for quite a while now – Conxa was much less concerned about it than her husband had been.

When the time came to go to bed, everything happened as if by design. The couple was given the best room at the inn and the chauffeur was to sleep two doors down. Antoni and Conxa left the door ajar. She began to undress, as did her husband. The chauffeur was whistling softly. In a state of exceptional excitement, his voice trembling, Antoni Mates called for the young man. He responded pleasantly, as always. Antoni Mates ordered him to come and the poor boy responded that he was about to get into bed. "It doesn't matter, come right away," Antoni Mates responded, his voice more and more subhuman. The chauffeur pulled on his pants and stopped in the doorway. "Come in," said Antoni Mates. Distraught, the boy went in. He was barefoot, wearing pants and a sleeveless undershirt. Conxa was lying almost naked on the bed. Antoni Mates took the chauffeur by the arm; the boy didn't understand; his head was spinning. But he didn't protest. Stupidly, he let himself be swallowed up by the same wave, and the three of them fell onto the bed.

From that time on, Antoni Mates was a happy man. Conxa tolerated, and even enjoyed, the absurd combination. The chauffeur, a bit horrified, soon understood, however, that this was a gold mine, and that it was in his interest to be discreet.

Their idyll lasted four years. During this time Antoni Mates became a sweeter man, more religious and more reactionary than ever. It was at this point that the couple began to give off that air of perfect unity, and husband and wife were joined like Siamese twins. The chauffeur lived like a prince. He exploited his masters and sang the praises of his position. He told his buddies that el Senyor Mates – the title of Baró had not yet been conferred on him – treated him like a son, and that his wife was the loveliest woman in Barcelona. And he said it all with a wink and an air suggesting that something or other might be going on between him and the lady.

The boy was careful not to compromise himself or anyone else. But four years, in he was beginning to feel not only disgusted but in truth even a bit sick.

Antoni Mates planned little trips and arranged things so that no one could suspect a thing. Blinded by his obsession, it would have been easy for him to be careless. But no one, absolutely no one, caught on.

The chauffeur's condition alarmed his masters. One day the poor boy vomited blood, and within four weeks he was in the cemetery.

A few days before the seizure that did Antoni Mates's chauffeur in, he had got together with a few other boys his age in a bar on Carrer d'Aribau. This usually happened on Saturday, and this was when he would usually boast of the marvels of his post. But that night, perhaps having drunk more than usual, or perhaps in a bad mood that presaged his imminent death, the boy, who was already quite ill, sang a little more than usual. He didn't tell the whole story, but he got very close. His friends didn't pay him much mind. They supposed it was a joke or a lie his drunken imagination had come up with. At the next table sat a shabby, gray and insignificant little man, who opened his ears as far as they would go. That little man was up on a great many things that went on in Barcelona. That night in the bar on Carrer d'Aribau, the only thing that mattered to him was to catch a name that he didn't know. He wanted the chauffeur to sing a name, and when he did, the man needed to hear no more. What the other fellows took to be a joke or a lie was an incredibly valuable revelation for the little gray man.

The reader will remember that when we spoke of Dorotea Palau's beginnings, we noted that in the days when she worked at Leocàdia's house, she used to be accompanied by a young man, a little older than she, whom Dorotea introduced as her brother. The little gray man who was listening in on the conversation of the chauffeur and his friends in the bar on Carrer d'Aribau was the very same young man who used to accompany Dorotea Palau twenty years earlier to the house of the Lloberolas.

It wasn't true that they were brother and sister. They had only a vague, distant kinship. The boy had grown up in the creepy, servile atmosphere of a cabaret, doing the duties of a servant and, to some extent, of a go-between. He was sickly, puny, and, according to the other service staff, totally impotent. Polite and accommodating to a fault, the useful little snoop inspired a particular sort of repugnance. He had been getting by without any particular success when he happened upon the conversation with the Mates's chauffeur. At that point, he had been working as a night porter for quite a few years at one of the most popular and comfortable *meublés* of Barcelona.

The man's name was Pere Ranalies, but he was known by his peers as "The Monk." Perhaps they came up with this name out of sarcasm, because no one had ever seen him with a woman. Pere Ranalies seemed to function with the cold, bitter head of a bar cat, the kind that, as if it were not enough to have been spayed, are only allowed to polish off the herring bones even the wagoners refuse to eat. Pere Ranalies had done great service to his relative Dorotea Palau, when she was a young woman with no connections and just muddling through between needlework and the labors of love. The Monk took particular pleasure in following both Dorotea's prostitution and that of others in which he had had a hand, unfailingly playing a despicable role. When Dorotea went to Paris, they had a falling-out that lasted years. On her return, they made peace, but the dressmaker was starting to feel her oats and she found conversation with her relative a bit repulsive. Still, she would tolerate him in certain places and at certain times of day, when the man's presence wouldn't jeopardize her, and Dorotea could squeeze out a little business and Pere Ranalies could pick up a good commission.

The Monk had gathered a considerable archive on the private life of Barcelona. He was on to the scandals and pecadilloes of many important gentlemen and no few notable ladies. His position in the *meublé* was one of utmost confidence. Everyone knew that his obligation was to keep silent and never lose his composure. The couples who were entrusted to him when they came for a room looked at him with the same serenity with which a murderer looks at a dog as he commits the crime, never doubting that the dog is mute and ignorant of the judge's address. Ranalies did not discharge his duties with the indifference of one who is simply making a living and doesn't care one way or another. He deposited in his woeful office all the sick voluptuosity of his impotence. He was a connoisseur of erotic slander but kept it all to himself. He enjoyed it in secret, and only used it for the sake of business. He became such a cold-blooded authority in this domain that certain gentlemen of Barcelona would seek him out to pull monstrous pranks. Ranalies, both on his own and in association with a cadre of adept middlewomen, found ways to supply what no one else could. The frigid heart of Pere Ranalies was the magical engineer of aberrations and deeds that defied belief, not precluding even the tenderest of morsels. He knew all the most rotten neighborhoods and slums by heart. He was the perfect cop, whose operations hinged on misery and the flesh of monsters. His silence, his honeyed smiles, and his acrobatic reverences had always been his salvation. The confessable part of his existence was that of an exemplary man of few means. He rented a room in a rooming house on Carrer de la Riereta in the heart of the Barri Xino and the landlady, who was a good woman, looked upon him as one of the family. He went to Mass every Sunday; he never got drunk. Thrifty and neat, he never caused a fuss. He was easygoing, his voice was unctuous with humility and veiled with resignation, and even in his speech he employed no interjections or bad words.

If on occasion a bit of important business came up that required preparation and expert collaboration, Pere Ranalies would seek out his relative, Dorotea Palau, for the dressmaker was also a voluptuary of such viands, with a special talent for their elaboration.

When Ranalies learned of the death of the chauffeur in the bar on Carrer d'Aribau, he went straight to Dorotea Palau and told her the whole story. The name Antoni Mates didn't appear on the Monk's list and he – who knew everything – had not till that moment had any suspicions regarding that well-known and well-respected gentleman. Ranalies thought that if the story were true – and he didn't doubt for a moment that it was – there was big money to be had. But it was an extremely delicate operation that would require great tact. Perhaps Dorotea Palau would find a more deft, natural and efficient way of navigating it. Dorotea thought it was superb, and clever as she was, and skillful as she was beginning to be, it wasn't hard for her to come up with a plan of attack.

Dorotea did not yet have the honor of counting la Senyora Mates among her devotees. She sent her a string of invitations, proposing impossibly low prices. She paid her several visits. Finally, Conxa received her and placed an order. Employing exquisite manners and the flourishes of a grand vedette, Dorotea won her client's heart. Since Antoni Mates had assumed the obligation of never leaving his wife's side, she began to win her client's husband's heart as well. One day, on her return from a trip to Paris, Dorotea regaled the Mates couple – on whom the barony had just been conferred – with a string of dazzling and fascinating stories. Her performance was so delightful, with just the right touch of understanding and delicacy, not to mention enthusiasm, that the couple lost all notion of space and time. Since the death of their chauffeur, life had gone dark again for the newly-minted Baron. Antoni Mates was feeling a combination of fear and remorse. He wanted to turn his back on all that. Above all it horrified him that anyone might suspect such a thing of him. Sensing from the gaze of the baron and the baronessa that she could now cast her hook into the water because the bait was irresistible, Dorotea made a few vague, extremely tenuous, gestures, as if the whole thing meant absolutely nothing to her. Among normal people, a situation like this is practically inconceivable. But Dorotea knew what kind of individuals she was dealing with, because Pere Ranalies had presented her with a textbook case and a perfect diagnosis. In the event Ranalies had slipped up, at most Dorotea might lose a client. But there was also a likely chance of gaining many more. If the Baronessa de Falset took her "under her wing" with the kind of protection she had in mind, Palau-Couture would soon reach the summit. Dorotea brought the red cape closer to the horns of the beast and waited a few seconds, during which her heart almost stopped beating. Instead of a mortal goring, she received an ovation. The barons surrendered before the stylist's tact, talent and discretion.

At first, the Monk supplied his relative with the necessary personnel. Material of excellent quality, in very good condition, and guaranteed to be safe. With the baronessa behind her, Dorotea Palau came to serve the most select clientele of Barcelona. Realizing that she should choose an apartment that met with the needs of the baron and baronessa, Dorotea moved. One day, Dorotea learned of the existence of a certain group of more or less elegant and dissolute young men. By chance, one of these young men came from a very good family. Dorotea had met him in a seigneurial mansion when she was a young girl and he was a ten year-old boy, very cute, and very diligent, with a sailor suit and curly hair that was irresistible to ladies' fingers. Dorotea also learned that the seigneurial family was practically in the poorhouse, that for a hundred-pesseta bill that boy was capable of doing a great many things, and she found an opportunity to bring a great lady with an excellent heart into her obligation by doing a "favor" for her son. Dorotea made a deal with the young man. She spoke clearly from the start, and the young man accepted the conditions. The readers already know the rest of the story of Dorotea, the young man and the Barons de Falset.

Up to that point, Pere Ranalies had been living off the fat of the land. However, starting with the negotations between Dorotea and Guillem de Lloberola, he began to note an inordinate negligence on the part of his relative. The Monk had become a nuisance to Dorotea, who no longer had any need for him. Not to mention that Dorotea was an absolute miser. The Monk asserted that the "she-beast" had cheated him, and demanded the money owed him. The Monk had fallen on hard times; all his savings had been wiped out in the notorious failure of a bank that had affected half of Barcelona. The Monk was ambitious by nature. He saw that he had lost, and he had a right to recover what he demanded of Dorotea. She refused, and she threatened to turn him over to the police for a whole pile of reasons. The

Monk, who was smarter than Dorotea, laughed in her face and said it was "hard to believe she was such a fool." When he saw that Dorotea wouldn't cough up the dough, the Monk vowed that he would kill her. She took it as a joke. She thought of Ranalies as a kind of repugnant, but inoffensive, mosquito.

Pere Ranalies bought a knife to kill Dorotea Palau with. He didn't know when or where it would happen, but he swore that his distant cousin would not get away with this. Ranalies believed in witches. A murder like the one he had in mind was a bit hard to carry off with absolute impunity. But Ranalies believed in witches. Besides, inhabited only by impotent monsters and vomitous aberrations, his brain demanded a special kind of cruelty. Ranalies had a sick mind, cold, calm, and fully conscious. He wanted to kill like a cat, without a sound, with clean hands and a smile on his face. When, and how? He was sure that luck would favor him. Dorotea would fall into his hands. He envisioned the moment, he savored the impunity of his crime, he heard the woman's muffled scream and smelled her viscous blood…With his soft, icy fingers he would sit and caress the knife. It was a five-spring stiletto, like the ones from the days of the hoodlums, the kind that plunge delicately into a man's body fat, like a diver with perfect style.

Luck or witchcraft did indeed watch over Ranalies the night porter. Dorotea had made a friend in France, an odd, shady guy with a blond moustache, a bowler hat, dirty fingernails, and a diamond on his pinky finger. He wore secondhand suits that had been painstakingly restored at the dyers', filmy *pochettes* in pastel colors, and metallic ties, with a gold pin in the knot that had a tooth – probably from a child who had been killed for his blood – set right in the middle. He was a rascal who liked to sing, drink red wine all day long, and dine al fresco, and he made love in a roguish, gallant, and theatrical way, like a character out of Beaumarchais. Dorotea had been thoroughly diddled by that strapping fellow, who continued to write her after she left Paris. He had some wine business in Perpinyà and on occasion he would cross the border and come to Barcelona to enjoy *"un dîner fin avec la belle Dorothée."*

On one of these getaways, Dorotea accompanied him to a quiet cafè near the Pla de Palau for a glass of Pernod; the Frenchman was in high spirits, and they continued on to the restaurant Can Soler on the Barceloneta. He liked the spattering of the frying oil, the slices of watermelon from the Passeig Nacional, and the whole petty trade in fishing, sailing and distilled liquor that reminded him of the port of Marseille. They dined on lobster in tomato sauce with an exhilarating allioli. *"Comme ça sent bon, ma belle!"* said the Frenchman, whose cheeks had gone dark, practically purple, like two veal kidneys.

The Frenchman had brought Dorotea *"quelque chose de très chic"*: a necklace of tiny glass seed beads that practically danced upon her fleshy neck with their peals of laughter.

Later they went to see a revue at the Teatre Còmic. The Frenchman found it dull and a little crass. Then they still found time for a drink, and the Frenchman began to think that despite Dorotea's excess pounds, her flirty gaze was still quite nice. The Frenchman was staying in a hotel by the Boqueria Market. They couldn't go there, and

Dorotea didn't want any compromising situations at her own house, so they adopted the most practical solution. The taxi driver pulled up to the *meublé* that was currently most in demand. After drawing the curtains behind them, a diminutive little man, gray and seedy, wearing the white jacket uniform of the house, opened the door for them. Dorotea was very put out, but she didn't let on. The Monk pretended not to recognize her. He led them to the lift and deposited them in room thirty-two. At that time of night there were three people on duty. As it was a weekday, the erotic temperature was not so high as on other nights, and the work wasn't killing them. The Monk was covering both the door and the telephone. The other two were doing their rounds on the upper floors. About two hours had gone by when the Frenchman called down and requested a taxi; in five minutes the cab was at the door. The Frenchman went downstairs and said he would be back within the half hour. When the Monk asked after the lady, the Frenchman, smiling and in the tone used by a man in his cups, responded: *"Elle dort, la belle Dorothée...Dommage de la réveiller...Je reviens tout à l'heure..."* What had happened to the Frenchman was quite natural. When Dorotea, fatigued and worn out by it all, began to nod off, the man realized that he had left certain papers he didn't want to lose in a jacket pocket in his lodgings. Since he was a distrustful type, and he, too, believed in witches, he got nervous. He dressed without a sound so as not to awaken Dorotea.

Once the Monk had closed the cab door on the Frenchman, he felt for his knife as he wondered whether the man had been so stupid as to leave the door to the chamber unlocked. He took advantage of a lull to go quickly upstairs, first ensuring that the other two were on duty and unaware of his maneuver. With great caution, he pushed on the door of room thirty-two, and it opened. Inside he found only darkness and the sound of Dorotea snoring. On tiptoe, the Monk turned on the red light. Dorotea continue to snore. He picked up a washcloth lying on the floor in case he had to muffle her voice, and gripped his knife. Dorotea let out a weak guttural groan that wouldn't have caused the slightest alarm because, in a house like that, the origins of the "ahhhs" were harmless, and no one paid them any mind. The knife pierced her heart and the hemorrhage bubbled up as if from a spring. The Monk left the knife in the wound; earlier, he had scrubbed it down, just in case, and he was wearing the white gloves they wore when taking a meal up to one of the higher-priced rooms. He pulled the sheet up over the dead woman's body, turned out the light, peeped out to make sure the hall was empty, and opened the door. Three minutes later he was back at the telephone. The maneuver had been perfect; there was not so much as a drop of blood on him anywhere. He looked in the mirror; he had the same gray face of an upstanding man as always.

A half or three-quarters of an hour later, the Frenchman returned. The Monk took him up to the room, and the Frenchman turned the lock on the door. He got undressed in the dark so as not to awaken Dorotea. When he got into bed, he felt the wet stickiness of the blood. The alarmed Frenchman must not have imagined that things could have reached such tragic proportions because he had the wherewithal to say, "*Voyons, ma belle! Pas de blague!…*" When he put his hand under her left breast he felt the knife. The excitable Frenchman squealed like a pig being pulled by the tail. He was naked, he was locked in that room with a dead woman, he was filthy with blood. Dorotea's body was still warm. The man wasn't so unthinking as not to realize that his situation was deeply compromised. By the time he got dressed, cried out, they would be upstairs…His mysterious errand was perhaps the only place where he could find a defense, yet in that moment he felt it simply made him look more guilty. The man felt defeated. He called downstairs, said two incomprehensible words, and dropped back down onto the bed, lacking the resolve to get dressed, staring at his hands, his chest, his stomach, his legs, his whole body, helpless and covered in blood.

Ranalies answered the phone and called for the police patrol who were just a few steps away from the *meublé*. A couple of *guàrdies civils*, always in the vicinity, also rushed right over. Ranalies called for the second servant, who was on the top floor. The third man on duty had already gone to answer the door, and he ran into Ranalies just as he came back from calling for the police. They all went up to the room. The Frenchman was screaming like a madman, crying, incapable of getting dressed, incapable of unlocking the door. The Frenchman said over and over again that he was innocent, but no one believed him. They tied him up, he went up before the judge in a state of exhaustion, and everything that happens in such cases happened…

The testimony of Ranalies and the other two servants left no room for doubt. Even worse, as the Frenchman told his story, the judge was laughing up his sleeve. Everything pointed to him, everything conspired against him. Who could doubt the staff, Ranalies in particular, who had been in service at that house for so long? What interest could any of the staff have in committing a crime like that? When the woman was identified and the newspapers said that the body belonged to Dorotea Palau, the well-known dressmaker, a great consternation spread among many ladies from the best families: "Poor Dorotea! Who could have imagined it? She seemed so decent, so utterly beyond reproach!"

The only person who breathed a bit easier on hearing of the crime was the Baró de Falset. Guillem de Lloberola wasn't the slightest bit moved, nor did it take him by surprise: "What other end could a hag like Dorotea come to?" is what Guillem thought.

Antoni Mates thought that Dorotea's disappearance left one less person to compromise him. Dorotea had been silenced forever more. Antoni Mates had stopped going to the Club Eqüestre. He hadn't seen Frederic in ages, and had no desire to run into him. Frederic felt the same way. Since Frederic had been saved, he had no interest in further analysis of the details, but when he was all by himself he couldn't help thinking that what he and his brother had done was not very clean. Frederic also did his best to avoid Guillem. Guillem, on the other hand, radiated satisfaction...A newcomer to actual fraud, he derived great pleasure from both the game and the adventure of it. He hadn't yet reached the stage of disappointment. We won't call it remorse because that would be excessive, but a sort of sadness of mere routine does ultimately take over, even for someone who is collecting a string of murders.

Guillem considered the Baró de Falset a repugnant and cowardly scorpion, without a drop of venom. He didn't merit a moment of regret. Guillem believed he was doing society a favor by morally eroding a man like the Baró de Falset, squeezing money from him as if from a sponge. Guillem was wielding the most vile and criminal of weapons, but he didn't see that, or preferred not to. He thought that high-stakes swindling put one in a brilliant position, as vivid and as human as allowing oneself to be nailed to a cross. He enjoyed the artistic voluptuosity of the game, and like a coward he accepted the venal turpitude and all the economic profit he could derive. Guillem was thirsty for fine suits and fine ties, dinners in fine restaurants, and sleeping with fine women. Once he had dared to blackmail a man of the category of the Baró de Falset, the scorn he felt for his father and for all his family's prejudices was only exacerbated. A satanic, but still immature, flora grew within the bookish depravity of the younger Lloberola. In men's hearts two phenomena carry tremendous sexual force: the first is the thrill of lowering oneself, of squatting like a dog, and suffering discomfort and physical pain to draw closer to divinity, the same idea of divinity and integral union with God that some mystics of monotheism have aspired to by means of these somewhat sadistic procedures. The other phenomenon, full of sensual intensity, consists of stifling within oneself any reminiscence of fear or mercy, any of the apparently irreducible religious and moral subconscious that is present even in frigid temperaments, until one has achieved the absolute absence of shame or scruples in the face of any situation. In his puerile, twisted and literary way, Guillem leaned toward the second of these phenomena.

Guillem decided to blackmail the Baró de Falset again. He formulated his plan in writing, a marvel of composition. Having the authentic letter from Antoni Mates in his possession, Guillem was able to pose the affair in such a way as to assign himself no role in the shameful events at the heart of the extortion. The document explained the carryings-on of the married couple with a third person, whose name did not appear, but whose existence Guillem could certify, as he had come to know the facts through the confession of the person in question. Moreover, in light of Antoni Mates's social position, the third person was of very little consequence. As proof, Guillem submitted the evidence of the previous extortion, and the irrefutable testimony of the baron's letter to his brother. In the event Antoni Mates didn't wish to deliver the amounts requested to Guillem, he would find a way to spread the defamatory news wherever it would be most prejudicial. Still, Guillem didn't believe he would have to go so far, and he always assumed that the baron would pay up.

Two days after hearing the news of Dorotea Palau's murder, Guillem requested another meeting with Antoni Mates. Flustered and practically jumping out of his own skin, naturally the baron conceded it to him. Guillem was paid a considerable sum. Mates handed it over with relative dignity, considering the panic and rage that consumed him. A short time later, Guillem turned the screws a little tighter. At that point the baron lost control, cried, groveled, threatened to kill Guillem and then begged Guillem to kill him, to free him of this torture. In the end, the baron gave in. Guillem performed

magnificent demonstrations of serenity, cold-bloodedness, soulless-
ness. After he had paid Guillem, the baron attended a very important
board meeting. They were preparing for the Exposició Internacional
on Montjuïc. Those were the days of the most unrestrained squandering of the dictatorship, and the Baró de Falset anticipated magnificent
returns. This was where his brilliant and splendid reality lay; he hid his
tortures, his fear and the secret and unutterable reality deep within
his breast. The baron wondered if he was the victim of strange hallucinations. When push came to shove, the young man could say
whatever he liked. What of it? Who would believe him? And if they
did believe him, then what? The baron would recover his serenity for
a few days but then, every so often, he would remember the letter he
had written and the fear would return. It was the infamous letter that
kept him up at night. He could have gone to Frederic and demanded
that he return the document, throwing in his face his indelicacy in
not having burned the letter, as he had requested. But he would soon
desist because that would have exposed him, and muddied the waters,
when what he most wanted was for the waters to stay nice and quiet,
and for not a word to be breathed.

To understand the intimidation of the Baró de Falset, the acute-
ness of his panic and the extent of his vulnerability, one must always
bear in mind the weakness and cowardice that stemmed from his
abnormality. The other thing that must also be kept in mind is the
kind of prestige he enjoyed and the kind of people he lived among.

Antoni Mates sought out a famous Jesuit priest. Mates had a reputation as a great Catholic and a great believer, even though at the core

his religiosity was a sham. But he tried. He made an attempt to see whether his religion could be a living, breathing thing, and whether he could find some kind of consolation in it, in the event of a catastrophe.

The Jesuit was an intelligent man, but he felt lost here. The Baró de Falset was a moral wreck. He had no faith, no resignation, no repentance, nothing; he had only the asphyxiating fear of a rabbit, and nothing more. Antoni Mates also realized this was not the path for him.

When a cowardly man finds himself in a blind alley, he is capable of who knows what foul things. So it was that the Baró de Falset had a grotesque, criminal idea. He was in good standing with shady elements of the Ministry of the Interior – the Minister was Martínez Anido – who was in contact with other even shadier elements, more given to, shall we say, "direct action." The Baró de Falset believed that, if he paid enough, there would be a way to make Guillem de Lloberola disappear, in an apparent accident or – why not? – a murder. So many had disappeared this way in Barcelona, what difference could one more make? He came very close to proposing the idea to a person who very possibly would have welcomed it, but he couldn't, he didn't have the guts. He didn't trust the person he had in mind.

Secure in his power, Guillem initiated a new attack. That day the baron's nerves were in better shape than usual. Guillem said:

"All right, it's your decision! I will do as I see fit."

Before the young man's resolute expression, the baron proposed a transaction, but then Guillem decided to up the ante, and with appalling aplomb he uttered:

"I don't give a damn about your money: it's you I want to ruin. I will risk it all, I don't care. I wouldn't keep silent even if you gave me your entire fortune, do you understand? You are contemptible, and since you have no imagination, you can't possibly comprehend the pleasure it would give me to annihilate a person like you. Even if I had to annihilate myself in the process, even if it meant the death of my father. As you can imagine, the death of a father, or anyone else, is nothing compared to the joy of ripping off a mask as well-anchored as the one attached to your face. What merit is there in destroying a worm, a wastrel, and a ne'er-do-well like me with a scandal? None at all. The merit lies in destroying the falsehoods of an imposter like you, surrounded by priests and bank accounts, flush with credit and consideration. To watch as this hypocritical society you belong to writhes disgustingly with joy and horror on hearing that one of the biggest fish in said society has been tarred with infamy and tossed into the gutter in his underwear. You must understand that if it is in my power to enjoy such a spectacle, I will not be so foolish as to let the occasion pass. I swear to you, everyone will know! Everyone will know who the Baró de Falset is, I swear it!"

Guillem's words left the baron utterly terrified, his response dying on his lips.

From that day on, Guillem took pleasure in elaborating a sort of cruel torment. He found a way to secure introductions to persons who had frequent dealings with the baron, and to others who were under his authority. He would show up in the company of those persons in strategic places where the baron would be sure to see him speaking with them, wearing a meaningful smile. He had the nerve to show up in the baron's own offices, and enter into conversation with his most important staff.

Antoni Mates thought he was done for. When he ran into someone who greeted him, when he chatted with someone else, he was utterly subject to suggestion. He thought he could sense that the person was already in on everything, that it had all been explained to him. He thought every word was an allusion; he perceived a double meaning in the most innocent things. In his office, on his most sensitive missions to the most notable members of society, on his many boards of administration, everywhere, he would discover imaginary eyes examining him, laughing at him, looking down on him as the lowest and most repugnant of perverts. And this fear, this terrible fear, began to leave its mark on his face. It altered his voice, his gestures, his way of walking. People who ran into him often, and, even more, those who had not seen him in a while, detected a bizarre uneasiness that they couldn't explain. As the days went by, the situation became darker and darker. In the end, everyone was aware, everyone realized that something very serious was wrong with him, and no one could figure out the cause. Only Guillem de Lloberola secretly reveled, silent as a dead man, as he contemplated the slow martyrdom of that poor man laden with millions, with stature, and with cowardice.

In their conjugal life the situation was even more unsavory. Conxa asked her husband what was happening to him. Since Guillem's first attack, Antoni Mates had manifested to Conxa his remorse for everything he had done, for the lengths he had gone to in degrading himself and degrading her. Conxa didn't understand. She was made up of a combination of cynicism and other things the baron couldn't suspect. She thought her husband had gone soft in the head, which for her, in truth, had long been true. But when his fear took on the dimensions of madness, Conxa became frightened. Antoni Mates didn't hint at Guillem's role in his disgrace and, naturally, Conxa didn't know a thing, nor would she ever know, about how Guillem was undermining her husband.

Conxa called in two or three doctors. Perhaps it was a case of *surmenage*, a temporary breakdown; perhaps it could be cured with a bit of repose. The more they treated Antoni Mates, the worse things got. He hadn't the slightest doubt that everyone was in on the story, and that he inspired disgust and pity. He once again considered the idea of making Guillem disappear, but by then it was too late. What good would it do? The death of that young man couldn't heal a thing, and would only compound the horror that was stalking him with the horror of a crime.

Antoni Mates was a total wreck. In three months, a man who had been famous for his aplomb and his sagacity in business, for his unassailable social position, had turned into a sort of drooping puppet, powerless to clear his lungs of the pus of imaginary infamy that kept him from breathing.

—.—.—

IT TOOK FREDERIC a long time to realize it, but in the end he understood that he had done a foolish thing. Bobby had been a good and trustworthy friend to him. A man as unsubstantial and overwrought as Frederic needed a passive and patient foil. Not everyone could treat him with Bobby's calm, cool nonchalance. If Frederic had been a thinking man, if he had been able to see himself in the mirror with critical good faith, without the passion and vanity that dominated him whenever his affairs were in question, perhaps he wouldn't have needed others so much. Above all he wouldn't have needed Bobby so much. For a man like Frederic, lacking in imagination and any kind of inner life, it is more troublesome to lose a friend of Bobby's caliber than it is to lose a lover, no matter how smitten he may be. Because people like Frederic see women as creatures who fulfill them and satisfy them on given days or hours, in their spare time, beyond the ordinary, gray hours of everyday. To the man who is experiencing it, a bond with a woman who makes your head spin can seem like a one-of-a-kind thing, tinged with a pearly suggestiveness, a red-hot eagerness. Oftentimes – indeed, most times – this suggestiveness, and this eagerness, can simply be replaced with another woman. It can even happen – also quite frequently – that for the moment there is no need to replace them. That is, they can be compensated for with a feeling of calm, of liberation, of repose, and of clarity. Gray everyday life can continue precisely on its way, perhaps a bit more transparently. Once eliminated and in the past, those moments of private life, of incandescence and lyricism, do not by a long shot possess the same lyricism and incandescence. On the contrary, they are perceived as an oppressive imposition that we have been fortunate to free ourselves of, and if we just persist a bit, it will not be at all difficult to pick up another imposition that will have the same lyrical and incandescent effect.

In contrast, if we are lazy by nature, once we have had as a friend, without realizing his worth – because we thought it was a natural thing, like having healthy teeth or clear eyes – a person who will put up with all the humbuggery of our particular way of being; who will go for a walk when we feel like it or sit down when we don't feel like walking; who has sufficient lack of initiative to go to the theater we want to go to, or not to go to the theater at all, if we fancy the Forty Hours' Devotion; a person who has the distinction of listening to us and of knowing how to listen, who contradicts us when we wish to be contradicted and is silent when we require silence; a person who never says no, but has the grace often to pretend to say it; a person with whom we have lived for years and years and who is as useful as a pair of old slippers to rest the feet after a very long walk; as soon as, by whatever chance, we find that this person disappears from our everyday dull routine, then what happens is that time becomes interminable, and our walk, our club, our confidences, our aperitif, our leisure time, and even our boredom are not what they used to be. They are missing the wedge that propped them up. Our life is like those annoying wobbly coffee tables on which no drink can be enjoyed. Someone who has been a friend since adolescence cannot be replaced by just anyone. The obstacles are much more difficult in nature than when it is simply a question of replacing one lover with another. The time of love, the life of the emotions, is always easy to resolve. In contrast, the dreary hours, life without rewards, the slow digestion of minutes stripped of pain or glory, or cloaked in the shadows of the sadness of desire, these are the hours that cannot be resolved just any old way. These are the hours when we most require, and hence most value, a disinterested collaboration.

Bobby was not precisely this ideal friend to Frederic, but of all his acquaintances he was the one who came closest, the one who gave him that feeling of repose, calm, and companionship. Frederic would never have given any thought to the value of friendship. Bobby offered him nothing more than patience and good manners, and Frederic absorbed these things – which came very easily to Bobby – as if they were the elements of a true friendship. Both as a single and a married man, Frederic had fallen out with everyone. Companions didn't last long with him because, in general, in order to take Frederic seriously you had to be just as trivial and oblivious as he was. Squabbles were common and intemperance was shared equally. Only Bobby, by virtue of being so different from Frederic, and so incapable of passion, abandon, or a vivid interest in anyone's fate, allowed Frederic, who was no psychologist, the gratification of believing that he was a faithful friend. At the same time, Frederic could indulge in the pleasure of considering himself far superior to Bobby.

After their foolish falling-out, Frederic thought he had lost the company of a first-rate fellow, the only one he considered a good friend. And for a ridiculous reason, in which the greater part of the fault lay with him. He discovered that he missed a number of things. He discovered that when he left the Banc Vitalici to take up his position at the sidewalk café of the Hotel Colon, he had no one to listen to him when he said the world was a mess, and this country was a piece of sh…, and Catalans were impossibly vulgar and ill-mannered people, and his neck was itchy, and marriage was absurd, and love didn't exist, and gentlemen here don't know how to behave like gentlemen, etc., etc. He discovered that, when he ran into a woman and winked at her, he couldn't run and gush into patient ears that he had just seen the most "stunning" woman, and he was the only man who knew how to deal with women like her, and she was a sure thing, and there was no one like him at flirting and leading them on. Frederic found that when his arms were itching for a string of caroms in a good game of billiards, he couldn't come up with a couple of intelligent and comprehending arms willing to let him win, if such was his mood. Or when someone had passed on some piece of juicy gossip, there was no sponge to absorb it all without protest, even managing to evince interest and curiosity. He discovered that when he just wanted to fool around, shooting bread balls at his friend's nose, sticking a toothpick into his ribs, or just calling him a "nincompoop," this guinea pig for his experiments in banality, silliness or conceit had fled his cage. The cage was just empty. His bridge partners were only good for bridge and nothing else; his officemates simply disgusted him; his family poisoned the very air he breathed; and the mere thought of his father made him hate life. There was only one door left through which he might escape, but the effects of his escape were unpredictable. The only door he had left was

Rosa Trènor. Why Rosa Trènor, in particular? The nocturnal adventure on Carrer de Muntaner had been a failure. It had been entangled with the anxiety of a promissory note, with an imminent battle with his father, with the fictional illusion of recovering his life of fifteen years before. Naturally, not even glue could hold all this together. Like everything concerning Frederic, it was skin-deep, and came and went without rhyme or reason. But after his falling-out with Bobby, Rosa Trènor's presence had neither sentimental nor erotic interest, nor the thrill of rebellion and scandal within the routine of a false and nauseating family peace. Rosa Trènor now represented the possibility of companionship and perhaps even friendship. When they had been lovers, years before, Frederic had turned Rosa into the repository of his egotism. He trusted her. He would consult her on anything from the color of a tie to guidance of a moral order on some issue he was looking into. Rosa knew him, she tolerated him, she understood him perfectly. Rosa was what Maria, Frederic's wife, had never known how to be. With the passing of time, she was spent, exhausted, and less demanding, and he was worn down, defeated, less fussy, and perhaps more indulgent with humiliation. So, perhaps, once she was stripped of her *femme fatale* patina and he was resigned to putting up with a few pains in the neck, they might achieve a sort of idyll without phony violins and with a merciful abundance of poultices.

And so it was. Rosa took a bit of distance from Mado, on account of the incompatibility between Frederic and Bobby, and she accepted her late night bouquets of camellias more and more infrequently, because Frederic advanced her all the money he could, and more.

Frederic became very familiar with Rosa's apartment on Carrer de Muntaner. He even came to find some charm in the spectral cat that licked the coffee cup, whose appetite knew no bounds. As Frederic came to discover, she paid her frequent visits by jumping in through the kitchen window. He found it amusing to see her perched on the quilt as he explained to Rosa Trènor, looking grotesque in pajamas the color of a white wine from Alella, some theory he had just come up with on the cultivation of peas or on how to carry out a risk-free abortion.

Frederic interceded on the cat's behalf. Rosa had the concierge bring her a bit of fish. And the cat got fatter and lost her spectral personality.

One day Rosa told Frederic the story of the stuffed dog. The dog's master had been a general born in Valladolid, a short, slight man with the voice of an angel, whose wife beat him. The general fell in love with Rosa, and every day they would talk a walk down to the Parc de la Ciutadella, past the monument to General Prim, and visit the zoo. At one o'clock on the dot the general would board the tram. The little dog was a sort of cross between a terrier and a seminarian. It would get ill-tempered and snappy as it walked along beside them. Rosa would bring a couple of sugar cubes for him, which he would catch mid-air, his mouth wide open and his eyes rolling back in his head like an opera singer's.

Eventually, the general's wife got wind of the story. The idyll came to an end, and the general died of sorrow. One day at dawn, as Rosa was leaving the Grill Room, she came across the little lost dog wandering up and down the Rambles. It jumped up and put its two little front paws on her beaver coat. Rosa was appalled at its boldness. She let out a shriek, but when she recognized the general's dog, she started to cry. She gently picked it up, lifted it into the taxi, and sat it on her lap with motherly affection. The dog lived with Rosa for two years until a car ran over it, leaving it stretched out on Carrer de Muntaner, its open eyes near bursting, with a rivulet of blood on its snout. Rosa was desolate. She kept a few garters she no longer used in a cardboard box, and she remembered clearly that one of those garters was the first thing the pitiful nails of the general had touched when she surrendered to their idyll. Rosa took the dog to a taxidermist near the school of the Brothers of the Christian Doctrine, by the Palau de la Música Catalana. He was an old man who desiccated small animals, and he did it on the cheap.

Once the dog had been stuffed, Rosa draped the historic garter around its neck and gave it a home in the place where she worked and slept.

Frederic didn't see the humor in that military memento perched on the armoire and he asked Rosa if she would sacrifice her souvenir of the general for love of him. Rosa put up a great resistance. One day when Frederic was a bit more recklessly lavish than usual, Rosa gave in to his entreaties, and the following day the ragman took the dog away.

Thanks to these innocent little larks, Frederic was able to forget his family situation and his wife's bitter laments. He would spend many nights away from home without offering any explanation. Maria didn't care any more. She felt entirely divorced from her husband and by nature made no sexual demands. Maria had everything she needed with the pipes of her mother's apocalyptic lungs. The children spent the day at school. The girl had just turned fifteen; the boys were dressing in golf clothes and chewing gum.

They didn't yet have ideas of their own, but Maria did everything in her power to enlist them in a sort of holy war against Frederic. Her mother went even further.

The idyll between Rosa Trènor and Frederic de Lloberola lasted four months and three days. More or less the same length of time as the demise of Antoni Mates, el Baró de Falset.

—·—·—

HORTÈNSIA PORTELL HAD a grand house with a garden on the Passeig de la Reina Elisenda. She had arranged the main floor of the house to receive visitors and accommodate large groups. There was a very spacious entrance hall with three salons and a dining room on the right, and yet another, smaller, salon on the left. On the upper floor were the rooms that corresponded to the more personal life of the house. The architecture was simple, done in rather good taste, but a little bit shoddy. It was one of those mass-produced houses that at first had looked like stage sets for an operetta and are now feeling the effects of film.

Hortènsia had vitrines full of objects inherited from her great-grandmothers: magnificent fans, tobacco cases, music boxes, slippers, ribbons, and items whose usefulness was a mystery to anyone who was not an expert in all the absurd, old, rancid, constipated, and marvelous bibelots that one keeps in a vitrine.

From the days of *modernisme*, or Art Nouveau, if you will, Hortènsia preserved a portrait of herself and her husband having hot chocolate in a garden. They are sitting in a couple of rustic chairs painted watering pot green.

Mixed in with the other paintings, there were fake El Grecos, fake Goyas, and fake Riberas. Not that she had a lot of fakes; lately she had been replacing them with fashionable contemporary paintings. She was the only lady in Barcelona with a Matisse and a Derain of the highest quality. From time to time she would purchase something at a local exhibition, on the advice of friends with some knowledge of the field. She was most pleased with her Picasso. The canvas portrayed a long, thin adolescent nude, which scandalized many of the ladies who came to the house. Hortènsia had given it pride of place.

Presiding over the main salon hung the Lloberolas' historic tapestry, which, as the reader knows, Hortènsia Portell had acquired quite some years before. It showed a scene from the Bible. Jacob, wearing sheepskin gloves, was kneeling at the feet of an Isaac whose hands were full of the fruits of the earth. Isaac had the aquiline nose of a notary public and hair like spaghetti. Rebecca was smiling at them both, holding a bird that looked sort of like a chicken by its feet.

In the background were depicted the sons and daughters of the chosen people. They were waving their arms in the air and making way for a hairy, ruddy, and corpulent man who carried a boar on his hip. It was Esau.

The most important piece in the salon, after the tapestry, was a Louis XVI sofa, admirably pure in its lines and fragile as a nymph. General Arbós, a cannibalistic sexagenarian who weighed one hundred forty-three kilos, developed a habit of sitting on that sofa. This caused the lady of the house great distress.

By this time, the widow Portell had gotten extremely fat. Her exaggeratedly blond hair, her tortoise-shell glasses, and her short round figure made her look like a character from one of those German plays that deal with social or pedagogical topics. Except for her somewhat harsh and loud way of speaking, which smacked of Carrer de la Princesa, Hortènsia didn't seem to be from here at all. Anyone who ran into her would have thought she was a product of international tourism.

Usually once a year, Hortènsia would throw a party in her home. The main attraction might be a tango singer or, from time to time, an artist of great stature, like Maria Barrientos, the soprano. Barrientos was a friend of Hortènsia's, though of late their relations seemed to have cooled. Sometimes, giving in to the entreaties of a handful of ladies, she would have a flamenco party in the garden, with *bunyols* and *xurros*, fried dough in the form of dumplings or bows, and they would all wear *mantons de Manila*, voluminous silk embroidered shawls that were a souvenir of the colonial days. This is what they most enjoyed draping over their décolletage, because, the truth be told, the ladies of Barcelona have always had a weakness for flamenco style and all its poses.

The party Hortènsia Portell threw at the high point of the Baró de Falset's personal persecution complex had no particular artistic theme. In truth, it was mostly an excuse to bring one hundred fifty individuals together to set the leaves on the trees to trembling with their sighs and peals of laughter. The jazz music would exasperate any couples who aspired to continue their conversations as they took a stab at dancing. It was mid-June, and the heat was sticky and tropical.

By eleven the salons were almost full. It was rumored that Primo de Rivera, the dictator, who was in Barcelona those days, might make an appearance. He would be dining at the Cercle de l'Exèrcit, the officer's club, and had promised to attend Hortènsia Portell's party afterwards.

A few newcomers, some of them extremely young, situated themselves strategically in the foyer so as not to miss anyone's entrance.

In the salons, the glow of arms and shoulders was dazzling. A sea of slow, wide waves slightly tinged with blood rose and fell with the rhythmic breathing of creamy rose flesh. From time to time, amid the waves an amphibious medusa would float by in the form of the nape of a neck.

The parade of necklines alternated between the sublime and the abominable. The fashion of the long skirt had not yet taken hold. The flowering of legs and ankles and the occasional distracted knee, and the gamut of chiffon stockings, brought to mind the image of a bar with light, fizzy, multicolored sodas.

In among legs of exquisite style swelled lamentable arthritic extremities, like the grotesque balloons given to children, or legs that were simply sedentary, deformed by consecutive pregnancies. Some of these legs had reached the point of elephantiasis. Salomé Roca, a heavyset woman in a very short silver tunic showed off everything she could with the aggressivity of a satyress.

Lace dresses dominated, especially in black. There were many splashes of white and pink. The occasional burgundy or pea green accompanied the most agile musculatures, and the slenderest arms and ankles of the "it" girls.

Costume jewelry had not yet been invented, and the gathering did not give off that air of later parties, at which ladies were draped in so much colored glass they looked like extras in a pharaonic operetta. At Hortènsia Portell's party only strings of pearls and well-set diamonds were admitted.

Many of the ladies on the guest list knew Hortènsia only vaguely. Others had very little contact with the world in evidence that evening. They were a bit lost, taking up positions in the corners of the entrance hall, not daring to display themselves under the lights beside the guests who had taken over the sofas and pillows.

The men were distributed between silk and skin, like little black chunks of truffle amid the pink and white flesh of a galantine. Many wandered off on their own, or a trio would corner a young woman and proceed to laugh their heads off. Others went off under the trees to have a smoke.

In the smaller salon there was an assembly of abdomens feeling a bit indignant at the strain of the tailcoat and the demands of the wing collar. These abdomens had to make do with the cheeks of sixty year-olds suffering from chronic bronchitis.

Every so often, some old-school gentleman would go and dip his white moustaches into the plump perfume of a more tender cleavage and return with an anecdote fluttering delicately between two fingers, like a butterfly. He would then release it between noses and laughter to spread a bit of honey and cynicism on their arteriosclerotic lack of imagination.

The dance floor was getting crowded, but many young men were not dancing. This was when saxophones were beginning to be intoxicated with the blues and the black bottom. The Charleston had moved on to skid row. This was the high point of the red-hot days of Josephine Baker. Half the men at Hortènsia Portell's that night had devoured "la Baker" at the Folies-Bergère, as she emerged from her silvery sphere to reveal the most dynamic India rubber haunches ever to be seen.

Many girls felt the same veneration for "la Baker" that their aunts had felt years before for the Virgin of Montserrat, whose image had been blackened by the smoke of centuries of candlelight. It was just a question of directing one's devotion to one black skin or another, and in Hortènsia Portell's milieu there were many more advocates in the ranks of colonial paganism. Milans del Bosch, the Civil Governor of

Barcelona, did not share with the tender dancers of the black bottom their veneration for Josephine Baker, and he ordered the removal of a portrait of the Negress on exhibit in a record store, on the grounds that it was pornographic.

Hortènsia Portell allowed her guests absolute freedom of movement. Groups formed according to the magnetic attraction of affinity and friendship. Many bridge partners gathered around a hope chest as if ready to play. Without the table and the cards, lacking an ace of clubs or a king of hearts to pinch between them, some guys' fingers were at a loss; they couldn't even manage to smoke. The most desperate fingers would dig into some sweet upper arm and drag it off to the garden to tell whatever latest story wasn't too corrosively blue to tell, making do with a few drops of curaçao in a glass of water.

With their décolletages and their nighttime coifs, the women lost personality. Their dresses had too many slits and openings and too much skin was left to the elements. Their souls, and even their malice, fell flat. Something like what happens at the beach. In general, women are much more skilled at sustaining their erotic magnetism on an afternoon stroll, at a hippodrome, or at twelve o'clock Mass than by the side of a swimming pool.

In the presence of so much cleavage on so many middle-aged women, such an unnatural pneumatic display, normal men feel as though they've been transported to one of those commercial brothels in the south of France in which all the flesh is high quality and no holds are barred. These things throw one's palate off, and end up producing contradictory sensations.

Even so, some admirable specimens still stood out between the overall provocation and the indistinguishable black tie. An unabashed collector of trophies of the fair sex might have admired anything from the arms of Clementina Botey, pure white with only a tenuous blush of pink, to the shoulder of the Comtessa de Mur, so criminally silken as to be almost metallic, and dense with an intense and fragrant pigment that brought to mind heated Caribbean hallucinations.

Hortènsia sat beneath the tapestry, on the Louis XVI sofa. The most respectable ladies were arrayed around her. The Widow Xuclà was wearing an old-fashioned egg yolk-colored dress of silk moiré, her bosom covered with constellations of diamonds. Rafaela Coll and her sister, the Marquesa de Cardó, two old poker players, flanked Pilar, guarding her like two prudent opponents in an exhibition game to be sure the widow didn't try any dangerous sprints. This group was dominated by the hippopotamian anatomy of la Senyora Valls-Darnius, who had vowed, ever since her husband pulled off a considerable swindle in a cement deal, never to utter another word in Catalan. She had also let the word get out that she was in the market for a young man who would give her a tickle from time to time, no matter what the price. This lady had something to say about every-thing and she could get a little tiresome. The most amusing member of the Restoration *équipe* – this team had been in the flower of its youth when Spain lost its colonies in 1998 – was Aurèlia Ribas, of the Ribas silk merchants, as they were known. She had three brothers, all of whom were marquises, but she had been left without a title. She was nothing but the widow of an insignificant lawyer. Aurèlia had the face of a fish; she called to mind the rigid, inexpressive, silvery profile of the porgy. She was seventy-eight years old and they had just removed a tumor from her uterus. Poor Aurèlia was so simpleminded that she cried over this misfortune, as a young woman would have cried if the operation had made it impossible for her to have more children. Needless to say, Aurèlia's whimpering about her uterus provoked the gentle laughter of the poker ladies.

The Comtessa de Sallent, the Widow Xuclà's sister-in-law, presided over a different group, composed of exemplars of the fusty nobility. These noble ladies, in general, dressed in a more lackluster fashion, and made less use of beauty salons than those whose titles were fresher. Some of these ladies were truly awful and positively turtle-like. The Comtessa de Sallent herself, despite proceeding directly from a lateral branch of the Cardonas, looked and dressed like a chestnut vendor and spoke a Castilian studded with as many hard, greasy expressions as lardons on a Lenten flatbread. Next to the Comtessa de Sallent, Teodora Macaia had the magnificent and unapproachable majesty of a bird of paradise. Others, like the old Marquesa de Figueres, were embarrassed by their ridiculous necklines exposing their deteriorated skin. They didn't dare look up, and they spoke in a whisper, as if they were saying the rosary.

Occasionally a blend of gardenias and bad faith would appear, laughing uproariously, brandishing the flaming helmet of her hair and mortifying the pearls on her breast. Such was the case of the young Baronessa de Moragues, a manufacturer of rubber objects, deeply vulgar, but also deeply exciting.

A jaunty team of young married ladies and single ladies at liberty made up the most numerous group, with the most male components. This group exuded an aroma of hard liquor and grass from the golf course. In general, this team was composed of the prettiest and the most risqué "music hall" toilettes. Among them, flashing sparkling teeth and cherry-pink gums, were a few young women from the high aristocracy of Madrid, newly married to Catalan nobles or local industrialists. These Madrilenyes had the delicate bitterness of a peach pit, and were better at sustaining a more off-color and perhaps more intelligent conversation.

For some reason, the Dictatorship had facilitated a feminine trade between Madrid and Barcelona in that world that called itself aristo-cratic. Thanks, too, to the Dictatorship there was a resurgence of gro-tesque pomp, exhibitionism, and traffic in noble titles. With parades of gold and uniforms and military fanfare, the regime of the time buttered up the base vanity of shopkeepers and petty nobles. Many of them had never been anyone, and their utter insignificance had had no other initiative than to collect the rent on their properties and redeem the coupons on their bonds, always pinching pennies and fear-ful of falling into poverty. In the years of the Dictadura, these people felt a sudden desire to spend and to show off, to see their names in the newspapers and their wives four meters from the queen, with a gigolo, and to sponsor a flag-raising in some little town on the coast. Their air of parvenus and bottom feeders rested like a spider web or a strip of leather from a carpet beater on the dress shirt of many of the gentlemen who sauntered through that party and the infinite public and private feasts that were taking place in those daysin Barcelona.

Some gentlemen from fusty families had come to realize they were no longer of any relevance and had been relegated to the dust bin by the democratic and industrial policies of the country. Those gentlemen who had been content during the war to cut down the forests on their estates as they bred canaries and did spiritual exercises, surfaced at the party with all the shiny hardware of their coats of armor and their inanity. Many of the children of these families held positions in the parasitic bureaucracy that sprang up in Barcelona as the 1929 Exposition drew near, with the proliferation of public works underway all over town. The people who worked in the Treasury, the Civil Government, the Bank, the Customs office, were almost all from the province of Extremadura. They lived a separate, resentful, life during that sentimental expansion of Barcelona. Under the dictatorship, they, too, invented titles and uniforms and they, too, introduced glossy, pneumatic wives and sassy, carnivalesque creatures who were accepted by the practical bourgeoisie.

Hortènsia Portell didn't sympathize by a long shot with the deluge of tawdry pomp of the times, but she found herself, and most of her friends and relations, caught up in the game. She was in her element, like almost all the fine bourgeois ladies of the period, with a taste for public display and exhibition. Hortènsia was a weak woman, and she couldn't say no to anyone. At heart she was very tolerant and liberal, but lacking in deep-rooted convictions. It was this temperament –

perfumed like her skin with superficiality and distraction – that invented those grand eclectic gatherings at her home.

Because that night on the Passeig de la Reina Elisenda, alongside that whole empty, déclassé world, Hortensia had also invited people who had played a role in the old Catalanist political life. These were men who stood apart from the masquerade, including the occasional sensible businessman, skeptical grayhair, or intelligent young mien.

Hortènsia had brought together exactly the sort of mélange that can always be found at pompous Barcelona gatherings. A mélange of this sort is the result of improvisation, rapid growth, and insufficient review of credentials. It is also the result of a somewhat material- istic world, in which the brand and price of an automobile is paid respect even before the person ensconced within has been identified. The occupant is then extended moral credit and elegance credit in proportion to the price and brand of said automobile. All this dress- ing up as aristocratic scarecrows that had been the consequence of the First World War was spurred on further by the mentality of the Dictatorship.

If the conversations of all the different groups had been placed side-by-side they might have produced the effect of Horace's monster, with the peculiarity that each of the monster's members would have been gnawing at the other.

The most peppery tongues belonged to those fifty years and over; the most airy lungs would glide back and forth from tangos to love and from love to tangos.

Most of the young men's dialogue centered on chassis, car bodies and gonorrhea. These conversations, in a Catalan spoken to the tune of a *zarzuela*, sounded like a bumblebee buzzing, smelled like mineral oil, and were tinted the color of permanganate.

Among the more serious political topics were timidly broached, and Romanesque art might be discussed, along with the half dozen most highly valued legs at the party. Great Barcelona events were spoken of with satisfaction, from the construction going forward on the Plaça de Catalunya to the two thousand priests from a whole range of Spanish dioceses who would be coming for the 1929 Exposició Universal. These canons would check out the objects on display in the *Palau Nacional*, the main exhibition space of the fair, and then stroll down the Rambla in mufti, smoking cigars. In certain male circles, anticlericalism was in vogue.

The ladies in the tapestry room were all aflutter. Many didn't believe the dictator would come. Hortènsia smoothed their feathers. Shrill as a parrot, the young Marquesa de León squawked in Spanish for everyone to hear: *"I saw Miguel this afternoon, and he assured me he was coming."* These particulars offered up by the marquesa caused a few old ladies to snicker, as it was going around that she and Primo de Rivera were in a dalliance.

The arrival of Conxa Pujol, the Baronessa de Falset, caused a commotion, as she was coming without her husband. She was escorted by her in-laws, who looked as if their only reason for coming to the party was to accompany her.

It was the first time that Conxa had attended such an event without her husband. She was at the peak of her great beauty. Conxa must have been thirty or thirty-five years old. All the men's eyes clung like leeches to her cleavage. Her skin was the most fascinatingly foreign and dreamy product ever to grace the streets of Barcelona.

Conxa's presence stirred up a great deal of commentary. The topic of Antoni Mates was vividly and impertinently present. Everyone had his own personal version of the famous cotton dealer's state of mind. Many claimed he had gone mad. In one group, they secretly exchanged shady references, but the explanations were completely off the mark. Without a doubt, the main source of these references was the Baró de Falset's own behavior, and, at most, some particular detail from the market scare, because, in fact, Guillem de Lloberola had not used any of his arsenal against the baron.

Conxa made her way over to the jaunty team after dropping a few crumbs for the old ladies and allowing herself to be subjected to a string of malicious questions.

Hortènsia escaped from the rheumatic team and went over to breathe in a bit of the fragrance of freshly-mown grass that surrounded Conxa Pujol. The baronessa's only explanation was that her husband was a bit weary, but she said she would not under any circumstances have missed Hortènsia's big night.

Among the men who decided to wag their tails in the vicinity of Conxa Pujol's stockings was a young man with curly hair and the face of a child who said a couple of words amid the hurly-burly of men who were melting over the baronessa's skin. Clearly that young man was not part of the scene, because many asked who he was.

Bobby was in one of those groups, He cleared it up for them:

"That's Guillem de Lloberola."

"De Lloberola?" said his interlocutor. "Ah, sure! The brother of that cad, right? Your former friend?"

"Precisely," added Bobby. Neither he nor his companion said another word.

But Guillem still triggered the following exchange between two other people in the group:

"Who are these Lloberolas?"

"How can I put it?.... I don't know..., just some old spongers..."

The Marquesa de Perpinyà de Bricall i de Sant Climent made another sensational entrance. She swept in like a dethroned queen, escorted by her son-in-law, a couple of colonels, and her sister-in-law, who was from Valencia and flaunted the title of Duquesa de Benicarló. The Marquesa de Perpinyà wore a very severe black dress with a golden shawl draped over her shoulders. She was ugly and misshapen and her skin was pitted and deathly white, as if coated with cheap stucco. The marquesa belonged to the most authentic nobility in the country. It was said that she had a decisive influence on all echelons of the regime. She could have Captain Generals removed from office, and in Madrid people paid her much mind. The Dictator stopped by her house for coffee every day. Ever since the coup d'état in 1923, the marquesa had puffed up like a bullfrog.

Legend had it that the coup was planned in her palace on Carrer de Carders.

The presence of this grande dame pacified a number of the ladies, because in effect it guaranteed that the dictator would be showing up at one point or another. Otherwise, the Marquesa de Perpinyà would not have bothered to attend Hortènsia Portell's party. The marquesa paraded stiffly among the files of the dumbfounded, and went over to sit under the tapestry, immersed in the poisonous pomp that was beginning to enter a comatose state. Generals bowed to kiss her hand with a cocky and liturgical flourish, and she alternated laughs and hiccups, producing a dry, infrahuman voice, reminiscent of the sound of walnuts rolling around in a sack. In one corner of the great hall there were two middle-aged men. One had a gray moustache and a disabused and absent air, and the other had a lively demeanor and the mouth of a jackal. When the one with the gray moustache caught sight of the Marquesa de Perpinyà, he said to his companion:

"Remember what we were saying about Barcelonism? Now, just take this woman. I know a little about her family history. Her father has gone over it with me many times. The marquesa's grandfather gave his all for the dynastic Carlists, in opposition to Queen Isabella II. He was in exile in France for ten years; he pawned everything but his shirt. The liberal government confiscated his properties, and he took it like a man…"

"A pointless, foolish enterprise…if you don't mind my saying so."

"Pointless and foolish as you like, but in those days people had a little more spine, they knew how to sacrifice, they took life more…"

"Yes, and I have it on good authority that she knows how to sacrifice, too. They say she sold a forest to pay for the party she threw last year for the king and queen…"

"Sure, that's exactly what she knows how to do, sell forests. You'll see how things go when she doesn't have any forests left to sell. And it's not all her fault, she's under the pressure of her son-in-law. What can you expect of a duke who's an ex-croupier and polo champion? He feeds his vanity with his mother-in-law's money."

"You can't deny that she's a lady who know how to be a lady. She has a certain majesty…"

"The majesty of the domicile."

"I don't follow you."

"Oh, sure you do. I mean, people like *La Perpinyà* and other families cut from the old cloth, if you take them out of the house they live in, they are nothing. They never move from their decaying old manors on the most anti-hygienic streets of Barcelona. The manors hold their gardens, their salons and their chapels. Do you know what it is to live in an immense apartment half taken up by rooms full of junk in which, to add insult to injury, there is a chapel and a chaplain who says Mass? All their tradition can be summed up in the leaks in the ceilings and the mildew on the walls. And beyond those walls, you see, extends the life they have never understood: Barcelona. What have all these people done for the country, what have they contributed? Absolutely nothing. As long as they have forests to cut down, a domestic priest at home to say Mass, and a couple of servants to dust the chairs, they keep going. When all this is gone, they're nobody. The marquesa has the same mentality as her house on Carrer de Carders. A sad and useless mentality. Her father was Catalan. He was a man who still spoke Catalan. What is she? How does this woman feel about her country and its oh-so-noble traditions? Well, this is how she feels: she marries her only daughter off to a ruined duke from Cartagena who seems to be nothing but a perfect swine, and she runs around like a madwoman behind the imbecile who is mucking things up for all of us…"

"Be careful, man, lower your voice."

"You tell me if I'm right or not, about this majesty of the domicile. Take the Lloberolas, for example. As long as the Marquès de Sitjar lived on Carrer de Sant Pere més Baix he seemed to be someone. Now he is penniless in an apartment that could just as easily belong to a shopkeeper, and he's poor Senyor Tomàs, and nothing more. They are people who are incapable of reacting, of living life as it comes. And the marquès's sons are worse than the sons of my shoemaker. Look at the younger one, over there, yes, the one who's chatting with the wife of old Mates. He's nothing but a rascal who will end up in jail."

"You're just saying that because you think the Catalan aristocracy has fallen short. But do you really think this pack of pork vendors with titles are any better?"

"Well, I'm not sure if they're better or worse. Morally, they may be worse, and that's saying a lot. But they combine their arriviste vanity with an interest in work, an interest, if you will, even in stealing and dirty business. That's at least something…"

"Well, thanks a lot!"

"Look, what I mean is that among these people, no matter how low-class they are, there are at least some who have initiative, ambition. They get factories rolling, they get banks rolling. They put the stomach of the country to work…Some of these ladies, the ones wearing the most diamonds and speaking the worst Castillian, because they grew up speaking Catalan and working, and never went to school, have husbands who still work twelve hours a day…"

"I find this line of reasoning unpersuasive. You're just a materialist…"

"And what of it!"

"In any case, all this hoi polloi with their new money earned who knows how, are also running after the dictator and the current regime just as fast as the old aristocrats you criticize."

"They're running even faster! They're chasing him because they can profit from it. And the women do it out of vanity. Since they're people without convictions, they don't waste any time. Now they're supporting this silly general, and tomorrow they'll throw their weight behind a republic or the communists, if it means a few *quartos*. Do you see all these gentlemen who are bowing and scraping and collaborating on everything that does the country the greatest harm? Many of them used to vote for *la Lliga de Catalunya* back when we could vote, and they dressed their daughters in the little white hoods of the *Pomells de Joventut* – the Catholic, Catalan bouquets of youth! – until the dictator dissolved the association."

"Well, you're right there. You Catalanists are certainly not making a very good show for yourselves…!"

"Real Catalanists are few and far between. Back in the glory days of Catalan politics, Prat de la Riba used to say there were no more than a hundred at most. And that's being generous."

"Prat de la Riba died in 1917. Hasn't there been any progress since then?"

"More than likely the number has gone down…Do you see that fellow devouring Aurora Batllori's cleavage? That fellow was as staunch and fierce a Catalanist as they come. Now he's accepted a very important commission the Marquès de Foronda procured for him, and some say he is a police informer…"

"Really?"

"I wouldn't be at all surprised. In any case, I'm going over there under the trees, because the 'beast' must be about to arrive…"

"Yes, and you continue to talk at the top of your lungs! I don't know why you even come to these places. A separatist like you! And tomorrow in the social pages of the paper your name will appear right beside the names of these people you find so disgusting…"

"You're probably right to criticize me. But what's a man to do? I came out of friendship with Hortènsia. Because I certainly don't have a good time at these affairs…In the end, though, each of us has his share of cowardice…"

Guillem de Lloberola had met Conxa Pujol just a few days before. They were introduced in a group standing at the Ritz. The baronessa didn't sense anything special about the boy; she didn't even notice him, just as she didn't notice him at Hortènsia's party. Many young men like Guillem had been introduced to Conxa, and they immediately faded from her memory. What happened to the Baró de Falset when he met Guillem didn't happen to Conxa: she didn't recall a voice, she didn't feel any panic, partly because the two shameful episodes in which Guillem had played a role were enveloped in an olio of darkness and mystery. And partly because after the *chantage,* those two shameful episodes represented the most chilling phantasm of Antoni Mates's life. For his wife they only represented two more shameful episodes among a multitude of shameful episodes.

In the days of the chauffeur, and even before then, Conxa had had her own feasts for the goddesses. Like a figure out of Juvenal, Conxa had paid many afternoon visits to houses of infamy, and had taken advantage of trips abroad to engage in a sport in whose practice someone from her world would never be recognized. She derived pleasure from being brutalized by scum. Fed up with endless flattery from all sides, she found a very special voluptuosity in the thrusting and biting of a drunken sailor. This creature whom evil tongues had claimed to see arch her back in the air like a grouper out of water, continued to arch her back like all the fish in the sea.

Her mysterious afternoon adventures left her with an ailment that required the intervention of Cuyàs, the dermatologist. Conxa had to offer him some explanation, but, like all good dermatologists, Cuyàs kept his professional counsel.

Cuyàs was one of Hortènsia's guests. He smiled at the Baronessa de Falset with utmost politeness. The two rather blond young men he was with had contradictory opinions about the baronessa.

"She's not such a big deal. We all know where she came from. I don't get all the whoop-de-doo about her."

"She's 'out of this world.'"

"Just another pretty face…"

"Come on, you're exaggerating. I say she's 'out of this world,' truly out of this world."

"I know another girl who's out of this world and nobody pays her any mind and she's available to anyone. Yeah, yeah, don't give me that look – she's just as 'out of this world' as this one."

"And what's the name of this beauty?"

"She has only one name: Camèlia."

"And her address?"

"Carrer de Demòstenes, 31. Every afternoon, from four to eight. Price: twenty-five pessetes."

Dr. Cuyàs smiled without saying a word, but his eyes were saying "This fool doesn't know the first thing about Carrer de Demòstenes. He just wants to play the *enfant terrible*. But, to be honest, maybe he's not that far off."

On the last stroke of twelve there was a great commotion and a sort of general "Aaaah…!" Five or six ramrod-straight individuals had just come into the house. Among them was a tall florid man with thin white hair. He was fatigued and ordinary, a cross between a police inspector and a canasta player, with a touch of the priest and a touch of the lion tamer. It was General Miguel Primo de Rivera.

Many ladies frankly threw themselves at him. Cuyàs the dermatologist whispered into his neighbor's ear:

"My God, how many of the young creatures here today wouldn't give anything in the world to be raped by that old goat?"

Primo de Rivera strode over to the most glittering and crusty group. His eyes popped at the sight of Teodora Macaia's supple skin, and his lips were coated with a dense saliva. Primo de Rivera had had a long day and he was tired. His cheeks wore the natural rouge of wine.

The ladies pawed at him. He proferred highly spiritual words in return. To his nearest and dearest, he told a filthy unexpurgated story from the barracks. The ladies choked with laughter.

The Marquesa de Lió, who didn't leave his side, said to him, in Spanish:

"*Ay, Miguel!* You are so funny, so salty, *saladísimo!*"

And amid the cackling of the old ladies, that *saladísimo* kept echoing, floating in the night air like a drowned man's shoe.

The merriment lasted till quarter to four in the morning.

——————

THE DAY AFTER Hortènsia's party, at a poker game played many afternoons at Rafaela Coll's house, a trip to the red light district off the Rambla known as the *Barri Xino* was organized. The name alluded and, in a way, paid homage, to the vice and filth of Chinatown in San Francisco. The co-conspirators for the escapade were Rafaela, Teodora Macaia, Teodora's best friend, Isabel Sabadell, Hortènsia, Bobby, the Comte de Sallès, Pep Arnau and Emili Borràs: two widows, two divorcées, three bachelors and one married man. Rafaela had been a widow the longest; she had already been to *La Criolla* and other dives. So had Hortènsia. Teodora and Isabel, the two divorcées, had not. Isabel and Teodora had been friends all their lives, and both had been unlucky in marriage. They were both a little tired of their own feelings. Teodora had very few illusions; Isabel, who was prettier and more sentimental, still believed in love and in the relative fidelity of her friend, Ferran Castelló. Among the men, the Comte de Sallès, the married one, was a most eccentric and charming fellow. He took the dress code, neckties and rouge very seriously. He was romantic, childish, and a little silly. When he took a paramour out for dinner, he would order roses for the table in the color of the soul of the woman he had invited. It was all the same if she was an interesting person or the most brazen turner of tricks, the count behaved towards her just as he would have behaved if the fates had conceded him the grace of dining with the mummies of Madame de Sévigné or Madame de Lafayette.

The Comte would speak of literature, politics, and international elegance with a certain innocent fancy, often unaware that he was boring the lady. They would tolerate him as one tolerated a child who was not only extremely polite but also paid very generously and always without offending. The childlike count had his stubborn side and his lyrical fugues. Sometimes he would stop mid-word in a conversation, and affect a sort of beatific smile. One could see a minuscule boat sailing through his blue eyes. It was the little boat that carried him off to glide through the dead waters of the moon. The count was a cross between an elegant and original man and a simpleton. He was misunderstood in his milieu. Society folk made fun of him behind his back. They thought he was a crashing bore, but at heart they appreciated him because he was a good person. To tell the truth, the count was far superior to all the people who would address him with the familiar "tu" when they found themselves having their hair cut next to him in the barbershop of the Club Eqüestre. With his great concern for aristocratic refinement, in Barcelona he was like Robinson Crusoe on the desert island. He would escape to Paris to see his friends at the Jockey Club. There he would seek out a mad duchess from the Faubourg St.-Germain, a veritable wax figure with whom he could talk of dogs, horses, religion, and the nobility, most particularly of Eugénie Montijo, the Spanish marquesa who became the last empress of the French when she married Napoleon III.

Emili Borràs was just as eccentric as the count. He was a mathematician who took a great interest in the visual arts and in women's fashion. He enjoyed this elegant and somewhat trashy world purely as spectacle. Cold, evasive, inconsistent, and fragile in a feminine sort of way, he never let down his guard. Some said he had no blood in his veins. He was the purest example of an intellectual to be found in Barcelona society in those years. Emili Borràs was very successful with women because of his special way of being chic, a bit negligent and apparently offhanded. He was well liked because his conversation was never vulgar. It fluctuated between disconcerting naiveté and putrid cynicism. Emili Borràs was Catholic, and he worked for a living.

Pep Arnau was another member of this group, as was Bobby. The reader will remember that we first ran into him playing baccarat at Mado's. When we recounted the events of that evening, we didn't pay much attention to Pep Arnau, nor will we do so now, because, as we said at the time, Pep Arnau's only distinguishing characteristic was to be fat and innocent as a pig.

Those ladies and those gentlemen parked their two cars in front of the Lion d'Or and went on foot down Carrer de l'Arc del Teatre. It was one o'clock in the morning and the street was simmering with milling shadows. It was full of ammoniac gases and from time to time you might step over a dead cat sleeping its eternal nausea atop a bed of orange peels on the ground.

The ladies were a bit alarmed as they stepped into garbage and repulsive liquids, but they were also full of anticipation, and thrilled to discover who knows what. Lost in inky vagueness, the corners and the narrow streets they were scrutinizing seemed less exciting arteries, feverish with vice than sites of dreadful poverty and filth, resigned and humble desolation. On Carrer de Peracamps, that leads to Carrer del Cid, they caught sight of the cheerless pharmacy-red letters of the great neon sign of La Criolla.

They continued down the street and found themselves on that stretch of Carrer del Cid that had been fixed up rather nicely by the Office of Tourism and Visitor Attraction. These neighborhoods were being spruced up for the 1929 Exhibition, and the procurers were busy hunting for Chinese, blacks, rough trade, and women snatched from the hospital morgue halfway through dissection. They would dress these women up in green skirts and gypsy shawls, pinning a couple of plumped-up chunks of salt cod to their sternums to imitate breasts, then they would hang them with a horseshoe nail to the doors of the most strategic houses.

Mixed in among those women extracted from the morgue, there were others, alive and in one piece, who nonetheless seemed to have visited a salon for dislocation and deformation. Occasionally there would be a sassy wench, or even a pretty one, but her lungs would be soaking in a pool of rotgut. This girl would let out a cry as hoarse as a seal in an aquarium when they toss a rotten sardine in its face. It would tie a knot in your stomach. There were all kinds of men, from perfectly normal sailors, mechanics and workingmen, to pederasts with painted lips, cheeks crusted with plaster and eyes laden with mascara. Among these people whose luck had been shattered sashayed a variety of paupers, cripples and pickpockets who can only be found in that kind of neighborhood. Or maybe it is the neighborhoods themselves that apply a special sort of maquillage. Maybe the very same men set down on the Rambla would be an entirely different thing. In that neighborhood you could see people of humble extraction, such as can be found anywhere, who were not at all picturesque. But there were others, in particular some women attired in smoke, scouring pads, and cats' skins who you could say might die like fish out of water if you took them away from there. In order to breathe, their veins required a continuous injection of uric acid and rotten cabbage. The taverns were all soaked in tincture of *cazalla*. This anisette moonshine extracted from the festering of stones may be the substance that best conveys the idea of a perpetual chain on the heart, an irredeemable brutalization. Next to the taverns there were prophylactics stores set off by blue and red lightbulbs, containing rubber, glass, and fabric objects, along with packages of cotton wool. All these things alluded to the catastrophes of sex in a way so vile, so lacking in lyricism, that, combined, they formed a sort of cynical sneer, a repulsive parody of Ecclesiastes, in the heart of the neighborhood. They sang of the vanity of it all, even of the vanity of that sincere, ragged, shameless and poverty-stricken vice.

As if to justify the name *Barri Xino*, at a bend in the street there was an authentic Chinese man. Old and faded, as if his body were made up entirely of layers of onionskin, he carried a tin can in his hand containing an inch of a black substance that looked like coffee. He seemed close to death. Vendors of substances meant to be chewed alternated mid-street with monstrous beggars exhibiting mutilations that burned the eyes, or some half-naked body with a withered arm twisted behind its back. It was the police, paid by the taverns, who brought these paupers here, to give the neighborhood its final touch of color.

Despite this accumulation of the stuff of pathology, the humanity that resided there seemed to make the most of life, in such a natural and oblivious way that it could easily be mistaken for optimism. Walking through those places, one didn't even feel the need to button up one's jacket out of caution. Those ladies and gentlemen at the door of La Criolla didn't stand out in any way. The neighborhood was accustomed to this kind of visitor. There was already quite a body of literature about the festering quality of the Districte 5è, the official name of the Barri Xino, and both foreigners and curious locals were welcomed at La Criolla with courtesy and normality. Once inside, particularly on the day before a holiday, which was the case that evening, you had to make your way down a compact gauntlet of cotton jerseys, caps, an occasional bowler hat, sailor's shirts, and even the random elegant trench coat escorting a pair of painted lips with a silver pistol. The visitor's nose found itself continually cutting through a fluid curtain woven of cigarette smoke, sweat and droplets of rum.

The ladies who had never been to that place before were a little bit disappointed. They had heard such barbaric things about it, and all they saw was a sort of café-club with pretensions to being a dance hall. The establishment was a converted warehouse. The old iron columns that held up the roof were painted to look like palm trees. The ceilings were painted to simulate leaves. The musicians sat in a sort of box. The orchestra was odd and disjointed. The trumpet player was the house eccentric, jumping around the box from one side to the other, and shaking everything up with his metallic convulsions. The eight visitors were given two tables right by to the stage. The dance hall was packed. In the audience there were workingmen from the neighborhood calmly drinking coffee and innocently dancing. They didn't pay any mind if their partners bumped into a couple of degenerates mid-dance, or into someone who had just stolen a bale of cotton in the port and was celebrating with a plate of blood sausage disguised as a woman. Scattered among the other tables, alongside the anonymous proletariat, were another kind of customer who cashed in on the prestige of the establishment. There weren't very many of them that night. Some of them wore intentionally effeminate clothing; others dressed like thugs. Some had sclerotic skin, others were disfigured by rickets or tuberculosis, so unrecognizable that you couldn't tell if they were women or adolescents, or beings from another planet, sadder and more brutal than our own.

Some of them sat among the women, others among the sailors. With the eyes of an astonished detective Teodora Macaia started picking them out, and then checking with Bobby to see if she was right. Bobby, who had little expertise in the trade, as well as no little disgust at it, gave her vague answers. At a certain point, the white light of the establishment shifted and a play of special lights began: picric acid yellow, methylene blue, permanganate red. All the colors were scandalously pharmaceutical, right out of a clinic for secret diseases. Under these chemical lights, the shady elements of the establishment were thrown into repulsive relief. Some were so expressionless as to make your skin crawl, and they called up thoughts of the gallows, the madhouse, the anthropometric chart. Teodora and Isabel were having the best time. Little by little, they discovered unsettling specimens among the couples on the dance floor. A boy in a trench coat with a red kerchief at his neck was wearing a full face of makeup and a woman's hairdo. Under the blue light, his image came into focus, and his cheekbones turned the gray-green of grass in a cemetery. He was so lean it seemed as if his bones would crumble or his lungs would collapse from one moment to the next. And his gaze was so disconsolate, so vague, so otherworldly that Teodora pressed her lips together, doused her perpetual smile, and looked the other way. The count was a bit vexed by the spectacle. Not by these more tenebrous aspects, as he was very modern and liberal-minded, but rather by the squalor, the distress, and the raucous screams and laughter. He had been willing to accompany the ladies to make Hortènsia happy, and because he didn't know how to say no, but even though he tried to dissemble, he was wracked with nerves.

Rafaela and Hortènsia were hanging avidly on Emili Borràs's comments. The mathematician looked upon it all with the eyes of Christian mercy. He was still sensitive, though, to the effects of color and volume and to the bizarre and literary bitterness of the ambiance. The only allure of those seamen, those inverts, and those prostitutes was the deeply desperate sexual sadness buried in their bones. Emili Borràs saw in them a gallery of the sincerity of human instinct, without the mask of cosmetics or perfume to make the horrid grimace of the beast more bearable. To Emili Borràs, this was what was truly authentic. The laughter, the sweat, the frictions and the encounters came about in a primary way, without shame or regrets. To Emili Borràs, the smiles of those pederasts – some of them former gunmen, many of them thieves by profession, yet others simple brothel fodder – were innocent, almost childlike, and their deviance was of no account in the face of a naturalness and unselfconsciouness more proper to madmen and children. Emili Borràs saw in this the quality of an etching. He quoted from Russian novels. Above all he quoted the Church fathers; he spoke of Jesus Christ…"It is essential to be able to comprehend these things, along with the *Confessions* of Saint Augustine, because neither Augustine nor Thomas à Kempis is precluded here. This is a profound human truth, an exemplary document, a practical lesson in spiritual exercise. I find it profoundly ascetic...And that mint-green kerchief is fascinating, simply fascinating..."

The conviction and pathos Emili Borràs infused in his words left an impression on Hortènsia, already so impressionable and susceptible to the lure of the literary. She listened to Emili's ideas and felt true sorrow, enormous pity for all those people who were entertaining themselves as best they could. Hortènsia had the heart of an angel. She would have chosen the most bedraggled, most syphilitic prostitute, called her over, and had her sit down at her table. Then, with the theatrical gesture of a princess in a children's play, she would have placed her necklace around the woman's neck! Hortènsia thought of Raskolnikov from Dostoevsky's *Crime and Punishment*, when he kneels at the feet of Marmaladov's daughter, who has become a piteous prostitute. She remembered the explosive monologue Dostoevsky puts in his criminal's mouth and she found a series of analogies between the world of vomit, mercy and suffering of the Russian author and the methylene blue light that made the faces in La Criolla more livid and the depravity more entomological. Hortènsia thought about the party the night before, and the money she had spent on champagne to water all her grotesque and pneumatic guests. She remembered that *saladísimo* that the Marquesa de Lió kept repeating to Primo de Rivera's abdomen. Hortènsia was miserable, and her eyes were misty, but she didn't say anything. She listened to Emili Borràs, who, in the midst of his own excitement, was making incisive points with considerable sensitivity.

Rafaela's only passion was poker. Accustomed to making hospital visits, she had a thicker skin in general, and she saw that world as so distant from her own that she didn't share a single iota of Hortènsia's tenderheartedness. Her greatest concern was that, as the dancing became more lively, no couple should come too close to their table and soil her skirt. The count was speaking of Verlaine, of Oscar Wilde, of Gide and of Proust, as he said: *"Dégoûtant, dégoûtant, tout à fait dégoûtant."* Pep Arnau was whispering into Isabel's ear, and Isabel laughed and cried out, "My boy, you are a monster, a perfect monster!" Bobby was putting up with it all with his usual forbearance. When the mathematician had finished his speech, who knows what a mental association led him to ask the widow Portell:

"By the way, Hortènsia, what did Conxa Mates have to say yesterday? Did she mention her husband?"

"No, not really," responded Hortènsia, "she just said he was fatigued."

"You'll understand why I asked," Bobby went on. "I've heard that Conxa is going to get a divorce. Uh-huh. That's why I was so surprised to see her at your house, because it seems that poor Antòni is really in a bad way."

"That's what everyone says," Hortènsia said, "but, you know, maybe not all that bad. It seems he's developed manias."

"It's a bit more than manias." Bobby said. "The situation is very serious, and I heard this directly from Lluís. You know he and Lluís used to be inseparable. So, the other day he called for him and he made a big scene. He cried, he said it was over, it was all over. And when Lluís said to him, 'My God, Antònio,' and tried to take him by the arm, he screamed like a madman and said, 'Don't touch me, please don't touch me, I bear the stigma of iniquity, of the most shameful iniquity of them all,' and he started to cry like a baby. Then he calmed down and it seemed as if he didn't remember a word of what he had said. Lluís found the whole thing very strange. Conxa is losing hope, and the worst thing is that the doctors say there's nothing wrong with him, he just has this strange and senseless fear. And it's only getting worse. That's why I was so surprised to see Conxa at your house. Either she's a heartless hussy…or I don't know what to think…"

"She's a hussy," Teodora jumped in, "nothing but a hussy. All that pretending to be in love with her husband…, all the times she criticized me…"

"Who can say what's behind all of this…" Hortènsia said. "But why did you think of it now?"

"I don't know, just a mental association," said Bobby. "I find Mates very unpleasant. I've never been able to stand him…"

"Neither have I."

"Ha, nor I."

"Nor I."

"Nor I, never," the four woman quickly chimed in.

"But wait, Bobby," said Pep Arnau. "A mental association? What do you mean? I don't get it."

"It doesn't really matter, Pep. How shall I put it? Aren't there times when you see a watering can and think of a toothache, or you see a priest and think of a lottery ticket?"

"No, that's never happened to me," responded Pep Arnau.

"Well, in that case, never mind," said Bobby with a smile, not wanting to go any further.

"Why don't we think about leaving?" asked the Count.

In response they paid and got up from their chairs. But Teodora hadn't had enough. She wanted more "sensations," and she asked Pep Arnau a question. His answer was:

"Oh, it's all right with me, I have no objection."

They went back down Carrer de Peracamps, which was deserted. Out of the tavern known as Cal Sagristà, the house of the sacristan, came a big man who started to follow them. He was horrible. He must have been around forty. His face was masked in rouge and his hair was impregnated with coconut oil. He came to a full stop in front of them and, moving his hips in a most atrocious way, he began to plead, in Spanish, in a high-pitched tone meant to imitate a woman's voice, with the unhurried, sibilant lisp of the professional invert: *No tenéis un cigarrillo para la Lolita?* The women found him absurd and bizarre, in an indefinable way. But the men, even beyond discomfort and disgust, felt actual panic. That big inoffensive man terrified them, and their fear prevented them from pushing him away or even answering him. The man went on demanding "a cigarette for la Lolita," as they tried to speed up and get away from him. But the man kept following them, whimpering and crying "Ay!" into their ears, intolerably, over and over again, as if imitating a female orgasm.

"When you come face to face with a thing like that," said Emili Borràs, "you don't know what to say. Your throat tightens up, you feel ashamed, you want to cry…"

"That's a bunch of poppycock," said Bobby, though he felt exactly the same shame and the same desire to cry as Emili Borràs.

Once they were back at the Arc del Teatre, they started to feel like themselves again. Pep Arnau said:

"Teodora wants to go to *La Sevillana*."

When the men seemed to hesitate, Isabel piped up, "You only live once."

"But you understand that the place is repugnant?" Bobby objected.

"We couldn't be more certain," responded Teodora.

"Well, if you all want to go, let's go, why not…" Hortènsia added.

"You asked for it," Bobby answered.

Teodora wouldn't let up:

"Come on, don't be so stuffy. Didn't we agree we would pull out all the stops tonight?"

They had barely reached an agreement when Pep Arnau headed straight for a sordid little entryway with neon lights that spelled out "La Sevillana." At the top of the stairs, a woman of a certain age opened the door. Bobby said a few words to her and the woman, momentarily stunned, caught on right away. It wasn't the first time a group from the high society had climbed the stairs to her repulsive brothel to see what was known as "the pictures."

Since Rafaela was impervious, it didn't make a bit of difference to her. Hortènsia had been softened up by the memory of Raskolnikov and Primo de Rivera, and by Rousseau and Émile. She wanted to feel more Russian. Teodora, like Isabel, had a different urge. She felt a little depleted, and her senses were dulled. This was a new thing. It was alive, and more graphic than a scene from a *garçonnière*. The thrill they anticipated was at once both childish and sick. The men trailed behind them like sheep.

The middle-aged woman led them into a sort of alcove, and set eight chairs in a circle. The alcove had been converted into a stage no bigger than a fist, the kind you find in neighborhood cultural centers in the slums. She switched on the battery-operated light, and four women and two beings who must have been men appeared. The actors and actresses were wearing nothing but their natural skin. The scenery was a few filthy cushions. The furniture, a couple of chairs. The middle-aged woman announced the titles of the "pictures." Some of the titles evoked Versailles, others a public urinal. Before her troupe, the woman of a certain age wore a bitter, maternal expression. Her voice was full of spiderwebs like that of a miniature dog trainer you might see at a circus. Each time she called out an allegorical title, the cast would recombine in a welter of bodies. At times the combination looked like a monster of boiled flesh with twelve arms and legs. It recalled a Brahmin divinity or an Aztec god who had lost his power and walked naked down the road, eating dust and being spat upon. The scene was too hard to bear for anyone who retained even a drop of compassion. The pornographic tableaux those poor women were attempting to reproduce were nothing but the fever dreams of a colonial barracks. The sad skin of those bodies erased any trace of what might have caused excitement. At times, when the troupe was down on all fours to perform a wicked scene, you had the impression that they had lost a ten cèntim coin and were trying to pick it up with their lips. Engaged in the most dulling mechanics of sex, the assemblage performed without the slightest enthusiasm. They had already been obliged to execute all these aberrations a thousand times, before an audience of idiots, towards which they felt absolute indifference. They were artists who acted without feeling, and with no sense of rebellion, their veins watered down by pallid routine, without the slightest spirit of rebellion. The thing was as glacial and inexpressive as the copulation of insects.

The spectacle required silence. Indeed, before a sight like that, even if at the outset there might be a titter or two, soon any secretion of amusement stops cold. Mouths close, cheeks contract, and eyes are sullied with a gray liquid that is either fever, sadness or shame. The troupe would let out a snort or a sigh. One of those poor girls was so close to being a quadruped, or who knows what, that she had a positive reaction. A pong of sweat and of the essences only found in poor whorehouses wafted from the stage.

The four gentlemen were filled with shame, unable to say a word. That little room gave one a sense of the infinite: the infinite sadness of the tears and bestiality we all carry inside. Emili Borràs was glued to this mirror that reflected back to him all the pus in his heart. The count tried to rise above it, but it was impossible. The ladies kept their composure at first, but soon they were overcome. They felt a heinous dizziness, as if a frog were hopping in their stomachs.

The stunt lasted no more than twenty minutes. Bobby gave the middle-aged woman a couple of bills and they went out into the street without taking a breath.

Emili Borràs said to Teodora:

"That was painful. You need the skin of a gorilla to tolerate such a spectacle. Still, it can't be denied that it's powerful. A consummate demonstration. Only the piety of a saint can comprehend such a thing. I would like to be so saintly, I would…but it's beyond me…"

"I don't know," said Teodora. "I think you're being much too philosophical. I just found it repugnant. As for them…well, that's how they earn their living."

"What kind of a living do you think they earn!"

"I don't imagine it's a place in heaven."

"What do you know? What do we know of those who truly earn a place in heaven?"

And Isabel added, "So, is this true depravity?"

"No, no, this is just the infinite poverty of the flesh, the infinite sadness of the flesh," Emili responded. "You won't find depravity in these neighborhoods. This is not depravity."

"So," said Teodora, "do you mean that the depraved ones are people…like us…?"

"Who knows, who knows," answered Emili Borràs.

They were a bit thirsty, so to round off the night they stopped off at Villa Rosa.

In those days, Villa Rosa was having a moment of splendor. In addition to the last dregs of the nighthawks and the quota from the cabarets, every night there was a group of air force officers who had recently discovered the establishment and went there to soak their wings in manzanilla sherry and raise the boorish ruckus characteristic of the military. They were good kids, tanned and mildly acrobatic, who had great success with the ladies. The German and Scandinavian element, and above all the Americans, looked after the Gypsies who performed there. They would turn red as bull's blood, and you had the impression their skin might burst. The boiled front of their uniform shirts would get positively soggy. Some of them turned almost gelatinous, like cooked cod tripe. That night there was a magnificent giant in attendance who could balance a glass of manzanilla on his nose, as two streams of liquid flowed down his face. Maybe it was rash to enter Villa Rosa stone sober on a night like that. To adapt to the boiling pitch of those souls, the prerequisite was a prior alcoholic fever and an undiscerning nose.

It had been a long time since Bobby had been to Villa Rosa. His last memory was awful. The Marquesa de Moragues had asked him to engage two chorines who worked there to dance at her house. The deal was done in the early afternoon, when the establishment was empty and the only thing floating there was the dense air left behind by the expansions of the stomachs and the bottles of wine that had been working at full tilt the night before. In the light of the early afternoon, Villa Rosa felt to Bobby like the state of cerebral sorrow and self-loathing that follows a tumultuous bender. By the side of the counter an extremely fat old Gypsy woman was crying. She had one foot propped up on a foot stool, in exactly the same position as Philip II in the Escorial. The woman's leg was deformed and wrapped top to toe in a dirty bandage. She was weeping because the pain was getting progressively worse. She said the cause of her ills was a bite from a rabid cat. A thin man, whose skin and clothing were both the color of tobacco juice, was inspecting the bandages and saying they might have to amputate her leg.

The sight of the Gypsy with the bandaged leg haunted Bobby for days. When he and his traveling companions entered Villa Rosa he could still see that old crone bitten by a rabid cat by the side of the counter.

Seated at a table with a bottle of solera sherry before them, Emili Borràs was still talking about Jesus Christ.

Hortènsia, who had traded in her good bourgeois egotism for a Russian soul, found the spectacle of the previous establishment artificial and perfectly commendable. She said everything they had just seen was the "pus from society's wounds." The Count, a fan of popular science, said that pus was necessary for the organism to defend itself. He mentioned leucocytes and dead bacteria. Isabel begged them to drop the topic of pus and stop talking about such disgusting things.

Teodora began casting insistent glances at an aeronautics officer who was a friend of hers. The officer was sucking on the nape of a twenty year-old hostess's neck. She was a bit drunk and very beautiful. When the officer realized that Teodora was watching him, he saluted her smartly, blushed and stopped.

When the Gypsies of the house caught sight of their posh guests, they went over to pay their compliments. Two of them, known as *La Tanguera* and *La Mogigonga* for their expertise in dancing and burlesque, finished off the wine the guests hadn't seen fit to drink. *La Tanguera* dedicated one of her sublime dances to them, duplicating the delicate and fragile tapping of a wounded partridge.

Emili Borràs made a few Germanic and Freudian comments about flamenco dancing. Hortènsia listened with delight. The Comte rattled on for a while like famed racconteur Garcia Sanchiz but the ladies didn't take him seriously. Bobby rubbed at his moustache, thinking that he and the ladies and the others and the entire crowd were all a bunch of fools.

They left Villa Rosa at four-thirty in the morning. When they got to the Rambla and jumped into their automobiles it was as if they were waking from a bad dream to find themselves between peaceful sheets, with a drawn bath. They sank into the upholstery, corroborating that indeed it was truly theirs and that nothing horrible had happened to them. Rafaela ran her fingers over her ears, her neck and her wrists to be sure no one had robbed her.

Hortènsia thought vaguely of Raskolnikov, of inverts, of Primo de Rivera, of the Russian soul, of the act at *La Sevillana*, of Antoni Mates's wife...But she was very tired and she rested her head on

Isabel's coat. Isabel still had the energy to refresh her lipstick and powder her rouged cheeks.

Just about the same time that Hortènsia Portell reached her house on Passeig de la Reina Elisenda, got undressed, wrapped herself in a Japanese robe, and dissolved two aspirins in a glass of water, in the Grill Room on Carrer d'Escudellers two pairs of police patrolmen were breaking up a group of onlookers who were standing at the door. Inside the establishment things were in disarray. The people sitting at the bar got down from their barstools and stuck their heads into the dining room of the restaurant. There you could see an upended table, and on the floor a sizable circle of wine, a broken bottle, half a filet mignon, a dozen potatoes, and a whole bowl of cheese soup which, sans plate and spread out on the carpet, looked pretty repulsive

In a corner, the restaurant staff and two women who had just arrived were holding up a young woman in the midst of an attack of hysteria, while an utterly ineffectual gentleman, his face blanched with dismay, was dabbing a towel soaked in cold water on his forehead to wipe the blood from a wound caused by a wine bottle. Another group of women was trying to calm a lady wearing a bedraggled beaver coat, her face full of scratches, and the polite gray man who accompanied her. Such a scene in the Grill Room of the time was not unusual, and no one paid it much mind. In the match that had just taken place, no bones had been broken, and the police saw no need to arrest anyone or to trouble any of the actors in the drama. All the owners wanted was to put the whole thing behind them, because there were not yet many people in the restaurant, but soon the regular clientele would begin to arrive.

The lady with the beaver coat and the scratches on her face was Rosa Trènor. Quick to recover, she disappeared in the company of the gray man and a young woman. She had gone there to make a scene, and her work at the Grill Room was done for the evening. The man with the cut on his forehead, Frederic de Lloberola, had them apply a taffeta strip to the wound, which was insignificant. The girl with him was over her attack of hysteria. The waiters cleaned the carpet, set the table with fresh tablecloths, and brought over another bottle of wine, another filet mignon, and another cheese soup.

Rosa Trènor wanted to break up with Frederic, but in her own particular way, which in fact would be like not breaking up. Frederic had had no intention of splitting with her because, oblivious as he was, and seeing other women behind her back as he did, he still found some kind of company and solace in being able to express all the vacuous thoughts that passed through his head to Rosa Trènor in conversations and over dinner. From time to time, a night with her was not all that bad. Frederic thought Rosa was perfectly satisfied with this arrangement, and that the money she had recently asked him for and that he had not been able to give her was of no consequence. Frederic thought her asking for cash was just a casual thing. He thought perhaps she didn't even need it, and even if she did, she could get along without it. He was convinced that Rosa was an altruist who put no price on her gratitude to Frederic for having renewed their friendship and chosen her as a confidante for such an important life as his.

For all these reasons, Frederic had begun to treat Rosa in a rather despotic way. Ever since the garbage collector had carted off the general's dog, Frederic had stopped being generous. That gesture of sacrifice was enough to give Frederic a perfect notion of his control over Rosa and of her unconditional devotion to him. Once in possession of this idea he allowed himself to relax his solicitude and treacly gallantry.

Naturally, Rosa saw things very differently from how Frederic imagined them. Rosa thought he pined for her and she had him in her grasp. She thought he was being unfaithful out of spite and revenge. It was his proper desperation – because Rosa considered Frederic a gentleman and she believed in "proper" desperation – in the face of her refusal to bestow certain favors that Frederic demanded and she did not allow. These favors existed only in Rosa's imagination. A month after they renewed their relations, Rosa and he pretended they could maintain an open-minded status quo. But since they were both romantics, Rosa forswore absolutely her early morning bouquets of camellias (so Frederic thought, at least). Before the sacrifice of the dog, they enjoyed two weeks of outright love. This put wind under Rosa's wings, but Frederic's refusal to give her money and his latest infidelities (that she, as we have said, considered unimportant and attributed to spite) obliged her to take some violent action, pull off some outrageous stunt. Frederic had not been to her house in a week, and Rosa was beginning to wonder. For the time being, Frederic was of very little use to her, but he could always turn out to be an ace in the hole, and even his economic situation could be susceptible to change. Don

Tomàs was a very old man. He could be carried off to heaven in a blink of the eye, and a bit of change would have to fall Frederic's way.

Rosa thought that if she broke up with him in a boring way perhaps Frederic, less ardent than she thought, would use the opportunity to end the whole thing. But, if she staged a theatrical break-up, with a bloody and scandalous sort of grandeur, she would impress Frederic and awaken a little rumble in his heart. She believed much more strongly in a kick to the head than in a cold shoulder to keep the pathos of love alive.

When Rosa learned that Frederic was pursuing a young girl from the Excelsior, a French girl who had just arrived in Barcelona, she organized a little police detail and surprised them at the Grill Room. So as not to go alone she had picked up a notary from Manresa whom she had captivated at the Colón, and she had him buy her a half dozen oysters and a chicken leg.

The scene was incredibly tawdry. Verbal abuse on the man's part; hairpulling on the woman's. The little French girl proved to have the claws of a cat and after the obligatory scratches she went into a hysterical fit. Frederic said a few harsh words to Rosa, and she decided to scrape his forehead a little with the neck of the previously broken wine bottle, taking great care not to hurt him too badly.

Frederic had found the scene very unpleasant, and the cut on his forehead was throbbing. Even so, once Rosa was gone, he was actually rather pleased. This was great publicity for a man of his age; it gave him a sort of gigolo's cachet, and infused him with dignity in the eyes of the staff of the restaurant. "Rosa is in love with me," he thought. "The proof is in the pudding; if she weren't hurt by my behavior, if she weren't utterly smitten, she wouldn't have risked such a scene. One thing is clear: this is the only way to deal with women." Thinking these optimistic thoughts, he sank his teeth into the filet mignon, which ceded to the pressure of his mandible, and swallowed the first slice of meat with cruelty. With another bit of cruelty, he lightly twisted the short hairs at the nape of the little French girl's neck, which triggered a voluptuous shriek from the girl and sent the first spoonful of cheese soup spurting from her pouty lips.

"This must have something to do with menopause," thought Frederic. "The last gasp of passion, the swan song. But I've had enough. It's not worth my while to be embarrassed or put out by an old bag like her." This was the chivalrous way in which the good gentleman of Lloberola referred to love. In the end, he wasn't entirely wrong and, in point of fact, he had had enough of Rosa Trènor. Their novel had come to an end.

People from the Excelsior were beginning to pour into the Grill Room. The florist at the door was selling bouquets of roses and work was piling up in the kitchen.

Two young men had just sat down at a table near the door, across from the bar. The waiter set down two whiskeys without so much as a word. He looked at them in a bitter, condescending way, as waiters do with unimportant clients who often neglect to bring enough money to pay the check.

One of the young men was a bit worked up and, though he was usually not excitable, that night the words tumbled out quickly and chaotically. His buddy followed him with bored, drooping eyelids. The excitable one said:

"I want to write a novel about a situation I've seen from close up and in detail. A really big deal…"

"Look, in Barcelona there are thousands of tall tales. I don't know what case you're referring to, but it would be enough for me just to tell my mother's story. The plot is the least of it. The real thing is to know how to write it. How to put things down, how to make them interesting and alive. I've tried it many times, but I've given up. I've found a simpler way to earn a living…"

"I'm not ready to give up yet. If I ever publish something, I know they'll say I'm resentful and deceitful, when in truth it's reality that's resentful and deceitful." When a novel states a fact that ties into another fact and another and another, as the chain goes on, the events begin to seem more and more extraordinary, and the characters take on a chiaroscuro effect without grays, and the melodrama builds, most people reading the novel will think it's a bunch of lies, and that such things are impossible in real life. And the truth is exactly the opposite: if you just wrote down the characters and the 'permutations' you can find in a city like ours – right here in Barcelona – and even within our own circle, you would be called an idiot. Believe me, there's no need to wait for a dark, sensational crime, the kind that scares concierges stiff when they read about them in the newspapers. These splashy, absurd crimes and criminals are not at all important, you see. But, if you could look inside the high society gentlemen and ladies who appear to lead perfectly gray and proper lives, whom no one would ever suspect of a thing, who appear incapable of a violent gesture or of any slightly spectacular and interesting act... If you could follow in their hideous footsteps, you would have more plots than you could ever know what to do with. And I'm talking about plots of the sort you couldn't spit out in public without running the risk of being drawn and quartered and banished from society like an undesirable villain."

"Yes, of course, no doubt about it. I couldn't agree with you more. But if I could write the way I would like to write, I wouldn't be deterred by anything they might say about me. I would forge ahead. The problem is that here in this country there is no one, at least no one so far, who conveys this direct and passionate connection to the lives of the people around us, with all their pettiness and also with whatever modicum of grandeur they might have. You say you have an interesting story to tell. So tell it. Prove it. I know I'm not the one to do it. I don't have it in me. I gave up long ago..."

"I want to find the way to say these things. Sometimes I think I'm somebody, and I feel I have the stuff to write a great novel. But then I remember how lazy and incompetent I am. I read a couple of lines I've written, and I find them trite. The style is clumsy, and couldn't even run on wheels. You've read a few of my poems – you know I've never dared publish a single one. My family would be scandalized. And even though I have nothing but contempt for my family, I do have a bit of respect for my mother and I can imagine her dismay. The worst thing would be for me to go on with this project I have now, this story I am so attached to that there are moments when I even frighten myself. I feel like some kind of monster. I don't know where this all came from. I mean, I'm not responsible for this. My grandfather or great-grandfather must have been quite out of the ordinary. Because I know perfectly well who my father is, and he is nothing but a silly puppet. My mother must be a saint; I've never dared to judge her."

"You're just a lazy bum. And you're full of baloney. It's okay to live like a bohemian for a while and pretend to be a cynic, but you should be working at something, anything. You can't spend your whole life pretending to be misunderstood and never producing so much as a handful of paragraphs. Just start something and stick with it for real. If it's no good, you throw it into the fire and you let it go, like me. I don't mean to make myself out to be a saint. I've been just as much of a deadbeat as you. And all those unpleasant and ignominious things have gone on in my house, too, and I've gone along with it, but one day you just say enough, that's behind me now. Now I'm working. I'm earning a good living, and I intend to get married. And you're no kid yourself. You're not stupid, either. You're healthy and good-looking. When you're a kid, no one can point a finger at you if you behave like a kid, and you can accept favors that would make a man blush, but the time comes when all of that is just not right. You're too old. I don't know if I should pry, but, from what you've told me, it seems you can't expect much from your family…"

"Much less than not much! And the saddest thing is that I'm in love now; yes, me, in love!"

"About time. But it's not the first time you've thought you were in love. This must be like the time you were in love with Glòria, that girl who used to buy you dinner every night at the Cafè Lion d'Or…"

"No, I swear, it's not like that at all! I am in love with the protagonist of my novel. A woman I've only seen four times, and spoken with twice. I never said anything special to her. I don't believe she would ever take notice of me. She is a very unusual woman, cold, twisted, bizarre…Cerebral in a way I don't believe anyone else in Barcelona is."

"You see what a bunch of nonsense this is? Do you hear how pretentious you sound? What do you mean, in love? Rotten romantic dime-store literature, that's all it is. You're thirty-one or thirty-two years old and you're still a kid, a rather sleazy kid, not to put too fine a point on it, but…"

"Maybe so. And maybe sleazier than you think. And I'm not ashamed to say so. I swear, there is a scandalous voluptuosity to my sleaziness – you can't even begin to imagine it. The first time I did something that seemed beneath contempt, I got a knot in my stomach. Later, I started seeking out that knot like a drug, a stimulant. And finally I no longer feel any knots at all, and I don't know what I'd have to do to feel one…"

"You're a damn fool. With all these obsessions with your family, with its atavistic past and its gloomy future, you're going to go so far around the bend that one day you'll go mad for real and you'll start wanting to suck children's blood…"

"I know I'm a damn fool. But I swear, from time to time I land a sweet piece of work. It's not that I deserve it, it happens by chance.

It's all a question of having a little nerve and grabbing the opportunity. If people here just had a little more nerve, amazing things could happen! Though, if you think about it, there's plenty of nerve to go around…Still, Barcelona could look like a tale from the *Scheherezade*…"

"I can't imagine what else you want to see happen. Right now it all seems like a perfect mess. Just in the past eight years, we've seen more than our share of things, of every variety and color in the rainbow…"

"Not to mention what we haven't seen yet. And then they say there are no novels to be written here."

Just as the excitable young man was saying this, a newsboy who was hawking *La Vanguardia* and *El Día Gráfico* stuck his head in the door. The young man with the drooping eyelids bought *La Vanguardia*. On the front page, among the day's obituaries, the excitable young man saw a name that made him jump up from the bench he was sitting on.

"How can this be? He's dead?"

"Yes, one of dozens; he's dead. He was no one to you. The fact that an extremely rich man, and a creep at that, has died, is no reason for you to get all worked up. I don't imagine he's left you any spare change…"

"Come on, hand it over, let me see. 'Has died,' it says, and nothing more. It doesn't mention the last rites, the sacraments. The guy must have croaked in an accident, or who knows how. Let me see the local news. Does it say anything about him? Yes, it does! Look here! What? How can this be! This is horrible! Obviously it must be a suicide. They don't quite come out and say it, of course, out of respect for the position of the deceased. They must have paid them to hush it up. But there can be no doubt...that pig committed suicide! Suicide!"

"All right, so he committed suicide. His business must be failing. What's eating you? What fault is it of yours if he committed suicide"

"It's very peculiar, believe me. And very interesting...I wouldn't have imagined this in a million years...Life is strange, huh? Very strange. Look, do you see what's going on there, in the other room? There's my brother, with a tart. And isn't she gorgeous? I don't know how Frederic does it...He does the family proud..."

"What? Listen, how many whiskeys have you had?"

"Just this one here in front of me. Why do you ask?"

"Because you're acting as if you were soused..."

"You know, believe me...No, don't be silly, I'm not soused. But really, life can sometimes turn out in such a way...When I tell you I'm afraid of myself, it's the absolute truth, and not just romantic dime-store literature, I swear..."

"Listen, kid, go home to bed. Jenny's stood you up today. When she's not here at this time of night...it's a sign she's picked up some guy...like your brother...Wait, look, he's leaving! Are you going to pretend not to see each other?"

"Don't be ridiculous!..."

Frederic de Lloberola had settled up and was helping the French girl into her coat. On their way out of the restaurant they passed by the table where the two young men were sitting. The excitable one grabbed Frederic by the arm. When Frederic saw him, he was a bit surprised, but he showed no concern at all for their being family. He said,

"What are you doing here? What's up?"

"Haven't you heard?"

"Heard what?"

"Look here: the Baró de Falset has committed suicide."

"What? How is that possible?"

"That's what I'm wondering."

"Well, to be frank, I'm not all that surprised. I heard he was going mad…Anyway, that's how it goes."

"Hey, what's that on your forehead?"

"Nothing serious, I got hit with a bottle…nothing to worry about."

"By the way, the girl is quite a looker."

"You're incorrigible."

"Do you have a plan in mind?"

"Stop, fool, stop. I'm just taking her home…"

"Okay, don't get mad. Good night…"

"Good night."

—·—·—

AS GUILLEM DE LLOBEROLA buttoned up his pajamas, he felt an eerie chill down his spine. His mouth was dry and he had a peculiar headache. In fact, he had a bit of a fever. He took his pulse. It was beating hard and fast. He lay down in bed and tried to read a book.

It was impossible, he couldn't see a single letter. He turned out the light and it seemed as if that repugnant individual were there in bed beside him. He took up all the space. There was barely enough room for Guillem to breathe. It was that very same man, cold and immobile, with a bullet hole through his cranium, and a distinctive little snort, an inhuman snort, still coming out of his mouth, a snort of shameful lust. He couldn't push him away, couldn't get him out of the bed. He was pinned there, rigid, in his greasy, white, dead nakedness.

Guillem had murdered him. That little hole in his cranium, that coagulated blood smeared on his face, was all Guillem's doing. The young man could never have imagined that things would go so far. He had played at depravity, had played at being a scoundrel, and had had the luck to come across a poor bastard who fell into his trap. It is entirely possible that another kind of man might have laughed off his blackmail scheme and tossed him down the stairs. Weak and cowardly as Guillem was, like all the Lloberolas, he had had the great good luck to run into a man who was even weaker and more cowardly than he. And Guillem, a creature without energy, without impetus of any kind, took pleasure in believing that he had taken up an important place in the brotherhood of cynics. Most deplorable of all was that that affair, that misunderstanding, that ridiculous hoax that poor Guillem de Lloberola had pulled on a defenseless man, miserably squeezing his money out of him, injecting the microbe of folly into his head, had all been for such a sad and despicable purpose. Callow and inexperienced as he was, Guillem could not have imagined that his prank would come to such a tragic end. He thought the aftermath of exploiting a pervert who had a very great deal to lose would be little more than the material profit that he extracted, and the gratification of dishing out a bit of humiliation to a person whose economic situation placed him in a position of superiority to Guillem. He had not suspected that the microbe of folly would perform with such grave efficacy and intensity. He had thought it was nothing but base and petty fear, and for that poor man the survival instinct would be stronger than anything else. Guillem – who was also a sad and abnormal man – hadn't taken into account the reactions that take place in the souls of the abnormal, even if they are millionaires, even if they are the Baró de Falset, and even if they are showered with the respect of their fellow humans. Guillem could also never have suspected that he had so much power. He had felt as if the fear produced by his little chantage contained a bit of condescension on the part of Antoni Mates, and that Antoni Mates had allowed himself to be swindled because he could afford to, as the amounts that Guillem had extracted from him meant very little to him. Guillem could not believe there could be such a great distance between his unscrupulous temperament and the spineless temperament of the Baró de Falset. He could not have believed that a man would take things so much to heart that he would forget everything else, completely lose his bearings, and kill himself. Since he could never have imagined coming to such an end, it filled him with dread. Above all else, he was surprised.

He felt the fear of a child on whom a pistol goes off in the midst of a game with another child, when he realizes he has actually taken his friend's life. This was not by any means what Guillem had wanted. But on the other hand he was perfectly aware that he had not overlooked a single detail, and that he had behaved with the luck and audacity of a criminal much more astute than he.

In all that affair, Guillem had fallen victim to a self-intoxication, to a drunken binge of literature and depravity. The day he left the house of el Baró de Falset with the promissory note for fifty thousand pessetes in his pocket, Guillem had patted his suit and his cheeks to assure himself that indeed it was he who had carried off that audacious fraud. And when he managed to keep the letter the baron had addressed to his brother, Guillem could hardly believe that the man had reached such an extreme of nullity and lack of foresight. After that, the events themselves had carried the two of them along. Just like Antoni Mates, Guillem was a puppet swept up by destiny. When he had told his friend Agustí Casals about the shameful mess he had protagonized, he did so with the morbid desire of deviants to proclaim their depravity aloud and without compunction, to tell the story with childish delight in such a way that no one can suspect it is their own.

From that day on Guillem had felt the urge to do everything it was in his power to do with a being as insignificant and morally wanting as Antoni Mates. The confidence expressed with impunity and entrusted to his friend spurred him on and convinced him to confront Antoni Mates, in that perfectly-wrought scene, worthy of a professional scoundrel.

Now, feverish and sleepless, he was the actual assassin of a supposed suicide whose monstrous cadaver lay in his bed, emitting the same bestial and lascivious little moan that Guillem recognized from another nightmarish bed in the apartment of Dorotea Palau, the dressmaker. No one would ever know that Guillem was the perpetrator of that crime. He would never have to make a statement, never have to explain a thing. He had shot a bullet from a great distance. There were no fingerprints on the handle of the pistol, nothing that could lead anyone to suspect that the murderer was Guillem. But that night, he possessed a faculty that bore some resemblance to a conscience. Wallowing in these dark thoughts, the green of graveyard nettles, Guillem realized that his pajamas were drenched. He ran his hand over his chest and his skin was dripping wet, too. His copious sweating had broken the fever. The cadaver with the lascivious moan was no longer lying at his side, robbing him of his breath. Guillem felt weak and exhausted. He wanted to take off his pajamas and put dry clothes against his skin, but he couldn't lift his arms, he was clamped to the bed, his mind in flight. Between dizziness and unconsciousness, he finally fell asleep like a log.

The next day it was quite late and Guillem had still not shown signs of life. Leocàdia went in to wake him up. She heard her son whimper and thrash about in bed as if troubled by an exceedingly distressing dream. Leocàdia rested her hand on his back and Guillem awoke with a terrible start. He had a splitting headache and it took him a few seconds to realize his mother was there.

Leocàdia asked him two or three questions. Guillem didn't answer. He just smiled, the fresh, open smile of a child who has been naughty and defends himself with the charm of his lips to avoid a scolding.

Leocàdia gazed at her son with ineffable tenderness. She saw his charming, naughty, slightly feminine face, his black eyes, his smoker's mouth. It was the face of an unregenerate scoundrel, with even, white, sharp, perfectly intact teeth. Leocàdia gazed upon his black hair curling in brash, romantic disorder, and his thin arms inside his red pajamas. That childlike smile was frozen on Guillem's face. Leocàdia felt her entire person being drawn into her son's smile, imprisoned in the fascinating net of her son's lips and teeth. Abruptly, Guillem's gaze went dark, his mouth contracted and he ground his teeth as if he had felt a stitch in his heart. Leocàdia's head snapped back, and she drew close enough to touch the border of his sheet. At that point, Guillem wrapped both arms around her neck, and sought comfort for his mouth and cheeks on the poor old woman's sunken breast. He needed to breathe. He felt as if his lungs were being torn from top to bottom, and he practically vomited an unrelenting hiccup, followed by one of the most vivid, unfettered, carnal crying spells possible, with loud and sonorous sobs much like those that babies let out unselfconsciously.

Leocàdia withstood the sobs of her son without saying a word, and without understanding a thing. And what good would it have done her to try and understand that child who struck fear in her soul?

Guillem quickly came to. He was terribly ashamed of what had just happened to him. He couldn't understand how he had fallen prey to such weakness, such strange tenderness in his mother's presence. It had been so many years since his heart had gone out to his mother, or to anyone else!

Guillem let go of Leocàdia, and made a beeline into the bathroom. He soaped himself up from head to toe, and let the cold shower fall with all its force onto his chest. Guillem stretched out his arms, clenched his jaw, and smiled. But this time it was a ruthless smile, with all the glee of a wild animal.

PART II

IT HAD BEEN FIVE years since the Baró de Falset drilled a bullet into his head. In those five years, the public life of the country had undergone quite an evolution. Events of glorious transcendence had taken place in Barcelona. The most brilliant moments were marked by the 1929 Exposició Universal in Montjuïc. The entire parade of souls the reader had occasion to contemplate one night at a party thrown by Hortènsia Portell completed the final lap of its peacock promenade. Firecrackers burst from their eyes and streamers flowed from their mouths. The summer of 1929 was a season of phosphorescence: the most lacquered chassis, the most pearlescent yachts festooned with the most profuse bunting combined to dazzle all the bootblacks from Almeria who bent to their trade at the foot of the Rambla around the monument to Columbus and on the sidewalk cafès of the Plaça de Catalunya. Cabarets once again exuded chilled champagne, as in the good old days of World War I. Barcelona's hotels were overwhelmed; anyone with an extra cot or a room ordinarily devoted to fleas had a canon from Extremadura or a fishmonger from Portbou as a boarder. Some even went so far as to lay mattresses on the rooftops and use the lightning rods for hangers. Barcelona was bubbling in a stew of grandeur and it was every man for himself. Eyes, cheeks, noses, and sexes found infinite room to play. Nocturnal parties during the exhibition were truly a dream, a prodigious sight that horrified the people of Barcelona. "Where will the millions come from to pay for such extravagance?" said the man on the street, carrying a child in each arm and a little dog sticking out of his vest pocket. And it's the man on the street who will have to pony up so that all the blue, green, and pink mystery of the colored fountains of the Palau Nacional can rain down *ballets russes*, St. Lorenzo's tears and otherworldly foam onto his necktie.

Dinners at Ambassadeurs, la Rosaleda, Miramar, and their more economical versions at the Hostal del Sol and La Pèrgola, together with the wine and roasted almonds of the Patio del Farolillo, served to expand the gastric unconsciousness of the country. Anyone with five duros, or even without them, went to Montjuïc to see the Exposition. At closing time, the Rambles and the cabarets were packed to the gills. At the end of the day the American fleet would spew out a stream of giant toy sailors dressed like children, who would gorge themselves on sweet sherry and the high-octane alcohol known as aiguardent, later toppling onto benches or carrying women around on piggy back. Then a squad of some kind of officers, spiffy and loose-limbed as a Charleston, would beat them down with billy clubs and pile them into a big old wagon. When they reached the Porta de la Pau they would toss them into the launches and the sailors would tumble in with a plop, like bales of wet cotton.

The inauguration of the stadium was a sublime fusion of aristocracy and democracy. Never had such a thing been seen. All the top hats of the king, his sons, his brother-in-law, all his gentlemen, all the dross from the municipalities and provinces, and all the parasitic bureaucrats of the moment, served as chimneys for the smoke of enthusiasm. Europe would be hard put to have witnessed on any other occasion a display of more resplendent top hats, their very skin composed of pure mineral coal. That afternoon the great belly of Primo de Rivera, wearing a paisley vest the color of cognac, rubbed up against the jackets of the people. Sixty thousand hats saluted the dictator and the kings of Spain. The royal daughters, *les infantes*, sat quietly in the central loge, wearing vaporous dresses made of strawberry ice: they were tall, subdued, somewhat sad young women.

The day of the inauguration, the brand-new Plaça d'Espanya saw humanity multiply as if people were ants, or as if all the ants in the country had been blown up with bicycle pumps and then rushed off to steal jackets and skirts from their respective haberdashers or dressmakers.

On that day were written the first lines of a hymn that seemed as if it would never have to end. It was the hymn of the sex and the belly of Barcelona. The laborers from Murcia who had come north to work in construction toiled to a java rhythm. These Murcian men, dark as coal, were too busy sweating blood to think about striking. The union heads who had escaped Martínez Anido's bullets were out of the country; the ones left behind to live high on the hog basically ogled the legs of showgirls on the Paral·lel and drank the anise water the chief of police would treat them to. Barcelona had forgotten all about the days of politics, pistols and bombs. It had forgotten about virility. Its only creed was those multicolored lights that shone every night from the Palau Nacional. People barely knew the names of their councilmen or provincial representatives. All they knew was that Foronda was in charge. Mariano de Foronda y González Bravo, the Marquès de Foronda, was a Grandee of Spain and the Director of the Exposició Internacional. Foronda was everything, greater than the dictator, greater than the king. The board of the Exposició Universal, under the direction of Milà i Camps and the Baró de Viver, would do anything that struck Foronda's fancy. Anyone who was more or less thick-skinned or willing to bow his head would be tossed a bone. Colonels, police, canons, and employees from the department of revenue all revealed their troglodytic rapacity with a despicable lack of shame. Milà i Camps, President of the Barcelona provincial government, went a little off his rocker and started to believe he was Lorenzo di Medici. He called in every possible painter, sculptor and goldsmith, and rendered his madness on the walls of the Palau de la Generalitat in the most awful and grotesque murals ever painted. A team of unscrupulous artists interpreted the most reactionary history of Spain to his personal taste. The worldview of this fanciful aristocrat became a sort of madhouse of Gothic peaks. Rubió i Bellver, the architect, pumped his head full of hot air to make his Gothic folly even more monstrous. Milà i Camps wanted the Toison d'Or, he wanted to be viceroy of Catalonia, and he wanted to enter the cathedral in a carriage drawn by all the lions in the zoo at the Parc de la Ciutadella. Back in Madrid they let him be distracted by all these twinkling childish amusements and gave their orders directly to Mariano de Foronda, who was not only the director of the Exposició Internacional but also, and more importantly, of the electric tramway company of Barcelona. At one point, the Baró de Viver was on the verge of being hanged from the prickly dyed moustaches of the Marquès de Foronda, lord and master of the trams and the money of Barcelona.

The image of the Sacred Heart of Jesus was enthroned in every military headquarters and officers' club. These were places where poker was played and the murder of prostitutes was primed. Like the time a poor girl was thrown off a balcony on the Passatge dels Escudellers, her kidneys run through with a sword that had made its name in the disastrous wars in Africa.

The bishops and archbishops fanned the flames of this reactionary orgy. The priests and canons they sent to Barcelona to survey the treasures of the Palau Nacional – over five thousand pieces of art from all over Spain – consumed two thousand liters of manzanilla sherry daily, and all the meat from all the bulls killed in the Monumental and Arenes bullrings was reserved for them in its entirety. A line of canons formed to eat a sandwich made from the first bull. The dictator resuscitated the mentality of the "dandy generals" who were the consorts of queens, and of the petty loyalist defenders of King Charles who turned up the heat on bordellos and sacristies to distract the people with incense or desire, according to their predilections. At heart, the dictator had the ridiculous charm of a Tartarin. In this regard, and in others, he put one in mind of General Francesc Savalls i Massot, the colorful and hapless leader of the Carlist wars who somehow always found a way to land on his feet.

Barcelona shimmered like an international shooting star. In the publicity published abroad about the Exposition, the financial "fiddling" of the magnates of the situation swelled to cosmic proportions. Anyone who didn't brazenly steal simply didn't have fingers, poor thing.

When it was over, people cringed, wondering how such things could have been tolerated. But the fact that they put up with it, and accepted it, was very natural. Politicians know that there is nothing so mutable, so easy to fool, so corruptible, as a mob. And in those days Barcelona, Catalonia and Spain were just that: a great mob of small intestines and rubberneckers. The Dictatorship filled shriveled stomachs with crusts of bread and offered up a bit of fireworks to cast a reflex of red happiness on their curious faces. Cowardice and stupidity on all sides contributed to the game, and yet it cannot be denied that Barcelona did have a brilliant, stupendously decorative moment.

The stale old aristocracy and the fresh new aristocracy that have popped up in this book felt as if they really were somebody. The pneumatic tires that the Hispanos-Suizas and Rolls-Royces set into motion had the grandeur of a Roman catapult. The upholstery might be a little the worse for wear, but it exuded a deeply human breath, like the breasts of slave times. The buttocks of the aristocrats that flattened it out on their return from kissing the hand of the queen would soak up the genuflections of all the workers of Murcia, ripping out rails and bursting pipes without the slightest fear of a rebel bullet.

But this happiness was not to last. Stocks began to wobble; currency began to wobble; the dictator was tired and everyone was tired of the dictator. The king gave him a kick in the belly, with the cold, geological cruelty that is the province of kings. As Primo de Rivera had the good fortune to die a dull and decent death in Paris, no one asked for his head. In a word, it was a blunt, primary, and not at all perverse sort of biology. A biology of the kind cultivated in a Spanish barracks, over a bottle of wine, a deck of cards, and a nameless chanteuse, a homegrown version of *la Bella Chelito*, doing a belly dance in a dressing gown festooned with ribbons and bows. The dictator sought to extend the nineteenth century military chaos that had been stemmed by the alternating two-party system imposed by Cánovas del Castillo. When Primo de Rivera left, not a single bone of either the military anarchy or the Cánovas system was left unbroken. The monarchy dragged its tail for a good long time, and no line it was thrown could help. In Jaca two captains with communist pipe dreams faced the firing squad, but things got even worse. A few months later, not a single city or town was left in Spain without a street or town square bearing the names of those two martyred captains. One fine day people woke up to find the Republic in the streets. People seized onto the Republic in childlike amazement, without bloodshed or vengeance. The Conde de Romanones went to the Escorial to send the queen off. The count sat on a wooden bench at the train station, with his moustache, his twisted hat, and his desolately historic eyes. Not far from his shoe stood an empty bottle of Sinalco, the oldest soft drink in Europe. In those days, in El Escorial, they still drank Sinalco.

The queen left Spain like a lady-in-waiting wearing a necklace of tears. No one dared steal even a petal of the disintegrating roses she held in a large, pallid, and misty bouquet, watered with the sobs of the aristocracy.

The king had fled hours before. In Barcelona the Catalan Republic was proclaimed, and the Plaça de Sant Jaume celebrated one of the most enthusiastic, sweaty and sublime days of its history.

In the five years that transpired between the 1929 Exposition and advent of the Republic, the daily uncertainties in the private life of the people we have met in the pages of this book continued to be resolved behind the blindfold destiny reserves for us all. Those were thorny days for the Lloberolas. The most brilliant moment of the Exposition coincided with the most bitter moment for don Tomàs: a failed inheritance.

Don Tomàs had a paternal aunt, his father's younger sister, known to at least four hundred Barcelonans as la Tia Paulina. Tia Paulina had been widowed at a very young age. With no surviving family on the side of the deceased, she inherited her husband's entire fortune free of taxes or obligations. Tia Paulina had sole possession of the cut she took away from the house of the Lloberolas because, even though Don Tomàs's father was the absolute heir, the part bequeathed to her as inalienable successor represented a considerable inheritance, which in time quintupled in value.

The only possible heirs to Tia Paulina were Don Tomàs, his sisters, and the Baró de Gresol, a second cousin to Don Tomàs. Despite being a more distant relation, the Baró de Gresol was Tia Paulina's godson. That good lady had always shown him great affection.

Tia Paulina had been born in 1840, at the ancestral home of the Lloberolas. Her birth was met with the scent of the last blasts of powder from the first civil war. She made her communion in a tiny hoop skirt that reached below her knees, beneath which you could see white silk pantaloons that covered her little partridge feet in hoops of lace trim. Tia Paulina had been a silent, anemic child, terrified of devils, freemasons, and the wayward ways of Queen Isabella II. She spent winters shut up in a school run by the Sisters of the Holy Family who had her sing songs under the trees of a damp garden and taught her to embroider on a *canemàs* – or *canyamàs*, as the ladies who did embroidery Catalanized the Spanish *cañamazo*. On this embroidery canvas Tia Paulina would stitch images of the baby Jesus, of General Zumalacárregui, and of the Lloberola family coat of arms in wool of many colors.

Tia Paulina spent the summers in a little town close to Perpignan where the Lloberolas had an estate. Most of the trip was made in enormous ramshackle stagecoaches. Tia Paulina would suffocate in the heat and turn fuchsia red. Once, the stagecoach was shot at and robbed by bandits as it made its way through the province of Girona. One of the thugs stuck his big hairy hand into the warmth of Tia Paulina's corset to see if she was hiding any jewels there. Her two small breasts were tiny and green as an almond hull. She fainted.

For four years after that she would tell the priests when she went to confession how a big thuggish man had touched her that way. At the Perpignan estate, Tia Paulina listened to the song of the crickets and the warblers. Her hair was combed every day, she was bathed twice a year, and her little body was enshrouded in a long gown made of something like sackcloth that reached down to her feet. Tia Paulina was very white and very sad. She read Chateaubriand's *Les martyrs* and a romantic little French novel called *La siège de la Rochelle*. That novel was the basis for her criteria on love.

At eighteen years of age she was married off to el Senyor de Llinàs. Out of family expediency, he sympathized with the Carlist cause, but in fact el Senyor de Llinàs was a somewhat brutal Voltairean; he moved with great ease from gunpowder to laughter. The wedding night was a monstrous affair for Tia Paulina; her mother's instructions proved utterly worthless.

After two years of marriage she began to feel a deep adoration for her husband. Even though the realization that el Senyor de Llinàs was not the slightest bit religious caused her great suffering, that apoplectic man's moustache – an exact copy of Napoleon III's – had pervaded her heart.

El Senyor de Llinàs impregnated every chambermaid and cook in their home, but he never managed to impregnate the womb of Tia Paulina.

When the condition of the maids in the service of el Senyor de Llinàs began to show – sometimes even earlier – they were let go and they would return to their villages. The illegitimate children of el

Senyor de Llinàs collected dung along the roads of all four provinces of Catalonia. One boy who turned out to be a little more clever than the rest entered the seminary. In time he would write a Month of May devotional and die like a little saint.

El Senyor de Llinàs was twenty-five years older than his wife. The only activities he felt any passion for were playing *tresillo*, a 19th century card game played with the Spanish deck, and eating the tender green walnuts they would send him from his estates. His house was located on Carrer de Mercaders, an immense old mansion with a square garden out of which two palm trees stretched their necks like two condemned men trapped in a well. El Senyor de Llinàs played cards every afternoon with three gentlemen: Don Josep Rocafiguera, a man from Aragon by the name of Ceballos, and the grandfather of the author of this book. Ceballos had the sexuality of a soldier and the soul of a swashbuckler. As the men played cards, Tia Paulina and the other ladies knit woolen socks for el Senyor de Llinàs, with a brazier at their feet and the song of a canary and the mewling of a discontented cat in their ears. Occasionally, they would embroider a mantle for a statue of the Virgin Mary or cut out underwear patterns for the poor of Saint Vincent de Paul.

Ceballos was in love with Tia Paulina, and someone let on about it to el Senyor de Llinàs. This gentleman was jealous in the extreme, more jealous than a tiger. Tia Paulina knew nothing of Ceballos's great passion, but she noticed that where her husband's moustache met his jowls it looked for all the world like a Florentine dagger. One day el Senyor de Llinàs said a few choice words to Ceballos. There was a duel. As luck would have it, Ceballos's bullet went straight to the heart of el Senyor de Llinàs. He dropped his top hat and pistol on the field of honor and fled like a madman. Not long afterwards, he got himself killed fighting for the Carlists in the Seu d'Urgell, just as Savalls was betraying the holy cause by reaching an accord with Martínez Campos at the Hostal de la Corda.

Tia Paulina was widowed at thirty-eight. She sensed that her husband's soul was destined for hell, but since she couldn't be entirely sure, she decided her time would be well spent if she devoted the rest of her life to praying for the eternal repose of el Senyor de Llinàs.

From then on, Tia Paulina's life could have been considered exemplary if the years had not turned her heart into a dried-up, yellowed and acidic artifact. Many thought she had a lemon where her heart ought to be. Where el Senyor de Llinàs had taken the maids down the path of iniquity, Tia Paulina had them singing the "Holy, Holy, Holy" even as they gutted fish entrails. From break of day till nine in the evening, when everyone went to bed, in Tia Paulina's immense old mansion you could hear the music of the scrub brush, the broom, the feather dusters, the washing bats in the laundry, and the fans for the kitchen fires, accompanying unschooled, tuneless voices endlessly repeating: "Holy God, almighty God, immortal God." Tia Paulina filled the apartment with birdcages. She had five parrots that also intoned "Holy, Holy, Holy," as well as a blackbird that whistled it. But Tia Paulina had to be on her guard, because the birds tended to forget the pious singsong as their hearts went out to a little tango popular in those days that went *"Cariño, ho hay mejor café que el de Puerto Rico..."*

Tia Paulina kept six or seven maids because she was a fanatic for cleanliness and her house was endless. There was always a lot of drama among them, because she would get jealous of one and develop an aversion to another. The maids used her, bamboozled her, and filled her ears with gossip and bad faith. When a new one arrived from the village, still warm from cows' breath and the tongue of a young buck, Tia Paulina would subdue her rebel breast with the wool of the scapulary. If she suspected that the girl had a boyfriend, Tia Paulina would shut herself up in a room with the girl and try to charm her like a serpent. If the girl was pliable, she would succumb to asceticism. If she rebelled, she had no choice but to close the door behind her. Tia Paulina cultivated a sort of special service of stunted, colorless and sexless young women: they all wore habits and they only went out at night once every twelve months, to attend midnight Mass on Christmas Eve.

Before the reformation of the old city of Barcelona, Tia Paulina had never been so far as the Plaça de Catalunya, and had barely set foot on the Rambla, where it meets Carrer de Portaferrissa. The streets she was familiar with were Mercaders, Pont de la Parra, Riera de Sant Joan, Sant Pere més Baix, Carders, Plaça Nova, l'Infern, Ripoll, Catedral, Santa Maria, el Pi, Sant Just and Sant Jaume, and the squares were the Plaça de les Beates and the Plaça Nova. In truth, she could go months and months without leaving the house except to go to mass at the chapel called Capella de l'Ajuda on Sant Pere més Baix. On

Sunday she would go twice, early in the morning and for noonday mass. When she went to church she always dragged along her own little folding chair because she didn't want to sit on the woven rush seats for fear of getting fleas. When white hair and rheumatism began to afflict her, she would have a maid carry the chair. At the noonday mass at l'Ajuda she would stop a while at the door to speak with the few acquaintances she frequented. One of them was Don Manuel Duran i Bas, who attended the same mass, on his wife's arm. Don Manuel Duran i Bas was Tia Paulina's lawyer and she doted on him. He was one of the last men in Barcelona to use the top hat in all its splendor. In old age, he had developed a hunchback, and the curvature made him seem very small. His eyes languished under his incredibly hairy and droopy eyebrows, and his moustache – the whitest and thickest in the land – fell over his mouth like a great curtain of sadness. Don Manuel could barely see. He would lift his head, which sank into the stiffness of his crooked back, and through gold-rimmed glasses poised on his nose he would contemplate that toasted almond known as Tia Paulina, puffed up with corsets, underskirts, and petticoats, and the blackest, bleakest fabric the world had ever seen. The four strands of whitish hair she had left had turned yellow as a smoker's fingers from the potions her hairdresser applied. Atop it all was a timid little mantilla, as forlorn as a hospice.

Tia Paulina talked with Don Manuel about mortgages and the old days. They would also mention a former friend of Don Manuel's, a girl who had gone to school with Tia Paulina and had died very young in a cholera epidemic.

When Tia Paulina felt the need to make an important confession, she would go to the cathedral and work her jaw for a couple of hours behind the screen of her father confessor. This man was a penitential priest, who could stand in as a surrogate for the bishop when assigning penance. When it was merely a question of what she called "making peace with herself," she would go directly to l'Ajuda and resolve it with any old parish priest.

The urban reformation of Barcelona had been hard on Tia Paulina. The havoc it had wreaked on her neighborhood obliged her to change her idea of the world's topography.

Don Tomàs de Lloberola was always very solicitous of his aunt, treating her with exceptional interest. His counterpart in the business of winning her over was Tia Paulina's godson, the Baró de Gresol.

They kept track of who had paid her more visits throughout the month, and who had sent her the best *botifarra* sausages when the pig was slaughtered in the fall. Or the biggest ring cake on the day of Saint Anthony of the Asses in June. Or the almond confection known as *panellets* that had most delighted her on All Souls' Day. Leocàdia would take the children to visit her. When they were small, Tia Paulina had terrified them. Without fail, their aunt would give them six *unces*, about three ounces, of candies from l'Abella. They were every bit as acidic as she was. This point counterpoint between Don Tomàs and the Baró ended in a fierce hatred between the two relatives that expressed itself in gossip and tales they would take to Tia Paulina regarding the discourtesies that one or the other of the aspirants to her inheritance had shown her.

Don Tomàs's two sisters, Clàudia, the spinster, and Anneta, who was married to Don Ramon de Francolí, each plotted while clinging to her aunt's skirts. Collectively, thanks to all her nieces and nephews, her feet never touched the ground. Despite her terrible avarice, when economic disaster befell Don Tomàs, Tia Paulina helped her nephew out a bit. As Don Tomàs didn't want to abuse her generosity, what he did was to multiply his acts of solicitousness and tenderness. He would say "Tia…" and "Ay, Tia…" and "But Tia…" as if angels were dictating to him. Don Tomàs would pet her and prance before her like a dog with honey on its tail.

Even before that period of economic anxiety, every summer the Lloberola nieces and nephews geared themselves up for Tia Paulina visit to their respective estates for some little part of the season.

When she was at the Lloberola house, Leocàdia was so eager to be the perfect hostess that it would make her sick. Nothing was ever to Tia Paulina's liking, and she had very special requirements. Every morning a battle raged between Leocàdia and the cook. Tia Paulina always complained of the cold. Even when the heat was asphyxiating, poor Leocàdia had to keep the balconies closed so her husband's aunt would not catch a chill. They went to the extreme of killing two pairs of peacocks because the birds' morning squawks were too raucous and disturbed her sleep. When they went for a walk down a country lane and saw a couple of farm laborers coming towards them, they would step to the side or fall back, to avert any unpleasantness for Tia Paulina in case one of the farmers slipped and used a coarse expression.

The last few years, Leocàdia had had to put up with tremendous rudeness and infinite oddities from Tia Paulina. Despite her extremely advanced age, she still had a clear head and provoked as much torment as ever. Don Tomàs de Lloberola's last hope lay in Tia Paulina's inheritance. Shut up in his apartment on Carrer de Mallorca and reduced to utter precariousness, Don Tomàs thought the inheritance might still set things right. His aunt didn't spend a cent, she simply amassed revenue. According to the Lloberolas' calculations she had a considerable fortune.

But neither Don Tomàs, nor his sisters, nor the Baró de Gresol could have foreseen the dark beast that would undo all their machinations. Naively, they did not take into account another person who, without paying visits, or sending ring cakes, or slitting defenseless peacocks' throats, still held the acidic lemon of Tia Paulina's heart in his hand. The hand was cold, unctuous, servile, and disposed to do whatever was necessary to squeeze that lemon dry. The person was Tia Paulina's confessor, Mossèn Claramunt, the penintential priest of the cathedral.

Mossèn Claramunt had been reared, one might say, on the teats of the Lloberolas, a product of the munificence of Don Tomàs's father, and of Don Tomàs himself. In Tia Paulina's final years of existence he exercised an absolute ascendancy over that good lady's heart. The sagacious priest delicately insinuated to her that all her relatives only loved her for the assets of her inheritance. While he was at it, he revived her fear of the possible damnation of el Senyor de Llinàs, leading her to believe that the life of chastity, devotion and sacrifice she had lived would not be sufficient to expiate the great sins of the deceased. When she made her confessions, the priest instilled terror in her, portraying her as a somewhat ungenerous person, too in love with her money, and lacking in devotion to charity and pious works. Fear spread throughout Tia Paulina's body. The sagacious priest hinted delicately at a subtle draft of a will and testament. Tia Paulina was so pleased with it, she committed it to memory, but the priest didn't entirely trust her, and he used her fear to press her further. Tia Paulina was on the far side of eighty and her mind was not what it used to be. She let herself be absolutely dominated by that fear and even came to have visions. E Senyor de Llinàs would appear to her, naked, with a chain around his neck, surrounded by flames. Instead of comforting her, the priest embellished the pathos of the apparition. When Tia Paulina went to the home of Martí i Beya, the notary, to write her will, the canon accompanied her. As if the will were not enough, Mossèn Claramunt started siphoning off money on the pretense of masses and charities, and Tia Paulina surrendered it to him, kissing his hands all the while. All her stocks and securities, and all her cash, found their way to the canon's bureau. Mossèn Claramunt had taken control, and as custodian he was free to distribute, as he saw fit and to his liking, an amount that came to more than a million pessetes.

Tia Paulina spent the last five years of her life completely disabled, in a mortifying state of semi-imbecility. The poor maids had to bathe her and do everything for her. They fed her sips of soup as if she were a child. Leocàdia and her sisters-in-law helped them out. Tia Paulina still recognized everyone. Though she could only speak with difficulty, she showed a great disaffection for all the women who were caring for her. Yet if Mossèn Claramunt ever came to see her, the eyes of that poor dim-witted old woman would show a bit of light and her sunken mouth, monstrously deformed by paralysis, would do its best to mimic a sort of smile.

Tia Paulina died two days after the inauguration of the Exposition on Montjuïc. She was eighty-eight years old and for four months she was nothing but a skeleton under a scrap of skin. All that was left of her was a fragment of lung that went through the motions of breathing, and bowels that couldn't digest a thing.

The priest anointed her with the holy oils and Leocàdia closed her eyelids. Her nieces, Clàudia and Anneta, took charge of dressing her in the habit of the Third Order of Saint Francis and placing the rosary from her first communion between her fingers.

When Martí i Beya, the notary, read Tia Paulina's will, Don Tomàs had a fit of ferocious rage. Then he simply crumpled. He could never have predicted this. He couldn't have imagined that Mossèn Claramunt would do such a thing to him. He could imagine it from his sisters, or from that finicky cold fish, the Baró de Gresol, but never from his priest. Tia Paulina had left everything, absolutely everything, for pious works and beneficence. Doctor Claramunt was the sole heir of confidence with absolute liberal faculties. Not one miserable legacy, not one mingy thought for anyone in the family, nothing. The poor maids who had sacrificed their lives for her, the unfortunate Carmeta who had served her for forty years – a dumb martyr to the brazen disrespect of the departed – there was nothing for them either. Fortunately Tia Paulina was already in her grave because the maids were so enraged that they would have spit upon her cadaver and cut out her heart to feed it to the cats.

Never has a dead woman gone to the other life to such a litany of shattered voices or such raw and direct indignation.

Claramunt the canon merely said: *"Bueno, bueno, bueno,* such a holy lady, such a pious lady, *bueno, bueno, bueno…"*

There was no way Don Tomàs could take it in. It was too much. His only hope, his only lifeline, wickedly burned, destroyed by a scheming clergyman dominated by the desire for money, by utterly sordid avarice!

The meeting of Don Tomàs and the priest was sublime. Never had such liturgical smiles and grimaces concealed such moldering hatred. Never had anyone seen the likes of the priest's gall and the marquis's indignation. It was the battle of the sea lion and the crocodile, an encounter between the ice of the Antarctic and the hot mud of African rivers.

It seemed impossible that two hidebound Catholics, two remnants of militant adherence to the Carlist cause, two pallid shades of reaction, one clad in the robes of the father confessor, the other in the stain-spattered jacket of a marquis, could be reduced to the incontinence of a dust-choked highway, to the fury of two bilious coachmen, tongues saturated with aïoli.

Tia Paulina's will was irrevocable. There was no recourse. This was the opinion of Martí i Beya, the notary, and all the lawyers.

Don Tomàs lost his head. He quoted to the canon from the novels of José María de Pereda and, in a phrase that resounds throughout Spanish literature from Quevedo on, ended up calling him an *inmunda sabandija*, a filthy louse, in Spanish. The canon let out a peal of hysterical laughter. He kept repeating his incessant *bueno, bueno, buenos*, and threatened Don Tomàs with the eternal damnation of hell for the sin of greed and for lack of respect toward the ministers of the Lord. Don Tomàs felt the need to do something. If Leocàdia hadn't stopped him, he was even considering a campaign in *El Diluvio*, a liberal, Republican, anti-monarchical, and anticlerical publication. His blind rage had reached this extreme.

Everyone thought he would die from the shock, but Providence still had other tests in store for the aggrieved soul of Don Tomàs.

The last of them was the proclamation of the Republic. It is not that Don Tomàs had considered his dreams fulfilled with the Dictatorship. Still, his brand of Carlism was pretty comatose, and in the Dictatorship he perceived, if nothing more, a pact between King Alfons XIII and the Sacred Heart of Jesus, between the monarchy and the Church. The mediator in this pact was General Miguel Primo de Rivera, and its nuances included the elevation of religion and morality and the annihilation of the things that most horrified Don Tomàs, which were anarcho-syndicalism, unionism, communism, and Catalanism. Don Tomàs believed that with a big enough dose of Martínez Anido and Cardinal Segura it would be possible to establish a tribunal in Spain that bore some resemblance to the hoary and Holy Office of the Inquisition.

The fall of the dictator set old Lloberola to trembling and, when he saw the Republic on the horizon, he used his last stores of energy to turn himself into a sea urchin. Don Tomàs remembered the revolution of 1869 and the Republic of 1873. He remembered the soldiers dancing on the altar of the Betlem parish church and all the horrible sacrileges of the 1800s.

What came with the second Republic seemed even more grim to him than the disasters of the first. Since the incident with his aunt's estate, Don Tomàs had become a listless little chick. He no longer saw anyone. In April 1931, the victory of the Republicans and ouster of the dictator put a little oil in the lamp of his heart. He joined with his closest relatives and his former acquaintances from Franciscan conferences, beneficent societies, parochial councils, perseverance leagues, and priests, rickety Carlists, decrepit piles with all four feet halfway in the grave, and former gunmen from the anti-union strikebreakers of the Free Syndicates, to take part in secret meetings held in sacristies and private homes. With legs that could barely hold him up and *El Correo Catalán* in his pocket, he felt like a conspirator. But the churches and convents that were being burned in Spain were like a dose of hemlock for poor old Don Tomàs. He shut himself up in his office to cry under his grandfather's effigy. Don Tomàs was vanquished. He didn't believe in the efficacy of the ultra-right wing *penyes blanques*; his only hope would have been lightning bolts from Mt. Sinai. The word went around one night that the convents of Barcelona would be targeted. That night Don Tomàs took two nuns into his home. They were distant relatives from the church of l'Esperança. Don Tomàs felt like a hero; it reminded him of Hernán Cortés's renowned "night of sorrows" in Mexico. Don Tomàs's ears brimmed with lurid fantasies: the groans of the religious martyred in the middle of the Plaça de Catalunya by the anarchists of the FAI and the independentists of *Estat Català*; Bishop Irurita burned to the quick in the house of Francesc Macià, as Dr. Aiguader, the Mayor of Barcelona, stoked the coals with the ferrule of his ceremonial scepter; Lluís Companys, then a member of the Chamber of Deputies, escorting four hundred naked women down the Rambla proclaiming free love and other barbarities. Don Tomàs imagined he heard and smelled these things as he contemplated his two cell-dwelling relatives, eating garlic soup next to silent, desolate Leocàdia. He feared that the monsters of anarchism would be showing up any minute to sack his house and rape the two nuns…but that would be over his dead body.

Mossèn Claramunt, who, as one can imagine, was on the outs with the Lloberolas, didn't take such a dark view as Don Tomàs. The first days of the Republic, he would say, "*Bueno, bueno, bueno*, as long as they leave the poor priests alone, as long as they don't attack religion, *bueno, bueno, bueno.*" Later, though, the Mossèn would join in the panic, which led him to attempt a reconciliation. Don Tomàs would not stoop so low.

When el Senyor de Lloberola saw in the rotogravures what had been done to some of the churches and convents of Spain, he said: "This is the end of the Republic! This cannot go on, by any means! This is communism, this is worse than Russia…much worse than Russia!"

A week after he had taken the two nuns in, Don Tomàs could no longer get up from bed. All his innards were failing. He had a high temperature; he was in constant delirium. Dreams of red terror were suffocating him. The communists were pulling off his sheets and stamping his belly with a red iron. Don Tomàs suffered and screamed for three days. A Carmelite priest gave him the sacraments. Leocàdia and his children hovered at the head of his bed. Leocàdia was already somewhat immune to his pain, and his children's only wish was for their father to finish dying and leave them in peace.

On the fourth day, he was greatly debilitated. He no longer spoke, he was barely conscious. Some time later came the death rattle, and then the final collapse.

The Carmelite brother who comforted him through the end coined this phrase: "A saint has died, assassinated by the Republic…"

Leocàdia wanted to dress him in the habits of the Church of La Mercè. Frederic fought with her and imposed the uniform of the *Maestrant de Saragossa*, the brotherhood of Saragossa cavalrymen. The gold and red uniform was too small for him. They cut the dress coat down the back and laced some ribbons through it to keep the split in the uniform together, turning the coat into a sort of corset, like those worn by chorines in the zarzuelas of the day.

In death, Don Tomàs appeared to be wearing a ghoulish disguise; he had been turned into a macabre doll at the insistence of a cad.

They were still able to afford a bit of pomp for the burial. A handful of people attended: the proverbial "quatre gats."

Thus ended the life of Don Tomàs de Lloberola i Serradell, de Genís i de Fontdeserta, seventh Marquès de Sitjar and fourth Marquès de Vallromana.

———.——.———

IN HORTÈNSIA PORTELL'S dining room a rather political dinner was taking place. Hortènsia had turned out to be a Republican of the firmest convictions. As her white teeth pulverized the fish course, she told funny anecdotes about the Marquesa de Perpinyà, the Baronessa de Moragues, the Marquesa de Lió, and the Baronessa de Sant Rafael, all the grand dames who used to be her friends. The advent of the Republic had thrown the infinite vacuity of their lives into even greater relief. The Marquesa de Perpinyà was weeping in France with the dethroned kings, following the lead of some of the ladies of the Madrid aristocracy. When she learned that Don Alfons had crossed the border, she fled her mansion and went to live in a modest little hotel under an assumed name. Naturally, everyone knew who she was, and the hotel staff thought she had gone mad.

That lady, like other personalities from her world, could think only of communism, and of selling off houses and estates to get their capital out of Spain. Laws prohibiting the exportation of money destroyed their plans, but they contrived to plot with people who engaged in contraband, and other unscrupulous folk. The Marquès de Puigvert had been among the most panic-stricken, and he wanted to carry an extremely large amount across the border. Hortènsia Portell told the story of how he had tried to enter France in a third-class car on a train through Puigcerdà, accompanied by a servant. When they were about to cross the border, both master and servant lost their nerve. A barber who lived in a town close by and plied many trades offered to smuggle forty thousand *duros* in bills right under the noses of the police. The marquis, the servant, and the barber, all three dressed in peasant caps and espadrilles, took their seats on the train. Lord knows where the very clever barber was hiding the marquis's forty thousand duros, but the fact is that neither the police nor the frontier guards intervened. Once they were over the border in France, when the marquis and his servant got ready to take possession of their capital once again, they discovered to their stupefaction that the barber had melted away. He hasn't been heard of to this day.

The marquis, desperate and ashamed, both by the loss of the money and by the swindle they had fallen prey to, was silent as a tomb. Not enough, however, to keep the news from Hortènsia Portell's ears.

The Marquesa de Lió was the subject of more delightful incidents. At the time of the revolutionary coup, the marquesa was true to her principles. She was prepared for the revolutionaries to come and rape her. She put on provocative pajamas and even left the door to her apartment ajar. She felt like a martyr for the monarchy. She didn't want to flee, she wanted to give her blood and her honor for the cause of the king. When the marquesa realized no one was coming to rape her, and the Republicans were a peaceful lot, she saw that she was making a fool of herself. She had her suitcases all packed to go to France when she was visited by a great friend, Don Lluís Figueres, one of the most brilliant minds of the Dictatorship. The marquesa thought Don Lluís would flee with her, but Don Lluís was very calm, and found the whole business of the Republic rather amusing. So the marquesa stayed on in Barcelona and within a few days was discussing feminist politics and her belief that women should play a role in the new regime. She even wangled an introduction to a member of the Parliament from the Republican Left party, and ended up thinking Niceto Alcalá Zamora was rather charming.

It was the hippopotamic senyora Valls-Darnius, though, who broke all records. We already met her at Hortènsia's party, precisely when she had sworn never to say another word in Catalan, as a consequence of her husband's great windfall thanks to his dirty dealings with the Dictatorship. To assure that the deal her husband had made would continue to render the same benefits under the Republic, she claimed to have felt Republican all her life and dated her Catalanism to before the 1892 *Bases de Manresa*, the cornerstone of the Catalan regional Constitution.

La Baronessa de Sant Rafael, who was more romantic than her poor husband, fled to eat the bread of exile with the other aristocrats. This is how she put it to her acquaintances. While the poor baron went and trawled for lipfish and sawfish in Palamós, the baronessa ran off to Biarritz with her gigolo to dance the tango. When her money ran out, she went home to shed her last monarchical tears.

As a rule, in fact, the local aristocracy didn't go very far, and didn't sell or cash in all that many assets. Most stayed home, biding their time, and many even adopted the Republican label. What they wanted, though, was a moderate, Catholic Republic, and when faced with what they called the demagoguery of the Constituent Courts, the response was a Homeric chorus of caterwauling. From the pulpit, the clergy saw to inflating their howls, preaching the apparition of the Beast of the Apocalypse in the land. Carlists and devotees of the dethroned king united in the common cause of opposing the Republic and celebrating solemn masses. When Don Jaume de Borbó died, they dedicated a magnificent funeral in the Barcelona cathedral to him. That funeral was one of the most brazen demonstrations of monarchist sentiment. In the aftermath, a few worshippers murdered a poor boy who was passing by, so that the solemn funeral would share in the prestige of shedding innocent blood. It appears some religious monarchists favored human sacrifice.

All the public and private events that took place throughout those days were of tremendous interest to Hortensia Portell. She was in her element in the Republic. It wasn't that she had fallen out with the opposition or the desperate; she felt the tears of those afflicted by the new regime, and occasionally she even humored them, but in both form and substance Hortènsia felt like a Republican. She believed in progress and evolution, and where modernity was concerned, no one was going to get the jump on her. This was why Hortènsia wanted to meet and get to know the Catalan Republican personalities, and that night Josep Safont would be coming to her house. She had also invited Rafaela Coll, Isabel Sabadell, and Bobby Xuclà. Isabel was already friendly with Josep Safont; she claimed to be even more Republican than Hortènsia.

Josep Safont held important posts. He was a volatile young man from a comfortable, bourgeois background, but he had felt like a revolutionary all his life. He had been a syndicalist and a communist, he had been in prison, and he had spent a good bit of time in exile. Once he held a position in the government Josep Safont decided to make overtures to the aristocracy, and he allowed it to be inferred that he had affairs with married ladies from the upper crust. Safont was short and thin and blond, with horn-rimmed glasses and a Levitical voice. He considered himself worldly and irresistible. He would wink an eye, and give only a partial account of his conquests, implying that he was quite the sensation. The ladies would poke fun at him, and, as you might expect, he didn't catch on. Isabel Sabadell pretended to be soft on Safont, and he declared that when the law permitting divorce was passed, he would probably marry her.

That night Safont was at the height of his brilliance. The ladies listened to him with delight. Hortènsia was the most sentimental of the group, and her eyes rolled back in her head when Safont disclosed the torments the police had subjected him to. He also told tales of struggles and death threats in the days of the pistol-packing union busters. Safont had never been tortured, and even in the midst of the turmoil he had always more or less had a good time. In Paris, his father sent him tons of money and Safont devoted more time to intense love affairs than to conspiring. Safont had the overheated imagination common to the southern climes, and in the presence of ladies he turned into a peacock.

Rafaela found him undistinguished. Rafaela thought all the men of the Republic were common and ill-mannered, and felt that no good could come of their ilk. She was among those who claimed that the city councilors and the officials of the Catalan government were a pack of thieves who had turned the Plaça de Sant Jaume, where both City Hall and the Generalitat were located, into Sodom and Gomorrah. In Hortènsia's house, Rafaela contained herself, and in truth she enjoyed hearing Safont go on, because she was curious and loved intrigue. She liked to have a finger in every pie.

Bobby was apathetic, pessimistic and polite. He believed in nothing. Not in the men of the Republic, nor in the ones who came before. He was an absolute skeptic. Politics disgusted him. In Bobby's eyes, Safont was as much of an arriviste as all the others, and he felt tremendous scorn for Hortènsia and Isabel, drooling over that short, blond man.

Along with the *potins* about the members of the fallen regime, there was beginning to be new and entertaining gossip about the personalities of the new regime. The brilliant folk of Barcelona have always been rather provincial in spirit, and the most stimulating gossip was always the chatter about things happening in Madrid. Rafaela would quote the words of Minister Indalecio Prieto to show what a boor he was; Isabel and Hortènsia found them very funny. Safont brought fresh stories that met with great approval. Of the morsels that circulated about Barcelona, the most sought-after were the ones about Senyora Casulleres. She was the wife of an important public figure, a beautiful, sassy, and vain brunette who had always lived in the deepest poverty, and was out of her depth with her husband's new position. Only a few months before, no one had ever heard of this woman, and yet in just days she had become the rage in Barcelona. Monstrous tales circulated about Senyora Casulleres among the ladies of the aristocratic circles that hated the Republic. Some of the things they said about her were true, and some were lies. There was also a lot of talk about Senyora Sabater, a poor, tacky, and grotesque woman who had pretensions to being Madame de Tallien. Senyora Sabater gave tea parties at which she recited poetry before a series of reptilian followers of communism. The prevailing topic among the aristocratic ladies was the debauchery and dirty business of the Republic. In this area, fantasy and calumny achieved the sublime. It was said that the wife of another public figure had purchased and paid cash for jewelry valued at one hundred thousand duros. There wasn't a single dressing room, confession box, *meublé*, or nuptial bedroom that hadn't heard the story of these jewels a thousand times over.

Many ladies were convinced that in order to be hired, the typists and secretaries in the offices of the public institutions had had to sacrifice their virginity to a councilman or a deputy. The most wicked backstairs gossip was the daily bread of spurned women and of ladies who believed that communism consisted of allowing traffic to circulate on Holy Thursday.

All these protests against the new regime, all this sadness at the suspension of military and religious parades, exuded an air of boiled cabbage and local cowardice. All in all, the climate had not changed all that much, and the sentimental life of the country was much the same as it had been before.

The topics that awakened the greatest passion were feminism, female suffrage, and, above all, divorce. As soon as the divorce law was passed, women in the kind of circles that formed around Hortènsia Portell started predicting likely imminent divorces. This led to tremendous conversations and arguments. Hortènsia was in favor of divorce, of women's suffrage, and of woman in government and anywhere else they might be useful.

A couple of young women asked Hortènsia to give a lecture, but she didn't have the nerve. They wanted her to talk about fashion and the Republic. When Rafaela heard about it she spread the word far and wide, maintaining that Hortènsia had accepted the invitation. For a few days Hortènsia was a laughingstock among her closest friends.

Isabel Sabadell, quite the Republican and quite a friend to Joan Safont, had not yet given up her old ways. Whenever she could she would seize the opportunity to speak Spanish and cozy up to a ring of young aristocrats who got together in a little apartment to conspire and play the royal march on a gramophone. The poor boys passed the time shouting *"¡Viva el rey!"* in Spanish at closing time in the cabarets, and proselytizing among prostitutes and bootblacks. Truth be told, they were utterly irrelevant, but since their families were very wealthy and had been prominent during the Dictatorship, Isabel Sabadell and other ladies like her couldn't help but have a soft spot in their hearts for them, even if afterwards they would delight in explaining their shortcomings.

Hortènsia, who wanted to be a pure Republican, reproached Isabel for this frailty, while Isabel was annoyed by Hortènsia's cruelty, because in the presence of Safont she presumed to being the most radical of them all, even a communist sympathizer.

Many ladies and many young women, spurred on by boys still wet behind the ears, spoke of Russia with grotesque enthusiasm. Most of these women had no idea what a five-year plan was, but it was considered to be a topic of the most chic and elegant conversation. They discovered their passion for Russia through the Soviet films that were being shown in those days in Barcelona. The local authorities were very open-minded about programming and they coddled this snobbish desire to be *à la page*. These special sessions where people came to see the most important films of Bolshevik propaganda were showcased by the Cinaes group. The audience was a mixture of the elegant set and those known as intellectuals and artists, but above all it was married ladies accompanied by athletic young men from good families, who applauded wildly at things that were sometimes childish and sometimes deplorable. They considered the monotony and doggedness of Soviet film to be the last word in good taste and refinement.

Despite all their talk, in the world of Hortènsia Portell and other fine ladies like her, everything that was going on in the country, all the changes, which were considerable, were viewed as spectacle. Deep down, none of it really mattered very much to them. Naturally they had a fear of strikes, and a fear of losing their money and their peace of mind, but even this fear was only relative. The sheer full-bellied optimism of these people was hard to subdue. That night at Hortènsia's house, Josep Safont was a spectacle. Even Isabel saw him this way, for she knew very well that this man was neither of her world nor of her atmosphere. Josep Safont just didn't fit in, in that air tainted by a bourgeoisie too steeped in the *ancien régime*. What truly concerned Hortènsia and those ladies was the world of tittle-tattle that unfolded in fifty Barcelona mansions. Still and all, Hortènsia had to be given some credit. She was an honest and generous woman. Her age precluded affairs, and in truth she didn't desire one. Hortènsia just needed to fill her life, and she did so by pretending to be extremely concerned about politics and the world of the intellect. She would apply a coat of three or four extremely unremarkable ideas to her skin, and the perfume of those ideas accompanied her wherever she went. At that point in time, she felt Republican, because that seemed to be the more intelligent choice and in Barcelona it was beginning to be fashionable for women to lean a bit toward the side of intelligence.

Hortènsia took no risks. If her aristocratic circle criticized her for having had Josep Safont and other revolutionaries and atheists to dinner, she would absolve herself, attributing the invitations to curiosity, the same curiosity that had steered her to the cabarets or the perverts at La Criolla. Hortènsia was Catholic, but very much in her own way and very little in the way of the priests. She believed that she was not a sinner, and that someone like her was beyond all that and could be exposed to all of life's spectacles. Hortènsia was a self-centered, conservative bourgeois lady. She had nothing to lose if at some point she appeared to espouse divorce and even free love. These questions didn't affect her in the slightest. Just as in other days she had had actresses with shady reputations, flamenco singers, and generals like Primo de Rivera to her house, now she could indulge herself by inviting a Communist or a Republican like Josep Safont over. Her virtue was not compromised at all.

Josep Safont retreated from the after-dinner conversation at eleven-thirty, on the pretext that he had a party meeting to attend. As soon as he was out the door, Rafaela began to tear him apart. To be contrary, Hortènsia defended him to the hilt. Isabel found him amusing, because she could see the self-importance and puerile vanity in the man's eyes. She didn't find Josep Safont at all attractive, physically, but she felt he was neither as foolish and common as Rafaela thought, nor as sublime as Hortènsia made him out to be. Within the governing Republican Party, Isabel thought there were more intelligent and spectacular young men than Safont, and she mentioned a couple of names.

Hortènsia didn't know any of them, and she was a bit put out, asking Isabel why, instead of Safont, she hadn't brought some of those men she thought were more remarkable. Bobby was satisfied, as always, to be in the midst of the ladies' conversation because, between the squabbles and the henpecking, he never had to express an opinion. He made a bit of cruel fun of Hortènsia, telling her that now she had no choice but to invite the two or three fellows Isabel had mentioned, and her devotion to the Republican cause was going to cost her a lot of money in dinners.

Bobby only spoke of politics when he was among his lady friends, out of courtesy to them, and nothing more.

Many of Bobby's aristocratic friends from the club had gone over to Alejandro Lerroux, the populist, anti-Catalanist leader of the Radical Republican Party. Bobby found this attitude ignoble. One aristocrat best known for how he had worshiped the monarch and kowtowed to the bygone dictator proposed to him that he join the radical party, because Senyor Lerroux was the only guarantee of their oysters on ice and their poker games. Bobby didn't want to argue. With just a stiff smile and a slow blink of the eyes he left him frozen in place.

There were some truly abhorrent elements in the *Cambra de la Propietat*, the real estate authority, and the *Foment del Treball Nacional*, a regional chamber of commerce. These individuals considered Mr. Lerroux to be such a good fellow that if they asked nicely enough he would bring back the king, reduce salaries to pre-war level, and send them a priest and a civil guard to rub their tummies on nights when they had indigestion.

During the Dictatorship, families that obstinately adhered to a strong morality had been shaken to the core by a kind of social contact that had already taken hold in Barcelona. In those days the world of the demimondaines had been admired only for its natural beauty and for its shamelessness, or for the stories brilliant playboys and disabused artists would tell. Now it was admired, tolerated and appreciated first-hand. A scandalous dancer, who once had merely been applauded from a theater box, would be received years later, not as a sensational number at a private party in someone's home, but as a close friend of the lady of the house.

Some of the ladies from Hortènsia Portell's clan, such as Teodora Macaia or the Baronessa de Moragues, started paying visits backstage and attending late-night dinners in questionable company. Things that a true lady of Barcelona or a respectable bourgeoise would not have dared to do a few years before without exposing herself to great scandal and absolute disrepute could now be done coolly and casually, as if it were the most natural thing in the world.

The finest actresses and dancers would go for tea or play bridge with the granddaughters of ladies who had embroidered flags for the Carlist army, ladies who would say an Our Father before fulfilling the intimate acts of the sacrament of matrimony and who saw love as a quasi-sacrifice in the service of the preservation of the species.

These contacts between different social atmospheres occasionally produced pathetic squalls. Still, in general the disasters they produced were nothing worse than a growing flexibility in certain lovely souls, a more peculiar cultivation of reckless behavior or of the unstoppable pursuit of the latest thing, and a more intense secretion in the glands of gossipmongers.

Straitlaced ladies, moralists, and priests preached against what had begun to be called the relaxing of customs. During the Dictatorship, with the aid of local authorities, bishops had imposed punishments and prohibitions with regard to women's clothing, how much skin could be revealed, and what things couldn't be done on beaches in the summer.

But despite the prohibitions and the spiritual exercises, what was emerging day by day was the temperament of a more physical, more sporty, more carefree, and, above all, less morally and economically conservative society. And it was not that this represented a rebellious stance, nor was it a rejection of principles. It was just something in the air. It was a system in evolution, and you could even say it happened in good faith. Attitudes and words that entailed a spark of audacity crept imperceptibly into the heart of even the most rigid houses.

With the advent of the Republic, that freedom of association took on an even more eccentric aroma. It was a potpourri of propaganda in favor of divorce and women's rights, a respect for personal merits that was not exactly under the control of the confessional, the relative muffling of the vociferations of the clergy, nudist and Bolshevik propaganda that circulated with impunity, the dissolution of the Jesuits, and the sense that adultery was not such a tragedy...Indeed, in certain nuclei, all this activated some very hardened tumors of protest and reaction. However, it gave ordinary, everyday people of lukewarm convictions, whose doctrine was limited to getting by, stronger lungs to breathe in whatever might present itself and a more tolerant retina that inclined them toward the refreshing new notion of keeping an open mind.

With the Republic, women of the merchant, middle, and petty bourgeois classes, who might have their own intellectual or journalistic leanings, or might be the daughters or wives of preeminent politicians, came to be fodder for community intrigues or the delicate foam of whisperings at five-pesseta tea parties. And these women might mix with some of the odalisques of the fallen regime who had painted their lips fire engine red to prowl the places of influence, either to try and captivate a public figure, or simply to strut their stuff.

In the society pages of the papers other ladies' names were added to the list of the two dozen top-drawer names approved by the arbiters of elegance. Having emerged from more modest temperatures, to position themselves for the social success they coveted, many abused the services of beauty institutes, stylists, magazine articles, gigolos, and eccentric cartwheels.

Ladies who had forsworn tea and taken up gin, would still perform a pantomime of disdain for Republican social climbers. Many ladies of the *ancien régime* stopped going to the Liceu opera house so as not to run into the families of the Republican authorities. It was a tame and thrifty sort of conspiracy.

But as we have said, ladies of a more conciliatory spirit, some of them the former clientele of the dictator's appetites, went over to the Republic. Under the pretext of concerts, art exhibits, charitable balls and cozier, more private parties, the snobberies of old were thrust together with the new.

All this exposition should serve to prepare the reader for the heterogeneous society that came together at the home of Níobe Casas, the dancer, a few nights after Josep Safont's debut at Hortènsia Portell's.

Níobe was the daughter of gypsies from Tarragona. As a child she had eaten grass and crushed tadpoles' heads amid the thorny and erotic vegetation that surrounds the *Pont del Diable*. That ancient aqueduct was known as Devil's Bridge because only the devil can build a bridge to last a thousand years. As long as she was making camp with the gypsies, she was no more significant than a coppery insect. A cat-eater like the rest of her family, at night she would lift her little pug nose to the stars and doze off in the company of a wicked and romantic cricket that would perch on the toasted parchment of her belly and sing songs to her.

One day, when the air held the peculiar pungent aroma of fox-tail amaranth, she was carried off in a sack. She spent days upon days confined in long indistinguishable rooms containing pianos, trapezes, horizontal bars, and other instruments of torture. When she was fifteen, not knowing where she came from or how, not knowing anything at all, she found herself dressed up in a tutu and dancing the "Dance of the Hours" in *La Gioconda*, at the Teatro di San Carlo in Naples.

But Níobe had ideas of her own, and an ambition that was as hard, red and shiny as a dove's heart cherry. It didn't take her long to find a Russian painter who ate mussels while listening to the guitars of Posilippo and hunted little scamps at a lira a head to replicate the intimate proclivities of the Emperor Tiberius. Níobe cast her tutu to the winds and coiled herself around the Russian's neck. He did her no harm, and he showed her how to twirl her spaghetti around her fork, and, en passant, the path to glory. Níobe made the leap to Moscow, and from Moscow to Paris, always coiled around the neck of someone who frequented fine restaurants. In Paris she became saturated with surrealism. The Countess of Noailles made her a gift of a pipe, and a woman from the Madrid aristocracy gave her a man's suit.

One day she realized that Paris was not good for her biliary secretions, and she ensconced herself in a cove on the Costa Brava to practice a little nudism in the company of two poets and two Pomeranians. From the Costa Brava she leapt to the Passeig de la Bonanova in Barcelona, where for four years now she has owned a bar, an operating room, and a swimming pool. At this point she began to host the heterogeneous society we recently mentioned.

Níobe Casas wasn't exactly sure why she was called Níobe, or why she was called Casas. As she tumbled from place to place she had used nomenclatures taken from botany, perfumery and distillery. In Barcelona she called herself Níobe Casas, and these two names were probably suggested to her by a professor of archaeology whose skin was as deeply tanned as his soul – much like the sand in the Swimming Club, to which the archaeologist was inseparably attached.

Physically, Níobe was sublime artifact. She was brown as a smoke-blackened pipe, with dark eyes that shone like a beetle's carapace with a near-violet metallic gleam. She had a brazen, somewhat brutish nose, broad at the base, a mouth from deep within a Gauguin painting, and hair like a great shock of platinum silk, as firmly disciplined by the comb a gigolo's. All of which made of Níobe's head an effigy to behold with squinting eyes, in a game of thrust and parry, while sucking in the rouged extract of heavenly savagery that radiated from her cheeks.

Níobe's body had nothing to do with humanity. Diminutive, compact, as tightly wound as a ball of twine, it bore a zoological kinship to a mongoose or to the mythical Madagascar maquis, half-human, half-ape. To a normal man's eyes, her arms and hips served up a paradox of attraction and repulsion. The fingers of her hands, long, black and slender, ended in ten silvery nails, a gaudy, horrible, offensive silver. Níobe wore a variety of clothes around the house. She was just as likely to wear pajamas pants with a nude torso, fastening around her breasts a pair of sporty goggles meant to be worn in a convertible, as a mechanic's overalls, or a long skirt paired with a discreet neckline. The décor of the apartment was done exclusively in glass and nickel, except for the piano, which was a standard Steinway. Her kitchen was the bar. Only cold food was served and drinks didn't stray from the Rips Bar book of cocktails, with illustrations by Paul Colin. As the reader can see, she lived and ate worse than a member of a chain gang. She spent many hours each day feeding tiny morsels of foie gras to her fish, or she sat by the swimming pool, wrapped in a terry cloth robe, wearing espadrilles with laces, blowing soap bubbles, chewing gum, or lying stretched out on the ground with a hot water bottle on her stomach.

Níobe spoke Catalan with a peculiar lisp, pronouncing her *esses* more like *shushes*, mixing in Gypsy expressions and French from la

Villette. She didn't practice any known religion and she made love exactly like an amoeba.

Níobe's dances had a relationship with the death penalty across climes and cultures. They were akin to industrial mechanics and the customs of insects. They required a minimum of music, a couple of South African chords and nothing more. She asserted that Stravinsky was a twit, and only barely tolerated Schönberg. She didn't wear any clothes at all when she danced; she would camouflage her skin, as they did with ships during the war. She did it with lively, matte colors, and more or less pre-Columbian motifs. If the audience required discretion, she would don the tiniest possible *cache-sexe* decorated with the wings of the Spanish fly. But if the audience was made up of regulars, she wore nothing.

All these delights made Níobe a powerful magnet for devotees of communism and transcendental nonsense. Níobe had two female friends: one was Amèlia Nebot, a young bourgeois woman who had left her husband to go off and study bel canto in Milan. She gave concerts at the Palau de la Música Catalana, wrote articles on feminism for radical weeklies, and attended a *penya*, a youth group devoted to cultivating cacti and to Soviet poetry. Among the members of that *penya* were two young sketch artists not precisely known for their virility. Amèlia Nebot was fat and common, and she practiced spiritualism. Níobe's other female friend, more an admirer than a friend, is already known to the reader: Teodora Macaia.

Teodora pressed for an invitation to one of Níobe's intimate gatherings, and never left. Teodora went to dinner with Níobe at the Colón and the Hostal del Sol. Níobe wouldn't touch anything but caviar and canned asparagus. Teodora wolfed her food down and, while she was at it, provided Níobe with new admirers. She introduced Níobe to Hortènsia Portell, but the widow didn't want anything to do with her. To her, the gypsy from Tarragona seemed like an overly crude tango.

With the coming of the Republic, Teodora let go even a little more than she had before. She had been separated from her husband for a long time now. She had an official lover. Not only that, when she went to Paris she spent her time chasing down chauffeurs. As Teodora came from one of the finest families, these things were no obstacle to her appearing at the forefront of all cultural and elegant solemnities. Teodora still had a welcoming voice and the bearing of a true lady. She was one of the few women left in Barcelona with whom a slightly skeptical gentleman could feel right at home.

For Teodora, admiration for Níobe was way to pass the time; for some of her female friends and relatives it was a reason to skin her alive.

Níobe kept an eclectic stew of admirers simmering. First among them was Professor Pinós. Pinós had studied Romance philology at Halle, and did a lot of work for the Fundació Bernat Metge for classical literature. His was the sappiest and most venal kind of erotic temperament. He was known to have some half dozen lovers, all forty or older. He spent all his time traveling to international conferences and eating at indigestible banquets. With the excuse of dancing a *chotis*, typical in Madrid, he would spend Sunday afternoons at the Ritz smelling every folkloric Spanish armpit that showed up. He attended all the rhythmic gymnastics festivals, was married to a nymphomaniac from Aragon, and had a son who wanted to be a priest.

Doctor Pinós compared Níobe Casas to the Orphic dancers, pre-Doric civilization, and Dionysian phallus worship. Níobe listened to him as if she were hearing a dog bark. He had tried to gain entry to the intimacy and delights of the gypsy woman, but Níobe would shrink back into her shell like the *Pagarus bernardus* crab; the only favor she would concede was to allow him to dive naked into her swimming pool and fish for a sponge with his teeth.

Her second admirer was Miquel, the essayist. Miquel was another academic full of twaddle. He made his living training typists in the ways of culture. Miquel was at the antipodes of an honorable man. Irascible and pedantic, he brooked no humor. Grafted onto his Catalan were strains of Homeric dialect and Argentine tango. Those who knew him asserted he was the most grotesque man in Barcelona.

Miquel adored Níobe, and had written fifty-two articles establishing parallels between the gypsy woman and Santa Teresa de Ávila. More than one young nincompoop who ventured to read this Molieresque charlatan would cut out his articles and read them to the poor wenches who went out to bare it all onstage at the Bataclán or the Moulin Rouge. Miquel the essayist also frequented the afternoon sessions at these places in the company of his wife, the daughter of a usurer, who had become more artful than her husband. With his wife's money, Miquel the essayist found a way to become a man of refinement without ever having to bend a single vertebra.

That night Miquel was going to read a longish essay on the thighs of Níobe Casas and the philosophy of imminent states. With all Miquel's philosophy, the most he came up with were garbled and unamusing obscenities that Amèlia Nebot found sublime.

Salazar the banker, whose parents were Castilian, was born in Roda. Rich, carefree, fat, and prone to laughter, he attended the session not so much to see the dancer as to see if he could get something going with Senyora Casulleres. One of Níobe's admirers was Renom, a deputy in Parliament, who was a lean, gray, and silent man. He had once secured funding for a dance recital that Níobe had done in the Palau de Projeccions theatre. He never lifted a finger after that, but he felt that gave him the right to spend hour after hour lying at Níobe's feet, with the face of a dessicated lion or tiger converted by the capitalist system into an expensive rug.

There were half a dozen poets at the session, too. Some of them were fine young men, unpretentious and full of good faith, who had no other defect than that of taking seriously the most poetic poet of them all, by the name of Sabartés. What Sabartés shared with Níobe was her blackness, but his was confined to his shirt, his cuffs, and his fingernails. Sabartés was a member of the *penya* of the desperate. He had pulled off forty-cèntim scams. Women would buy him half a *cafè au lait*. You could say he was the Barcelona equivalent of the kind of poetic bohemians who still frequent the Café Universal or the Café Colonial in Madrid. Sabartés performed in establishments off the Rambla; midway down Carrer Sant Pau, Carrer de la Unió, Carrer Nou, or Carrer d'Escudellers. However, he didn't dare pontificate as yet at the sidewalk café of the Lion or the Cafè del Liceu, or La Granja, or Gambrinus. The world of intellectuals who couldn't quite make it to the Rambla was quite sizeable at the time. Many had been to jail, and not precisely in the section reserved for political prisoners. Sabartés had not yet suffered this fate. In a word, he was a poor devil whose tongue and heart were made of pus. Two of the poets in Sabartés's orbit were members of the Swimming Club and owned a car, but they never let him ride in it.

Cascante, the musician, and Corminola and Saladrigues, the sketch artists, completed the one hundred per cent transcendental sector of the meeting. Saladrigues did lead pencil reproductions of well-known pornographic postcards at a very good price. Corminola only drew gas burners. The two of them were famous for something else, but they were both excellent young men. Cascante played exclusively for Níobe, and in the summer he played the saxophone under the tents at neighborhood and village fairs.

Alongside all those characters there were people like the Comte de Sallès. No one could ever have imagined how that delicate man would react to the Republic. When he saw the royal disaster, the count, who had been a close friend of the deposed king, and of the few kings still standing in Europe, had adopted an intelligent and tolerant attitude. Instead of making a fuss and rushing to dry the tears of the Marquesa de Perpinyà at the Portbou border crossing, the count betook himself to the Hotel Formentor in Mallorca in the company of a young Chilean woman. There he meditated copiously on love and politics, and after mulling it over a good while he decided that things weren't going all that badly and that the best thing an aristocrat could do was to aid in the consolidation of the Republic and advocate for full-blown Catalanism. Naturally he did neither of these things. On his return from Mallorca, he settled into an armchair at the Club Eqüestre and tickled his beard, just as he had always done. On the occasions when he took a break from his armchair, he would water the orchids in his garden and tend to his scientific correspondence. Teodora Macaia convinced him that Níobe was just the thing for him. The count, deferential and extremely polite to all the scoundrels and paupers who congregated around Níobe, opted for enthusiasm, wiping his British nose with a handkerchief and assuming a cosmetic smile that lasted all night long.

Another of those society admirers was Senyora Sabater, the wife of the prestigious politician of the same name who, as we said in previous pages, gave communist teas and recited her own poems between cookie and cookie. This woman had a very large head and was such a font of idiotic conversation that the two lovers she'd had didn't have the heart to extend the relationship beyond a month.

The most exultant of the Republican ladies, the one with the most opinions, the one who attained the greatest heights of verbal incoherence and wasn't afraid to shoot off her mouth on any topic at all, was Senyora Casulleres. Salazar the banker devoured her with his eyes. Senyora Rull and her daughters Adela and Conxita were particular friends of Níobe's. Adela and Conxita were fresh, doughy young women, with all the flavor of a legume salad, who were open to the generosity of any fingers in their vicinity.

Aside from Teodora Macaia there were a couple more whom the reader is familiar with: Conxa Pujol, the widow Baronessa de Falset, and Guillem de Lloberola. The baronessa was the last to arrive. Níobe allowed her to stroke her silvery fingernails gently, and soon after the concert began.

Amèlia Nebot, standing, and Cascante, sitting at the Steinway, interpreted the following program: "Berceuse juive," de Darius Milhaud; "Villancico del corazón asesinado por las penillas del alma," a cantata by Cuérnigas, an Andalusian composer; "Egloga piscatoria," by Respighi; "Rondeau," by Machault; and a sort of blues for saxophone, piano and voice by Sagristà. This fledgling musician had put music to a lyric from Ausiàs March, the Valencian renaissance poet who warned that only sad lovers need read his writings: *Qui no és trist de mos dictats no cur.* Young Sagristà was on the saxophone.

The audience listened to the concert with vehement passion and Pliocenic sadness. The favorite piece of the evening was the villancico.

When the concert began, Níobe fled so as not to have to listen to Amèlia Nebot, and to prepare for her own dances. She appeared cloaked in a trench coat of pumpkin-colored leather, which she quickly removed. She didn't end up entirely naked. Out of concern for the neophytes she had put on the Spanish fly cache-sexe. The paintings she had applied to her skin were pipes, Pernod bottles, decks of cards and bowler hats, all in black and white, interpreted in the cubist mode of Juan Gris.

Cascante never strayed from a single run of chords: an obsessive South African monotone he had come up with himself. According to experts, Cascante had lifted it from an American film titled *Trader Horn*. Níobe did three dances: *"La fumeuse d'étoiles," "Paprika,"* and *"L'artério-sclérose."* In the midst of this cosmic absurdity, Níobe had a few moments of graceful lubricity. All the considerable bulk of Miquel, the essayist, was sweating medulla and bay leaves. Some of the ladies were overcome, and they covered Níobe in kisses; their lips were left coated in cubist paint. Senyora Sabater declared that thanks to the Republic, Barcelona would come to be the most refined city in the world. Not even the Comtessa de Noailles had ever dreamt of such a jewel, such a feast for the eyes. The Comte de Sallés undertook to object, as he was a good friend of the Comtessa de Noailles and had attended a private screening of *L'âge d'or* at her home.

When the commentaries died down, Miquel the essayist, his face illuminated by a watermelon-red light, set to reading his mind-numbing piece. Níobe, Amèlia, Teodora, Senyora Sabater and the Comte made a great effort to read the papers. Ten minutes into the reading, all the air had left the room. But in the dark hallways of the Passeig de la Bonanova, amid clinical porcelains and atop examination tables, the entire crew of poets and idlers, including Conxita, Adela, and two married ladies, applied themselves to reproducing Níobe's dances. Off in a corner, one of Senyora Casulleres's nieces and Sabartés the poet channeled her rhythms in a much more human fashion. The niece let out a shriek like that of a wounded swallow.

Miquel the essayist was on page forty-three and the Comte de Sallès had still not lost his polite composure. When the essayist finished, the whole apartment trembled in a Sardanapalian shudder. Salazar the banker had not wasted any of his time with Senyora Casulleres. Níobe was pleased with her success.

The widow Baronessa de Falset was the first to take her leave, escorted by Guillem de Lloberola. They got into the baronessa's car and went to a studio on Carrer de Casanova.

On the way, Guillem said to the baronessa:

"I don't know how you put up with this rubbish. Never again, I swear, never. You're a big girl. If you find these things entertaining, you can go by yourself. I'm not going to be part of it. I can understand why Teodora would enjoy it. She's played all her cards, it would be hard for her to find someone who treated her as she might like, so naturally she's not very particular about where she finds her entertainment. But you...You're much too intelligent, too thoughtful, to mix with all this scum.

People with a little taste and common sense just laugh all of this off. Níobe is no one and nothing. Any tart who dances in a music hall is cleverer than she is. If it weren't for Miquel's pedantic articles no one would even know she existed. Have you ever seen such a pompous ass? Do you think such claptrap should be tolerated in times like this? After all, who are these people who decided that Níobe was a sensation? Is there a single serious person among them? Teodora, poor Teodora, just wants to be in vogue...what does she know? And Professor Pinós is a fool, and Casulleres an idiot! Do you think I enjoy hearing a bunch of chars and gossips pretending to be refined? No,

I swear, never again. Ask what you want of me, but not this. When I see you smile and take an interest in trashy pornography like this Níobe, you seem ridiculous, disgusting..."

The more overwrought Guillem got, the cruder his language got, and the widow baronessa drew first her neck, then her cheek, then her lips close to Guillem's lips. Swayed by the perfection of her skin, Guillem loosened up until all his cholera dissolved into closed eyes and a slow kiss.

———·———·———

AFTER THE SUICIDE OF the Baró de Falset, Guillem's life began to make sense to him. That dose of cold water to his pectorals flushed the lymph from his soul. Till then he had been a child playing at perversity. When he came to, he entered a danger zone: he could sink into a grotesque remorse, continuing to behave like a debauched child, as before, but now with the sham of tears and smarmy cowardice. There was also the danger of his accepting in good faith that he had been the murderer of the Baró de Falset. Fortunately, a well-timed cold shower had made a man of him. Not a good man, by any means. Guillem carried all the mildew of the Lloberola family in his heart.

When Guillem had been with Conxa Pujol at the stylist's house, he had perceived a magnificent body, a dazzling criolla. But other things interfered. The affair was too base and contemptible for Guillem's thoughts to have been elevated toward a luminous sphere.

It wasn't until Hortènsia Portell's party that Guillem understood who the baronessa was. He had had to see the reaction the woman produced in an elegant cage. To see how men's virility responded to the sight of her, the admiring tremble in their eyes, the contained desire in their breath. He had had to observe how the baronessa took a punch in that silent, polite sexual bout, to see how her arms, her lips and her diamonds counterpunched, giving no ground, dashing every hope. It was there, in her evening gown, with all the restraint of formal dress, and all her solitary strength, without the shameful appendix of her husband, that the Baronessa de Falset fully revealed herself to a young man who, camouflaged in the scouring rags of sordid abjection, had still been able to appreciate like no one else there the full effect of the implacable tragedy of a beautiful woman. That night Guillem's true struggle began. He had no baggage, for this combat was non-existent, because Guillem's familiarity with the baronessa was limited to two afternoons, and nothing more. Guillem didn't know what kind of beast he was risking his happiness on. With Conxa Pujol Guillem had only his instincts to rely on, and Conxa was no ordinary woman.

The death of her husband had almost scuttled the whole thing, but Guillem's ambitions found the right response. His pain was evaporating; the specter of the Baró de Falset had disappeared. In his insomnia, Guillem never again felt the presence of that cadaver by his side, snoring lubriciously, with a thread of blood trickling from the bullet hole. In his moments of insomnia, in the place of that terrifying neighbor Guillem sensed by his side a dense bouquet of gardenias with the smell of a woman.

The baronessa had been a widow for three months. The scandal of her husband's suicide had been the subject of much and varied commentary. In some conversations, people had gotten pretty warm, coming fairly close to the motive behind the catastrophe. But it was only in a vague way, with no precise details, because in point of fact none of them knew anything beyond the ravings of the baron a few days before he put the bullet in his head. It was natural that no one lent any credence to these ravings, because everyone thought the baron had gone mad. The cause of his mental disorder was a secret known to only one person, and this person, as we have said, kept silent at the time and forever after. After the first stage, things began to be forgotten. The widow baronessa slowly began to regain her own natural color and the characteristic color of her makeup. Teodora, Hortènsia, and other friends kept her company. She found ways to distract herself and not speak of the tragedy. In her heart of hearts, Conxa had been freed of the most disagreeable weight upon her life and began breathing freely. Her black mourning clothes made her all the more fascinating.

Three months after the suicide, Guillem de Lloberola pounced. The baronessa hardly knew him. At the Ritz and at Hortènsia's party, Guillem had only crossed a few words with her. He was just one among the very many, and he supposed that Conxa would not remember him.

The way he approached Conxa was not at all dramatic. He stopped her in the middle of the street, positioning himself by her side, like those ne'er-do-wells who go after the first girl who comes along, trying to start a dialogue that rarely goes beyond a sad, brief monologue, because the woman doesn't even bother to turn her head. Guillem did just that, in front of a shop window, when Conxa stopped to examine some refrigerators. For a practitioner of storefront eroticism, the objects that had caught Conxa's interest in the shop window would have offered an opportunity to speak of the cold shoulder and the frozen heart of an insensitive woman. Guillem almost succumbed to the temptation of the visual suggestions and images, but he didn't say any of those things. He simply showed her a fifty-pesseta bill, assuring her that he had seen it fall from her purse. Conxa glanced at her purse, the clasp in place. She opened it, checked the money in it, and thanked Guillem, insisting he was mistaken.

Guillem didn't budge from his stubborn insistence on giving her the bill. Not understanding his determination, Conxa laughed in his face, just to have something to do. Guillem looked down and turned cherry red. Conxa found the situation amusing and asked him, with no little aplomb:

"Sir, do you pull this trick with the fifty-pesseta bill with all the ladies?"

Guillem raised his eyes and, facing her with the full brunt of his insolence, responded:

"Not all of them, no. If I think they are worth less than fifty pessetes, I show them a twenty-five pesseta bill; and if I think they're worth less than five duros, I take care not even to notice them."

Right up until the last word, Conxa hadn't recognized him, but the fact was, they had been introduced. What was his name…? Not losing her composure, and even being rather pleasant, she added:

"Listen here, I know you…your name is…"

"Yes, senyora. My name is Guillem de Lloberola. I had the pleasure of meeting you the day…"

"Do you mind telling me what angel inspired you to attempt something so crass with a lady you…"

"It was no angel! I have done this thing you call crass in the hope that you would not recognize me, wouldn't remember me at all. It was within the realm of possibility not to be recognized. The dark, the suddenness of my approach, worked in my favor. And I thought… well, that you, a lady whom everyone knows, and everyone is familiar with, might perhaps, how shall I put it, enjoy running into a man who not only didn't recognize her, but even took her for a…"

"How bizarre…"

"No, senyora, it is entirely natural. It's so normal, in fact, as to be embarrassing, because your opinion of me…I mean, I have no interest in your taking me for a big shot or for an idiot. Your opinion doesn't matter to me at all…"

"Well, then, what it is you're after? I don't understand this whole business. Why have you taken the trouble to…"

"It was an act of kindness, senyora, pure kindness…"

"Kindness?"

"Yes, senyora, to give you a little thrill, a moment of distraction…"

"I don't understand."

"Naturally, senyora. I said it was a 'kindness,' and I am not backing down. I didn't do it in my own interest, but in yours, yours entirely. It's quite simple. I can imagine how unbearable it must be for a person like you to play this incessantly passive role in the game of admiration and enthusiasm. To be known to everyone, and now, after your husband's suicide, even more well known, and more highly esteemed. I imagine it must be a torment for you (well, perhaps torment is an exaggeration, but it must be tedious, at very least) to realize that you can never stop playing this one role, and that when you meet someone you have no choice but to put on this mask that others have assigned you. Because, if you are beautiful and interesting, and I am not denying that, of course, your interest and your beauty and your elegance become a sort of cliché, something everyone takes for granted, and this voice of everyone and general admiration and popularity – even if no aspect of the term 'popular' is exact or apt, in your case – are the elements that make up your way of being, or the role you play. And you are a slave to it all, to what you are and to what others have added to your innate prestige. There is absolutely no escape for you. At first, when one becomes cognizant of this power, of the power of this kind of stature, I have no doubt it must be rather amusing. But later, a person with all your gifts has to tire of it, and lose all pleasure in it, in this constant enthusiasm, in the acclaim and desire you see in everyone's eyes. Look here, Baronessa, I am sure that a king, for example, or an eminent man, who enjoys extraordinary popularity, must feel the desire to evade his majesty or his fame and one day have the pleasure of not being recognized by anyone, or respected or admired by anyone, of being just an anonymous person walking down the street. Do you see? And a woman like you is a player in this prestige of royalty. Most of the men who approach you, do so from below, like dogs, one could say, the same way they would approach a king or a genius, the same way they treat men who have such a public, notorious figure that they cannot escape their own skins, no matter how much they would like to. Baronessa, since I consider you to be a sensitive person, I imagine this is to some extent the way you must feel as well. And hence, believe me, my motive was not to be crass, but to be monstrous, to be atrocious, in pretending that I didn't know who you were. It was out of kindness, senyora, that I wanted you to have the delight (perhaps I am mistaken, my dear senyora, but I think there must be some delight on your part) of seeing that a man like me, a man from Barcelona who doesn't seem to be some kind of hayseed, not only doesn't recognize you, not only offers you the thrill of ceasing to be la Senyora Baronessa, Viuda de Falset (please note, senyora, that I have called you 'widow'), but rather takes her for a woman who can be bought, whom I think I can buy for fifty pessetes. In doing this, senyora, I am doing you the kindness, the immense service, of allowing you a change of personality, of granting you a way to leave behind that skin beautified for the admiration of all who know you to be the Baronessa de Falset, so that you can put on the skin of a common prostitute, in a world as far away as possible from yours, breathing an air that you will never, ever, be able to breathe. Never! Do you see? By saying that crass thing I said, I was opening a new door for you. Your curiosity would have shown me whether the door was tempting or not. I know that you, and not your curiosity, will say that never in this life could a door like that be tempting, and as a favor to me you will say I've gone mad, that is if you are forgiving or merciful enough not to say right off the bat that I am a scoundrel, or simply indecent. But that's what the lady playing her role would say, not what sincerity would say, don't you see? Not the intimate truth of a woman obliged to act in a play, and who finds this act to be a burden…"

"Excuse me…"

"Yes…"

"Well, this is all very…bizarre…and, indeed, it is all very interesting…"

"I haven't quite finished, senyora."

"But it's getting late, you know. I would be pleased to go on listening, but…"

"Well, when you are not in a hurry, I am at your disposal to finish my explanation…"

"Tomorrow at five?"

"Perfect. Where?"

"On Gran Via, at the corner of Carrer del Bruc…Is that all right?"

Guillem de Lloberola kissed the baronessa's hand, and she noticed a slight dampness on her skin. Even though it was now quite dark, when Guillem raised his head, the baronessa could see that his eyes were full of tears.

Guillem was quite pleased with himself. His relatively Pirandellian monologue – Pirandello was in vogue in Barcelona in those days – very possibly may have made an impression on the baronessa.

If Guillem's vague knowledge of Conxa Pujol's flesh of had included a few of the tidbits of information that came up as we told the tale of Hortènsia Portell's party in the first part of this story, if he had known of the forbidden escapades and whoring pursuits of his idol, perhaps he wouldn't have played up that bit about the world "as far away as possible from yours" or that other bit about the "new door."

If Conxa Pujol had not been something more than a mere dilettante, or a simple chlorotic tourist of the kind who are roused by the *gabinetto pornografico* of the National Museum of Naples and don't go any farther, in a word, if Conxa Pujol had not been exactly who she was, she might simply have called a cop at the start of Guillem's aggressive and insolent speech. Accustomed to more slimy and much more dimwitted admirers than Guillem, Conxa Pujol felt neither slighted nor persuaded, and the following day she showed up punctually for their appointment.

With a precision that even he was astounded by, Guillem continued tacking back and forth between a literary cynicism full of anisette and arnica and the genuine and childlike passion of a sardana dancer. After ten months at this game, Conxa agreed to undress in his presence and get into bed with him. For the time being, Conxa was fairly persuaded and Guillem began to come into his own. The fact that the body of the widow baronessa was a magic box, with all the springs and trap doors of the most corrosive voluptuosity in the hands of a talented juggler, would not have been sufficient to make Guillem feel so swallowed up, so evaporated amidst the leaves of that sublime agave. It was Conxa's disconcerting, bewildering, and tormenting mind that infused Guillem's cheeks with the burning pallor of an impassioned pilgrim. Conxa was half-persuaded, for the moment, because that was precisely what she wanted: a man in a constant feverish state, a perpetually aroused sexuality, forever initiating more devious snares, aspiring to more effective tricks, like a hunter of impossible monsters, and always with that air of defeat combined with a hope of triumph. Because Conxa always slipped away. There was no way he could dominate that undulating perfumed weakness. If for a moment he sensed he was dominating her, she would elude him through the most impracticable crevices. Sometimes the crevice would consist of all the profound brutality of a monosyllable spoken tenuously with the phonetics of an angel. Sometimes it was simply a puff of air from her lungs that Conxa, closing her mouth, would direct through her nose, accompanied by a vitreous, absent gaze and the mere beginnings of a smile, but it would sink into Guillem's heart like a ferret's incisors. Guillem found himself in all of this, because the only justification he could find for the monotonous activity of sex was the anxiety of contingency, the constant playing and losing, the stimulus of defeat, and that stuff of hatred and destruction veiled by a gelatin of tears that makes the skin of male and female creatures interesting. All in all, what each felt at the core of the other was a touch of sadism. Guillem was inured to the life of a successful gigolo. He had aplomb and utter self-confidence. Desperately virile, he was also desperately feminine. He had an unfathomable facility for adapting to the detail and the nuance of all the women he had contact with. An ordinary prostitute could find in him the same base echo of meticulous wickedness and rouged gossip that she could have found in a fellow prostitute. He was the ideal character to dally with a woman and sweet talk her. He never moved too fast, he always sensed the perfect moment. He displayed lovely absences, delicate reluctance, and a cool and tender passivity in awaiting the right move. He wasn't easily put off, he wasn't jealous, and he was willing to play roles that a more resolute man who wants to pay and wants to dominate would never tolerate. Discreet and reserved in his triumphs, he had a fertile imagination when it came to lying. And all of this came hand in hand with an unquestionable charm and a reliable and accommodating physiology.

This aptitude for conquest had given Guillem a very bad opinion of women. All he saw in them was the part that served his selfish ends: their likelihood of succumbing to Guillem's prestige. All they represented for him was their purely animal aspect of adoration or of jealousy; he appreciated them for their skin and for their intimate reactions, and that was it. Guillem had never been in love, and at times he wondered if he was even capable of falling in love, of feeling that profound luxuriance, lyrical with anguish, enthusiasm, and sidereal scintillation that he imagined love to be. Women had never provided Guillem the opportunity to infuse a little spirituality into his flesh, at least not the women he had dealt with so far. Sensitive as he was, the young man was perfectly aware of all that, aware even of how he had been brutalized by his conquests. He was running the risk of becoming a physiological machine mounted on a dissatisfied spirit. Despite his youth, he already had an excess of experience. The time for great emotional arias had passed him by; his weakness for debauchery and his lack of scruples had shielded his skin with a layer of skepticism. Guillem saw all this with no little melancholy. Another young man would have considered the profusion and diversity amassed in his erotic register to be of inestimable value. And it is not that Guillem derived no satisfaction from it, but he was beginning to feel fatigued, to find no merit in it, and to discover all the gray brushstrokes of monotony. So, the presence of Conxa Pujol renewed him. His fear of failure, his loss of confidence in himself, his need to refine all his powers in order to dominate an elusive skin, his pain at uncertainty, his renewed self-respect, his secret tears, the sensorial density of their encounters, and above all the superior perfume of the inconsistent and contradictory biology he was engaging with his muscles and his breath offered Guillem the possibility of something that, if nothing more, was a reasonable simulacrum of the flaming vestments of a true, pathetic love.

On occasion, powerless to unravel her mystery, in the face of her unceasing battle, Guillem had suspected that Conxa Pujol would never entirely surrender herself to him or to any man. Physically, this woman's case was not one of coldness or indifference; quite the contrary. Guillem sensed volcanic possibilities in her that he, however, had not managed to ignite. Nor could he accept the thesis that the baronessa belonged to that species of women whose sensibilities have been drained by constant and varied brutalization. A woman who was married at such a young age to the man she had been married to, and who until now had not been known to have a lover, led one to suppose a more or less undamaged temperament. Guillem would have liked to connect their present intimacies with those two shameful episodes in which he had taken part, but those episodes did not offer any pattern. One would have had to know the extent of the baronessa's intention in all of that. One would have to separate her responsibility from her husband's with great care, and that was impossible. In moments of obfuscation and defeat, when Guillem thought his desire was unattainable, he came very close to confessing to the baronessa. He tried to explain his double personality with perfect cynicism, but he realized that such an explanation would probably have closed all doors to him. As unusual as the baronessa was, Guillem was not certain how she would react on learning that this Guillem de Lloberola was the very same derelict her dressmaker had procured for her. Later on, when Conxa yielded, when an absolute intimacy had been established between the two of them, in moments of depression Guillem once again felt the desire to produce a dramatic effect by recounting to the baronessa the details of Dorotea's "scene of the crime." But then, too, he held back, and was assailed by yet another doubt: what if what he had accepted in good faith, his certainty that the baronessa had not recognized him, were just an illusion? Guillem came to fear that Conxa, much more astute than her departed husband and with a sharper memory, had been dissembling, had turned a blind eye, on recognizing Guillem de Lloberola to be the same subject procured by her dressmaker. This aspect of Guillem's fear was groundless, because Conxa Pujol never recognized him nor did she suspect for a moment that Guillem had been a party to those secret events.

As we were saying, Guillem imagined that Conxa would never truly surrender herself, to him or to any man. Guillem began to fear that in the mystery of his lover there was another woman, and that all her fissures and evasions and the unassailable integral possession of her body, her soul, her will, and even her unhappiness could only be understood as a natural or acquired corruption of her temperament. He feared Conxa was a lesbian, and that the fullness of her passion would never belong to him, because Conxa was saving it for a woman.

The fear of lesbianism in the life of "ladykillers" is one of the most ludicrous and unfounded. When a man who considers himself irresistible sees that a woman does not utterly give in to him, and retains a mystery that he cannot divine, he soon accuses the woman of an abnormal vice. The pride or vanity of men often leads them to see things, and in the case of the baronessa, Guillem was definitely seeing things. Conxa was bizarre and perverse, with a perplexing temperament, but she considered intimacy with another woman to be unequivocally disgusting.

This was not where danger lay. Conxa assented to Guillem's fever, in part just because, and in part because Guillem seemed different from her other admirers. The rudeness of Guillem's first dialogue allowed her to glimpse a "case study." A "case study" like those she had pursued through her own deformation and her adventures between abject sheets. Conxa dreamed that perhaps Guillem could provide for her what she had achieved by "slipping into someone else's skin" – that is, by doing precisely what Guillem had proposed she do in his monologue – without any need for her to undergo a metamorphosis, and accepting her as the widow of a millionaire cotton merchant and baron. Conxa realized, though, that despite his bookish cynicism, when push came to shove he was just as inexpert as the other pretty boys who infected her environment. What's more, the baronessa was able to perceive in her intimate dealings with Guillem that he had only been involved with women who were utterly lacking in substance. In her logbook of adventures, Conxa had recorded a night in Hamburg, in the company of a fascinating savage, on which she had experienced the complete detachment of body and soul and the most fiery of spasms. Each of the savage's gestures was unforeseeable and a work of art. Conxa had not had many experiences like that. She was not so foolish as to believe that this was something that could be found around any corner, or, even more, that a person from Guillem's environment and education could provide such a thing. She didn't demand this of him, but, if nothing more, she did want him to discover her, to feel his way with her. Since Guillem didn't make her feel the way she hoped, the baronessa always maintained the upper hand with him. She disconcerted and humiliated him, and laughed at him in moments when a man is incapable of laughing, in those intimate moments when laughter is worse than an insult and exposes all the grotesquerie of an incandescent physiology. Desperate, Guillem could not by any means shake off his fascination with Conxa Pujol. He was unrecognizable. His apprehensions began to draw blood. And Conxa sustained this unbearable state with feigned tenderness and facile concessions, only to retreat to aloofness and withdrawal, baring the most inhuman teeth of the femme fatale, all in the hope that Guillem would find his way to where she hoped he would go, instinctively and under his own impetus.

Something even worse made it impossible for Guillem to get to where Conxa would have liked him to go. It was his adoration of Conxa's beauty. She was so marvelously assembled, the quality of her skin and her countenance were so otherworldly, that Guillem was left feeling openmouthed and unworthy in her presence. When he embraced her, the emotion Conxa produced in him suffused his nerves with all the vacillations and clumsiness of a novice. And so, what for a normal and tenderly feminine woman would have been cause for absolute surrender and an exchange of panting and secret melody between the man and the woman, was, in the case of Conxa Pujol, a disgusted desperation and a cause for laughter that shamed the disappointed lover.

To the eye of a cold observer, Conxa could have appeared on those occasions to be a pure and simple vixen. In truth, Conxa's suffering and desire were just as strong as Guillem's. If she had confessed her erotic ideal, and Guillem had attempted to satisfy it, perhaps then Conxa could have experienced moments more to her liking, but they would have come about artificially. To satisfy her, Guillem would have donned a disguise that she had suggested. Conxa, to her own recollection, was too good a collector of authentic brutalities to be content with the dramas and farces of a luxury bordello. To confess would be unworthy. Conxa possessed the romantic kind of dignity that required that a woman never reveal anything, allowing herself to be ravished with closed eyes and clenched teeth. Any other way was not amusing.

At the start of their intimate relationship, Conxa and Guillem saw each other at most once a week, in a secret place no one would ever discover. Neither he nor she offered any reason to suspect their liaison. This state of affairs went on for at least two years after the baron's suicide. Always unsatisfied and more and more enamored of Conxa Pujol, Guillem underwent every imaginable torment. He always affected great dignity in her presence; he spoke very little of his family and his life before her, and this made it easier to keep her from learning about the sad economic situation they faced.

After those two years of battle, Conxa began to be aware of Guillem's failure. At the outset, Guillem had been in his element because the anxiety Conxa produced in him was the only justification he could find for the monotony of sex, yet he also realized his anxiety was to no avail, and Conxa was, indeed, unassailable.

At this disappointing juncture, an exceedingly ordinary event changed things absolutely. In even the most abnormal or absurd erotic dramas, a decisive role is often played by an element as pedestrian and unliterary as money.

A diffuse ill humor suffused Guillem's digestive system, assaulting his head and giving him no quarter. For days now he had abandoned the fantasy of possessing Conxa. She had become inured to his constant adoration and he knew all the hospitable facets of his lover's skin by heart. Guillem required a large amount of money. Not because he was in debt or otherwise compromised, but for the pleasure of having it and spending it. He got it into his head that it was precisely that woman, with whom he had always been unfailingly polite, who ought to give it to him. It amused him to stand before Conxa in the guise of an unscrupulous profiteer. Maybe this would be the pretext for a definitive breakup that would put an end to their misery.

With utter sangfroid, and in the presence of her nudity, he asked Conxa for money. Conxa eyes lit up, and she said she would be delighted to give him whatever he asked, and he shouldn't deny himself a thing. Guillem found strange not only Conxa's excessive generosity but also the fact that she considered his request to be so natural. Soon, though, Conxa's attitude shifted, and using language Guillem had never heard from her before, she launched into a sarcastic monologue. She informed him that his style of lovemaking was too puerile for him to be asking for money for his services, but despite this she didn't mind giving him whatever he needed, and even keeping him, and paying for shirts and socks for him that were more elegant than the ones he usually wore. She said she looked upon him as a boy, for whom she was beginning to feel a kind of maternal affection, but as a gigolo he was a dud.

Guillem had suffered this kind of humiliation before, but never with such ferocity and malice. And that day, Guillem was incensed. So, when Conxa finally ran out of steam with her immoral tatters, Guillem rose to his feet before her. All his muscles were tense and flushed with blood. Conxa summoned him with an icy smile and, without so much as by your leave, he gave her two slaps in the face with all his might. Conxa blanched, but she resisted the blows without the slightest peep of protest, just a deep sigh that dilated her ribcage and made the erect tips of her breasts stand upright. Guillem saw a mysterious breath that resembled her soul begin to emerge from between her lips. The glass of his lover's eyes was no longer hard; her pupils had a more liquid, more human consistency; her cheeks had turned a cadaverous white, and her rouge marked a rough discontinuous patch on her bloodless skin. Guillem was furious, and he followed the first two slaps with a direct blow to her mouth; her lips contracted in pain, but then immediately reacted with a weak and exceedingly tender smile of complete beatitude. Conxa sank back onto the bed, and Guillem, his spine rigid as a cat's, felt a burning liquor running through his medulla, perhaps the contained rage of his two years of failure, perhaps the atavic memory of a Lloberola who in days of yore had eaten human flesh.

Guillem sank his teeth into her shoulder. Conxa howled with a bestial enthusiasm, and both he and she experienced the most important erotic moment of their lives.

Conxa's night in Hamburg had had nothing on this. Like a marvelous sea anemone found at water's bottom, with wary contractile antennae full of corrosive viscosities that open up at a given moment and expand in a multicolored swoon that brings to mind perfectly denatured chrysanthemums and perfectly artificial orchids, so was the soul of that woman, and her sex and her ferocity and her joy and her enthusiasm and her tenderness began to liquefy, released and rendered in a gelatinous mystery of effusion, in a sighing melody beyond physiology, in a perspiration perfumed with the whole gamut of ultramarine atavisms and dark nights lit by the glow of shooting stars. Her skin, till now dry, insatiable, and cold as the belly of an iguana, was now softened, porous, hot, drenched by the thousands of internal arterioles that follow the rhythm of sincerity, that hold fast to the skin of men, and communicate from one heart to another all the anguish concentrated in the moments of sterile orgasm and unsatisfied desire.

Guillem and Conxa got up from bed certain of their triumph. Without a word or a comment. Everything that had just happened to them had nothing to do with the world of logic. Nor did it have anything to do with the world of physiology. It would be very sad to have to stop believing that in the skin of men and women there is occasionally something like a flash of divinity, in which gods mingle with monsters, and the gods laugh delicately at morality and reason.

The following day Guillem received double the amount he had demanded of his lover. Guillem did not attempt to refuse it, or even to say thank you. He kept the money, just as a wolf would have done.

From that time on, Guillem was Conxa's absolute master. Little by little her temperament and his underwent a change. Conxa began day by day to feel more tender, more feminine, more inferior; Guillem, in contrast, felt more and more self-possessed, he recovered his aplomb, his coldness and his hard surface. Guillem's disdain distressed the baronessa, but she could no longer do without him. After the first inebriation, Conxa no longer had the strength to judge or analyze. In her eyes, Guillem became more worthy of adoration by the day. Conxa tasted the bitter effects of jealousy and came to know the entire gamut of tears.

Their relationship went on in secret and Guillem exploited Conxa in every way. When Don Tomàs de Lloberola died, Conxa and Guillem's situation was that of a woman ruined by passion and a common gigolo.

At this point, Conxa began to lose her shame, and on occasion she appeared in his company in public; the woman in her circle saw nothing wrong with it. Conxa always denied it, but everyone knew the truth.

Guillem de Lloberola, more and more independent of and distant from his family, came to be a fashionable figure. His economic future was assured.

———·——

"THE ENTRYWAY WAS probably right there: natural stone, no paint, no plaster, no mixtures. The ashlars must have come from the Gusi quarry, or maybe even farther away. The blocks of stone were lashed with straps to the backs of the very hairy men who transported them. The backs and the kidneys of those men must have made a cracking sound, like a snapping tendon, with every step they took. They would stop only to breathe and to scratch the hair on their chests. Between the hairs there was sand and clay and crushed fleabane leaves and maybe a grasshopper scraping at their nipples with the saw of its legs. As they flicked the grasshopper off with a fingernail, and wiped the sweat from their eyes, they would feel a prick on their thighs, and it would be a boxwood goad with an iron spike that had no other purpose than to poke men's thighs. It was wielded by a long, lean man with bad lungs. From time to time those pricks sliced through the flesh and did real harm. At night some of the thighs slashed by the boxwood goad would swell up terribly, and the wounded man would get dry mouth and see red lights flashing, and begin to wail. The other men who were packed in beside him, sleeping flesh against flesh under a big overhang on top of a couple of blades of straw and nothing more, would land a good punch on him and the wound would swell even more. The following day they would find him dead and no one would take the trouble to bury him. They had too much work hauling ashlars. They would toss his body out in back, probably in Mr. Domingo's gully. There he would be eaten by ants, praying mantises, beetles and earwigs. Herons would take a little taste and no more. Herons built their nests in that wasteland, which at the time was full of black pines."

"The men who hauled the stone on their backs must not have been from here. Some had spent ten years in the galleys, others, even more. Their skin was tough. They were petty criminals, the kind who stole a wineskin full of sweet *vi ranci* or grabbed a girl by the leg and had at it on a haystack. All in all, they were men who were only good for lugging rocks. If they hadn't been able to haul the ashlars from the Gusi quarry as someone prodded their thighs, they surely would have died of sorrow. These things were natural in those days."

"How many hands high must the wall in front have been? Who knows! Above the main entrance were the arrow slits. There was a bit of a moat and a drawbridge. Though no sign of any of this remains, it was impossible for there not to have been a drawbridge."

"To raise such a castle no few years were necessary, and perhaps more than a hundred infected legs. It had to be this way; this was the way of the times."

"It must have been terribly cold inside the castle. Who knows if the chimney had been invented. Probably. What they hadn't invented yet were the brazier and the bed warmer. Portable foot warmers came much later. Inside, the walls were also bare stone. They probably didn't spend much money on wall hangings, because our tapestry, which was from France, was from many years later, the sixteenth century, I think, and tapestries weren't even produced in Spain until later."

"What must the first Senyor de Lloberola to wander the corridors of this castle have been like? He didn't yet use our shield. The three wolves and three pines. According to Papà, this shield is from the seventeenth century. Papà was exaggerating; I think it must be much older. If not, what's the point?"

"After the first Senyor de Lloberola must have come the second, the third, the fourth, perhaps up to twenty or thirty…No, thirty is too many. Thirty generations would mean seven hundred years. The Lloberolas must have lived here two or three hundred years at most. When a son was born, they would no doubt bring in a wet nurse from Moià, or from some neighboring masia that owed them vassalage. It would be interesting to know whether they also inserted a clove of garlic into the umbilical cords of the Senyors of Lloberola and tied them up with the lacings from an espadrille as they still do in some farm houses even now. That must be a very ancient custom, and the pagesos probably learned it from the senyors."

"I think the first Senyor de Lloberola, or the second, it doesn't matter, must have been terribly bored. As a matter of fact, they must not have been much good for anything. They probably had never in all their lives so much as picked up a blade of straw from the ground, just like papà. When it came to not doing a stitch of work, papà was every inch a senyor. When he died, his nose didn't turn yellow. It was just as red and swollen as when he was alive; maybe even more. It must have been just the same with these folks up here. Maybe it will also be like that with me, though my nose is finer and more noble than my father's was…"

"In any case, to be a Lloberola back then was more interesting than to be who I am, for example. To be a Senyor de Lloberola in a position to dispose of the life and property of others rather than smelling the stench of the hallways in that apartment on Carrer de Bailèn! They're not going to see much more of me in that apartment. Here you have the smell of the stables, but it is all more ventilated…To be a Senyor de Lloberola! A Senyor de Lloberola!…All these thoughts I'm thinking are a little ridiculous, but sort of thrilling, too. For one's blood to be tied to these stones, to this history…No matter what the newspapers say…No matter that President Companys and the *rabassaires* have decided that the master should no longer receive his shares of the crops…Tenant farmers!…*Rabassaires!*…Oh, if only one could…If only one had the Civil Guard at his disposal…The only good thing papà did in all his life was to die in time not to see all this nastiness…The Republic! A bunch of crooks! What the devil! For all I'm going to see of this…Bring on the *rabassaires*, bring on Companys himself! They can have it all. But not the house, the house no, that's ours to keep, I mean mine to keep…Of course the house isn't, shall we say, very old…Papà said it was from the eighteenth century. I can't really tell…In any case, I don't care if it's from the eighteenth century, you can lead a much better life, much better, than in that apartment in Barcelona…Let them have it!…They're the kind who breathe better in an apartment. My children don't understand all this…They're more like their mother…I'm still a Senyor de Lloberola, after all, yes indeed! Lloberola is a diminutive of *llobera*, which means wolf's den… at least I think it does. So Lloberola is a little den…everything is little: little wolves, little den. That's what we are, wolves with no food, with dull claws, with no courage…I've always felt that the Lloberolas were cowards. But why? We're like everyone else. The difference between us and all the rest of the cowards is that we are still senyors. Not people who think they're senyors, but actual senyors! We have a sort of seigneurial delicacy…A disregard…Nowadays what used to be called disdain is called disregard…Catalan is a horrible language; or rather, the Catalanists have made it horrible…They will never be senyors, not them!…What do you have to say about all this? What do you think, standing there drooling, with that expression on your face? Answer me? Am I not a true Lloberola?…"

His only response was a long, drawn-out "Moooooo…" because the creature being interpellated by that historical, political, and philological commentary was none other than a cow who was chewing on a few blades of tender Johnson grass. What remained of the supposed castle of the Lloberolas were a few vague reminiscences of a dry stone wall, in an untended field overlooking the masia.

Frederic's imaginings upon the story of those stones may be perfectly gratuitous. That pile had probably never been a castle, nor had it belonged to a Lloberola. It is possible that none of it was medieval, and it was just a piece of a big ramshackle house, abandoned, like so many in the landscape of this land, to end up as shelters for cattle and farm animals and points of encounter between lizards and brambles. It was Don Tomàs who discovered, no one knows how or with what tools of erudition, that that was in fact the castle of the Lloberolas, the lords of that stretch of land since the mid-twelfth century. The Lloberolas clearly had been rich pagesos, farmers who three centuries earlier had come to occupy the masia now known as Can Lloberola. The farmhouse had previously belonged to some other farmers whose name was Sitjar, and one of the first daughters to inherit – the firstborn daughter, la pubilla Sitjar – had married a Lloberola son, but not the firstborn. The firstborn Lloberola of the time died without progeny and all his property was absorbed by the owner of the farmhouse where Frederic lived with the masovers, the caretakers who looked after the mas.

Early in the 18th century, the Lloberolas went to take up residence in Barcelona, and that was when the King Ferdinand VI conceded them the title of the Marquès de Sitjar. The coat of arms of the rupestrian Lloberolas, who before being marquesses had borne the title of "honored citizens" and, not long after, of "gentlemen," had not exactly been the one with the wolves and the pines. Their coat of arms consisted of a cross and a ram's head with great horns, as it appears that the wealth of the ancient Lloberolas had derived from the sheep wool trade. But a king of arms, of the many who existed in the eighteenth century, hoodwinking farmers with mythological ascendencies, offered them the three green pines and three black wolves on a field of gold for their approval, on the basis that those ram horns seemed a bit indiscreet among marquesses in wigs and dress coats, stuffed with money and addled with airs.

Frederic was ignorant of the modest titled history of his line. He preferred to adopt the fantasies of Don Tomàs and the king of arms, and to believe that the handful of stones scattered half an hour from his ancestral home, his casa pairal, the home of his forefathers, had been the brilliant lair of all the romantic legends of Lloberolas wearing chain mail and helmets, disemboweling ferocious Berbers, ravishing perfumed Saracen women, and doing their worst to a downtrodden multitude of serfs.

No one but Frederic ever went up to the barren field of the castle. He spent many afternoons there. On the slope leading down to the masia, there was a good stretch of meadow grass. Occasionally, the smattering of cows that belonged to the masover of Can Lloberola would be led there so they could breathe some air beyond the stable and enjoy the scraps of green the land offered them free of cost.

Can Lloberola had been a very important estate, the best in the county, but in his decline Don Tomàs had overseen its fragmentation. The plots were divvied up and ended up in many hands. On Don Tomàs's death Frederic was left the house and a few jornals. A jornal is the plot of land a man can work in a day's time, and the masover worked them to his own advantage, while paying a pittance in rent.

In Don Tomàs's better days, the house had come to be quite a fine place. A good deal of money went into renovating and furnishing it properly as a summerhouse where they could receive guests. Later everything was allowed to deteriorate. Nothing was left of the garden. The masovers were pagesos, good farmer stock who saw no need for aesthetics or superfluous things, and they turned anything that was merely decorative into utilitarian land. They took over the owners' furniture and little by little invaded the rooms meant for the senyors. When Frederic picked up the dregs of his father's estate, he found that if he wanted to live in Can Lloberola he practically had to behave like a tenant. Despite the discomforts and the rural duplicity, Frederic was able to feel like a true gentleman there. The masover, who was shrewd, had known Frederic since he was a boy – he was ten years older than his employer. He would humor him and look the other way when Frederic had Soledat, the farmer's eldest daughter, untie his leggings when he got back from hunting. Soledat, who was no farmer girl, wore rouge and chiffon stockings, and as she went about untying his laces, Frederic's eyes pointed like two medieval hounds into the well of the girl's décolletage, within which sighed, somewhat rebelliously, the fresh lemons of her breasts.

It saddened Frederic to see how modernization had turned those noble rural walls into something ordinary and conventional. The masover had a gramophone and a radio, with an undomesticated speaker that let out squeaks and squawks and tangos and speeches by deputies from the Republican Left, while the stable boys dug the hay from their ears and Francisca hung a great cauldron of navy beans from the pothook over the hearth in the kitchen.

Nighttime conversation around the table of the masovers and the stable boys revolved around tenant farming, soccer, the politics of Macià and Companys, and Greta Garbo. They were all members of Esquerra Republicana, the party of the anti-monarchist pro-Catalan left, except for two farmhands from the FAI, the Federació Anarquista Ibèrica, who went out to dig potatoes with a copy of *Solidaridad Obrera*, the anarchist paper, stuck in their waistbands. These things drove Frederic mad. He saw disaffection in the eyes of the farmworkers; they barely bade him good day and good night. In town everyone knew he was ruined, he didn't have a cent, and the masover held more title than he, and soon he would not even be owed even his little bit of rent. On Sunday afternoons, when he went to the cafè, el Senyor de Can Lloberola was hardly afforded more consideration than the men wearing working caps and the sashes, known as faixes, that the Catalan farmworkers still wore around their waists. He had to forget about bridge; he played the local card games, burro and tuti subhastat, with the secretary and two farmers. To be in harmony with the table, he had to pretend to have read the newspapers and abstain from saying everything he thought about the Republic.

Frederic was having a sort of affair with a married woman in the district. She was a bright young girl who had gone to school in Manresa; she was fairly scrupulous with regard to hygiene, and sordidly banal with regard to every other topic under the sun. Her name was Montserrat. Her husband had a wine business and spent many days in Barcelona. As a girl, and even as an adult, Montserrat had been nourished on the innocent and popular Catalanist literature of Josep Maria Folch i Torres. Her husband had corrupted her morally and cultivated in her a taste for vaudeville and broad humor. She fell in love with Frederic because he was a tragic figure and a member of the nobility. He visited her fairly often. It was a topic of general gossip in town, but the wine merchant was one of those people who have ears and do not hear.

Frederic had always had a great fondness for the Can Lloberola estate. In its days of splendor, the hunting expeditions of Frederic and his friends were famous. On occasion, women had gone along, and the masover had done whatever was necessary so Don Tomàs would never learn of their carousing.

Three years before his father died, on the pretext of looking after the estate, Frederic began to spend long periods there, all by himself, leaving his wife and children behind in the apartment on Carrer de Bailèn. With his father's death and the coming of the Republic, Frederic was determined to extend his stay as long as he could. In truth, he and Maria behaved as if they were divorced. Like all the Lloberolas, Frederic had a mad streak, and ever since he had broken up with Rosa Trènor, he had been subject to a sort of grotesque melancholy, to appearing enigmatic, to registering absurd complaints and making grand scenes before his wife and children. Instead of smoothing things over, Maria tensed the cord even further on her end, and those last four years of marriage had been unbearable. As for the Republic, Frederic was just as indignant as his father, if not more so. But instead of wasting his time on clerical intrigues and cheap conspiracies, Frederic was invaded by sadness, and disgusted with the people of Barcelona who followed politics and went around causing democratic upheaval. His children were already grown, and they were the last straw. Ferran had finished school and begun to study architecture and dared, timidly, to express his opinions in front of his father. Frederic's blend of melancholy and nonsense came together in the form of an acute crisis. One day he threw a bottle at his son's head and hurt him rather badly. Another day he threatened to throw him out of the house. Maria always took the side of the little weasel against her husband, and la Senyora Carreres, who was even more necessary than ever from an economic standpoint, went so far as to call her son-in-law a monster and a bad man. She said that if he wasn't capable of educating and maintaining a family, he should go away and leave them in peace.

These scenes at the apartment on Carrer de Bailèn were among the most deplorable and idiotic of all the similar scenes that took place in the private life of the bourgeoisie of our country, often for irrational causes. Nothing could console Frederic. He stopped caring about his clothing; his friends at the Club Eqüestre avoided him. Sometimes he would while away a boring afternoon all by himself in a neighborhood cafè. Don Tomàs's will left no doubt that the Lloberolas had inherited a pittance, and Frederic couldn't bear any more humiliations and favors from his in-laws. All he had left was the estate and the company of the masovers who had always been loyal to him. For them he had started out as the young master, el senyoret, and gone on to be "Don Frederic." He had that pile of rocks in a barren wasteland in which the quixotic Frederic could envisage the castle of his past glory and the justification of his pride and his sadness. He had a red and white spotted cow who listened to his speeches on the grandeur and decadence of human vanity as she munched on the grass. Frederic was not just any old poor devil, as many – including Bobby, with whom he was never reconciled – believed. Frederic had a germ of madness, like all the Lloberolas, and it was that germ that sent him off alone, practically a tenant of the caretakers of his own property, putting up with the whistling and crackling of the radio and the opinions on communism of the handful of farmworkers stuffed with navy beans, reeking of the natural and repulsive odor of agriculture.

In the meantime, back home, things were peaceful. When you came right down to it, Frederic was an unusual case. There are men who go through this world without leaving anything of worth behind, without having had the slightest influence on anything. When they die, no one remembers them, nor does anyone need them. For as long as their contact with others lasts, neither on the surface nor in passing can so much as a blasted anecdote be told. What little effect they have is purely negative, even on themselves. They devote their time to spending, to destroying, to embittering, to making every minute unpleasant. They are usually serious to no end; they are incapable of humor, of laughter, of anything exuding a pleasant warmth. It might seem as if the most natural thing would be for no one to take note of such men, for them to be avoided so that they could not be a stumbling block for a single project, for in point of fact neither their judgment nor their value, nor even their volume bears any weight. But the strange thing is that this type of man is particularly annoying, and a source of concern to others. They behave like specters that intercept movement. Sometimes it even seems as if they rob all the air from a room, allowing no one to breathe. Their eyes, which are expressionless and reveal no special gaze, are more inquisitive than the eyes of others, and their tongues contradict for the pleasure of contradicting. Faced with such characters, some people give them a wide berth, or leave off what they're doing in order to avoid that stupid, inoffensive, entirely irrelevant contradiction that, for some inexplicable reason, is intolerably exasperating. Frederic was one of these men, at home, among his friends, among his relations; this is the kind of man he was. His arrogant illiteracy was irritating; inclined to opine on anything, to stick his nose in anywhere, he never knew when to keep his countenance, he kept arguments going, he overcomplicated absurd things, not to be insulting, but because he felt possessed of a divine inspiration, as if he were clairvoyant. Those who just depended on him, out of friendship or acquaintance, did their best to avoid him. If they ran into him on the street, they were always running late, or they would seek out a third person so as not to have to carry on a face-to-face dialogue with him. Frederic was a polite man, a rather decent and well-bred individual, he even had some sophistication, but despite that, he was annoying, unbearably annoying, in a class by himself. Don Tomàs's saving point had been his quaintness, his pathos, his theatricality. He had had a Molieresque quality – along the lines of an Orgon or an Imaginary Invalid – that imbued his nose, his moustache and his scarf. Don Tomàs was of another era, with all his clownish ways and all the absurd penitence that could be summed up in the conical cucurulla hat he would wear in the Holy Week processions. As pure spectacle, he could be tolerated, for a while. Not Frederic; Frederic was gray and sad, without contrast on the surface or in the soul. He was the proverbial bitter pill to swallow.

A man like this in the midst of a family, even an impassive family without an ounce of critical sense, ends up filling every room with corrosive vapors. His wife had many of her own defects but in a less strident way, more muted, one might say. She was dull, whiny, sniveling, hypocritical, vague, acidic, but even her acid was diluted with a great deal of water. Frederic's wife didn't realize who he was; she rebuffed him for reasons that were not exactly what made him so impossible – his infidelities, reproofs, bugbears, and lack of money – all of which could have been tolerated if Frederic simply hadn't been such a bore. And the most painful part is that he was no ordinary bore, oh no. If Frederic had been an ordinary man, as normal, sad and insignificant as you like, perhaps he would still have been tolerable. Frederic, in his own way of being, was an exceptional man, an original. An exceptional bore, despicable and gentlemanly, innocent and suspicious, generous and miserly, irresponsible, insubstantial, loud, false, and cowardly. Full of the most quixotic and most sublime illusions, defeated and self-important, he had been disarmed by life like no other.

His influence on his children was disastrous. If ever there was a man who didn't have the slightest idea of what it meant to educate a child, it was Frederic. When Don Tomàs had educated Frederic, he had believed in a few norms. His criteria might be good or bad, he might cling to asceticism, or morality, or nobility, or to the Sunday parish letter, or whatever, but between hassocks and cuffs to the back of the head, he followed those criteria. The results of his method were terrible, but it was a method. Not Frederic. He had reached the point of having no shame with regard to his children, and he would swing back and forth between punishment, shouting, and violence, and letting them do whatever they pleased. His children had no respect for him; bitterness and conjugal battle were their daily spectacle. Doubtless some of the things that were passed on to the progeny of Frederic de Lloberola and Maria Carreres, which the reader who continues to read this story will hear about, were caused by the terrible education and poor example of a household whose head was a failure as a father and in every other way.

Not that we can have a great deal of faith, in this world, in pedagogy or the healthy influence of parents on their children, because every home is a world unto itself and every technique fails. But what is certain is that, for temperaments like those of the Lloberola family, the pressure of a man like Frederic comes to produce the most absolute demoralization: the demoralization of exhaustion, smothering, and loss of respect. It cannot be said of Frederic that he is a criminal or a thief or excessively debauched, or an alcoholic, or black of heart, or anything like that. Indeed, such vices, when present in the father, have been known to behave as reactants, making the children resistant to vice. Frederic is simply a bore, simply a pain, simply insignificant, simply wretched, and the end result is the desire for the disappearance or death of a person whom by nature one ought to love and respect.

And this is what Frederic's children felt, spurred on even more by Maria's sourpuss expression and all the sighs and lamentations of Grandmother Carreres. The one who bore the most guilt for all that disaffection and exhaustion was Frederic. He had brought three children into the world without a drop of enthusiasm because, when he lost his illusions about his wife, he lost his illusions about paternity. It's not that he didn't love them, nor that he hadn't suffered when as little ones they bumped their knees against the corner of a table. But he loved them in a very peculiar way; his distress came more from the annoyance of hearing them cry than from tenderness and compassion for a child who has hurt himself. In truth, they got on his nerves, and he fled the house whenever he could. His children never required any effort, or gave him any headaches. They had their mother, their grandparents, their nannies, and he had plenty to do, gambling at the Eqüestre, or trying out an automobile, or chasing after a woman, or being a monumental pain, or arguing, or sitting around. When things started really going badly for him, when he ought to have behaved with humility, when he had to accept a sad salary at the Banc Vitalici, he would take his cowardly egotism out on his blameless children, depending on the mood he was in.

Since he needed to be seen as the wisest of them all, a gesture made by one of his children in all innocence – a shrug of the shoulders, for example – would be seen by Frederic as proof of a terrible instinct for depravity that had to be corrected. He would impose a disturbing, humiliating and unsuitable punishment on the child. The child would carry it out, not innocently, but rather with a resignation full of hatred for his father, taking note of his father's wretchedness, showing obedience so that the wretchedness would not go any farther. Children often have more common sense and flexibility than adults.

Clearly when Frederic had his attack of rural melancholy and liberated himself by forgetting about his family, everyone breathed more easily in the apartment on Carrer de Bailèn.

Frederic thought of them occasionally, above all of Maria Lluïsa, his eldest daughter, who was almost twenty. Not that his thinking of her had anything to do with regret for his own behavior, or with baring his soul before his own conscience…Much to the contrary, he believed that his children didn't love him because his wife had inculcated hatred for their father in them. He was a victim of his children, just as he had been a victim of his father. In his quarrels and fallings-out with Don Tomàs, it never occurred to Frederic that guilt is always two-sided, and that often no one is actually guilty but pure fate, the blind and contradictory biology that creates risible conflicts that, to some eyes, appear to be unassailable mountains. Frederic saw himself as pure, well-meaning, and angelic, and it was others who were his enemies and who were to blame for everything. This was not persecution mania. It was just emptyheadedness.

One of the clearest endorsements of Rosa Trènor's patience or stupidity was her having put up with him as a lover. As we know, it was Bobby's peculiar temperament and ennui that made him impervious to Frederic's monologues and effrontery.

Back at Can Lloberola, Frederic was getting a little coarser by the day. He began to enjoy the radio, and the farmhands' arguments about communism didn't get on his nerves the way they used to. He would go three days without shaving. He would feel an agrarian tenderness when Soledat untied his leggings, and he would go red in the face if Francisca caught on. The farmers who played cards with him no longer called him Don Frederic; they called him Senyor Frederico, and one of them even called him Senyor Frederiquet, diminishing him with the diminutive. He just kept his eyes on the cards and didn't move a muscle.

After dinner, when there was moonlight, he would wander around among the old castle stones. His heart bucolic and his belly full, he would listen to the crickets sing with tawdry sentimentalism. The castle stones took him back to the clouds of idealism. Alone, in the evening dew that was beginning to reveal the effects of arthritis, he would stiffen up and adopt the proper bearing of a Lloberola who speaks with the medieval shades of his ancestors. There he was, against all democracy, against all socialism, defending the traditions of a country to which he had never paid the slightest mind. For him, to have been born in Catalonia and to be called Lloberola meant to play bridge, to bring children into the world because that's what one did, to lose a fortune, and to put on a new tie for the first time. Everything else was a waste of time. In the presence of the ruins, these criteria underwent some modification. He was disgusted by the bridge games, the children, the fortune, and the ties. He was suffused with the solemnity of paellas and salads prepared in the fields, the delightful sight of Soledat's breasts, the stench of the stables, the chirping of the crickets, and the immutable pale yellow moon that cast a theatrical chiaroscuro over his ancestral ruins.

At nightfall, Frederic would visit the wine merchant's wife. He was getting a little tired. His abdomen, his gray hair, his wrinkles all gave him away. In the games of love with the wine merchant's wife he couldn't be much more prodigal than with his fortune. Frederic was almost finished. Premature impotence was common among the Lloberolas, and Frederic was beginning to feel the effects of that family flaw. He wasn't old: he had just turned forty-eight. But day by day in his intimate physiology Frederic began to notice alarming symptoms. The wine merchant's wife enveloped him in a cheap, tacky sentimentalism. Soledat, with her rouge and her chiffon stockings, and all the young bucks in town pressing up against her in the dance hall, was a finer prey. But Frederic needed to be flattered, and consoled. The wine merchant's wife knew how to console him, and it thrilled her that a bona fide Senyor de Lloberola would deign to lie in her bed, in a bedroom that smelled of sheepskins, of the brotherhood of the Virgin of Pain, and of cheap cologne.

Frederic's nose and heart were becoming accustomed to all this squalor. He even reached the point at which he found the appeal in a silk print nightgown the wine merchant's wife wore. It was a black fabric with a pattern of orange-colored babies that looked as if they had been stolen from an orphanage.

———·——·———

AFTER HER HUSBAND'S death, Leocàdia moved out of the apartment on Carrer de Mallorca. Guillem would just as soon live in a hotel as in a pension, since no one knew where he would be sleeping or keeping his clothes. Leocàdia spent the first few months at Josefina's house, but the poor woman wasn't comfortable with the Marquesas de Forcadell. There was too much bustle and noise in their house. Josefina always had guests, the children were rowdy, and the marquis showed no signs of affection to his mother-in-law. Leocàdia was an early riser. She was accustomed to eating promptly at midday and dining early in the evening. In contrast, her daughter's house was subject to constant disorder. The marquis would keep them waiting until ten p.m. and then telephone to say he wouldn't be home for dinner. Josefina had developed an absolute passion for golf and many days she would stay in Sant Cugat for lunch. Leocàdia was flustered by all this, and she proposed to her daughter and son-in-law that she would be better off retreating to the abbey at Cluny. The Sisters of St. Joseph of Cluny took into their convent women who had been left alone by manic disorder, widowhood, or earthquake. In the convent, they didn't exactly find Baudelairian *"luxe, calme et volupté,"* but they did find order, repose, and discipline, and enough comfort to satisfy their needs. In general, the ladies who retired with the Sisters of Cluny were from good families and highly educated, but wanting in fortune and affection.

Josefina and her husband didn't find Leocàdia's proposal acceptable. They thought their friends would be critical. It wasn't right for the widow Marquesas de Sitjar, with two sons and a daughter married to a well-placed man, to be retiring to a nunnery like a poor widow or an ordinary spinster. When Josefina expressed this opinion, it was not because she had felt any particular pleasure in having Leocàdia under her roof; she was concerned mostly with what people would say. Don Tomàs's will assigned Leocàdia a number of shares that produced at most a rent of some four hundred pessetes a month. This was sufficient for Leocàdia to pay her board at Cluny and cover her expenses, which were insignificant. Despite the frankly weak opposition of the Marquesas de Forcadell, Leocàdia installed herself in a pleasant cell at the convent, arranged her things there, and lived with more independence and tranquility than in the pompous and obstreperous apartment of her son-in-law.

Some old people, perhaps the immense majority of old people, who lived in harmony during a particular period of their lives, having felt an identification with a fashion or a set of ideas now considered passé, endure the latter years and changes not without protest and incomprehension. In truth, they are the survivors of their times, their fashions, or their ideas.

Old folk who have experienced a good moment in the past maintain a constant controversy with the new life that emerges day by day. If they say that something in the present is bad, it is not exactly for the reasons they adduce. It is bad for them, because the current thing is different from another bygone thing they considered to be good. If an old man affirms that women with short hair are less exciting than women with long hair, it is because back when he was prone to excitement, women wore their hair long. And if an old woman affirms that a man looks better with a beard and moustache, it is because the first man for whom she had feelings had a beard and moustache.

The more intense and fulfilling the bygone age of an old person was, the stronger the controversy, harsher the incomprehension, and more obdurate the protest before the evolution of things.

This criterion, which can be applied to the majority of respectable elders, could not be applied to Leocàdia, for the simple reason that Leocàdia had not lived any period of her life intensely. Leocàdia had always been a mere receptive vessel, without opinions or passions of any kind.

This is why Leocàdia was a delightful old lady. When her daughter was playing golf, not for a moment did she stop to think that between the days of her daughter and the days of her youth there was a notable difference, and she incorporated the word "golf" into her vocabulary beyond time and space. The only objection she had to the sport was that it was the reason lunch was served late or the reason she had to have lunch without her daughter. And she felt the same way about everything else as she did about golf. When her granddaughter

Maria Lluïsa showed up to visit her wrapped in a trench coat, alone, after work in an office where she was employed as a secretary, the widow Marquesa de Sitjar didn't complain or find anything strange in her granddaughter's situation, even though in her youth no young woman of her class would go out in the street by herself, or wear a trench coat, or take a job as a secretary to earn her living.

If Leocàdia had not enjoyed this sweet numbness, her later years would have been much grimmer, because the same lady who had taken so many pains with all the family furniture and relics of the splendor of the Lloberolas in the apartment on Carrer de Mallorca later sold off most of that furniture with great indifference. This can only be explained by accepting that her earlier pains and care were only a reflection of the importance her husband attributed to the furniture. Once Don Tomàs disappeared, along with the pathetic and grandiose exaltation he applied to anything that made reference to his past history, Leocàdia felt as passive and indifferent to the furniture as she did to everything else. As we have already said in another part of this story, Leocàdia's marriage had had a sort of mimetic quality, and she had adapted to it and completely annulled herself. As we have also already said, Leocàdia's protests regarding her husband's profligacy and wild-eyed notions were very feeble, responding only to a woman's natural instinct for preservation.

Thanks to this temperament, Leocàdia wasn't the slightest bit humiliated by living as a boarder in the Cluny convent. And, since in this world the same causes produce morally contradictory effects on different individuals, perhaps it was also as a result of the hereditary transfer of Leocàdia's temperament to her son Guillem that he too felt no sense of humiliation on accepting three hundred pessetes from Dorotea Palau, the dressmaker, and on later accepting whatever he required from the widow Baronessa de Falset.

The family member to whom Leocàdia was closest was Maria Lluïsa, Frederic's daughter. Maria Lluïsa loved her grandmother because she never divined in her clear blue eyes the slightest drop of bitterness or surprise. Leocàdia was like a child without enthusiasm. Maria Lluïsa was a passionate child. Leocàdia's feelings for her granddaughter were exactly the same as her feelings for her son, Guillem: tremendous tenderness, mixed with fear. That twenty year-old girl, as determined as she was reserved, as affectionate as she was elusive, gave her grandmother the shivers. Leocàdia never said a word to Maria Lluïsa, never gave her a sermon or tried to understand her. Leocàdia sensed that nothing would come of it.

Maria Lluïsa was twenty years old, and her sentimental life had already begun to enter a state of decomposition. As Voltaire's famous verses to the Marquesa du Châtelet put it, *"Qui n'a pas l'esprit de son âge / de son âge a tout le malheur."* But even an aphorism that seems so astute can fail to hold true for some people. Maria Lluïsa, for example. She possessed the spirit of her times and of her age in a brutal way, and perhaps it was this excess of the spirit of the times that was her downfall.

In every family there is an individual who maintains the qualities and defects intrinsic to the family, exaggerated and concentrated to the point of being grotesque and distasteful. This individual is usually a bachelor uncle who has had a bastard child with the cook. In addition to this farcical character, every family also seems to produce an individual in whom the most dashing, piquant and fragrant part of the family is distilled, and in whose skin the very defects become elements of grace, sparkle and elegance. This individual is usually a girl, and within the crusty, festering, and reactionary gratinée of the Lloberolas, the person chosen to play the role of fruit sherbet and marvelous perfume was Maria Lluïsa.

If an abandoned, fussy, and unfriendly womb could not produce models of vitality as trembling and out of the blue as the impromptu clash of melodies produced by birds washing their faces, if ladies like Maria Carreres could not have daughters like Maria Lluïsa, the logic of this world would be so unbearable as to oblige us all to close up shop.

Maria Lluïsa had been confined in a convent school in Sarrià, like most of the girls of her stock. At a time when children feel their puberty bursting like an unpleasant carnation, awakening scruples and desire, Maria Lluïsa had not been prey to any of those disorders that afflict sex in the life of boarders. She didn't fall in love with a nun, or with an effigy in the chapel, nor did a kiss on the not very hygienic fuzz of another girl's cheek infect her with nebulous and repressed intentions of the kind that are marked by a dopey tenderness in the voice and a bluish shadow under the eyes. Rest assured that when Maria Lluïsa put on her nightgown, that fragile fabric didn't hide anything but a sterilized, independent adolescence.

At the age of sixteen, Maria Lluïsa had mahogany red hair and eyes like two frozen grapes. She gave the piano a solemn kick in the keys because she had no talent for music, and she decided that a girl who had the misfortune of being born to a father like Frederic de Lloberola and a mother like Maria Carreres had no other recourse than to figure things out for herself and find a way to earn a living. This decision was the cause of great outrage, but Maria Lluïsa was the only Lloberola lacking in the two defects that were peculiar to all the rest: weakness and cowardice. Maria Lluïsa prevailed, and by eighteen she was working as a secretary in a bank on Carrer de Fontanella.

That was when her sentimental life began to get complicated. Till that moment, Maria Lluïsa had lived far from the fire. This is not to say, however, that she was innocent or didn't know the score. She understood perfectly well that her natural grace was sufficient justification for boxes of bonbons, bouquets of flowers, invitations and requests to ride up the Diagonal or around Montjuïc Park in a very sleek and shiny little car, and that these were simply veiled ways of seeking her body. But up till then no one had ever touched Maria Lluïsa, nor had she fallen in love with anyone. Her temperament was rather chilly; sex demanded nothing more of her than a shower, a racket, and a bit of makeup on her face. When it was time to dance, she listened to the music and nothing more. She responded reflexively and smiled instinctively without her heart's secreting any of the idyllic substances that throw one's rhythm off and keep one awake at night.

At eighteen, Maria Lluïsa stopped practicing her religion. When it was time for Mass, she would slip away from her mother with the excuse of exercise and sport, and she would tell as many lies as were needed to put up a proper front and avoid scandalizing the family. It can be said with certainty that by her last year in high school Maria Lluïsa no longer believed anything the nuns and priests told her. What most infuriated her was to have to do spiritual exercises and play a role she didn't believe in.

A few months after Maria Lluïsa took the secretarial job at the bank, she spent her first summer vacation with a couple of cousins at the seashore.

Under no circumstance did Frederic want to let his daughter go unescorted to the beach at Llafranc. He was opposed to it, as he had been opposed to her working in an office, not for any good reason, but simply out of prejudice and Lloberola vanity, and because of his uncomprehending and draining inclination to disagree. But by then Frederic no longer had any shame, and it had become more than clear that he found his family intolerable. To be contrary, Maria had taken Maria Lluïsa's side, and it all ended up with a big scene between father, mother, and daughter, and with the girl on the afternoon express to Flaçà, the closest station, and from there to Llafranc in her cousins' car.

The cousins were from the Carreres side of the family, daughters of one of Maria's sisters, who was married to a solid merchant from the French Midi who spent seasons in Paris and seasons in L'Empordà, where they were now.

The girls' names were Henriette and Suzanne. One of them was twenty-one years old and the other nineteen, but they were identical, and if you weren't used to them, you couldn't tell them apart. They had a very delicate complexion, with blood very close to the surface, and subject to fever blisters. They were somewhat gigantic in shape. They inherited this tendency from their father, Gaston, a Frenchman with a vaudeville cuckold's black moustache and cheeks. From their mother they had inherited a chlorotic tenderness and a devotion to the Virgin of Montserrat. Henriette and Suzanne were fresh-faced, with big eyes and big mouths. They were well-liked, but they were not exciting. Long of arm and leg, on the fleshy side, lacking in femininity, it seemed as if all their inner piquancy must have evaporated through their pores and been lost between laughter and sea water without germinating in any virile gaze. Their father had bought them a mint green Talbot and they passed the wheel from one to the other, making sensational turns and coughing and squawking like moorhens when the intercity bus left their mascara full of dust.

Henriette and Suzanne received Maria Lluïsa with an explosion of a bottle of "extra dry" from a good year. Maria Lluïsa cried with joy. The three girls spread out enough pajamas, maillots, rubber penguins and panthers, balls, hats, scarves, and terry cloth robes to drive all the beaches in the world wild. They had a canoe and two water sleds, and a friend of all three by the name of Dionísia Balcells, who summered with her mother in Llafranc. Dionísia was one of those delightful snub-nosed girls whose faces continue all their lives to be a little comical and girlish: a wide mouth, bright, partridge eyes, and peroxide blonde hair cut and combed like a boy's. Her legs were slender and firm, she was narrow in the chest and hips, and her entire musculature was made for rapid movement and wild gesticulation, and for a laugh that reached all the way down to her toenails. She was one of those girls so intentionally *à la page*, so innocently in command of the flirtatious gesture and the eccentric moue that when they give in to love there is nothing left of them but a warm spoonful of honey that trickles out with a primary physiological tenderness.

Dionísia may have been the youngest of the four, but she was also the most modern and free. She had a degree in Natural Sciences, she had spent long periods in Madrid and Algiers, and she had spent the past winter in Paris. Despite her youth, Dionísia had been one of the most outspoken and feminist inhabitants of the Residencia de Estudiantes in Madrid. She was a friend of the surrealist poets, the psychiatrists, and the Mexican painters who also lived there. Her insides were glazed with whiskey and her lungs with Lucky Strikes. Even though she chattered like a magpie and the saliva of self-importance glistened on her teeth, this young lass was extraordinarily attractive and charming, and her femininity was of the most authentic and disconcerting kind.

Dionísia and Maria Lluïsa were made for confidences and commentaries, and they got along very well. Henriette and Suzanne tended to live for sports. The four of them made up eight hips of a modern girl, not homogeneous, but so well-endowed in water and flesh that the world's best milieus had nothing on them.

Early in the morning, the four of them would escape in the canoe to deserted beaches in hidden inlets. The colorful knit fabrics clinging to their bodies and the entire traveling circus of rubber creatures left no few knives of tropical lust in the eyes of the fishermen, as the canoe cut through the waves in the bay spreading a trail of diamond excelsior.

In the deserted inlets the four girls would bathe and sunbathe in the nude, throw stones at the sea gulls, and eat strips of cured ham, pinching them between shiny and dangerous red fingernails, dirty with grains of sand. They liked to feel the transparency of the submarine landscape on their bellies, with all the gelatinous and corrosive greens of the vegetation and the zoophytes that clung to the rocks. They did the crawl with their eyes open underwater and the white skin on the soles of their feet floated nervously and in rhythmic jolts like roses attached to the tail of a mechanical fish.

On the jetties, the broom flowers were lit up by the last gaslights, where the bumblebees flocked to burn. A deeply fragrant gas, opaque, the color of Hollandaise sauce.

The four young women, to keep in shape, would do fifty sit-ups every day, keeping their legs rigid and touching the tips of their toes with the palms of their hands. At some point in the arc of the exercise their breasts would hang from their torsos like two little pear-shaped lanterns. Later, when they lifted their heads and their mussed hair was back in place, a struggle between sweat, smiles and fatigue was outlined on their faces.

At peak time, they would go back to the beach, their eyes glassy with the burning of the sun, their pupils bearing the dreams and the prestige of their adventures in the deserted inlets. All this went straight to the spinal cord of the sun-black boys lolling on the sand, who sensed a mysterious something in the laughter of the four young women that was both brutal and innocent and wicked and exciting.

Salt water sports are among the most corrupting and most given to blood-gorged adolescent rebellion. The deceptive coolness of the water and the reptilian innocence of sunlight inject into the skin and cauterize in the bones all the infected wounds of ideas, awakening a budding melancholy, and intercepting the broad animal breathing with tears of decay. They fill evenings and nights with dreams of disaster and shipwreck, and visions of dark and quiet waters where ripped-out teeth, coral sex organs, and rootless roses drift.

Four girls together on a boat, secretly bound by the webs of rubber toy animals, terry cloth robes, salt-laden maillots, and calisthenics, laughing with utter impunity, bend over to pull up an anchor, revealing, even for a couple of seconds, the possibility of a perfect nipple trying to penetrate the wool fabric. Yielding to nothing, defending one another, complicit in their virgin animal joy, they are four flashes of lightning that strike the soft backbone of banality and docile lust without mercy.

A woman who has been spent and explored, whether she is the most celestial and world-weary adulteress who delivers herself up to a violet-strewn affair or the saddest, drabbest tramp who, amid the coals on a dock, reconnoiters through the misery of cotton and alcohol thieves, will always be a spent and explored woman. Always the monotonous repetition of everything, from which nothing, neither love nor madness, can free us.

In spent and explored women, even the most skeptical man can find a glimmer of starlight, without so much as a single star from the immense night escaping her eyes. But this will always be done on the basis of comprehension, humiliation, renunciation, and compulsion. A spent and explored woman, for the strict connoisseur of authentic sensuality, can never touch the compact mystery of four young women on a boat, with their bathing suits, their rubber toys, the laughter that burns in their mouths, physically assaulting all the piety scattered throughout the world with the absolute immodesty of their hidden, virgin vulvas. Four young women on a boat, joined together by the sweat of their sit-ups, their nettles, their jellyfish, their unconscious coral reefs. Joined together by their own deeply irresponsible springtime. Maria Lluïsa, Dionísia, Suzanne, Henriette arrived on the beach at peak time, which was the time of the hairy sun-black legs of the boys in counterpoint to their own less sun-black and perfectly hairless legs, hanging from the white wood of the paddle boat, imitating the back-and-forth motion of the legs of aquatic birds.

The paddle boat would suddenly start to shudder, as if undergoing some kind of internal catastrophe, and a pea green, butter yellow and tar-colored swimsuit would plummet into the water with a shriek. Then the hands of a boy accustomed to the oars, trembling a bit, arms contracting, would pull out a fruit of naked skin peeled in places by the sun's grill. The young man's fingers slipped on the underarms, periodically visited by the razor, and that spiky contact that lasted as long as he liked was replaced by the shock of two elastic lemons wrapped in colorful wool, crushed for a moment against the boy's naked thorax. The breath and the laughter of the girl rubbed up against the pained and concealed sigh of the oarsman, and, one leg here, one leg there, the rhythm was reestablished. To kill the silence, the antipathy or the excited flesh, girls and boys together would sing one of the Cuban rumbas that were in vogue those days in the cabarets.

The youngest brother of Isabel Sabadell, known as Pat, had come to spend a few days in Llafranc with some friends. His name was Patrici, but no one called him by such an archaeological and pretentious moniker, so unsuited to the aesthetic of heavy oil engines.

Pat was twenty-five at the time. He was boyish and fresh-faced, with shiny, deep black hair and very white teeth. Pat spent his days winning first prizes in nautical challenges and punishing his lungs on his outboard motorboat that was the color of fish entrails. His ears were full of gas explosions and he cultivated his musculature as if he were a show dog.

Pat shot straight as a bullet for Maria Lluïsa's smile. The day after he first saw her, Pat told her his life story, his ambitions, and his ideas.

On the third day, when the beaches were full of people, Pat and Maria Lluïsa went a little farther out; Pat's slightly rough hand, accustomed to water sports, slipped inside her maillot and visited its secrets, which with the help of the cool water felt like fresh fruit and flesh without a soul. Maria Lluïsa didn't protest, nor did she laugh. Altruistically, and for no particular reason, she allowed the boy's nerves to take in through her wet skin the intact electricity of her body.

It was the first time in Maria Lluïsa's life that she had felt that sort of generosity. She was not at all sentimental; she didn't feel any attachment to that boy's well-distributed and well-iodized physique; it was simply a moment of female generosity. She wasn't looking for moral compensation; she wasn't looking for anything. Animals that have never been to college and gods not subject to any doctrine regarding sex must also enjoy this splendid license to be visited by a hand that sweeps diplomacy aside.

Pat was a bit weak with emotion and gratitude. They were only a few strokes from the beach, and Pat floated on his back by her side for a while. Maria Lluïsa felt the joy of the philanthropist. Nothing is as satisfying to the ego as an act of pure charity. In the gaze of the man or woman who has just done an act of charity there is a tiny flash, as insignificant as you wish, of that brilliance that theologians claim appears in the eyes of the blessed in the presence of the Supreme Being.

Pat and Maria Lluïsa reached the beach a bit exhausted from their exercise. They fell onto the sand breathing heavily. Dionísia slipped lit Camels between his lips and between her lips.

Pat was stupidly mesmerized by Maria Lluïsa's toenails. Usually, when a girl has been subject to the pain and deformation of shoes, the spectacle of her wet, naked, sand-encrusted feet after swimming is a disappointment. But under the implacable shower of the sun, his eyes half-closed, Pat felt a muted desire to kiss Maria Lluïsa's little feet, to nibble softly at the whitish flesh of her heel, right there where the flesh gets hard and the skin has an insensitive thickness. In the desire of that kiss Pat would have liked to deposit a liquid tenderness, like a teardrop of gratitude, of adoration, of effusion…

In the evening, before dinner, Pat and Maria Lluïsa were having a Picon aperitif in a bar decorated with pine branches, as the sea was turning black. Maria Lluïsa considered Pat to be a conventional, self-centered and visceral creature, who thought only of the efficiency of his outboard motorboat and his father's spinning mill. Pat told her that his father made him get up at nine a.m. when he had only gone to bed two hours before, stealing into the house with red eyes and a stomach full of whiskey. Pat had made love with the prettiest vamps who frequented the hour of the aperitif at the bar of the Hotel Colón. In his Chrysler, he had looked suicide in the face on the curves of the coastal highway of the Garraf, wearing on his tie all the rouge that could rub off a cheek. Pat wanted to bare his heart to Maria Lluïsa, and he told her these things with a touch of puerile vanity and a touch of Tolstoyan transcendence. Pat's speech drew on the grammar of the sporty gigolo, using catch phrases, some of which were mindless translations from Spanish, some of which proceeded without translation directly from the music-hall. You could see the influence of the movies, of avant-garde decoration, and of some vague familiarity with the intelligent, pleasant and superficial writing of the day in both his mentality and his manner of speaking. Pat was comfortable with these things because they were fashionable among some of his more sensitive friends.

At one point, between smiles and drags on their cigarettes, Maria Lluïsa's hand mussed Pat's thick black hair. She shook his cranium and Pat's cheek brushed against Maria Lluïsa's neck. But it was nothing more than a moment she desired and engineered. Pat went on talking about movies and other affairs. He was only interested in talking about himself and his thoughts, with the unconscious selfishness of a child. Maria Lluïsa was there in front of him and he didn't need to know anything about her. Pat didn't believe in women's sincerity. He had absorbed the somewhat brutal theory of athletic young men, who are used to feeling love in a purely physiological sense, through their constant dealings with vamps who, seeking a break from the abdomens and bronchitis of their official boyfriends, take up with the members of the Swimming Club. Pat was sweetly vulgar with the girls, and sometimes even inconsiderate. This was considered to be chic and tony among his friends, and this was the way many brilliant young men of the time interpreted romance.

But despite this muscular and mechanical way of behaving, Pat and other young men like him displayed the most baptismal innocence. Sometimes their callow ingenuousness turned them into characters right out of *The Lady of the Camellias*. Motor cars, whiskey, and the fatigued pubises of fashionable lovelies had not entirely broken the shell of their good-boy upbringings. Inside this shell made up of maternal cares, family comforts and even fatherly talkings-to, the ladyfingers boys like Pat dipped into their hot chocolate were crafted of the most conservative essences of the country. Maria Lluïsa saw Pat for the selfish, common and visceral child he was, but he was a child she found appealing, if only physically. Maria Lluïsa had not yet analyzed any aspect of what she felt for that young man. But the conversation, the aperitif and the tanned arms coming out of the white shirt matched the color of the boy's soul. It was the first time in her life that she was freeing herself of something she couldn't quite define. She found Pat to be good company. When the boy followed all four of them back to her cousins' cream-colored chalet, a few steps from the bar, Maria Lluïsa restrained her heart as if it were a fluttering swallow. She laughed heartily at the table and ate with an optimistic appetite. She might even have eaten more than her cousins, who never said no, and weighed twice as much as she did.

After dinner, Maria Lluïsa and Dionísia chatted. Maria Lluïsa didn't want to let on. As innocent as Pat, Dionísia was only interested in his ideas.

"He's very cute, but I think he's awfully rough around the edges. For a three-day fling, *bueno*," she punctuated in Spanish. "But three days and no more. On the fourth day, I think he'd start to be a pain. If we only got together on the beach, okay, because he's cute undressed. He has loads of sex appeal. But, as soon as he starts walking, he goes downhill, don't you think? And I wonder if you noticed another thing: when he crosses his legs, he could drive you crazy, he's always touching and jiggling his foot. As far as I'm concerned he's not the slightest bit interesting. He's not my type, and this morning I sort of let him know…"

"Well, I couldn't agree less! I think he's kind of cute precisely because he's so rough and such a child…"

"But they're all the same! Still, he does have a sort of flair for talking nonsense…, and he's likable enough…"

"What more do you want? You say he's funny, he's cute, he's likeable…"

"Yes, he's plenty *mono*," she said, now using the Spanish word for "cute." "His eyes are very expressive and he has a nice body; but I swear he's a dope…"

"All right, you win. But it seems to me you don't need a philosopher to go to the beach. You deal with intelligent men all day long… How are things going with the sex appeal of the wise men at the Athenaeum of Madrid?"

"There are all kinds. And I don't really care about their physique, you know. I like to talk with men who have interesting things to say, and this guy would get tiresome really quickly. The only thing he can talk about is cars. That's fine for your cousins, who are wild about wheels, but I don't know what you see in him…"

"I think you're being very hard on my catch! And here I was so delighted…"

"Liar. You like Pat because, of all the swells here, he's the only one worth the time of day. And you know what? He's a cheeky devil. Do you know what he asked Suzanne and me? If he could come with us in the boat to do calisthenics! He says that at the inlet we go to he'll have more freedom to show us how to perfect our crawl...I told him that we go to the inlet to practice nudism."

"You're kidding! Don't you think that's a bit extreme?"

"Of course. And he got even more persistent about coming with us. I told him we'd think about it, that all four of us had to agree to it..."

"Dionísia!"

"Well, I don't mind a bit if he comes with us. We'd make him sit with his back to us, staring at the rocks, and he would enjoy a wonderful view, because I think he's pretty tame and not some kind of satyr. We spent a little time on the paddleboat today, and that's the conclusion I came to...If I didn't think the Colls and the Banúses and the Jiménez girls would skin me alive, I would send for him tomorrow morning and take him off in the boat. No, really, would you mind if he came with us?"

"If he came with us, not at all, on the contrary. But you do see that then it would be an entirely different *plan*," and she used a word in Spanish for the first time. "We would all be much less lively and spontaneous in our exercises. Besides, it would get boring with him alone. What do you want with just one guy?"

"If the *plan* were just to be buddies and get in shape? It doesn't matter to me at all, not one bit. I don't know why we're supposed to do anything different, just for a boy...He'll be, I don't know, just like one of us..."

"With one small difference..."

"Pretty small."

"Don't be fresh now."

"I said the plan was just to go as buddies…"

"You tell him that, and let's see what he thinks, especially the part about what you said about the small difference…"

"I think he knows how to behave…"

"Listen, are you just talking to get me to talk, or have you gone mad?"

"I've told you many times that I have my own ideas about the question of sex. In Paris, two friends of mine, two very good friends, eh?, belong to a nudist club and on Sunday boys and girls get together and…it's all just fine."

"But have you ever gone with these friends, have you ever tested it for yourself?"

"No, but I've been tempted. I swear, it wouldn't matter to me at all."

"Sure, but the fact is, you've never done it…"

"Maybe I just wasn't in the mood. They get up too early in the morning and they're full of nonsense. Most of them are vegetarians."

"They must be utterly charming."

"Enough! You're way behind the times. Let's just let it go. So you don't want Pat to come with us, then."

"Of course I don't. And what's more, what would our aunt say… if she found out?"

"She'll never know. And neither will mamà. And, look, it would be something new and different. We spend our days here like shrinking violets. Most of the boys are dimwits, and when one comes along with a bit of spark, we should take advantage…Unless what you want is to have him all to yourself…"

"Come on, Dionísia! What's got into you…?"

"No, sweetie. Don't get mad, I just said it as a joke. I know Pat is just another boy to you. I don't wish him on you for a minute. He's a garden variety bore. I swear, not one of the guys here has made the slightest impression on me. And I imagine you feel the same way, and your little conquest of Pat is just…But, you know, that's not what he thinks…"

"What do you mean? What does he think?"

"He thinks you're sweet on him. Not that he's said as much, poor thing. But since you…"

"Since I what? I don't follow you."

"Yes you do. You and he, over the aperitifs, were having a real tête-à-tête. And it looked like you were really involved, and that's just natural, because he's so cute…", and here, again, she said *mono*. "And he knows it, and he takes every advantage…You didn't notice it, but he was looking at you like a real playboy who already…"

"Oh, Dionísia, you're always…"

"Wait, just a second."

"What?"

"Today, after lunch, I was reading for a while in the garden and he passed by and saw the book I'm just about to finish, and he asked me to lend it to him when I was done, and I'm not sure what to do…"

"Why not? What were you reading?"

"That book by Lawrence. What would you do? Would you lend it to him?"

"He's a big boy. Too bad for him if he finds it shocking."

"I'm not concerned about him. I'm asking for me, because just imagine…"

"For you? You mean so he won't get the wrong idea…? Oh, Dionísia, you see? I would never even have thought about it. Maybe I am more innocent than you, but if he had asked me to lend him that book I would have done it without thinking twice, like the most natural thing in the world. Really."

"Well, it's just a little too dirty. I really like dirty books…but there are a few details…that I find…well, I don't know, Lawrence could just have kept them to himself…There's no need to spell everything out like that…with a bit of imagination…"

"Yes, it's pretty smutty. Still, I found it very interesting. But it is possible that Pat would only be interested in the dirty parts. These athletic types are like that. But, sure, lend it to him…Maybe…"

"You mean maybe he'll wise up a bit when he reads it?"

"Don't go thinking he'll turn into a satyr! There's no danger of that, Dionísia. I don't believe that reading is a stimulus. Those are just things that happen in school…The sea is much more exciting than any book…And I don't know, every day I'm more and more afraid that I am a cold fish…, a little too cerebral, you know?"

"You may be cold, or you may imagine you are, though I think you're just dreaming. But you can't assume the same of Pat, or even guess at the impression books may make on him. Since I have the impression he reads very little, for that very reason reading must make a bigger impression on him than it does on you or me, who devour novels all day long...Two days after I read a book I don't remember a thing about the plot. I'm just ready to start a new one."

"You know what I think?"

"What?'

"I think we've been talking about Pat for half an hour."

"Hey, we were talking about books!"

"Yes, now try and deny it...I just think we could talk about something more interesting..."

"Does it bother you to talk about him?"

"No, but we're spending too much time on him."

That night, Maria Lluïsa began to have feelings that were quite new to her. Dionísia just infuriated her. What did Dionísia have in mind? What did he think of her friend Dionísia? Maria Lluïsa would have liked for Dionísia to have a flaw in her skin that made her repulsive, or for her voice to be extremely disagreeable, or for her body to have unimaginable deformities. Was Dionísia was in love with Pat? Did she just want to toy with him and take him away from her? Was she telling the truth? No. Maria Lluïsa was sure it was just the opposite. She thought her friend had been covering up even more than she had. But what did Dionísia have to offer? What did Pat see in her? Maria Lluïsa started comparing, she analyzed her figure in the mirror. She was secure about her beauty and her grace, and she knew she was chic. Dionísia was a lesser beauty, her face was less refined, her skin was less exciting. It was impossible for Pat to prefer Dionísia to her.

But Maria Lluïsa was frightened, she was full of fear. Why? Hadn't she been convinced just a few hours ago that Pat was a selfish, common creature, a boy like any other? What had happened that morning was an incident of no importance. Their conversation over the aperitif had been completely banal, but even so, now, in bed, Maria Lluïsa ran her hand over those corners of her body that had been visited by the audacity of the swimmer. She realized then that the morning scene had not been an act of generosity on her part. In the warmth between her sheets, her skin pearled with sweat, she realized that the one who had been magnanimous was he. He had favored her with the contact of his hand, his slightly rough hand, on the sleeping irrelevance of her eighteen year-old belly. Pat had done her the favor of awakening her to the flush of a world she hadn't suspected. Maria Lluïsa stroked her own skin with her hand and thought that Pat could never find that feverish and welcoming tremble in Dionísia's flesh. Her hatred for Dionísia became more and more intense. Lying in bed, her pajamas open, her entire body saturated with darkness and silence, with the unconscious breathing of her cousins two steps away, Maria Lluïsa was horrified at herself. How could she be having such feelings? She had known so very many boys just like that aquatic seducer, and none of them had had any effect on her. And he, more common, more childish, more insignificant than many of her friends, had swept her off her feet in less than twenty-four hours. In truth, what was there between them? Very little. She couldn't rely on a single feeling that boy might have. She realized that her heart was beating at an absurd rate. But Maria Lluïsa insisted that it was not precisely her heart, that she wasn't the slightest bit enamored. Maria Lluïsa wanted to convince herself that all that was not love. She wanted to believe it had all started with the conversation with Dionísia. The false nonchalance with which her friend had spoken of him had awakened her fear that Dionísia might interest Pat more than she did. She feared that in those four days there had been some real contact between Dionísia and him, and that she, in her innocence, had not realized it. Dionísia was capable of having robbed her of that iodized physique in the most underhanded way. Because when Maria Lluïsa thought of her swimmer, she could only see his belly, his torso, his arms, his naked smile, and his coal-black gaze. She lingered over his skin, over the sensual irradiation of the charm of his words...

Maria Lluïsa was astonished that she could think all those thoughts, with no shame, with all that animal desire, with such a lack of concern for her friend that she would have wished her dead. And all for what? For a boy to whom, as Dionísia said, they were paying more attention than he deserved.

Henriette heard Maria Lluïsa's noticeable sighs. Perhaps she might have heard a sob, and she sprang from her bed to see what was wrong. Maria Lluïsa grabbed her by the hand; Henriette felt a feverish contact, but her cousin didn't say a word, she just clung to her hand, she drew her closer, she put her arm around her waist and made her lie down with her. Maria Lluïsa needed company, she needed a warm skin next to her own, a generous flesh. Henriette didn't know what was going on, and she kissed Maria Lluïsa. Under her kisses, Maria Lluïsa broke into abundant silent tears, hiding her head against Henriette's hard, vibrant breasts. The wet warmth of Maria Lluïsa's tears pervaded her cousin with a strange voluptuosity. When she had found some release through her tears, Maria Lluïsa felt as if a cord tying her lungs had been broken. Henriette got out of Maria Lluïsa's bed and slipped back into her own sheets a bit amazed and a bit ashamed of what had happened.

———·———

FOUR MONTHS AFTER those scenes on the beach, Maria Lluïsa rested her head enveloped in her mane of tangled hair on Pat's gray jacket. In her left hand she was holding a black velvet cap; with her right hand she was taking a cigarette stained with red from her lips. Maria Lluïsa half-closed her eyes lashed by a cold wind and ran the wet end of the cigarette over the tip of her nose. Maria Lluïsa's smile was made of the same clean, cold gold as that December morning. His fingers on the steering wheel, Pat had one eye on the highway and one on Maria Lluïsa's cheek. Maria Lluïsa's head bobbled delightfully on Pat's collarbone, following the rhythm of the suspension. Pat could sense her ideas, resting on the wool of his jacket, but he didn't understand them. A special light flowed through Maria Lluïsa's eyelashes, as if her thoughts were pearly fish wriggling among the mysterious flora of an aquarium, and a bit of the glint of their scales escaped through her pupils.

On one side of the highway, a red gas pump stood out against the dying silver of a hedge. Pat stopped to get ten litres. Maria Lluïsa used the time spent in this maneuver to fix her hair, her cheeks and her lips. When the motor started up again, a fragment of a melody of a java song no longer in fashion knocked Maria Lluïsa in the teeth. Most likely the blood red gash on the tip of her cigarette suggested the blood red color of the song. For Maria Lluïsa, java was an atmosphere: exposed nerve endings with a tremulous erotic voracity, *cassis*-tinted foulards, and a blade retreating like a squid through the smoke, slippery with the green moss of peppermint liqueur. For Maria Lluïsa, java music was a sort of protest against the bare landscape lacking in ambition on either side of the road, against Pat's gray jacket, against the perfect symmetry of the steering wheel, and against the little mirror in which she could see Pat's mouth, just as bare and lacking in ambition as the landscape. Maria Lluïsa turned off the song and rubbed her forehead on her friend's lapel, just as one might wipe a tool or a drill bit off on a sheepskin rag before making an incision.

"Pat, you'll never guess what I'm thinking."

"What?"

"I'm tired of being a virgin."

"Shocking…" Pat said this in English.

Since that dark night on which Maria Lluïsa would have liked to see Dionísia turn into a monster, Pat had eased up on his audacity. In the water, their contact had been so epidermal and so entwined with laughter that Maria Lluïsa started down a via crucis of disappointment. Pat, on the other hand, fell into a contemplative tenderness in the presence of her natural blessings. The young man's behavior knew no middle ground between animalistic assault and delicately inane lyricism. But Maria Lluïsa liked him a lot, and she liked him even more when he tore himself away from them and struggled all by himself with his outboard motorboat, filling the blue waters with thunderous noise. Then the young man was someone, he represented a bountiful living element in a landscape of muscles and machines, without an ounce of brains or ill will. It broke Maria Lluïsa's heart.

In Barcelona, she and Pat began to meet up and drive around in the Chrysler. Maria Lluïsa noticed Pat's timidity: he preferred to circumvent her in a dangerous calculus of twists and turns, always sidestepping the real issue. Pat's kisses seemed perfunctory, performed completely out of touch with his nervous system. But she could tell that he wanted her, even as he felt a great respect for her. The young man was afraid of Maria Lluïsa, and he was afraid of an intense affair with her. At first he thought he was simply in love with her. Then he found her to be too much of a woman for him. Maria Lluïsa disconcerted him. The young woman ran rings around him. Pat had a primitive idea of love, a romantic notion he had drawn from books. Pat thought there was an incredible emotional abyss between the kind of women with whom he had been intimate and the girls of his class. With a girl from his class whom he didn't particularly care for, he felt he could take liberties and try a few moves that didn't go anywhere, like those aquatic fantasies in Llafranc. They were ways of passing time that didn't compromise anyone and could be snatched like a delightful prank. But when he started to take an interest in a girl of his class, Pat imagined that love was swaddled in such complicated veils and required such solemn genuflections that he felt totally lost.

And this is why Maria Lluïsa's way of being, so direct, simple, and unceremonious, was so disconcerting. She would take his arm, muss his hair, and kiss him on the lips so very naturally, as if it were the least important thing in the world, as if Pat were a doll on her sofa or a little pedigreed dog. When Maria Lluïsa was being effusive in this way, Pat felt inhibited, and his response to her coquetries was stilted and fearful. If Maria Lluïsa's behavior with him had been reserved and a little hypocritical, doubtless Pat would have become incandescent, and his impulse, always under the restraints of his archangelic idea of love, would have manifested itself with more nerve. It was Maria Lluïsa's temperament that disconcerted Pat and kept him from doing cartwheels. He, who was fed up with escorting all kinds of women affecting the disenchanted punctiliousness of the *amant de coeur*, didn't know what to do with a woman like Maria Lluïsa. The fact is, it was the first time in his life that he found himself in such a situation.

When Maria Lluïsa told him she was tired of being a virgin, Pat took it to be one of her *boutades*, a simple wish to play the *enfant terrible*, and he smiled, certain that those words meant no more to her than if she had said she found the smell of his hair lotion unpleasant. Pat could not conceive by any means that Maria Lluïsa had said those words seriously, because the idea he had about girls like her required him to apply an inflexible formula that allowed for no exceptions. At heart, Pat was an innocent. Like many boys of his class, he had become fully sexually active before he knew it, and his bourgeois education had imposed strict criteria on him for the classification of the women of this world.

Pat didn't realize that the essential character of a person can't be found in her position in life or in the opinions others may have of her, but rather that the essential character is hidden in her core, independent of time and space, or of morality and prejudices. Pat's error was to believe that by the mere token of living off her body a prostitute could not be, deep down, more sensitive and a better person than his sisters. And he was also mistaken in believing that a girl of Maria Lluïsa's class and education, solely by virtue of being of that class, could not be serious in saying, purposefully and sincerely, that she was tired of being a virgin.

These fatal errors led Pat to believe he had the right to treat all prostitutes with contempt and the obligation to consider it a simple extravagance that a girl like Maria Lluïsa should express such an a shameless concept.

In fact, Maria Lluïsa, swept along by a suggestion as banal as the java song that had knocked her in the teeth, was saying something bound to an authentic desire, to an experience she considered to be a prime necessity.

Maria Lluïsa was incapable of formulating an idea like that, by making use of the emotional circumstances of a moment that could be historic in her life. Maria Lluïsa chose an indifferent temperature and landscape, she chose a tone of voice without chiaroscuro, and even a smile that neutralized the transcendence of what she had just said. Maria Lluïsa had learned quite a few things in those few months. She had become good friends with a young woman who worked at the bank with her. This young woman, of black extraction, overcame the high yellow whiff of her family's origins with the oceanic play of her hips and a hairdresser equipped with solvents. This girl was the lover of the assistant director, and she carried this role with the aloof and dissembling dignity of a girl who doesn't beat around the bush. She had already had two abortions and she was ready to do it again, with aplomb. Maria Lluïsa took everything that came from her friend's lips to be an article of faith, and when she turned out the light in her bedroom in the apartment on Carrer Bailèn, she had those subversive goods in her baggage. Gifted in the realistic analysis that women tend to perform instinctively, Maria Lluïsa could see the moral catastrophe of her ancestors. She saw the hysterical, petty and hypocritical ineptitude of Maria Carreres and the abusive and egotistical blubber of her maternal grandmother. Maria Lluïsa felt just as foreign next to her mother's bleached hair as she did beside the raffia moustache of a Congolese divinity.

In our country there are families in full productivity, in which parents and children live as if they were bound together by a fever of collaboration, helping one another, the parents filling the children's feeder with the last crumbs of their meal. They have a family spirit, sometimes aggressive, sometimes defensive. These are people who are still infused with the ferment of the workingman or the cringing of the shopkeeper that can bend their backbone. In contrast, there are families of long tradition that are so evaporated, squeezed so dry, whose social productivity is so nullified that their members feel a fatal desire to separate, to flee from the paternal path, to destroy the family spirit. The Lloberolas, and other ancient houses like theirs, had been attacked by the latter microbe. Before her parents, Maria Lluïsa felt the same thing Frederic, Josefina and Guillem felt before Don Tomàs de Lloberola. All of them fled for their own reasons, and all of them hated and rejected their parents' ideas and feelings in their own ways. Maria Lluïsa was just the same. She didn't want to have anything to do with the tearful, leather-bound moral cowardice of her mother. She felt an inhuman contempt for Frederic. She wanted to be herself, a Maria Lluïsa in touch with her heart, whose name perforce was Lloberola, but who didn't have anything to do with them.

The same anarchic sentiment that moved Frederic to choose Rosa Trènor as his lover, the same anarchic sentiment that made it tolerable for Guillem to don his vagabond rags and accept Dorotea Palau's three hundred pessetes, was at the heart of the feeling of disintegration, destruction and disdain that compelled Maria Lluïsa to say that she was tired of being a virgin.

And it was not just words. Maria Lluïsa had thought these things through in her own way. She was aware that, in those times, materialism, as some saw it, or a more rational and understanding vision, as others saw it, had undermined certain principles that the pre-war bourgeoisie defended tooth and nail, including the principles having to do with modesty and sex. In this world, female figures who dispensed with modesty were well thought of, welcomed, and admired, even if it was only at a distance, even if it was only in their existence in film and theater. The remoteness of this consideration was shrinking so steadily that it was reaching as far as personal relations, practically even direct contact. Maria Lluïsa discovered cases she had only seen in novels in close proximity, on her own street, at her own workplace, a meter away from her own typewriter. Maria Lluïsa knew single women, the daughters of bourgeois families, who had lovers, and enjoyed the shadiest of intimate interludes. Some of them became emancipated in good faith, others out of passion, and others coldly, in pursuit of a utilitarian end or a perversion with no material compensation.

Not that everyone Maria Lluïsa frequented was like this. One step away there was still passive resistance, the world of numb silence, prejudice, routine and sanctimonious devotion, servile imitation, fear, solitary vices. That was the system advocated by her mother, by the Lloberolas, that is, the family phantasm that was smothering Maria Lluïsa and from which she wanted to free herself by leaping into the field of liberty and lack of shame, accepting all the risks and all the potential catastrophes.

It isn't that Maria Lluïsa had a vocation for perversity, or an ideal of unrestrained libertinage. Maria Lluïsa still believed in a trace of heroism, in delicate and ardent possibilities, if she decided to break the intact urn of her maidenhood. Maria Lluïsa saw that if she took her mother's tack, she exposed herself above all to wasting time waiting for the one who would decide to marry her, and she exposed herself, even more, to that decision's never taking place, and she exposed herself to the possibility that the man who did take possession would be wrong in every way. In a word, in her mother's tack, Maria Lluïsa saw only an ominous dependency upon marriage. Maria Lluïsa reasoned this out in a childish and unsophisticated way, as many girls might do. But at very least, she was consistent in her ideas and did her best to be straightforward. In rejecting her mother's technique, obeying that feeling of disintegration and destruction, Maria Lluïsa accepted as a certainty that the importance of virginity was quite relative. Once she had accepted that, her decorum saw no obstacle in offering it to someone she herself had chosen, a young man who was physically pleasing and agreeable, and with whom she hoped to experience Dionysian moments, with no strings attached. And she wanted to give herself to that young man sitting by her side at the wheel because, as very limited and full of flaws as he was, he had not pursued her voraciously and incontinently. Pat had not taken any initiative in this regard. After that morning in Llafranc, Maria Lluïsa was a bit disappointed, but at the same time, the boy's passivity gave her a reason to keep observing him, to analyze quietly if he was the right boy on whom to gamble her deepest intimacy. Maria Lluïsa felt the pleasure of choosing her own man, without any lasting ties, when the time was ripe, and when her desire was sweetest. Maria Lluïsa, at eighteen, dreamed of all these things. Naturally they had their risks and dangers, but as we have already said, the Lloberola cowardice was one of the family flaws Maria Lluïsa had avoided.

When Pat said the word "shocking," Maria Lluïsa blanched, her eyes clouded over, and her mouth clenched in a grimace of sadness. Pat stopped the Chrysler and looked closely at Maria Lluïsa's face. The boy was beginning to discover a new hemisphere, the hemisphere in which all the paradoxical constellations of a girl's nerves spin. With the disconcerted tenderness of a porter accustomed to carrying sacks on his back who finds a newborn baby in his hands, he took Maria Lluïsa's head in his trembling hands and said "Forgive me," in an almost inaudible voice. Maria Lluïsa relaxed her teeth, and through the opening between those two rows of enameled snow, Pat slipped his tongue, burning with thirst.

Maria Lluïsa was the first to react. Pat's eyes were wet with tears and she dried his face with her scarf.

"No tragedies, Pat, do you understand?"

The young man felt ashamed and humiliated. They drove all the way to the Diagonal without saying a word. Maria Lluïsa kept singing her java song. Pat was frightened by the decision he had just made. When he dropped Maria Lluïsa off near her house, his inexperience led him to say these words:

"Listen, Maria Lluïsa. Are you sure you're not making fun of me?"

Maria Lluïsa responded with a fresh, natural smile. They agreed to meet at six p.m.

Pat had told his friends that Maria Lluïsa was a girl who liked to pretend to be modern, and whose head was full of hot air. Whenever someone insinuated that anything definitive might have gone on between them, Pat would get indignant and say:

"Get out of here! What are you thinking?"

Pat's twenty-five years had given him great arrogance and aplomb in his judgment of women. He knew perfectly well how far he could get with this one and that one. But he wasn't quite sure whether Maria Lluïsa wanted to entrap him, or if she just wanted to have a good time and amuse herself. He also wasn't quite sure whether he would let himself be entrapped or if he would merely collaborate in having a good time with Maria Lluïsa. Pat was convinced of one thing, and that was that if by chance he were so foolhardy as to take Maria Lluïsa into a room with a bed at the ready, Maria Lluïsa would defend herself heroically and never again look him in the face. The events of the afternoon demonstrated quite the opposite. They showed that Pat's certainty had been entirely unwarranted.

Pat went to pick Maria Lluïsa up at the arranged time, still not sure of anything, still believing that she was sort of toying with him. Pat couldn't bring himself to accept that Maria Lluïsa would hatch such an important plan so lightly, but what filled him with misgivings were the color of her face and the perplexing mystery in her eyes after he had spoken the word "shocking." For Pat, Maria Lluïsa continued to be the same enigmatic girl who frightened him. That afternoon, though, Pat was feeling virile; he wanted to solve the problem with all his being, no matter what. They met up at six.

"Where do you want to go?" Pat said.

"Wherever you want," she answered.

As a precaution, Pat had left the Chrysler in the garage. A taxi would be less noticeable in the event she agreed to go to a *meublé*.

Until Pat closed the door of the room with a key she said nothing. In the taxi she was rather nervous, her heart was beating violently, and her eyes were wet and shiny. Pat took her arm with a trembling, sweaty hand, and from time to time he kissed her hair and her ears. When they were alone in the room, Maria Lluïsa parted her lips to tell him:

"If you want me to get undressed, you'll have to turn out the light."

The room was completely dark, and between the panting and excitement that were only natural, the job of unbuttoning went a little slowly. A soft hiss of silks and wool, a grotesque clang of keys and coins, of shoes, which in situations like this are noisy as clogs, and then the peculiar squeak of the mattress springs and the protests of the metal fittings of the bed at that moment when two disconcerted bodies fall onto it. The integral dialogue of their two naked bodies was imbued with the madness of discovery. Words did not achieve expression; contact electrified them from their lips to their toes. Their bodies tangled and intertwined, and their hands would have liked to reach beyond their ribs. When Pat's eyes reached the right glassiness and phosphorescence, he destroyed what Maria Lluïsa had tired of. With a girl as athletic and flexible as Maria Lluïsa, the job was already half done. Pat found himself in a natural situation; he practically didn't notice the difference. She moaned, but only softly. The feeling was not as intense as she had imagined. Later, with Pat's arm around Maria Lluïsa's waist, when he felt the wetness of her cheeks cooling his breast, he experienced a moment that was more tender, sweet, and full of reverence than any other in his life. In a daze he kissed her forehead over and over. His lips didn't form the shape of a kiss, but Maria Lluïsa felt them in every drop of her blood.

In truth, what had just happened to them replaced the air in the room with a gas of sadness and incomprehension. Those two naked children wanted to laugh, but they had no strength, and the mouth of the one sought refuge in the mouth of the other. Then Maria Lluïsa shut herself into the bathroom, and Pat lit a cigarette. At that point Pat realized that he was satisfied; the oil of vanity breathed through the pores of his skin.

From that day on their intimate encounters at the *meublé* multiplied. Maria Lluïsa came to have a perfect naturalness, approaching indifference. She came to realize that she was not the temperamental type. Pat was full of enthusiasm but also so full of fear that he could have jumped out of his skin. He couldn't help but tell two or three of his friends about the deal that had fallen into his hands. At first, Pat experienced sensational moments, but soon he was invaded by qualms and misgivings. Above all, by the fear that the whole thing could get complicated, that a moment of carelessness on his part or a lack of hygienic experience on hers might end up creating a conflict. Maria Lluïsa had never spoken of even the remotest commitment or obligation; she hardly even mentioned love. Maria Lluïsa was satisfied; it was she who had wanted this. From their first afternoon in the *meublé*, when she went home for dinner she looked at her mother with more self-assured eyes, and her smile was colder and more self-satisfied. Her friend from the bank cauterized any of the insignificant remnants of a scruple she might harbor in her heart. She managed to flee from sentimentalism as if from a contagious disease and, despite all this, Maria Lluïsa felt her dependency upon Pat, she felt that she loved him, but she didn't want to confess it under any circumstances. She wanted to believe that Pat was an instrument for her own private use, to resolve a need in her intimate life, and nothing more.

As things became routine, Pat began detaching himself from all the poetry of their contacts and came to see Maria Lluïsa's body as just one of many. They became so familiar with each other that love slipped away into the physiological routine. Pat wasn't a boy with the imagination to refresh situations, to enhance new onslaughts with a touch of lyricism. No matter what literature says, the practice of love is monotonous. If there isn't a faith and a tenderness underlying it, sex becomes mechanical and boredom waters down the veins. To compensate for this, Pat tried to rough up the scenes a bit. Maria Lluïsa followed him effortlessly. Pat was too accustomed to treating only one kind of woman to stray from the acquired procedure, and he applied to Maria Lluïsa's flesh the practices of the others. His language was pure at first; salty or crass words alluding to the erotic function were far from his thoughts. Later, those words and those thoughts appeared one by one, at first timidly, and later with insolence. Finally they were just normal and had lost all their spice. Maria Lluïsa was becoming intoxicated with a gas characteristic of brothels. Pat obliviously allowed her to become intoxicated. As Maria Lluïsa relinquished her last traces of modesty, Pat felt more composed. Each of them was beyond the danger of falling in love. A few months had gone by and everything was smooth as silk. They met a couple of times each week. Maria Lluïsa averted all the family dangers, and Pat no longer bothered to pretend when people alluded to his *collage*, smiling with the affable vanity of a self-indulgent child.

At the bank where Maria Lluïsa worked it seems that someone hinted at things about her and someone high up in the establishment took a greater interest in her. Maria Lluïsa's friend told her not to be a fool, but she hadn't yet come to this conclusion. Much to the contrary. Ever since Maria Lluïsa and Pat were lovers, she had become much more reserved with other men. She wasn't doing it to be faithful to him. It was more out of self-preservation, to defend the willful demise of her moral sense behind a mask of correctness.

Ten months had gone by since the scenes at the beach in Llafranc, and the change in Maria Lluïsa's soul was inconceivable. The truth be told, this was only a rapid and astonishing growth of the seeds Maria Lluïsa unwittingly carried inside. The strangest thing was that, through the whole affair, Maria Lluïsa was destroying any trace of sentimentalism day by day. She even realized that she didn't feel the slightest bit jealous if she saw that Pat was feeding her a couple of lies to cover up his involvement with other women. Maria Lluïsa had turned her relationship with him into a bit of sport. It was true that she had tired of her virginity, and her sustained commerce with a fresh, muscular, and well-groomed young man gave Maria Lluïsa more aplomb and allowed her to walk in the world with more satisfaction, appetite, and joy. Pat found in her all the advantages of a delicious vamp, without any of the drawbacks or annoyances because, in addition, Maria Lluïsa was docile and undemanding. If on occasion it wasn't good for Pat to go out with her, Maria Lluïsa didn't protest in the least and always understood.

The Lloberola tarnish had produced in Maria Lluïsa a variation on her uncle Guillem. Not for nothing did Leocàdia feel the same tenderness and the same fear when she looked at her younger son and her older granddaughter.

When things had been going on like that for a year, when Pat had lost any trace of scruples or fears, the conflict arose. More than two months had gone by since Maria Lluïsa had had what ladies call their period. The young woman was a bit unnerved. The symptoms were quite clear: pain in the kidneys, upset stomach, some swelling in the ankles, and an aversion to cigarettes and to strong smells. Maria Lluïsa kept silent, hoping for a solution, but ended up telling her friend at the bank. The girl gave her a remedy that was nothing but a strong purgative. Maria Lluïsa had a very unpleasant reaction but it didn't solve anything. Then Maria Lluïsa told Pat. It fell on him like a bombshell. The first few months it had been all he thought about, but after a year it didn't seem possible any more. He had become accustomed to the thought that this danger didn't exist. When she saw Pat's anxiety and desperation, Maria Lluïsa started laughing in his face like a madwoman.

"I always thought you were a chicken."

"Oh, sure, a chicken. What do you expect me to do?"

"Nothing, Pat. I don't want you to do anything."

Pat had in fact started to be fed up with their relations; they no longer held any interest for him. All that was left was servile routine and Pat was distracted by other things. Marrying Maria Lluïsa was the farthest thing from his mind. For the time being Pat didn't want to marry anyone, much less Maria Lluïsa. His idea of matrimony was ultraconservative. One thing was a lover, but a potential legitimate wife was something entirely different. Maria Lluïsa was, to him, an absurd, insecure, morally-depraved girl. He had contributed to her supposed depravation, but that was of no importance. Pat didn't even realize it. If his back were up against the wall, he wouldn't have hesitated to affirm that he was blameless in the case of Maria Lluïsa, and that it was she who had ravished him. Pat didn't have the guts to tell his father about the problem; he would have been furious. Maria Lluïsa came from a noble family, but they were absolutely ruined. In his house they had no social standing. She was earning her living in a bank as an ordinary typist. Pat thought of his sister Isabel, of the aristocratic pretensions of the Sabadells, of his father's millions, his factory, his outboard motorboat, his friends in the Club Nàutic and the Club Eqüestre. It was monstrous, it was impossible. On the other hand, the girl had known no other man than he and Pat unquestionably had to confess he was the father of the child she was carrying in her womb. Not that the Sabadell mentality gave no credence to considerations of conscience. Pat was perfectly aware of the question of conscience and of his duty as a gentleman and a man, but, terrified and in a panic, he said nothing. Wide-eyed before Maria Lluïsa's bitter smile, he was incapable of making a decision. He was afraid to propose an abortion to her. Such a thing would have to be her idea, and an operation could be dangerous. Pat didn't know anything about such things. His ideas about obstetrics were very vague, but he had heard that such procedures, in addition to being a crime, were dangerous and sometimes fatal. The idea of an infanticide was repugnant to his sentimental, bourgeois mentality, but even more repugnant was the idea of confessing to the whole affair and marrying Maria Lluïsa. Pat was a weak, spoiled child, a creature who could drown in a glass of water.

Maria Lluïsa watched him without saying a word. She could deduce the path of Pat's thoughts as if a malignant spirit were inscribing them on his forehead as they emerged. Maria Lluïsa understood everything. She saw his rejection, and his cowardice. His scandalously conservative twenty-six years of age, and his industrialist's soul with no capacity for uncertainty. Pat didn't dare break the silence, and almost by force he tried to draw Maria Lluïsa to his breast and embrace her dramatically. With great delicacy, Maria Lluïsa resisted.

"What solution do you suggest for me, Pat? What do you think I should do? What do you think you should do?"

Pat didn't answer. He shrugged his shoulders and finally expelled an "I don't know" so profoundly strained it could have been uttered by a fifty year-old man, and not by a boy with suntanned skin who had enameled his teeth with sea air and paroxysms of sport. Maria Lluïsa put her hand on his shoulder and, decisively and maternally, said:

"Don't worry your head about it, Pat. Don't give it another thought."

Pat sniveled:

"What will you think of me, Maria Lluïsa?"

"What else can I think? That you're a baby…just a wretched baby…"

When Maria Lluïsa was alone again, the scene with Pat began to sink in. She had certainly expected something along those lines from him, but not that bad. Then she began to realize that despite her desire to stifle sentimentalism, she did love Pat, she had believed in him a little. This had been an acute disappointment. Maria Lluïsa had never supposed that marriage would be the solution to her problem, it wasn't that. But she did expect a bit more generosity on his part, some compassion, at least some goodwill. Maria Lluïsa was perfectly aware, and she blamed herself, that she was the one who had wanted this, and she had no intention of demanding anything at all from her lover. But women, even the most realistic of them, always retain a bit of romantic illusion, they always believe in the possibility of a gentleman who will know how to make a gentleman's gesture. And that boy from the outboard motorboat perhaps was just not enough of a gentleman. However, since Maria Lluïsa was a decisive young woman, she let Pat be. She would never demean herself by asking for anything. For a moment – Maria Lluïsa was a girl of nineteen – she entertained the idea of a sincere maternity with all the consequences. But that just couldn't be. Maria Lluïsa envisioned her family panorama. Such a scandal could by no means take place in a climate so bitter, shattered, and lacking in comfort as their apartment on Carrer Bailèn. The humiliation would be too great. The disdain Maria Lluïsa felt for her mother and for all her kin, the independence she had imposed on herself as her primary obligation, made it impossible for her to lose face before them. In her house, the word "dishonor" was the only applicable word in this case. And she found this word to be so stupid, so inhuman, that she would rather die than accept it. The romantic thought of running away, breaking with all their prejudices, keeping her job and looking for someone to help her out also passed through Maria Lluïsa's head, but she was too pretty and she believed too truly in a sporting and decorative idea of life to be prepared to make such sacrifices. Besides, as yet she had no sense of motherhood; it was pure literature to her. What she felt was apprehension, horror at her situation, and the desire to free herself at any cost. This wasn't motherhood. No inner light had shone, there had been no metamorphosis of affection. What she was going through was simply shame and misfortune. Of all the possible solutions, Maria Lluïsa chose the one that was most shabby, expeditious, and in keeping with her moral temperature. Her friend from the bank made the arrangements. She needed around a thousand pessetes. Maria Lluïsa didn't have so much money and even though she hated to ask Pat for it, she didn't have any choice. Pat dispensed the money with a philanthropic pomposity, and he felt that those thousand pessetes absolved him of all obligation. Maria Lluïsa accepted the money with the proviso that she would return it and made him swear he would accept it when the time came.

Her friend accompanied her early one afternoon to the home of an acquaintance in whom she had utter confidence. She was a woman of around forty-five, with a pretty face, but much the worse for wear. She had an apartment on Carrer de Rosselló, decorated with airs of refinement, in which a slightly offensive scent of smut prevailed. The woman was neither a midwife nor in the trade, but she dealt in resolving the untimely conflicts of love with discretion and a modicum of safety. The woman's assistant was a man of around thirty, a medical doctor, lean, with a sallow complexion, and somewhat repulsive. He treated the patients with cloying sweetness and double entendres.

Though Maria Lluïsa answered the questions the lady asked her with naturalness, the woman was clearly affected.

The sallow doctor took up his duties in a chamber expressly equipped to be like a clinic. The operation went off relatively easily and with a satisfactory outcome. It was very painful, but Maria Lluïsa bore it with that endurance peculiar to women.

After the operation, she lay in the proprietor's bed for four hours. The good woman offered advice and tried to give her guidance. Maria Lluïsa listened vaguely, but her head was weak. When the doctor returned it was nine in the evening. He took Maria Lluïsa's pulse, said it was safe to go home, but that she should be very careful, and prescribed a prophylactic treatment for a few days.

The run-down woman with the pretty face took Maria Lluïsa and her friend to the door. When they said goodbye, she kissed Maria Lluïsa on the cheeks with great effusiveness. The woman's name was Rosa Trènor.

—·—·—

MARIA LLUÏSA'S BRAIN was voracious for negative ideas. It had destroyed the possibility of a love that would move the sun and the stars. It didn't believe in the appearance of some St. George in a suit, much less in the dragon he would slay.

For her the world was a mass of putty, stupidly come into existence. Since she had been born of this mass, she didn't protest. It was the salty, blue water in which her arms could become skilled in the perfect crawl. Maria Lluïsa accepted the most brilliant, amoral and metallic aspects of her time. Her landscape still allowed for the presence of enraptured souls and of souls who enraptured. She wanted to be one of the ones who enraptured. She vaguely recalled that her grandfather had been a man of principle. Her grandfather's principles seemed just as anachronistic and offensive to her as a boy who went to sunbathe on the beach dressed up as a little shepherd or a devil from *Els Pastorets*, the Christmas play. Maria Lluïsa felt a passion for resplendent trash. Her imagination was like those great luminous advertisements that flash on and off, lashed to symmetrical cages of stone and cement, fascinating millions of men who drag their dread down asphalt streets and breathe in a night heavy with alcohol, perfume, ambition and misery. Maria Lluïsa's tactic was that of many of her time: improvisation. This way of grabbing onto the antennae of life was the strongest imprint left by the war on a society that only began to evolve in the 1920's. Improvisation was exactly the same as living day to day. Barcelona suffered greatly from this, particularly in the most spectacular arenas. The way fortunes were made and unmade, and the ease of acquiring a sort of universal pass for being seated in the front row of the grand world, without concern for the moral antecedents or the condition of the subjects' shirts were the surest signs of the general reigning confusion and vain intestinal spirit of survival. Some periods take into account the name and family traditions of a person before conceding him any status; in other, more democratic, and perhaps more understanding periods, they have stressed intelligence, ingenuity, and even physical beauty, always valuing the clean and well-groomed person. Other, more recent, periods, in order to come to a judgment about a person, only make note of his shirt-maker, her stylist, their dog, or their automobile. Maria Lluïsa belonged to one of those periods in which the value of the person took only second or third place. In first place ranked the crease in one's trousers or the quality of one's stockings.

To affirm that a lady was sublime neither her witticisms, nor her acts of philanthropy, nor the anatomical perfection of her hips were mentioned. The only thing worthy of comment was the color or make of the dress she wore to this party or that concert. In general, people limited their vocabulary to the words "nice" or "not nice." The words "just," "honest," "brave," "contemptible," or "ignorant," were not in good form over the green of a golf course or a bridge table. It was very easy to be nice, because Maria Lluïsa's era was also one of the less demanding, and the dimension of the glands secreting niceness were four times the size of the liver.

After her year of sexual apprenticeship, Maria Lluïsa was perfectly equipped to calculate the value of all her physical attributes without falling into the traps set for shy, inexpert or innocent girls. Fortunately, Pat was so inferior to her that he had not left any trace of himself or any kind of depravity in the blue and pink regions of her soul. When the moment of disenchantment arrived, in the face of Pat's selfishness and cowardice, the bit of affection Maria Lluïsa had felt for him allowed her to react without violence. So it was that her blood absorbed a few injections of bitter skepticism and she developed – and in this she was quite mistaken – an absolutely pejorative notion of men's emotions. Maria Lluïsa believed that all the boys of her day with a bit of decorative value, like Pat, would behave the same way, and that a girl like her could not harbor any illusions of finding anything better. Maria Lluïsa did not suffer the nerves of many women her age, who dream of a great love and, unsatisfied and disillusioned, don't realize they have failed until they find their hearts dried up in their fingers like a useless object. Maria Lluïsa was lucky enough to sense the presence of delightful topics in the world that were not precisely the death of Isolde or the imitation of that death as it is carried out between an infinity of sheets in public houses and private homes. Even at the start of her relations with Pat, Maria Lluïsa had realized she was not at all temperamental. Maria Lluïsa's sensibility resided as much or more in her eyes, her skin, and her palate, and, above all, in her imagination, as it did in the secret corners nature has destined for the most celestial and nebulous of joys. Maria Lluïsa felt that a very furry, flexible, and Machiavellian fox coat or a flawless diamond were much more intense things than the fifth Canto of the Divine Comedy. And this theory of Maria Lluïsa's should not be seen with overly scrupulous eyes; it was a perfectly human theory, shared by numerous illustrious personalities of the time.

One of Maria Lluïsa's characteristics was her lack of dignity. This became more pronounced after the intervention at Rosa Trènor's house. Maria Lluïsa's era emphasized pure economics, a consequence of which was a relaxation of the sentiment of personal dignity. In Maria Lluïsa, though, this relaxation was aggravated by family circumstances. It's curious to see how a working-class family or a craftsman or mechanic's family, or even someone from the middle class working to make a place for himself, feels a sort of gratification, and pride, and most definitely a sense of dignity that families from the grand tradition, accustomed to not working, and for whom the easy life has taken the place of initiative, do not feel, just as economic catastrophe is launching a stage of moral decay. In such families the lack of dignity can sometimes reach unimaginable extremes.

We have already indicated some similarities between Maria Lluïsa and her uncle, Guillem de Lloberola. In fairness to Maria Lluïsa, it must be noted that her family couldn't offer her any shining examples. The spectacle of her father and mother only served to unleash shamelessness and disaffection. When Maria Lluïsa was able to get a bit free of them, the bank where she worked, the staff she worked for, and her friends were all people who used toothbrushes and worked to fill their stomachs. Pat had pretty clear ideas about sports, but his concept of human dignity was mean and anemic, suffocated by mufflers, sports shirts, and insurance policies.

Maria Lluïsa had experienced these climes, excellent breeding grounds for the fatty existence of the microbe they carry in their blood, a microbe that was nothing more than atavistic fatalism and the natural consequence of the decomposition of the Lloberola family.

Maria Lluïsa's flaws, in the days when she was nearing her twentieth birthday, were hidden under her ever-so-tender skin, her luminous and artless smile, her natural, soaring way of doing things, and her quality of pure blood and distinction that adhered even to the drabbest and most conventional sweater restraining the rigid joy of her breasts.

It was both the flaws and gifts of that young woman that brought into her life people the reader is already acquainted with. The pages to come will explain how, in human existence, whether by chance, by fate, or by predestination, names that had been separated come to be joined again. An invisible thread of some kind ties their souls together against their wills, and in the end men and women realize that they have staked all their blood on a useless farce of a game. The only thing left of it is a bit of a bad taste in the mouth and a few steps forward on the road to death.

The name of the friend who had had the two abortions was Teresa Martínez. She was older than Maria Lluïsa, and had been frequenting Rosa Trènor's apartment for a good while. Since we abandoned Rosa Trènor at the entrance to the Grill Room, after she slashed Frederic's face and wrapped herself in the balding skin of her beaver coat, her life had taken quite a few turns. She had cloaked her life of revelry and sentimentality in tones of respectability. When she realized that the exploitation of her body was a losing business, Rosa Trènor opted to exploit others' bodies.

Rosa Trènor established her business with the utmost discretion. Secrecy and mystery were her accomplices. The friends of her youth and the pleasant clients of her autumn years visited Rosa Trènor's house on the pretext of having a glass of champagne or a cup of tea.

Everything else was up to Rosa Trènor, and her friends were utterly satisfied. The staff she chose for the business were girls from needy homes and even some from good families. From typists to members of the tennis club: a bit of everything. A very small and perfectly reliable staff.

At the time of the Exposició Universal, Rosa established a great friendship with an extremely important person, a general. Rosa's every wish was his desire. At that point she expanded other facets of her little business. She bought a few thousand meters of pornographic film and she installed a baccarat table. Rosa Trènor's apartment was on the second floor of the building, the traditional noble floor, where one would least expect such a place. A plaque on the door that read "La Aseguradora Agrícola, S. A.," lent the landing an aura of actuarial and agricultural normalcy. The neighborhood watchman knew the score and his palm was well-greased. The attendees at Rosa Trènor's place were the crème de la crème of Barcelona.

In that new phase of her life, Rosa Trènor was able to put her entire pretentious grande dame repertoire to use. The way she received her clients was worthy of admiration, and the blasé aristocratic smirk that settled onto her plump velvety cheeks so as to play down the importance of things, particularly when the time came to set a price, was also worthy of admiration. To enter Rosa Trènor's apartment, one had to meet a goodly number of requirements. But for a gentleman known to some degree for his honorability and for the solidity of his bank account, it was sufficient just to present his card. The pornographic films were one of Rosa's great ruses for reaching other things from which she could derive fatter earnings, particularly the gaming table. The Dictatorship had prohibited gambling throughout Spain, and the fact was that wagering aficionados would have done just about anything to be able to place a decent bet. Rosa Trènor's baccarat cured no few neurasthenias among the gentry of the time. She had clients who went exclusively for the pornographic films; they tended to be all false teeth and hair more white than black. Rosa Trènor tolerated the parasites of the industry because among them were some who were considered to be the most gelatinous and influential. When the obscene film sessions in Rosa Trènor's apartment were over, occasionally a retired general or an ancient marquis and president of a religious association would have to grab onto the banister so they wouldn't fall down the stairs. The doctors registered many burst arteries among the most illustrious elders as a consequence of those films.

From time to time Rosa Trènor would organize custom-made sessions that she said were "for the family." At those times the only people allowed in were certain gentlemen and ladies who were party to a secret pledge. The ladies who had the good fortune to attend one of those sessions would only refer to them with an exquisite vagueness, never going into detail. Some husbands who happened upon the lair never in their lives learned that the night before, their wives had been indisposed by a glass of lemonade owing to the upset stomach produced by the viewing of one of the most positively filthy scenes a commercial imagination can invent. Such tender and mysterious questions of chance in the life of married couples seem to have bestowed some interest on the elegant set of the times.

With the fall of the dictator, Rosa Trènor suffered serious damages. She was reported by the police and she was fortunate enough to be able to make the baccarat table and the projector of indecencies disappear in time. If she hadn't, it was quite possible that with all her airs of grandeur she would have ended up at the prison on Carrer d'Amàlia.

In fact, Rosa avoided any substantial mishaps, and one particularly well-informed gentleman in the most sepulchral ring of a circle prone to arthritis, affirmed that Rosa Trènor had been saved by the freemasons.

With the coming of the Republic, Rosa confined herself to maintaining her best clients, who came for sentimental reasons. On Sunday afternoons Rosa would go to the Ritz, always in the company of a couple of "nieces." Even among young men well-versed in the riddles of courtship there were many unaware of the true meaning of Rosa Trènor's table. In that somewhat hybrid and pretentious Sunday air, Rosa played a very dignified role. Her dresses were even elegant, and her makeup was very appropriate to her forty-five skeptical years of age. When some young man would ask one of her "nieces" to dance, Rosa would cast him a maternal glance of the kind that asks the boy not to get fresh and to be considerate of the purity and excellent upbringing of the young woman who yields to his embrace to take in five minutes of tango.

Occasionally, a husband who was a client of Rosa's would attend the Sunday session with his wife and daughters. Generally, husbands who went for tea with their families turned out to be particularly depraved. Rosa knew this very well, and between her and the husband a half hour's dialogue would take place consisting only of three glances exchanged in such a way that not a single detail was left hanging. Many ladies went to the Ritz with a pure innocence. They were oblivious to the fact that when their husbands offered a chocolate *éclair* to the blondest girl in that domestic convoy, with a simple blink of the eyes he had just signed off on a conspiracy punishable by law with that dark lady across the table, who picked up a fluted *neula* wafer with a virginal gesture, as if she were drawing a Madonna lily close to the powdered environs of her nose.

When she took the daughter of her ex-lover into her home as a patient, Rosa Trènor's friendship with Níobe Casas had just begun. As a result she had begun to see Bobby Xuclà with some frequency, because Bobby, to the stupefaction of his acquaintances, had taken the disconcerting gypsy woman under his wing. Teodora Macaia had been the one to introduce Bobby, as she had done with the Comte de Sallés. Bobby found the dances, and the people who surrounded Níobe, to be revoltingly stupid, but the belly and the armpits of the dancer had made an unsurpassable impression on him. Níobe accepted Bobby without realizing that she had acquired the most decent, liberal, and polite patron in Barcelona. She took advantage of him in a way that did not give the lie to her gypsy origins, but Bobby didn't like to argue, and his checking account was fat and prodigal. When she wasn't onstage, Níobe was a voracious eccentric with a positively efficient conservative and bourgeois core. The surrealist gypsy turned out to be a farce, and

Bobby caught on to her right away. Her horror at diamonds was only for public display, and after a while it became clear that Níobe cared a great deal more for diamonds than for the spider wings of her cache-sexe. It was precisely for the purpose of purchasing some of those gems that Níobe came to meet Rosa Trènor, because if from time to time a fairly decent deal fell into Rosa's hands, she wouldn't say no to it. Even some ladies of unquestionable honor had had dealings with her to acquire a fox coat or a string of pearls at a good price.

Some nights Bobby and Níobe would go to the Pingouin. Rosa Trènor was a fairly assiduous client of that establishment. She didn't usually take any "nieces" there; instead, generally, she was accompanied by a gentleman of a certain age. Every so often, even a professional dancer or some very young boy whom no one knew would sit at her table.

Bobby really liked that early morning haunt, because everything there was to his taste and his way of being. Níobe forgot all about her dances, and curled all her coppery skin up in a corner. Far from her literary admirers, the dancer's teeth might even risk a sandwich of filet mignon or a portion of Italian pasta.

Of all the new things produced in Barcelona during the Republic, none was as successful and delightful as the Pingouin. No one knows why, but in those days the habitués of the wee hours felt a great attraction to the blood-red velvet divans and slightly pharmaceutical bar of that outfit on Carrer d'Escudellers. The Pingouin owed its allure to a gramophone with a mute, and to the priceless décor. The walls were hung with wallpaper showing wine-colored flowers against a background dark as squid's ink that might have been meant for a skilled laborer's bedroom in 1893. The Pingouin offered a gallery of unreachable boxed seats, where no one ever sat. Decked out in a green lamé fabric, they seemed made to order for a wizard to murder astral bodies or cook up an ectoplasm paella. The ceiling and the columns that held it up still preserved the filthy paint from the former warehouse turned into a dive for night crawlers. From the ceiling hung a naïf decoration. The owner had strung up a few lengths of wire holding wallpaper that showed peach blossom branches in flower. They formed a picture of innocence, a symmetrical green and pink spider web over the gray waves of stale smoke.

The music at the Pingouin was topnotch. Waltzes from before the war and contemporary rumbas, combined with Hawaiian guitars, Russian balalaikas and Tyrolean ocarinas, and dive-y accordions from Argentina and from riffraff the world over. The music, whatever music it was, picked up the rhythm of the establishment: a rhythm of boiled bones sloughing off their flesh, in lyrical and philanthropic convulsions, and above all a rhythm of silent sloth, distracted and barely conscious, the kind of lazy patience for which a quarter of an hour or an hour are all the same. The kind that watches the roses wilt on the tables as the sun climbs high in the sky and the street-cleaning hoses have used up all the water in the street.

Women came to the Pingouin with evening escorts already arranged, or with their current squeeze. They were relaxed and unassuming, their makeup often a ruin, with whiskey starting to trickle down hairdos tortured by bleach and marcel waves. Any arrangements made once inside were either a last resort or the result of the influence of the red of the roses and the sickly amber of the gin. Somewhere between six and seven in the morning a woman perched on a barstool, her tongue nebulous with drink, might cling to the arm of a solitary Scandinavian who had probably taken a vow of chastity. At the Pingouin anything was possible at closing time. Conversations there could just as easily be liquid and vaporous as lucid, uncompromising and realistic, without a shadow of mercy. Many couples would drop in at the Pingouin before going off to bed in order to capture a few whiffs of madness or resignation that would add a little greenery to the sad flesh of copulation.

The audience at the Pingouin was a mix of delicate and austere people, well-meaning poets, and certified drunks, not to mention bilge rats, men who lived off the flesh of women, and boatswains with no strings attached, who had arrived in the morning aboard a cargo ship and were carrying bank notes pressed like dead butterflies between their bellies and their belts. These sailors would hire an interpreter who had most likely been a gunslinger for some union, who would dart quickly in and out, with canine eyes, wearing a cheap suit, to let the sailors know that outside four women, like four phosphorescent mermaids, were awaiting them, when it truth it was only the four most faded souls from the bottom of Carrer de la Unió o Carrer de Sant Pau.

There were always two or three couples dancing at the Pingouin. Occasionally, revelers full of good humor and good manners would come in and concoct some eccentric dance steps. Other times a refined, but entirely drunk, gentlemen from a Nordic clime would start dancing all by himself, bowing to everyone and bothering no one. The Pingouin's salient feature was its great tolerance. Only with great difficulty could one come to fists or to fingernails. Within those walls alcohol became metaphysical, full of comprehension and soul. Everything moved to the rhythm of the music, everything was muted, everything had the flexibility of a rumba and the water of the port brewing in the belly of the gramophone.

Few people grasped as Bobby did the slippery jellyfish delight that floated in the air of the Pingouin. He would greet the better class of kept women, who arrived arms full of fresh roses and hungry as tigers, with a gray smile. Every so often he would order a bottle of Pommery to be uncorked to give the place a little grandeur. Bobby couldn't stand the stuff; for him champagne was only good for wetting the tips of his moustache. Even when Níobe didn't come along, Bobby would go to the Pinguoin with a friend, or a select married couple he had picked up at the Hollywood, a high-octane cabaret that had got its start around the same time, where many tender bourgeois ladies of Barcelona would go with their husbands to contemplate the celestial breasts of the Cuban women and dance bawdy, Tabarinesque dances, surrounded by the sultry aroma of the prostitutes.

One night at the Pingouin, Rosa Trènor took the opportunity to speak with Bobby about a little business deal with a smidgen of drama. That motley, absent, and dead ambiance seemed the most appropriate to her for concocting a scene in which she and he would play the role of specters that emerged from another atmosphere.

The topic was Maria Lluïsa de Lloberola. By the intercession of her friend Teresa, Maria Lluïsa had confided in Rosa Trènor. Rosa didn't let her get away. That marvelous creature bore the same blood as a man with strong ties to Rosa Trènor's history, and Rosa, who was just as silly, romantic, and transcendental as ever, grabbed hold of what chance had placed within her grasp to extricate that chapter that is usually titled "Twenty Years Later," in which the heart of the protagonist, bloated with memories and emotions, is about to burst. Rosa did not consider the possibility of exploiting Maria Lluïsa for one of her discreet and excellent latter day concerns. The woman's dreadfully trashy mentality perceived in Maria Lluïsa's blithe disposition a vengeance of destiny, the final act of a drama in which Rosa Trènor believed she had deposited her heart, when in truth she had deposited nothing but a little bit of stomach.

The only man who could be of use to Rosa in her perverse plot was Bobby. Another high-class client would have turned the scene into a banal anecdote of no importance. Bobby listened with his eyes half-closed as Rosa told her story. He said neither yes nor no. Bobby was a pretty decent guy. All his life long no one could accuse him of anything malicious or mean spirited, nothing that would sully a man's elegance. But like most people from his circle, skeptical and disabused, lacking in passion, every so often it amused him to try a taste of something that might seem perverse or even have a touch of evil. Since Bobby had broken off relations with Frederic, he hadn't thought for a moment of making peace with that smug and tedious man, but neither did he bear him the slightest hatred. Frederic's affronts to Bobby's mother were nothing new to him. He was aware of the opinion many ungenerous people had of the Widow Xuclà. Frederic meant nothing to Bobby. His economic disasters, the absurd life he was living on his estate, didn't affect him in the slightest. But Rosa Trènor's insinuations piqued his curiosity. Bobby also saw something of a final curtain in the affair at hand, and he realized he could act with impunity, playing the role of a traitor. Unseemly though it may be, sometimes this is the role a spectator would most enjoy playing.

Maria Lluïsa had only a vague notion of who Bobby was, but she was aware of the friendship he had once had with her father, and of the reputation that bitter and scrupulously polite bachelor enjoyed among the elegant set. Maria Lluïsa shared the ideas of some young women of her time regarding mature men and callow boys. It had become fashionable to disparage "cute" and athletic boys, with their vanity in their physiques. They were considered lightweights, lacking in interest and discernment. They were attacked for their empty chitchat and their inability to show a path to the stars. Young women like Maria Lluïsa preferred a man of substance, more polished and more experienced, to a speed demon or a tango dancer with slicked-back hair. Young woman like Maria Lluïsa liked to be taken seriously, to be treated with respect. If they were out to infatuate, they preferred a victim with stature and history to a gigolo whose only concern was how to dress, and how to get undressed in staler latitudes.

Maria Lluïsa and Bobby met one day at Rosa Trènor's house, and something happened to Bobby that had never happened to him before: he fell in love like a little kid.

He swapped the role of the traitor for that of the gallant young man, tender and pure, right out of a romantic love story. Bobby hid his feelings and tried to play the cynic, the paternal yet despicable man of the world who reveals that the whole plot revolves around a superficial fantasy. His behavior delighted Maria Lluïsa. She found him extraordinarily charming. His fifty years of age weren't the slightest obstacle. Maria Lluïsa wanted to be more and more modern, and his gray hair was a perfect fit for her state of mind. Bobby conducted himself splendidly with her, accentuating his generosity with a cool amiability that allowed her to retreat.

Maria Lluïsa didn't stop to weigh the consequences. Her habit of improvisation and living day to day allowed her to accept Bobby's friendship at face value, without having to think about what would happen tomorrow. All she had to do was pretend, and justify Bobby's attentions. Maria Lluïsa had achieved considerable independence from her mother, but it was important to her, above all, to avoid any kind of scandal. The rumor had reached Maria Carreres' ears that her daughter's ways might be a little too modern, but Maria Carreres felt impotent in the face of her daughter's power. Frederic, at that point, was completely divorced from his family. He had no authority over his children, nor did he care to. Frederic was a lost cause. When Maria Lluïsa met Bobby, it hadn't been long since Don Tomàs had died, and Frederic was adrift in the arms of the wine merchant's wife and the delirium of her black nightgown with the pumpkin-colored babies' print. Breathing in the dust from the stones of his castle, Frederic had no desire to see his wife or their apartment on Carrer de Bailèn ever again. Nor was he aware of the little temperature he had every evening. The people in the town said he was going mad. What was really going on in Frederic's body was tuberculosis, which would send him to his grave only a few years later. In Barcelona no one knew anything about this, and Maria Lluïsa didn't miss her father's lectures or his baloney a single bit. Without her father around, the air was cleared for her to spin out the golden thread of her dreams.

One day, Maria Carreres spoke to her daughter about a few things, some rumors she had heard, but Maria Lluïsa played her part to perfection, and her mother had no choice but to exclaim: "God be with you! It's in your hands now, Maria Lluïsa! You'll be sorry." In a word, all the things a mother says when she sees that nothing can be done.

Not only that, Maria Lluïsa's mother didn't allow Grandmother Carreres to stick her nose in these affairs. Economically, the apartment on Carrer de Bailèn depended on Grandmother Carreres. Yet Frederic's insipid wife, aware of her impotence with regard to her daughter, thought it was more sensible to play along and mask the situation. This was her way of averting scenes by the grandmother that, instead of convincing Maria Lluïsa, would only have strained the atmosphere. Over the years Maria Carreres had become a woman of frayed morals. Like an old garter, her morals applied no pressure and held nothing up. Whimpering all the way, she accepted her mother's favors and swallowed all the old woman's foul and contemptuous remarks. She preferred not to see things, letting herself be deceived and convinced for the sake of peace. The woman's psychology, like the fabric of her dress, had the look of a hand-me-down. The strategy Maria

Carreres had learned from the Lloberolas was to keep up appearances and bury her head in the sand like an ostrich. With a happy, shameless smile, she would make her round of visits, giving news of her own as if she were speaking of the Holy Family, when everyone knew about Frederic's absurd life, and knew that her daughter worked in a bank, and wore a string of pearls – of the kind that bode no good and are fodder for gossip among more pious souls – around her neck.

Bobby received Maria Lluïsa in the little apartment he kept for affairs of the heart. The girl planted a few fuchsias, some red geraniums and a number of violets in Bobby the skeptic's small spiritual garden, heretofore lacking in light or water or the slightest drop of hope. Maria Lluïsa's freshness, her exceptional grace, the way she had of alternating modesty and impudence, were things that Bobby had thought no longer existed in this world. When he rediscovered them in Maria Lluïsa's skin, he began to fear that he had been mistaken, that his idea of life and of women had served to create a reputation for him among the most elegant and boring sets as a polite man who never gets ruffled or surrenders himself entirely, but had probably ruined him for feeling all the flavor of madness in a pure and simple mouth that besides communicating the warm breath of another's lungs, also delivers the uncontrollable mystery of a soul.

In his heart of hearts what was happening was that Bobby was getting old and starting to dodder.

—·—·—

"MY HUSBAND EXHAUSTED all his available kindness on me. If he didn't do more, it was because he simply didn't have the wherewithal. He was not to blame for his medullary disease; he was a specter who fell in love with me, never suspecting his condition. Everyone lied to my husband; I was the only one who didn't lie to him. My mother was not the kind of woman who could understand what I was doing, what she practically obliged me to do. Our marriage was just one of the many marriages of the time. It was also not my husband's fault that on our return from Venice, one month after we were married, I, who was living in a dream, had to resign myself to being a nurse to a dying man. My husband had a nobility that I have not sensed in any other man. With his gaze he asked me only one thing, always the same thing: he asked me to forgive him for having married me, to forgive him for having turned me into a nurse. Perhaps the only worthwhile thing I have done is to understand that request for forgiveness and to feel grateful for it, more grateful than for any of the embraces of an irresistible seducer. At that point to be anything less than true to him would have been the greatest ignominy, in my eyes. If I had found myself by the side of a healthy, dominant husband, the kind who kill a woman with kindness but basically keep her in her place, I might very well have been unfaithful. At this stage, I don't think so, but I couldn't swear to it. What I can indeed swear to is that it never even remotely occurred to me to offend my husband. I find that for most women, nothing can be more compelling than a pair of impotent, supplicating eyes that see in us the prestige of a mother, that feel the confidence our hand bestows when we place it on a forehead for the sole purpose of transmitting our disinterested womanly spirit. My husband's gaze was that of a sick child, a child fifteen years older than I, and I was only twenty at the time. I felt an obligation to those eyes."

"I am writing these lines to console myself a bit. To remember that at twenty I wasn't an entirely stupid girl, and I knew how to capture all the mortified adoration in the gaze of a sick man."

"When my husband died, I put on an act. I didn't know you could produce tears without feeling anything. But I realized it was possible. The funereal faces of everyone around me, in addition to my own nervous exhaustion, made it easy for me to behave accordingly. I cried, I cried a lot, but it was entirely artificial. I would be lying if I said that I didn't feel great tenderness toward my husband. But I would also be lying if I tried to pretend that I wasn't hoping for him to die. What I don't understand is why I wanted it so badly, if in the end it didn't solve anything for me. As long as my husband was alive, his gaze kept me company, it even satisfied my ego to discover I was useful and to offer that poor sick man consolation. Once he was dead, even that was gone. I confess that when they carried him off, it seemed as if they were removing a bad dream from my heart. But years later, I must also confess that I missed that bad dream."

"I was never beautiful. I was never one of those women men find exciting. I don't want to kid myself. I'm certain of this. In my youth, I had enough intuition and enough presence of mind to realize it. Since my husband died, I have had thousands of opportunities to realize that my material fortune was of no little consequence, much more than my natural endowments. By twenty-five I was a widow and completely free. My mother was dead and I held one of the most brilliant positions in Barcelona. In those days, I had an obsession. I thought no one liked me, and I made every effort, I even humiliated myself, to be nice to people. But I could see it was all for nothing. They would show kindness in many different ways, they would flatter me to excess, but it all seemed fake to me. Now that I'm sixty years old, I think maybe I was imagining things. It's possible someone might have fallen in love with me in all good faith, if I hadn't been so standoffish with men when the time came for a *tête-à-tête*, and even more so if I hadn't been the victim of that peculiar melancholy that obliged me to distance myself from people. Now that I'm looking back with a cool head, the air I adopted seems frankly stupid. Not that what was happening to me at that point was my fault. Since my first marriage had been a disaster, I didn't want to expose myself to a second. In those days I couldn't help but think that my great fortune was sufficient for any man to have faked the most vivid love without a second thought. I don't think I was so mistaken about this. Despite the opinion of most of my friends, I am rather gullible; even now anyone can take me in. Nowadays, naturally, I couldn't care less, because I have nothing to lose, but at age twenty-five I had more than enough reasons to be mistrustful and to be protective of my own innocence. Since I had started to know myself a bit, I was afraid that if I allowed myself to risk being deceived, they would almost certainly deceive me. And this was why, on the one hand, I made such an effort to be nice and to conquer the dislike I believed I inspired in others, and on the other, if I started a conversation with a man, I did my best to avoid any insinuations."

"Now there are times when I think that all the pains I took in those days were quite unwarranted, and perhaps I might have done better to let myself be deceived. And other times I think exactly the opposite, and I believe I behaved perfectly, because, living alone as I have, with such independence, I have been able to see the word and take advantage of opportunities that I probably wouldn't have had if I had married. Still, one thing or the other, it's all the same, because I'm sixty now and there's nothing I can do about it. I find it very idiotic when people spend so much time worrying about the things they've left behind and the mistakes they've made. I think things turned out this way because this was the only way they could turn out, and that maybe my reasons for not marrying are entirely different, and have nothing to do with the way I explain things to myself."

"It's strange, though. By the time I was thirty I had completely abandoned the idea of a new marriage. I've had plenty of opportunities to do what a number of my friends of mine have done, but I've resisted. Maybe I've been cold, but I've always felt that unless there is real love, the other part is disgusting. As for real love, I doubt I've inspired it in anyone. If I haven't done what so many other women have done, I don't think it was out of any moral scruples; I think I could have overcome all kinds of scruples, because in other respects I haven't had any at all. That's just the way it was, and clearly this is how my life was supposed to turn out. I have it on good authority that all kinds of lies are told about me. People don't believe that a person as free as I am, who has always done whatever she wanted, who has traveled half the world and not been religious or a prude, has denied herself the pleasure of sleeping with a man. Everyone who thinks this about me is mistaken: I haven't known any other man than my poor husband, and I can even swear that I knew him very little, almost not at all. A few friends and a few books have explained to me what love in its most secret intimacies is like. I can affirm that I know nothing of all this: I am almost as innocent as a child before puberty."

"Nor has any religious idea been behind this. Because I believe in the religion my mother taught me, but I have never wanted to give it much thought. I am certain that if I started to think too hard about it I would end up losing my faith; the faith I have today is just as weak as it was when I was twenty. I have kept it this way all my life. Perhaps my chastity has allowed me to continue going to confession twice a year. I have very little love lost for priests, and if I had found myself under compulsion to tell them certain things, it's possible I would have stopped practicing. Since I've never done anyone a bad turn, my confessions are very brief, and I make it a point to find a priest who doesn't know me and will make quick work of it."

"Not all the things I have accomplished in this world have been exclusively out of vanity. I know that vanity is my worst defect, but I feel that I have often invested my actions with generosity and even idealism. If my life has any grace at all it is in not having succumbed to the routine of the majority of women of my class. I know people have considered me a snob. Maybe there is some truth in it: maybe I have been a slave to fashion. But I like to think that I have been sincere much more often. And, above all, that my actions have obeyed a natural impulse. Perhaps the circumstances of my life and the freedom I have always enjoyed have helped me be exactly who I am."

"What interested me were books and traveling and people with a certain spirit, just as what interested me in fashion and human relations were their most ephemeral charms and their most sensitive details. In my home I have sought to arrange things so that an intelligent person can find corners on which to rest his eyes. And I have sought out the conversation and company of these intelligent people, just as I confess that I have sought out the company of people who are no less brilliant for having been the worst idiots in the futile life of our country. There have been times when I have not wanted anyone to get the better of me, which has left me open to accusations of being an eccentric or even a madwoman, and even of being what I have never been: an unnatural woman."

"I believe that a woman who is not very feminine has no place in the world. It is true that in one essential sense of life I haven't been at all feminine: I mean I have not been a mother. But in all the other ways, externally, spectacularly, I have wanted to be more feminine and more exigent than the rest. I have looked at myself in the mirror many times, and I know perfectly well how to separate beauty from elegance. Perhaps it is also my particular sin of vanity to believe that elegance is more important than beauty."

"If I have not had children, if I have not been able to love a man as I had dreamed of doing, I have made sure to do innumerable favors and to be a true friend. At sixty years of age, I realize exactly how naïve I have been and how far I have taken my lack of cynicism…"

"With all the favors I've done, I am sure none has been met with gratitude. The women I have felt closest to and had the most affection for, the persons I have aided morally and materially, are the ones who have criticized me the most and invented the most lies about me. I know that my society and my class is the least imaginative and most malicious of them all. If I have tried to play a more active and personal part in works of culture and beneficence than most of these ladies, they have only seen in my actions the desire to stand out and be praised. On occasion, and in all innocence, I have traveled in the company of men, good, discreet friends of mine, because I find that I can talk about anything with men, and it doesn't get boring, as it does with my close women friends. And some of these men, while still dispensing all the attentions a lady deserves, have come to treat me in the cordial and evenhanded way they would any companion. The long journeys I have made in these conditions have been some of the loveliest moments of my life. Later I learned how the most spiritual and refined ladies I received in my home had criticized me. I've had one good fortune: I have not been very affected by what people said or thought about me. I get this spirit of independence of from Mamà."

"I know my culture is very shallow, and there have been those, more sincere or less pleasant than the rest, who have made it clear to me that I am a perfectly ordinary woman whose ideas are sadly banal. I have never pretended to be wise, and I do not envy anyone his talent. I have enjoyed life in my own way, and I have felt great emotion. Even if I was not a person one might call sensitive, I have endeavored to listen to people I found sensitive, in order to modify my taste, and I have learned to enjoy things I felt impervious to by nature. If artists and men of letters have had some regard for me, it has been owing to my inclination to listen and learn and my willingness to modify my own criteria. I know I have been considered grotesque, ridiculous, and pretentious. But by behaving as I did, I have saved myself from boredom and, along the way, either with my name or my money, I have done a bit of good for my country."

"What has most harmed me has been my lack of discretion, particularly in conversation. Though this has been interpreted as duplicity on my part, I am convinced, sadly, that it is simply the fruit of my ingenuousness and my belief that others are as well-meaning as I. My friend X has said so many times; naturally, I protested. Later, with the passage of time, I have concluded that my friend X was absolutely right. I have been and continue to be nauseatingly innocent."

"At sixty years of age, I find myself desperately alone. My fortune has dwindled greatly, and I must make an effort to save. Many people have left my side, but I still have a weakness for wanting to know what is going on, in particular for the latest thing, and for what can bring about a change in my country. Many of my friends criticize me for supporting the Republican government. They say I'm an old woman and I should be ashamed of being so juvenile, and I'd be better off shutting myself up at home. The truth is, I've been shut up in my home for years, and I am never so happy as when I am sitting by the fireside, surrounded by my memories and in the company of my thoughts. When someone comes to take me out for a little trip, or some escapade, it embarrasses me to confess that I'm no young woman any more, and I get tired, or that I'm in no mood to be disturbed, and out of vanity, pure and simple vanity, I still go out as if I were twenty-five. But I'm less and less in the mood."

"I would have liked to know how to write. I would have liked to be of use to my world by writing my memories of everything I've seen in this life, because in my position, I have met many people, and seen much grandeur and much misery. Writing a memoir is a constant temptation for me. Some people have urged me to do it, in good faith, I think. Today I've written down these things about myself to see if I am inspired to continue writing what I know of others. I have tried to start a story with a series of disorderly confessions. I am only at the start and I'm already fading. I wonder if, in the little bit I have written so far, I have been honest with myself. Maybe I have portrayed myself as too much of a victim, maybe I have neglected to say that both at heart and on the surface I am nothing but a selfish woman…"

Hortènsia Portell had just read the words "selfish woman." She was holding a few sheets of thick, broad, and dramatic, paper, written in a careless and affectedly virile hand. Disillusioned, she reread what she had conceived of a few months ago, and had left off in the moment she penned the phrase "selfish woman." Ever since she had stored it in a drawer with other intimate items, Hortènsia hadn't had the heart to go over it. Manuscript in hand, Hortènsia had realized that her attempt to write her memoir had been a childish act. Why do it? What could she gain from it? Hortènsia Portell's survivors would see her memoir as a posthumous extravagance. They wouldn't even leave her cadaver in peace. Hortènsia didn't want to give them the satisfaction. Moreover, nothing she might have to say about her life and times would be of interest to anyone. That's what Hortènsia was thinking in those moments as she weighed her manuscript, with a grimace of disgust as she considered what she had written about herself in a moment of weakness and innocence.

At the time, Hortènsia was facing a series of sumptuary and economic headaches. She had sold some of her paintings and intended to let go of many other things. Hortènsia proposed to retire to a more tranquil domicile that would not entail such great expense.

The manuscript Hortènsia was holding in her hands ended up, page by page, in the flames of the chimney. This literary auto-da-fè was carried out in silence, secretly, not without the executioner's feeling the detachment of four dog-eared roses from the tip of her heart as she carried out the sacrifice.

When Hortènsia had completely destroyed her work, the doorbell rang, and the servant announced the widow Baronessa de Falset.

Conxa would often visit Hortènsia's house in the afternoon, not so much to keep her company as to consult with her on things related to the new house the baronessa was building. Hortènsia had a reputation for good taste, and Conxa had faith in her judgment. At that stage, Conxa was absolutely immersed in the project, and in fact didn't give her architect a moment's rest. She wanted the building to be modern and brilliant, and the toast of all Barcelona. Conxa wanted to squeeze life down to the dregs. For days an idea had been spinning in her head and she hadn't dared broach it with Hortènsia. But that afternoon she finally found the mettle. It was an idea related to the décor of her new house, and related above all to another person who was the axis around which all of Conxa Pujol's feelings and illusions revolved.

"Listen, Hortènsia, what do you intend to do with your tapestry?"

"Frankly, if someone wanted to buy it…"

"The thing is, to tell the truth, I've been looking for a tapestry for quite some time now, but not just any old thing. I want something with a bit of style, you see? It's for the entrance, and I think yours is the perfect size. It would fit there as if it had been made to order. Forgive me, Hortènsia, but it's only because you say you want to sell all this, and that the house has got too big for you, that I dare to ask…"

"Do you know the story of my tapestry?"

"Vaguely…"

"Sure, you were just a child then…Really and truly, this is precisely the one you want?"

"But, what do you mean, Hortènsia? This is the one, yes. I think it's magnificent, I really like it…I can understand how hard it may be for you to let go of it…"

"No, it's not hard for me, that's not it. The idea of selling this treasure is very recent, because until a short time ago, I intended to leave the Lloberola tapestry to the museum. Almost as an act of conscience. But lately things have taken a turn for the worse, and I need everything I can get. I can't be too generous. That's why I said that if I found a buyer I would also let go of this tapestry…"

"I'm sorry, Hortènsia. My question has put you out. I've made you think of sad things…"

"No, no, my dear. On the contrary. I don't mean to make any profit on the tapestry. I just want to get back what it cost me, nothing more. I assure you it doesn't make me sad at all. To be honest with you, I have never enjoyed seeing it on these walls, because it did make the previous owners very sad to have to sell it. The Marquès de Sitjar, God bless him, was a poor devil, a fool, if you wish, but he was a gentleman. Yes, yes, a gentleman of the kind you can probably no longer find in Barcelona. I remember the day I acquired the tapestry as if it were today. Twenty years ago, just imagine. My way of thinking was very different in those days. You can also imagine that twenty years ago the people of Barcelona were very different and things they considered to be important would make people laugh nowadays. Nowadays, I appear to be old-fashioned and moralistic, but back then, for the Lloberolas and people of their stripe, I was just short of a devil. Just think what it meant to him for his tapestry, the crown jewel of his family, to end up in my house! Imagine how sad they must have been! The marquès came to see me out of absolute necessity. The poor man was polite to a fault. And I had the cheek to haggle with him, down to the penny. Clearly he wasn't used to this, and he gave it to me at the price I wanted, even if I had offered him half as much. And even so the time came when the poor man started to cry. Just think how humiliating that must have been for a person with his airs! To cry in front of me! And he wasn't play-acting, not at all. I confess I was a little harsh with him. More than anything else, it was pride that made me want to buy the tapestry from them. Then I had a change of heart and began to have misgivings. I felt as if the tapestry had been stolen, and the eyes of those biblical figures nailed to my wall were protesting, as if thanks to me they were in prison. What can I say, Conxa, I'm romantic and sentimental, and a bit of a fool. When all is said and done, if they had sold it to an antiquarian he would have swindled them left and right, and God knows where the wretched tapestry would be now. This is why I'm telling you that my intention was to leave it to the museum, but lately I've seen so many changes all around, I've seen that nothing matters any more, and life is so hard, so full of bad faith and indifference, that it is all the same to me if the tapestry disappears, just as the character of one family after another has disappeared. You see, Conxa, I turned sixty this summer, around the Feast of the Assumption. I know, no one thinks I look my age, but that's how old I am. And at my age, just imagine…you're just a child. You're still thrilled about your new house and you're in the best of all worlds. So, if you want the tapestry, as I said, I don't want to make any profit from it; nowadays it's worth ten times what I paid for it…"

"No, no, Hortènsia, I will buy it for what it's worth…for what it's worth today…"

"Stop, dear. I've always been a little extravagant. I think I'm a little too old for a change of temperament now."

It must be noted that Hortènsia was having a very dark afternoon. It must also be noted that Hortènsia knew perfectly well what was going on between Conxa Pujol and Guillem de Lloberola, but for some reason Hortènsia was a sentimental creature with a penchant for drama. And this is why Hortènsia proceeded to speak in this way:

"But be frank with me, now: you're interested in the Lloberola tapestry for something more important than its size…"

"I told you, it means a lot to me…".

"Forgive me if I'm sticking my nose where it's not wanted, but I'm almost twice your age, Conxa. What I mean to say is that I'm on my way out, and I may have a bit of a right to give you some advice, as a good friend…"

"You know you're the only one I consider to be a good friend. But I don't know what you have in mind…"

"Oh no, Conxa, I have nothing in mind. It just occurred to me that perhaps the person who is really interested in this tapestry might not be you, exactly…"

"You're mistaken, Hortènsia. And if some slander has reached your ears, I will speak to you with my heart in my hand…"

"Oh no, Conxa, please, by no means…Forgive me…Not at all…"

"The person you imagine…"

"No, no, no, you don't have to explain anything to me. I believe you, of course I do…"

"But I want to tell you. The person you have in mind doesn't know a thing about any of this. It's possible he doesn't even remember that this tapestry that belonged to his grandparents exists…The family doesn't concern him at all…"

"Well, I don't know him. I think he came to a party here once, many years ago. Yes, a short time before your husband's death. The current generation, you might say I've lost sight of them entirely. His sister Josefina is the only one I occasionally run into at the golf club… As you can imagine, anything I might know is just hearsay…"

"In our world, Hortènsia, hearsay is usually vilification. You know that better than I do."

"Indeed, indeed. I know it only too well, imagine…"

"Well, for that very reason, Hortènsia. I have always admired you because you've been an independent woman, because you've laughed off other people's criticism. And as for me, I have done my best, indeed, I am doing my best, to follow in your footsteps. I don't give a hoot if people criticize me. They can say whatever they want. Your tapestry means something to me because if I have it in my house, I will never think of it as 'stolen,' you see? I'm thirty-six years old, Hortènsia, and I think I can still have a child who will bear the same name as that old gentleman, do you understand? That old man who cried…"

"But it's true then, Conxa?"

"It's true. I'm going to marry him. Or to be precise, we will be married in four months; that's what we've decided…"

"Forgive me for saying so, Conxa, but I think you're making a terrible mistake."

"Do you know him?"

"No, no, I've already told you I don't. But I don't see any need for you to get married. You are running the risk of being very, very, miserable…"

"I don't understand."

"Listen. Is this young man your lover, yes or no? Are you ashamed to admit it? If my question is a bit too crude, forgive me…but at my age I think you can forgive me for being direct."

"All right, Hortènsia, I have no reason to deny it…He is my lover."

"Well, then, Conxa, what more do you want? What need do you have to complicate things? Isn't he yours? Isn't he truly yours? Didn't you tell me that you don't care what people say?"

"To a point, Hortènsia, only to a point."

"No, you're not being honest with me. If you're marrying him it's because you feel obligated by something that is not precisely public opinion. I am naive, Conxa, but not that naive."

"You will never understand this, but I will try to explain why I am getting married. Guillem is in a world of his own, I see this. Sometimes he eludes me, I can't control him, and I need to keep him close to me, by my side. And he needs me, too, for many reasons, do you see? If he is my husband, our situation will change, he will be more centered, he will feel more attached to me than he does now…"

"Or just the opposite, Conxa, just the opposite. I'm starting to realize that you're more romantic than I am…"

"Maybe I am. But there's something else. As long as we're being frank, I'm not ashamed to tell you. I have noticed that some people, no matter how they try to hide it, can't help but look askance and give us the cold shoulder when they see me talking with him somewhere. I've heard talk about the reputation he's earned and the reputation I'm earning…"

"But, Conxa, didn't you say all that didn't matter? For God's sake, don't go on…"

"Well, now it's a question of pride. I want him to be accepted as my husband in everyone's eyes, with my head held high. I want the satisfaction of seeing everyone who goes around calling him an unscrupulous gigolo and me a degenerate having to invite him into their homes and fawn over him. Don't you see? They'll have to respect him, even if it's only for my money, because, as you know, Guillem is penniless."

"You are getting married…Or to put it another way, you are using your money to buy a husband, to buy your reputation and that of a man whom you can't do without. In this regard, then, well, my way of thinking was, indeed, more romantic…You are a modern woman, Conxa, oh yes, much more modern than I! You think that in a year, or two, or perhaps less, this fellow will be respected as your husband and no one will think of him as your gigolo…"

"They can think what they want, but I will be serene and satisfied. And he'll be tied to me, he'll be mine…"

"He'll be tied to you by your money…?"

"Can't you believe that he really loves me, that we really love each other?"

"I have doubts about everything, Conxa. I can see you're in a huff. Since I have never in my life experienced such a passion…"

"Naturally, Hortènsia, I already said you wouldn't be able to understand what's happened to me. Maybe I am making a big mistake. I've made quite a few mistakes in life. Believe me, one more won't make a difference…"

"All right, Conxa. My tapestry is at your disposal. You realize that after all you've told me I feel more obligated than ever to indulge you."

"Hortènsia, I'd be grateful if you…"

"You mean I can't say anything about all this? Conxa, it will be very hard for me. I'm a gossip, I can't help myself. I spend my days airing dirty laundry over lunch, over tea, at the golf course, at the theater. Imagine how hard it will be for me not to be able to tell people, and you know who they are, at least a little smidgen of the conversation we've had. What do you expect us to talk about? What could possibly interest us more than dishing the dirt…As I see it, the topic of your wedding would be a bombshell, a trophy I would carry off this very evening at the Hostal del Sol, where I'm going to have dinner with Teodora Macaia, Bobby, and the Moragueses and I think even that flirt Titina and her in-laws will be there. Just think how hard it will be on me to be silent as a tomb, Conxa! But I promise I won't say a word… I promise…"

—·—·—

TWO MONTHS AFTER this conversation, the news of the wedding of Conxa Pujol, the widow Baronessa de Falset, to Guillem de Lloberola did indeed fall like a bombshell in the world of the posh.

In the men's circles, you could hear the following comments: "What brass!" "How cynical!" "What a loose woman!" "What a crook!" "What a tart!" and other comments that decency doesn't allow us to write down.

To be sure, Guillem de Lloberola accepted the baronessa's proposition in order to secure his situation. Guillem would not have been capable of taking the initiative himself, nor did it ever cross his mind, when he initiated his assault, that that adventure could end in marriage. Gullem had many defects, but a Lloberola could never have plotted so far in advance. If Guillem had foreseen the value of his play from the outset, he could have been qualified as a good diplomat. But Guillem was more of a wastrel, a bohemian, who lived day-to-day. The first time Conxa brought up the idea of marriage, Guillem wrinkled his nose. He had stooped really low and he had lost all shame: in point of fact, he was a *maquereau*. He took money from Conxa, but that all happened in the murky, irregular world where Guillem drowsed. He found the thought of exchanging that place for a bright world in the full light of day, the thought of becoming a legal *maquereau*, by means of a grotesque ceremony, presided over by the Catholic Church and the current Civil Code, to be a little disgusting. Once in a blue moon, Guillem felt like a Lloberola, and Conxa's marriage proposal seemed despicable to him. In addition to veiling the madness of a depraved woman and a man with no illusions in a shroud of propriety, for Guillem such a marriage meant becoming the master of the fortune of a man he had practically murdered. Guillem would be acquiring a certificate of grandeur and esteem by means of a series of base, criminal actions. But Conxa, despite her pirate, Creole blood, was intoxicated by the cowardly air of her social circle, and she wanted to have the pleasure of turning the bite marks of the bordello into the satisfaction of a twelve o'clock Mass to the sound of the municipal band. Conxa persisted, and Conxa demanded. Guillem blinked his eyes and began to get used to the idea of being Conxa's husband, having a great fortune and the best automobiles at his disposal, and to procuring for himself the most wonderful escapades, out of sight of the sadistic and unnerving sexuality of Conxa Pujol.

In Guillem's time, protests were ephemeral and people had adopted a general devil-may-care attitude of conformity and acquiescence. The only person Guillem sought some counsel from was his friend, Agustí Casals.

With the coming of the Republic, Agustí Casals had achieved great status. His friendship with Josep Safont and other public figures, his gift for oratory and, above all, his elegance in positioning himself, gave him a splendid standing. Agustí Casals was a good person, and for a while now he had been concerned about Guillem. He wanted to find something, some position, that Guillem could defend. He said Guillem was being ruined, and it was a shame for him to be facing a future with no prospects. When Guillem told him about the wedding project, Agustí reacted more as a lawyer than as a moralist. Agustí knew Guillem, even if he was ignorant of the darkest details of his life, but he knew perfectly well what kind of man he was. If it had been any other kind of person, a more redeemable kind, Agustí would have said to him that the first thing a man must preserve was his dignity. But Agustí could see that Guillem possessed a cancerous morality that had no chance of redemption. As a good lawyer, Agustí saw this as an excellent business plan that, with a minimal concern for appearances, assured his friend of a great position. Agustí advised him to waste no time on scruples he would get no credit for. And if anyone criticized him it would just be a case of the green-eyed monster…

Guillem married, and within four months he was on the board of the Club Eqüestre. He fabricated the thick skin of an ideal husband for himself, and he never took it off, not even at bedtime.

After lunch, he would sit and smoke a magnificent Havana cigar in full view of the historic Lloberola tapestry. He gazed at Conxa with gratitude for her delicacy in rescuing it. He saw himself in the figure of the warlike Jacob, bamboozling Isaac and everyone else with his youthful profile. While hairy and ruddy Esau brought to mind the image of his dimwit brother, Frederic, ensnared in wretchedness and confusion, playing cards amid the faded, acidic weeds, and nursing a case of tuberculosis in the bed of a wine merchant's wife.

—·—·—

ON CARRER DE BARBERÀ a man has just been killed. He saw how two policemen carried the man off to the clinic. Amid the cobblestones, the man's warm trampled blood was transferred from the valves of a heart to the soles of anonymous shoes and espadrilles. The desecration of human blood is a thing the civil codes of modern countries do not punish. That day, on Carrer de Barberà, there was no little blood to be desecrated, as criminals often use bullets with no sense of decorum. The faces of the people at the door to the clinic wore that common, yellowing, and congested expression the Barcelona public adopts when a man has been murdered in the middle of the street.

He had heard the shots as he went down the stairs, the well-worn and despicable steps that had the elasticity of rubber to the soles of his feet. To hear shots at that moment seemed impossible to him. He didn't even suspect that was what they were, and he continued down the stairs. When he reached the doorway, he found himself before the vision of a dead man suspended between two policemen, and the running, gesticulating and rubbernecking people.

Any other time, a spontaneous show of that sort would have punctured his flesh like an unconscious bite with no wish to hurt him or do him harm. But in the situation he found himself in, he felt as if the crime were premeditated, timed precisely so that he would find himself face to face with the dead man's eyes and the ochre cheekbones of the policemen on going out that door.

He was eighteen years old and had just left a brothel. It was the first time he had been with a woman.

He had had enough of the spectacle in the street; what he had seen was that a stain from such acids is not easy to wash away. But fifty meters from the clinic, the mobile indifference of the faces, the shoes, the hats and the shirts was reconstituted. As he walked toward the Rambla, the walls and the storefronts took on a gray and reserved air, like a man who adjusts his sleeves and cuffs after a fight. At the corner of Carrer de la Unió the tables of the venerable Orxateria Valenciana, where four generations of Barcelonans had sipped on tigernut milk, exuded the sugar, *xufles* and modesty of its comforting legacy. It was seven p.m. and, under a tent of fog, a sudden June heat was in the air.

On the Rambla, the carnations bursting out on the stands of the flower vendors and the round bellies of the sparrows plumped in the forks of the tree branches seemed more human and all-embracing to him.

At least these creatures didn't spit the aggressive egotism of the passing eyes in his face. Thousands of eyes. The Rambla was full of them. Eyes full of selfishness and lack of compassion and the tendency to hear only their own voices that walking on the Rambla at any time of day tends to produce. No one was to blame if they saw him as just another guy, with no interest in who he was or what had just happened to him.

He sat down at a sidewalk cafè and ordered a beer. He had twenty cèntims left in his pocket: just enough for the beer and a tip.

In every man's life there is a moment that is usually hidden in a fog of fear and shame or, if word gets out among his cronies, tinged with insincere, infantile and rude blustering. Years go by, and the negligent man, either unconscious or full of himself, manages to store the moment we are alluding to in the zone of infelicity, in a place where actions lose their flavor and color and are accepted as the bland eventualities of our existence. There is no record of any illustrious academic, solemn professor, or fashionable speaker who has chosen this moment as the topic of a dissertation before a select audience.

And despite this, that guilty moment contains so much festering poetry, condensed melancholy, or naked joy that it would be difficult, if one were sincere – if men can, indeed, be sincere – to find any equal to it in intensity. It is the moment when a young virgin boy overcomes his fear and delivers himself up to all the consequences of a brothel.

It is useless for the straightest of straitjackets, the most metaphysical of conversations, the darkest of Soviet enthusiasms, or the most terrifying of hymns from the hereafter to try and separate us from the millenary vibration of sex. It is pointless for intellectual or ecclesiastic good breeding to evoke the images of a panther, a pig, a serpent, or a frog with regard to the question of sex. The naked flesh of Siegfried will always leap over the flames when the time comes to pursue the flesh of the sleeping Brunhilde. And this will always be the axis on which men of all climes – the weak, thinking reed, as the sublime ascetic of the ruined bowels with a passion for abstract ideas put it – will spin.

Sexual life, depending on the person, can either be colored the gray of lymph or have an intense and hallucinatory polychromatic muscularity. But when even the most imaginative and skillful man reaches his plenitude and maturity, it will have an air of habit and routine. The poetic grandeur of sexual life, the place where it retains all its unpredictability and its dramatic interest, resides in the moment of initiation and discovery.

Poets, preachers, and aging pettifoggers speak of adolescence as the golden core of our path through this world, an enviable time, and they look at the human soul at that point when it is a green grape with all its juice still to be defined and channeled, as if it were a suit more full of flowers and hope than any we wear upon our bones. Where there is neither experience, nor a sense of responsibility, nor economic loss, nor calculated and mature incisions with a knife, there can be no pain. This is accepted by academic literature and by the heads of families. The definition of the *imberbis juvenis* as defined by Horace is still current when it comes to observing the sad university student, the sad rugby fan, the sad detector of brothels, the sad utter hypocrite up against paternal interrogations. When this sad creature is only seventeen he carries around a red and black confusion in the form of a monster that never leaves the zone of the pubis, the zone of the heart, or the zone of the brain.

Adolescents laugh and leap and dance, but no one wants to admit the adolescent's sexual sadness. He himself is embarrassed by it, and he will never confess it to anyone else. And when the years have gone by, he will assert that that sexual sadness is a lie.

In the solitary hours of adolescence, discoveries comes little by little. In our innocence and limitations – more pedantic at that age than at any other – we prefer to twirl the moustaches of wickedness, prefer to pretend we fear nothing, while our hearts tremble like poplar leaves. Reading allows for the morbid efficacy of masturbation; dreams are more full of alcohol than at any other time of life, and the only brutally poetic dreams are those of adolescence. Dreams that take direct revenge on the cowardice of unexplored flesh, icy spines and disgust at nocturnal pollutions. Pollutions without enthusiasm, without joy, that often even feel like a punishment. *Nec polluantur corpora*, says a bitter liturgical hymn that Catholic priests intone at the approach of spring.

Neither swimming pools, nor sports, nor maternal kisses, nor the four black peaks of the biretta worn by those who administer spiritual exercises are sufficient to combat the savage erection. When shameless friends come along – because among adolescents, too, there are the purely gastric types, who digest such preoccupations as if they were a basket of cherries – the shameless friends laugh their shameless laugh at the fear, the cowardice, or the voluntary chasteness of the shameful. Often, remorse accompanies the delirium of imagination, and time slips by without a decision. The champagne goblet modeled on Helen's tremulous breast is a cup that serves all drinks. The teeth of adolescent boys collide at every turn with that non-existent perfect goblet. The phallic totem of the most remote tribes is the very same totem of today's high schools and universities. The adolescent has been made to believe in the existence of sin. The case is presented to him factually, with its horrible material consequences. Some pedagogues employ convincing images. They have no compunction about projecting the catastrophes of secret maladies, with all their repugnant secretions and deformations and all their unbearable pain. But it is all for nothing: at some point shame and cowardice are gone. Temptation is too cruel, and the naked flesh of Siegfried will leap over the flames.

To reach this point, the adolescent has drunk the bile of sadness and confusion. No one has prepared him for this moment with solemn veils, or crowns of roses, or magical incense. He will arrive in secret, as if committing a crime, affecting indifference, but with his insides pulsating like the clapper of a bell. There will be no sublime figure for the adolescent to choose, no Venusberg mountain. He may squat among the orange peels and the stench of ammonia on the vilest street corner. He may have no choice but to pierce the shadow of whatever staircase corresponds to the limited sum of money he holds in his fingers. It is very sad, but this is the way it is. These are the pathways to the revelation of Helen's vulva. We all know it. It is so very common that to carry off the pretense that we don't give a damn, we make sure to tie a perfect knot in our neckties and we write a few poems that will move the more gelatinous ladies to tears.

The adolescent who pierces the shadow for the first time in his life may laugh at our poems and our neckties. He accepts as a celestial grace the smile of a woman who earns her living at the most despicable trade that exists. This woman is the guardian of the treasure. It is she who escorts him to the foyer of the brothel and she who presents the three goddesses to him. One in a green slip, one in a yellow slip, and one in a red slip. Then, in one of the fifty thousand disgusting brothels of the world, the judgment of Paris is reenacted. The apple this tortured Paris brings to offer to the most beautiful of the three is the whole mystery of his adolescence, all his desire shamefully compressed. Paris's choice is quick and feverish; he has blood-dark circles under his eyes. In an hour of mercantile physiology, in which she deposits a soul as indifferent as the roasted viands meant to kill the hunger of the impassioned pilgrim, he, the adolescent boy inexpertly and innocently hears for the first time the fateful symphony of sex, which the devil's coarse bow plays on the tense strings of our nerves.

As the years go by, the adolescent boy may become more demanding, may become cruel and idiotic with these women and with himself. But the temperature of the first time does not allow for anything like this. On that occasion, the most pitiful prostitute's womb might as well be composed of the most tender petals of the most tender roses, like the womb of Chloe under the inexpert thrusting of Daphnis.

And perhaps – because these useless paradoxes are the stuff of the spider web from which we all hang – the last prostitute, when faced in the most mechanical and primeval way with the latest inept Daphnis of all epochs, will exude a core of human mercy and an apparently wicked diligence, mingled with a blend of servility and maternity, a blend of angel and beast, in whose embrace the feverish adolescent will feel so close to the stars that never again in his life will the love of any woman be able to offer him a higher plateau.

As time goes by, the adolescent boy made man will not want to think about this; he will forget about his first Chloe, his anonymous Chloe of however many (naturally very few) pessetes. He will consider it to be the vilest dishonor to value the intensity of his first adventure over the intensity and pomp of later, much more literary, loves. Yet it is possible that what he considers to be a dishonor is the truth, a truth men never want to confess because their pride does not admit useless paradoxes.

The young man who had heard the two shots that killed a man on Carrer de Barberà, and who later devoted all his capital to the foaming topaz of a sad beer, had just experienced this shady and poetic moment of his existence. Like Paris, he had chosen from among the three goddesses a sordid Italian girl of twenty-five, the kind whose lungs live in a cistern, breathing in only the vegetation of the sewer, but whose continual ephemeral contacts had not managed to crush her siren's breast, nor had they burned the two moist and delicately hospitable violets out of her eyes.

He was eighteen years old and he was embarrassed to admit the truth, but she understood him perfectly. If the young woman had not been in a hurry, she would have done him all the honors, but in that house on Carrer de Barberà there was work to be done and there were people waiting. The prostitute limited herself to giving free rein to the boy's rapture, without protest, and to anointing his lips with the kind of cold, servile tenderness found on the snouts of ruminants.

The fact of having a woman all to himself, in a room with a door, without witnesses, without censors, without limits, drove him wild. His two years of hesitation and, above all, fear of a repugnant illness, howled like a dog atop a cushion of devastated flesh in the form of a woman. The selfish creature sought vengeance on moral pieties in pursuit of the revelation of pleasure. He said nothing, he simply listened to his sensations, noting the secret nervous harmony that begins to blossom into a fierce rhythm, till it reaches the desperate violins of a spasm that expires in a slow, flat and deflated chord. Biology coldly explains these things that the most fundamental modesty silences. But with his nails sunk into Helen's flesh and his eyes sinking in the well of her eyes, in that *crescendo* that for the first time in his life made his lungs bounce off the wall of his ribs, electrified by the unexpected sensation, nothing shamed him, and his only desire was to cry out long and hard, for everyone to hear him, to hear the joyous bellow of an eighteen year-old male who has a woman all to himself, even if it is a woman who clings at night to the threadbare jacket of a day worker, even if it's just for an hour, even if it's in a brothel, none of that mattered. None of that was enough to water down his cry of joy. The filthiest bed sheet, the flesh of the most enslaved body, can reproduce any myth.

After the desire to shout, after the great discovery, he began buttoning his shirt, with trembling fingers, wishing he could respond to her tawdry words with his own tawdry words, the words of a real man, a character who has seen it all before. But his heart, still bursting with the wine of enthusiasm, spoiled his words with a child's luminous and inexpert syllables.

On the staircase, he heard the shots, and he saw that dead man carried by the two policemen, at the very moment when he, *generosus puer*, thought he had just taken possession of life. Later, his pockets empty and his lips white with beer foam, his childish brain superimposed contradictory images: chiffon stockings, the patent leather of the policeman's cap, the blood on the cobblestones, a toothbrush stained with blood-colored toothpaste, the soapy inexpressiveness of the water in the bidet, the man's dirty jacket hanging from the arms of the two guards, the woman's sex and the dead man's mouth, and all of this projected onto the moving curtain of the Rambla, onto that backdrop of mechanical faces, rubber cheeks, eyes with a nebulous destination: onto anonymous, ordinary, inexplicable life.

Life and death side by side, as in the prelude to Tristan. An incomparably cheap and shameful love; an insignificant criminal murdered by another criminal; all of this in a festering neighborhood and in his eighteen year-old heart, protected by a castoff jacket dyed black because he was still in mourning for his grandfather. Only six months before he had seen him laid out in a uniform let out in the back, with moth-eaten red satin lapels. His grandfather! A being from a very distant clime. His dead grandfather was a wax figure, a repulsive old doll, who left no impression on him. But that dead man on Carrer de Barberà, he was the real thing, with his open eyes and his hair full of blood.

He paid for the beer. In an apartment on Carrer de Pelai, a classmate was waiting for him with the notes from Mathematical Analysis. Because that eighteen year-old boy was a student at the School of Architecture, a communist, by the name of Ferran de Lloberola.

—·—·—

IN ONE YEAR MANY thoughts had run through Ferran de Lloberola's mind.

When he graduated from the Jesuit high school, he was a tender, affectionate boy, of inordinate vanity and innocence. Ferran didn't realize what kind of house he lived in. He had never given a thought to his father or his mother, nor did he have the slightest idea about Don Tomàs and the family catastrophe. Ferran had lived the life of a boy into whom the fathers of the Company of Jesus, finding fertile ground, had injected their whole system. Ferran made off with the highest honors at school. With a normal intelligence and a prodigious memory, he left everyone else behind, and as one grade followed another, his position as a model student was a sort of sinecure that no one disputed. As for discipline, he carried the rule book at sword's point and only on very rare occasions had he been subject to punishment. He was the prefect of the Congregation of Sant Lluís and a brigadier in three different brigades. Though he didn't tend to fawn, nor was he particularly given to the virtues of spying, Ferran's mentality had been malleable to the Ignatian fingers, heirs to the rigid *ratio studiorum*.

Ferran's faith was fairly skin-deep, and he was about as chaste as a normal healthy boy can be when puberty blooms. It had never occurred to Ferran to doubt what the Jesuits taught him in their conversations, readings and, above all, retreats. Ferran didn't find the sort of theological indoctrination that occurred at the beginning of the school year – against a great black backdrop, to the lugubrious wheezing of a harmonium and a "Veni Creator Spiritus" sung in the teary drone of boy sopranos – particularly upsetting. The science in the sermons spat out by the father who conducted the operetta of the pain of adolescent boys was a science Ferran was accustomed to. The conversations on death, on eternal damnation, on the horrible vision of carnal sin, streamed through the brain of that young boy with the freshness of an idyllic spring. He agreed wholeheartedly with everything, and he already knew that in order for those things to have any effect on the distracted, the rebellious, or the devil's disciples they had to exaggerate a bit. Ferran's humble, tender eyes looked at the sunken cheekbones and ascetic shadows under the eyes of this father or that without any malice, as if to say: "You and I are in on the secret and we understand each other perfectly. You can push as much as you want, and I will take communion with the minimum of faith and minimum of enthusiasm required to be a perfect student."

Ferran's world was limited to the school, from the resplendent and theatrical communions to the ball thrown, with perfect bad faith, at the nose of the fattest and stupidest boy during recess. It was precisely in these free periods, more or less devoted to sports, that the Jesuit technique was most pronounced and the spirit of Ignatius of Loyola was most evident. Their purpose was to allow the young man whose head had been swollen for his personal merits, or his place in class, or the esteem in which his teachers held him, to behave like a despot toward the classmate beaten down by bad fortune or bad conduct. You could distinguish the perfect products of Ignatian technique from the incorrigible ones by their way of playing, of kicking each other, or of humiliating a classmate, and Ferran was a prodigy. The father prefect of the school could take great pride in him. Even when he was harming a classmate, he did it with unctuousness, and a phony smile of mercy and impunity. And it wasn't that he was a hypocrite, or mean, or heartless…On the contrary, he simply believed that this was the normal and proper way to behave, and the only way to be an exemplary student.

When he left school, he ran into the world of the streets and into other boys who came from other atmospheres that had nothing to do with St. Ignatius. That was when Ferran began to understand a bit who his family was. He observed his father's wretchedness and ineptitude and the economic penury that surrounded them with horror. The Jesuits had inculcated an entirely useless and puerile vanity in him. In his first year at the university, it only took a few underhanded punches to shatter his vanity and bring him down to earth. He was a ductile boy and a quick study. He understood that the false world the Jesuit school had created was pointless. His religious faith was quickly reduced to a bare minimum. He was still chaste, more out of fear than anything else. He would go to exciting shows with other boys like himself, but he didn't dare breach certain doors. The contacts he maintained with the Jesuits were purely perfunctory; he was even a bit offended when he realized that a former teacher wanted to snare him for a religious vocation that couldn't have been farther from his mind.

Life in the apartment on Carrer de Bailèn became odious to Ferran. He couldn't abide the air that wafted from his mother's coiffure or the clerical gesticulations of Grandmother Carreres. He thought that, in time, he could come to be an architect of some originality, a man of good standing and reputation, and this wasn't with the puerile vanity of high school, but with a pride that was growing in him little by little. Ferran's pride grew alongside the spirit of family disintegration, the same spirit that drove his sister Maria Lluïsa. After three centuries,

Ferran was the first of the Lloberolas to feel absolute contempt for the name he bore and for everything his family had stood for.

Ten months before Ferran found himself face to face with a dead man on leaving a brothel on Carrer de Barberà, he had a crisis that could have traced a definitive trajectory for him.

It had been just over a year since that veneer of faith and moral prejudice he had picked up in school had begun to fade. Ferran was practically indifferent to it all, and on the verge of risking the modicum of shame and the three drops of chastity he still had on the first eyes he came upon around the first corner he turned. If he hadn't made his move it was because the right opportunity hadn't presented itself. But just when his religious faith and moral tenacity were at their most tepid, a strange event disoriented him. Ferran believed that a supernatural event had occurred within him, in his innermost life. And this supernatural event turned Ferran's soul toward a very particular ambition. For a few months he stopped dreaming of being a great architect. What he wanted for himself was the glory of Christ's shepherd, Saint Paul. He thought he had a right to that glory, because what happened to him seemed analogous to what had happened, according to legend, to that storied apostle on the road to Damascus.

When Ferran told Pare Mainou, of the Company of Jesus, about these innermost impressions, not even he could organize them logically. The fact was that he was never able to give a precise account of what had happened to him. The only thing that was clear was the radical change that took place in his feelings and actions. Ferran imagined that, during a night of erotic turbulence, he must have fallen asleep after assuaging his secret misery, and a few hours later he was awakened by a very unusual light. He couldn't be sure if it was part of a dream or a real light. He was under the impression, though, that it was a real, physical light that had penetrated his bedroom. By this light, Ferran thought he had distinguished images of an angelic nature, forms in keeping with his purely infantile visual idea of the world of the blessed. The vision he was certain he had had was fleeting, it lasted just a moment, between waking and sleep. But it so impressed Ferran that he didn't hesitate to imagine that what had happened to him was of transcendent importance. Ferran was certain that God had called him in a way that went beyond the ordinary path, and that what he had seen with his own eyes was precisely what theologians call a miracle.

He stayed in bed for a few hours, unable to sleep, turning over his supposed vision in his mind. The consequences he derived from the event compelled him to get up early, head for the church of the Jesuits, and throw himself like a dog at the foot of Pare Mainou's confessional.

Pare Mainou listened to him and told him with perfect aplomb that God had worked a miracle to convert him. Ferran was dismayed. He made a horrible confession. With sadistic fruition, he accused himself of every carnal misery, chewing over the tiny details that are the hardest to tell, against which shame most rebels. The child felt the voluptuosity of lowering himself and humiliating himself with all the force of his seventeen year-old blood.

From that day on, Ferran wallowed in a pathological mysticism, with a nervous oversensitivity and a tendency to cry that would have been heartbreaking had he not made every last effort to conceal what was happening to him so that no one would realize what a state he was in, or suspect what he was going through.

He only calmed down during the time he spent with Pare Mainou. In the morning, he would seek him out in the confessional, and in the afternoon, he would plant himself at the door of his cell. There, he could cry and strip bare the puerility of his soul without compunction. Pare Mainou felt edified by his conversion, by that life soft as warm wax flowing through his fingers.

Pare Mainou was a very good person, but in Ferran's case he was a bit misguided. Not realizing that the whole thing was a childish fantasy, he put too much faith in the boy's words, and he let himself be carried away on the warm and fascinating wings of the miracle. Pare Mainou didn't advise calm or serenity. The readings he prescribed for Ferran were like a drug that exacerbated his pathological state. The *Confessions* of Saint Augustine, in particular, spread like a trail of gunpowder down the entire length of Ferran's spine. Some people think that no book can produce such acute sensual upheaval in an adolescent as directly erotic reading. Ferran's case could easily disprove such an unsophisticated opinion. St. Augustine's *Confessions* or the *Imitation of Christ* produced spasms and indescribable sensations in him. People well-versed in the history of the mystics know something about the terrible and monstrous explosions caused by the desire for divine contact. A being who finds himself in Ferran's situation seeks this contact in any way he can, and the most vivid and sensitive course is almost always through physical pain. To experience such pain and calibrate it to the limit of one's resistance is to feel an ineffable pleasure, a fruition that cannot be explained, nor can it be understood by a person who has not undergone similar moments. By an entirely different and apparently pure path, one can reach the most vicious masochism, the ruination and shredding of the flesh.

That boy was the victim of this evil, and Pare Mainou, in the greatest of good faith, did nothing but make it worse. Ferran began by analyzing all the things – even the most insignificant things – he found enjoyable, and started forgoing them one after the other. He started depriving himself of everything in such an absurd way that if he was thirsty he would not drink until he couldn't bear it any longer, valuing the physical torture of his thirst. In any area related to vanity and to the relationship with his classmates he reached extremes of sleight-of-hand to avoid suspicion. Sometimes the puerility of Ferran's sacrifices would have been laughable if he had not truly been suffering. His nights were tragic. He slept in a bedroom with his brother Lluís, two years younger than he, a soft, unsuspecting child who didn't imagine a thing.

In bed, Ferran felt a well-being he found offensive. When it became unbearable, he would kneel down on the bare tiles. This position, which quickly progressed from humiliation to pain, soothed him. He managed to remain immobile, and when the pain in his knees began to stab him with an insolent sharpness it seemed as if Ferran's lungs breathed more joyful breaths. Any boy who was not undergoing such a moral breakdown, could not under any circumstances have withstood two hours of kneeling on a tile floor like Ferran, who reached an unbearable degree of torment. Sometimes his brother would wake up and see him in that position. Naturally, he couldn't resist a few gibes at Ferran's expense. Instead of answering back, Ferran would hide in his bed, utterly ashamed, as if he had been caught doing something disgusting. Then he would finally fall asleep, content at having experienced both intense pain and humiliation, in the mockery and sharp words of his brother.

He felt the greatest fruition in the mornings when he received communion. As a child, even in his most tender and celestial years, Ferran had practiced this Catholic ritual in a fairly unconscious, if not completely unconscious, way. Spiritual withdrawal and respect had been the consequence of a fear imposed from without. All the magic of the sacrament escaped him, and ten minutes later, he would happily break his fast, without a single thought for mystery or the supernatural. Having to receive communion irritated him a little, because beforehand he would have to go and confess his sins. Except for this, it was just one of the many events of childhood. Later, he had ended up losing what little respect he had for it. When his "conversion" took place, it had been a little over a year since he'd last approached a confessional. When he began to change, Ferran discovered all the deep force of the sacrament. He came to take communion with a burning, shattering passion, with a shivering sensuality. That act was the only sedative for the irresistible stinging of his soul.

At first, after his conversion, Ferran would occasionally fall into the habit of a solitary vice that, naturally, he wanted to forswear entirely. He reacted with desperation to these lapses, which he could not overcome. Pare Mainou couldn't find the words to comfort him and make him understand that the flesh is weak and those unfortunate lapses were no cause for him to consider himself the most vile and unhappy of men.

Ferran wanted to bring order to the turmoil of his doubts. He wanted to draw a map of his path and of the direction his life would have to take. Amid all his grand denials, puerile vanity still had him in its grasp. Ferran dreamt of being an apostle of Christ, an awakener of souls, even of becoming a martyr, if need be. A literary proclivity led him to fall in love with the uncomfortable habit of the Capuchin friars. He imagined himself with a beard, wearing a hood, preaching the Gospel in the most inclement climes. When he told Pare Mainou these thoughts, the priest suggested that he would find the greatest renunciation, the maximum humility, and the maximum sacrifice in the Company of Jesus. He told Ferran that no other order had such severe rules and such strict practices as the order of Ignatius of Loyola, and said that for one who was readying himself with all his strength to achieve sainthood, no other institution could offer him greater security than the Jesuits.

Ferran was swayed. From then on in he began preparing for the novitiate. Pare Mainou put him in the hands of Pare Masdeu, the head of novices from Gandia, who by chance was in Barcelona at the time. Pare Masdeu had his feet much more firmly on the ground than Pare

Mainou. He examined the young man from head to toe and realized that, in his case, there was at least fifty percent of suggestion and misdirected sensuality.

With Pare Masdeu, Ferran restrained his lyricism. In Ferran's vocation, there was an element he didn't dare confess even to himself. This element proceeded from the weakness and cowardice inherited from the Lloberolas. It was passivity and inaptitude for struggle, bred in a depleted family that had not lifted a blade of straw from the ground in two hundred years.

After high school, Ferran understood the failure and destitution of his household, and if he entertained the pride of being a great architect and man of personal value, his enthusiasm soon waned, and in the marrow of his bones he felt the indolence and weakness characteristic of his father, his uncle, and his grandfather, Don Tomàs. Like all the Lloberolas, Ferran was afraid of life, and as soon as he decided to enter a religious order, this problem of life and the struggle to live was solved. The order would provide for him, and would make his decisions for him. Ferran's vocation was fifty percent egoism, and it is very possible that under the scrutiny of a capable and discerning man such as Pare Masdeu this fifty percent did not go unnoticed.

Despite Pare Masdeu's misgivings, which at times verged on positive skepticism, the headmaster of the novitiate didn't want to discourage him. Ferran seemed more and more determined, and Pare Masdeu said that in another month he could go to Gandia, not to join the novitiate, but to have a good look. There he would try to put his vocation to the test, and if it was a true vocation, there would be no reason not to admit him.

Ferran had kept his counsel and not said anything to anyone. He accepted the month imposed by Pare Masdeu, and looked for an excuse to make a trip to Gandia. But one day he lost control, and he told a friend who was older than he, in whom he had utmost confidence, about his situation and all his plans. Ferran's friend couldn't believe his ears, but when he realized it wasn't just a bad joke, he gave him a talking-to. Among other things, he said that his vocation was no such thing, and above all he was being a coward. Ferran cried his heart out. His friend understood the state of weakness and of moral unraveling to which his own suggestibility and the influence of Pare Mainou had reduced him.

Ferran's friend tried to get him to react. He was intelligent enough to see that Ferran was the victim of a collusion of absurd eventualities and that, in the best of good faith, he was about to commit moral suicide.

His friend sought the aid of a very famous Capuchin priest who was in vogue at the time. The Capuchin father spoke with Ferran and gave him the most sensible advice possible, in the course of which, even so, the spirit of rivalry between Franciscans and Jesuits was not entirely absent. What became clear was that Ferran's vocation was so shallow that the Capuchin father's arguments were able to reduce it by half in the first round.

Ferran spent two days meditating and looking at himself in the mirror, without setting foot in the convent on Carrer de Casp. Oddly, all the castles in the air he had built over the past couple of months, along with all his convictions of sainthood and sacrifice, were slowly turning into pale shadows. Still, Ferran had inherited his father's pride and stubbornness, and it was very hard for him to give in and confess that he had made a mistake.

On his visits to Pare Masdeu, Ferran couldn't find the words, and it wasn't long before Pare Masdeu grasped the child's unhappiness. He told him not to torture himself, not to worry. He could be just as holy and just as perfect living in the world and having a career as wearing on his head the four black peaks of the Jesuit biretta. Ferran didn't want to give in. He still protested, he tried new experiments in pain, he clung like a man possessed to the pages of the *Imitation of Christ*, but it was all pure willfulness, pitiful mental masturbation. Pare Masdeu told him not to persist. The provincial head would never admit him to the Company of Jesus, and he should go out in the fresh air and enjoy himself.

Ferran followed his instructions to a tee, and for the first time in his life, he felt all the strength, all the joy of liberation. Ferran felt exactly as if a chain that oppressed his breast and kept him physically from breathing had been broken. He went back to his puerile vanities, to the happiness of his classmates, and to giving free rein to his senses. As practical as he was, Pare Masdeu never suspected that such sublime faith would disappear in four months.

Not only did Ferran abandon his saintly projects, he completely abandoned religion. It seemed impossible to him that he had been the victim of those monstrous hallucinations. He felt deeply indignant on remembering the hours he had spent kneeling on the tile floor. He called himself stupid and idiotic. He was truly embarrassed by his unspeakable immaturity. And he extended his indignation to Pare Mainou, who had put the finishing touches on his delusion. True as it was that Pare Mainou was somewhat guilty, he was not nearly as guilty as Ferran liked to think.

In time, his hatred extended to the entire Jesuit Order, the whole Catholic Church, and all of Christianity. The marvelous thing he had found in the Sermon on the Mount and other passages from the Gospels turned into a feeling of disgust. Ferran began to read books he would never before have dared to open. He found these authors just as enthralling as he had found the *Confessions* of St. Augustine just a short time before. The *Antichrist* of Nietzsche, translated into Castilian, which he bought for just *a ral*, a quarter of a pesseta, at the used bookstand on Santa Madrona, revealed a bright new world to him where his ideas could wander.

By hating the doctrine he had learned since childhood, he felt as if he were avenging all the bad dreams and all the sufferings of those months of torture. He considered Pare Mainou, a saintly and dignified man, to be the most abject criminal in the world. One day, in the Sant Sebastià bathhouse, he realized that his first communion medallion was hanging from gold chain around his neck. Ferran whipped off this last sign of slavery. He hesitated for a moment, wondering whether he should sell it or pawn it, but he decided to throw it into the sea. An absurd puerility led him to believe he was carrying out an act of heroism by throwing that little medallion away.

When the Republic came, and later, when the Jesuit order was dissolved, Ferran was as happy as a dog with a bone, because his family was outraged, and, more to the point, because the Jesuits were his enemies, who had almost led him to perdition. In those days, like many students of his time, he was a communist, and he only liked Soviet films.

In this period of hatreds and inoffensive vengeances, Ferran was still afraid of women and brothels.

The day he made his decision, you might say he was perfectly calm. After the afternoon of the murder on Carrer de Barberà, Ferran turned on a dime. He made a series of important discoveries. One of them was the existence of his sister, Maria Lluïsa.

Indeed, the young man had been too busy inventing himself, first as a mystical farce, and then as a demagogical farce, to be able to experience his natural character in an ordinary way. It took the jolt of contact with a prostitute and the sight of a murdered man to plant his feet on the ground.

Ferran had never seen his sister. As children, when they played together, Maria Lluïsa was nothing to Ferran but someone a little older, a little more delicate and a little weaker than he was. Then life at school separated them completely, and Maria Lluïsa's emancipation, and the fact that she treated her brother like a child, did the rest. Ferran found her intolerable, he found her affected and overbearing, a person who did nothing but talk back to their mother over lunch and dinner. Maria Lluïsa and Ferran knew absolutely nothing about each other.

Ferran was in love with love. He was going through that stage young men his age go through in which a kind of sentimental and erotic desire is latent in every idea their brains can elaborate, and in all the impressions they receive from the outside world. The man is in love, and he doesn't quite know what he loves, or what he wants. All the subjective elements are mixed up in a tender and confused way, and what is missing is the concrete person who can channel and rearrange those elements. The woman has not yet appeared, but he can sense her perfume, in the daylight, in music, in every girl's gaze, in an inexplicable melancholy, in nighttime dreams, in cool bathwater, and in the flight of a swallow. The man lives in love with love.

One evening, in this peculiar state, Ferran looked at his sister, Maria Lluïsa. The life of this young woman was a mystery to Ferran. Her feminine climate was hermetically sealed in a world whose existence Ferran knew nothing of. He sensed, though, that a specific thing united him and his sister: their anti-family spirit, the aversion both of them felt to that apartment on Carrer de Bailèn and to the Lloberola name.

For the first time in his life, Ferran spoke of these things with his sister. Maria Lluïsa listened with discretion, appearing not to pay much attention. For her, that boy was the child she still envisioned in a sailor's suit or in golf knickers, and it was impossible for her to take him seriously. It is very hard for a brother and sister to crack the shell of family intimacy, which is precisely the least cordial, least communicative and least human relationship that exists. In a family, affection and coexistence have an inevitable, instinctive cohesion that can be observed in a brood of chicks in a nest or in an ant colony, but the elective affection, that spark of friendship or love, that something that free will and feelings create as they go through the world and sort out affinities and connections, is missing.

And it is precisely because of that instinctive and inevitable factor in family relations that the betrayal of a sibling is always more painful than that of a friend, even if one believes oneself to be much more identified with the friend than with the sibling. The betrayal of a sibling brings on a pain that is almost physical, and physical pain, despite the poets, entails obsession and prejudice far beyond any moral pain.

With Ferran, Maria Lluïsa had adopted that very attitude of lack of cordiality and communication. She had no doubt that the very last person who might be able to understand her was that eighteen-year-old whippersnapper. Nevertheless, as the conversation continued throughout the evening, Maria Lluïsa shifted from a state of impatience to a state of attention. She began to see something personal in that young man; above all, the desire to be a man, and the trace of a spirit of inquiry. And what Maria Lluïsa saw, and this was what most surprised her, was the interest he took in her, a tenderness and affection that were not a question of habit, that didn't correspond to their years of coexistence, or even to their common blood. The very unusual sound of a human voice that speaks to a person well known to it in some aspects but absolutely unknown in other, more important, ones. And all at once the inflection of this voice changes as it addresses those more important aspects, which it has just divined as if by miracle.

Maria Lluïsa saw Ferran progress from the – according to her – infrahuman condition of brother, to the condition of man.

Maria Lluïsa did not see that Ferran's feelings for her were the consequence of that state of being in love with love, nor that in a sister like Maria Lluïsa he found reflections of that inchoate thing his nerves were demanding of him. Maria Lluïsa didn't know anything about these things. If she herself gone through a moment like that, she hadn't been aware of it and, being more realistic, as befits a woman, she had quickly found other conduits. Ferran spoke to Maria Lluïsa with intense passion, he almost told her intimate details of his life – always with the shyness and politeness with which one speaks to a sister – that Maria Lluïsa didn't know how to construe. Maria Lluïsa thought that this brother who for her had just become a young man might perhaps be too much of a man, and his language might be too fervent and too casual. A painful thought crossed Maria Lluïsa's mind. She had a much less nebulous idea of the world than her brother. Maria Lluïsa, at that point in time – she was in the midst of her selfish adventure with Bobby – didn't know what it meant to be in love with love, but she did know that between brothers and sisters an event condemned by moralists, known as incest, sometimes occurred. Maria Lluïsa considered the possibility that that eighteen year-old creature who was still caught up in a state of sexual confusion and inexperience might, for some strange reason, one of which could very well be Maria Lluïsa's own grace and beauty, might be the victim of a frankly incestuous inclination.

When, in the course of one of his confidences, Ferran innocently took Maria Lluïsa by her bare arm, and she felt his slightly sweaty palm molding itself to her cool skin, she flinched. Unable to hide her repulsion or disgust, she pulled away. Ferran was left with his hand hanging in the air in the middle of that room, as inexpressive and incongruous as the wing of a wounded bird. Ferran looked into his sister's eyes to try to understand that instinctive rejection, that bitter gesture in the face of his candor and enthusiasm. He had taken his sister by the arm and kissed her on the cheek thousands of times, without provoking the slightest shadow or cloud in his or her eyes. And at the very moment when Ferran was breaking the ice, when he was seeking the human collaboration of his sister, when he was asking her to elevate him to the category of a good friend, what Ferran found in Maria Lluïsa was an attack of disgust or fear, or some indefinable detachment.

Then, despite his innocence, Ferran thought he could divine the explanation for that incongruity in Maria Lluïsa's eyes. Her monstrous idea in some vague way impressed itself upon the boy's brain. His explanation seemed as indelicate, as almost monstrous, as the thing itself. Ferran froze. Maria Lluïsa was still terrified, because Ferran's hesitation, his air of bewilderment at the possibility that Maria Lluïsa might imagine that of him, only impressed the idea more vividly upon her.

The two siblings remained silent. It was impossible to say anything about something as ridiculous as what had just happened, about such an absurd misunderstanding. Ferran, who was much weaker and much more sincere than Maria Lluïsa, felt the unbearable convulsion of a sob, and he hid his head in his hands, unable to choke back his tears.

Maria Lluïsa's distress was intense. The boy's tears, each nuance of his behavior, served only to bolster the tenebrous idea. Far from feeling repelled, Maria Lluïsa began to feel an extremely curious pity for that child, whom she saw as the victim of a sick and deviant affection. But she was unable to come up with so much as half a word. For such a case as she was imagining, she had not anticipated a response. Anything she said might have seemed offensive to him. Ferran, conversely, found himself in a parallel situation. How was it possible that malice or misunderstanding on his sister's part could have produced an idea of him that was so incompatible with his nature?

What could the boy say, what kind of clarification could he imagine when, tender and inexpert as he was, with the juvenile and magical idea he had of his sister's purity, any syllable with which he might attempt to defend himself would seem like a sacrilege? His face still hidden, Ferran hoped he might have misinterpreted Maria Lluïsa's gesture, but if "that" was not what her gesture was saying, if "that" was not what her eyes, chillingly diaphanous, were saying, were saying, then what was it, in fact, that had happened to his sister?

Maria Lluïsa interpreted Ferran's tears and obstructed nerves as his reaction – his noble reaction, of course – to a faux pas. If his tears had been followed by imprecations and revelations, Maria Lluïsa's situation would have been even more compromised. Any reaction, despite the fact that this was her own eighteen year-old brother, seemed impossible to her. Ferran's silence allowed her, even obliged her, in a way, to say something. Maria Lluïsa had to offer a response to those tears, to make some comment; she couldn't remain mute, she couldn't allow this pathetically shattering and absurd scene to drag on. Maria Lluïsa believed that the best thing she could do was to erase the ill effect her gesture of repulsion had caused, and imply that none of this mattered in the slightest and she hadn't noticed a thing. Of course this was a farce, and Ferran wouldn't swallow it either, but women often believe in the efficacy of lies and dissembling right to one's face. This is the most suitable stance for salvaging catastrophes, and perhaps momentarily the most effective. Later, time and reflection could provide tranquilizers, slow and numbing cauterizers that could heal any wound.

Maria Lluïsa spoke to Ferran, expressing bewilderment at his tears, asking him what was the matter. She attributed his state to an overabundance of nerves and advised him to go to bed. She said they could continue talking later about all those things that she found so very interesting. Maria Lluïsa even made an effort to give him a kiss – and at that moment, her brother's skin produced horror in her – and to treat him like a child, the child he had always been, who had begun to entertain the obsessions of a man.

Ferran calmed down and left his sister alone. By lying and pretending, Maria Lluïsa had released him from a moment of anguish, which he could not have found a way out of. The moment was behind them. Never again would Maria Lluïsa and Ferran make reference to that event, which to an outside observer might have appeared to be entirely insignificant, but which had just opened an abyss between brother and sister. Later, they would be able to pretend, and even to forget, and support each other mutually in a polite and distant way, but it would be very difficult for intimacy and understanding to evolve between the two of them, so long as they were under the influence of the memory of that event.

Ferran was terribly disappointed. With regard to every aspect of his house and the human relationships in it, the only welcoming sanctuary Ferran had found was in his sister. He sensed in her the most vivid and noble qualities of his family, and the same desire to escape it and to live her own life that he himself felt. That sister, who had always seen him as a child, would have been able to understand him as a man. Little by little, he could have aspired to be Maria Lluïsa's confidant. He had hopes of being able to help her, and to provide for her, if necessary, through his work. With Maria Lluïsa by his side, her shadow of protective femininity could have projected itself with ineffable sweetness over all his thoughts. Having coupled with a prostitute and repeated the adventure with other women, it could be said that Ferran had become acquainted with the most dramatic and intense aspect of his flesh in the contest with the flesh of women. The taste of Helen had entered his marrow and his belly, but it had left a sordid stain in the bluish liquid of his dreams. Ferran didn't know where to find a woman with that blend of angel and beast, who would make that visceral sensation even more intense with the compensation of the infinite melody of great emotion.

Ferran saw his sister as a guarantee. He wanted her by his side, as his confidante. He needed her gentleness, her confidence. Maria Lluïsa's presence demonstrated to him that he would be able to find in this world a woman like her, with her eyes and her grace, but with a burning sexuality and veins intoxicated with passion for him. Never, though, could Ferran have been able to imagine any feeling of desire or the most remote intention of animal rebellion mixed up with the almost mystical idea he had of his sister. Ferran realized that it was a misunderstanding on Maria Lluïsa's part, an excess of suspicion, which had destroyed the possibility of such an equilibrium of affection.

Ferran didn't understand that when he had opened his heart to his sister, speaking to her of his desires, his doubts, and his melancholy, perhaps he had done so with an unwitting vehemence. Perhaps he had approached her in a way that Maria Lluïsa had not been able to anticipate, and perhaps predictably it had taken her by surprise. Ferran was still a boy, and, heeding the counsel of his own inexperience, he still approached things head-on. He considered this to be the most normal and natural thing in the world. This is why it was impossible for him to assume even a modicum of guilt or responsibility in what had just happened between his sister and him.

Ferran was distressed for hours; he could see no way out. Maria Lluïsa would never be able to erase her impression, no one would ever dissuade her from her certainty. She would see any explanation as an excuse, and nothing more than an excuse. A fictional cordiality, thanks to which brother and sister could live as strangers, side by side. This was the most Ferran could aspire to. The dream he had imagined was now impossible.

Ferran had a lily-white notion of Maria Lluïsa. If he had suspected who his sister was at heart, if he had known only a particle of the true state of moral decomposition Maria Lluïsa was in, perhaps he would have considered all the pain that absurd incident had caused him to be for naught. Ferran's pain would probably have been different, not so gentle, not so much in love with love, but indeed more concrete, more positive, much more human. He would have had the same taste in his teeth that any skeptical explorer of the acid caverns of life tastes when he bites down on bitter rue.

—·——·—

AS THE DAYS WENT BY, Maria Lluïsa started thinking that she might have been mistaken. Maybe Ferran's behavior didn't mean "that." Maria Lluïsa treated her little brother with pleasant cordiality, but Ferran maintained a distant and exceedingly polite attitude. Ferran was finding other things down the road. One of those things was the prettiest shoe store clerk to be found those days on the streets of Barcelona. With this girl, Ferran had a hint of the kind of love that moves the sun and the stars. The clerk, who seemed much more natural and kind to him than Maria Lluïsa, smacked of popular taste, unpleasant and slightly tacky, occasionally ragtag and greedy, but she was sincere, uncomplicated, and alive. This was love, with the eternally corny delights of paper lanterns, neighborhood bands, and slices of watermelon. In the armpit of the shoe clerk Ferran the communist found the integral perfume of anonymous flesh with no pretensions to nobility, idleness, or the gold frames bearing the dust of misery that pained his sight in the apartment on Carrer de Bailèn.

Maria Lluïsa received a letter from her father. With that letter, Frederic was testing the waters. He didn't dare write to his wife. He was hoping Maria Lluïsa would be the best go-between for a reconciliation. Frederic was beginning to feel very sick. The wine merchant's wife and the farmer's daughter had impoverished him body and soul. The doctor in Moià told him his illness was no joke. Proud and inconsistent, Frederic Lloberola had decided to sell at any price what little was left of his estate and prostrate himself at the feet of Maria Carreres.

Frederic's return to the house on Carrer de Bailèn was silly and theatrical. Husband and wife shed tears, and mother-in-law Carreres had to drink great quantities of linden tea for her nerves. In Ferran's eyes, his father was unspeakably odious and grotesque.

Old Leocàdia had been flickering like a votive candle in the Cluny convent. They kept Frederic's illness and any other unpleasant news from her so she wouldn't worry. Leocàdia lived in that sweet, transparent egocentrism of the old, when they become like children and their only concern is for their devotions and other petty details.

From the opulence of Conxa Pujol's bed, Guillem responded to the servile and unlettered missives of his brother Frederic with the occasional banknote.

The Lloberola anachronism had become a frayed tightrope on which to walk heel to toe, amid admissions of defeat, without principles or dignity of any kind.

Frederic rejoined the Club Eqüestre. When he fell behind on his accounts, his brother, who was on the board, paid them without a word.

Frederic did everything he could to ignore his children's lives and his wife's bitterness. He was terrified of dying, and the doctors patched up his illness with injections and warnings.

Maria Lluïsa abused Bobby's affection, she cheated on him shamelessly, and her name was on the verge of losing what little prestige it had left. Many were aware of the concrete facts of her irregular conduct. Maria Lluïsa even came to question her own comportment. She began to fear that all this living for today and broadmindedness would lead to disaster in the long run. Considering the scope of her ambitions, she couldn't even have gotten a start on what she earned at the bank.

Maria Lluïsa had fantasized about a carefree life of limitless freedom. She had thought that the people she kept company with would accept such a moral position. This was an overly optimistic view of society. The literature and the conversations Maria Lluïsa sought out could digest anything. They gave the impression that the people of our country had taken a considerable turn, but even the young men who cited her as the very model of a modern girl and danced with her to the point of collapse as they whispered lewd phrases in her ear, criticized her from head to toe when they were on their own. None of them would have wanted a girl who behaved like Maria Lluïsa for a fiancée or a sister.

Bobby spoke seriously with her about getting married, and in principle Maria Lluïsa accepted. Bobby didn't see a thing. He was convinced of the girl's affection and sincerity. When Maria Lluïsa understood the softening of principles she had brought about in that distant and genteel man, instead of slowing down a bit she became childishly conceited. She saw Bobby as a sort of Lewis Stone. Maria Lluïsa admired that fine American actor who so admirably played the role of the understanding modern spouse. She imagined that Bobby would also be happy to live by her side in a modish film in which Maria Lluïsa would play the role of Greta Garbo.

Bobby had one of the most solid fortunes of Barcelona, and Maria Lluïsa saw herself sailing on a yacht overflowing with tangos, cocktail shakers, and spiritual gigolos, as she distributed orchids, smiles and fatalities on the arm of a husband who was as imperturbable as the Eternal Father.

Enthralled, Bobby said yes to her every wish, until one day he started to see certain things. In his dialogues with his conscience, Bobby tried to justify Maria Lluïsa and stifle his doubts. But one evening, a little scandal took place at the sidewalk cafè of the Hotel

Colon, and among the many people who heard about it, more than one went off to tell Bobby what had happened in full detail. Maria Lluïsa and two other girls were sitting at a table at the height of the hour of the aperitif. When they were at their most merry, a very well-known lady of the evening who plied her trade at the bar of the hotel appeared at their table and addressed a string of withering insults to Maria Lluïsa. In addition to the insults she tried to get her nails on Maria Lluïsa's face, and she swore she would kill her if Maria Lluïsa did not leave a certain person alone. According to the experts, it was said that the person in question was an officer in the Air Force, one of the most well-groomed and most alcoholic. Maria Lluïsa was quite vexed, but she more than held her own in the noisy exchange.

That incident was the straw that broke Bobby's enamored heart, overflowing with good intentions. He didn't stage any scenes of jealousy, he didn't even complain, but everything Maria Lluïsa needed to note to understand that Bobby had tired of her was perfectly clear.

Rosa Trènor, whom Maria Lluïsa saw on occasion, didn't despair of finding her a substitute along the same lines as Bobby. But Maria Lluïsa shuddered at the thought of continuing down that road. A second act, following Bobby, would place her on a lower rung, and soon Maria Lluïsa would no longer be able to sustain her equivocal situation. Things would just be too evident, and retreat would be impossible.

Maria Lluïsa preferred to step back a bit, and manage her adventures with more discretion. She performed a sort of examination of conscience, which left her feeling bitter, practically convinced she was a failure.

Maria Lluïsa saw that her job at the bank was an unbearable burden that became more and more tedious with each passing day. She had imagined she was capable of feeling the joy of labor and emancipation from the family. She had dreamed of living life *à l'américaine* within the climate of Barcelona. Maria Lluïsa only knew the movie version of America. She saw it all through "weekends" with strawberry ice cream, exciting bathing suits, and millionaires' sons, whose naiveté and tenderness were foolproof, who fell in love and signed checks and marriage licenses and divorce papers without batting an eye. Her adventure with Pat had not opened her eyes, much to the contrary. Not only had Maria Lluïsa accepted Bobby's attentions – and Bobby, in the long run, was a man of parts – but in a most unthinking way, she had gotten involved with other, absolutely deplorable men, who spared no details in explaining intimate particulars about Maria Lluïsa. Since there are always people in this world ready and willing to stick their feet in their mouths, on one occasion Frederic was essentially a hair's breadth away from hearing right to his face an appalling anecdote about his daughter that couldn't have left him unscathed.

Maria Lluïsa finally came to realize that, in the end, nothing good had come of all her emancipation and her modern ways. She didn't have a superior mentality or better taste, or more knowledge than most girls of her class. She was just as common and selfish as Pat. The only science in which she could show a bit of aptitude was one that did her no favors. It was extremely painful to admit that in Maria

Lluïsa's case, her two years of freedom and eccentricity had served only for her to lose her reputation, and a good portion of her personal delicacy and sparkle.

Even so, Maria Lluïsa couldn't have been less inclined to make peace with her mother's standards, or to resign herself to a path completely opposed to the one she had followed to that point. Maria Lluïsa's case was not unique among her acquaintances. Even if her behavior had been scandalous, most of her female friends continued to spend time with her as if nothing had happened, and perhaps Maria Lluïsa even had in her favor, in contrast to other young women like her, that she had allowed herself certain liberties without hypocrisy, and without going out of her way to keep it all secret. In a word, Maria Lluïsa was frank, and maybe it was asking too much of her frankness to want her to behave with absolute sincerity with Bobby. If Bobby hadn't had the misfortune of falling in love with Maria Lluïsa the way he had, he would have been able to anticipate that meeting a girl like her in the circumstances in which he had met her did not guarantee him a virgin out of Roman martyrology. But in this world, the most experienced and skeptical of men can also be the most gullible.

For a time, Maria Lluïsa felt rather sad and benumbed. Her affairs, which she carried on with great caution, didn't amuse her. She found the fellows more and more selfish, and only interested in one thing, which she was indifferent to. Without a modicum of passion, she found the episodes of the *garconnière* and the *meublé* stupid and monotonous. At twenty years of age, Maria Lluïsa was beginning to be tired of it all.

On the day that Maria Lluïsa, resting her chin on the lapel of Pat's jacket, said that she was tired of being a virgin as if it were the most natural thing in the world, it is very possible that she viewed with true horror the panorama of ladyfingers and anisette that awaited an unassuming bourgeois marriage, coping with marital flaws and economic constraints. Two years later, a bourgeois marriage along those lines didn't burst onto her imagination with the sudden flash of a meteor, but perhaps it seemed to be the only practical way out of the dismal impasse she'd reached. Maria Lluïsa had not had the courage to break things off completely with the age-old unctuosity of her family. She had only gone halfway in her freedom and her perversion. If she had resigned herself to living brutally and poetically, for as long as necessary, accepting all the consequences, Maria Lluïsa's behavior might have seemed suicidal to many eyes, but respectable, in the end.

When her inner sadness began to be visible on her face, and a slight muscular relaxation in her body revealed the anatomical melancholy of the disenchanted, Frederic received a visit from a young man from Bilbao who had come to ask for his daughter's hand.

He was a youngish man, getting on a bit, but tall and well-built, and he seemed like an excellent fellow. Some business with the metallurgical industry had brought him to Barcelona, and he had been staying at the Nouvel Hôtel on Carrer de Santa Anna for three months now.

The young man from Bilbao had met Maria Lluïsa at the bank where she worked. He followed her, he spoke to her, and he fell in love with her like a lap dog. He was a simple and expeditious man.

Maria Lluïsa found him suitable, and what most enticed her was a change of climate, a change of décor, and a definitive escape from Carrer de Bailèn. The position of the young man from Bilbao seemed brilliant, and the world in which he moved was much more lively and interesting than the office, the family, the parties at the Club Marítim, the officers in the Air Force and the sordid gossip about Maria Lluïsa's skin and bloodlines. A short time later, Maria Lluïsa emigrated from Barcelona and married as the good Lord intended, her eyes somewhat tinged with the green of hope, and her cheek a bit wet from three tears from Maria Carreres's eyes.

Ferran was truly happy about his sister's marriage. Since the night of their confidences and their misunderstanding, Maria Lluïsa's presence had weighed on his heart.

At the bar of the Hotel Colón, a few guys placed bets on the shape and number of horns the young man from Bilbao would end up wearing, with the same good humor with which they wagered three shots of London dry gin as they shook the dice cup.

———·——·——

AS BOBBY SMOKED HIS last pipe after lunch, he was hard put to understand how he could have been so foolish as to fall in love with Maria Lluïsa. Bobby smiled and wanted to put on a good front, but the truth be told his disappointment in that love affair had left him pretty crushed. The people who had supper with him at the Cercle del Liceu noticed a touch of intemperance and a bitterness they were not accustomed to. Bobby spoke of the youth of this country, and the young fledglings just starting out, with a scorn that was perhaps a bit self-serving. For him, the tone of Barcelona had become about as flimsy and flighty as it could be.

Bobby spent a lot of time at home, reading. The only things that interested him, though, were history books. Conservative and skeptical as he was, he savored the tales of the most derelict and critical periods, and the most contemptible characters, all mixed in with the smoke from his pipe.

When Bobby left the Cercle del Liceu, he liked to wander lazily through the neighborhoods of Barcelona he most loved. He would turn onto Carrer Ample and breathe in the air that drifted over from the docks. The Passatge de la Pau and the streets that led to the Plaça Reial, which in those days was called Plaça de Francesc Macià, after the current President of the Catalan government, revived in him the flavor of a Barcelona devoted to commerce and decked out in posh velvet. A Barcelona made up of dignified and thrifty people, who had an audacity and drive he didn't find in the people of his day. What's more, Bobby appreciated the capacious and seigneurial taste in everything his grandparents had done, with no pretensions to originality and without a shadow of impertinence. Those cobblestones impregnated with drugs and colonial merchandise held the breath of the sails that set out for America to seek sugar and coffee, and of those other ships that came back from the port of Liverpool freighted with cotton bales. The The gray air that clung to their wood had transmitted a polite sort of British morality to the commerce at home.

Bobby would confer with the palm trees of the Plaça Reial and the Passeig d'Isabel Segona. He didn't understand how the men of his generation had developed an antipathy toward palm trees. He thought that one of Barcelona's lovely qualities was the possibility of sustaining in its natural climate a tree of such legendary symmetry and such a gently rocking swoon as to have been the pride of the gardens of all the gentlemen of the country. To Bobby, palm trees felt like a living reminder of the lost colonies. Bobby, the skeptic, was an enthusiast for things with an elegiac air. He found a thousand flavors on the Rambles. Bobby's Barcelonism was entirely soft on the Rambles. He couldn't even be a skeptic there. He believed with all his faith that in no other city in the world was there a street as original, as alive, and as human as the Rambles of Barcelona.

The state of the Palau de la Virreina caused him some distress. He would have liked to see even a religious respect and consideration for that palace. The story of the Virreina was related to his mother's family history. Don Manuel d'Amat i Junyent, the man who built that palace, was the brother-in-law of his great-grandparents, the Comtes de Sallent, and he was related to the Castellbell and Maldà families. Bobby knew the life and miracles of el Virrei Amat, and all the tricks and energies he put into being the Viceroy of Peru. He knew about the relations the Viceroy maintained with a dancer called Micaela Villegas, whose nickname was "la Perricholi." Immortalized by Offenbach as "La Périchole," she seems to have been a dominant and extraordinarily beautiful woman. With the money he salvaged from her kisses, Viceroy Amat built the noblest house in Barcelona.

Bobby imagined La Perricholi with the eyes and skin of Maria Lluïsa. His relative, Amat, less skeptical than he, probably dragged her home to the docks of Barcelona and locked her up in that palace on the Rambla, not realizing that, in the ship that had brought her from Peru, the dancer had been unfaithful to him with a young man from Cadiz or Cartagena, experienced in the ways of women and the sea.

Though Bobby was almost always silent, when the topic of Barcelona came up he liked to show off his erudition regarding the old stones and history of our city. Bobby's ennui, his passivity and his smile were not unlike a pleasant cemetery, where at a given moment the shades of the dead would promenade bedecked in their wigs, their egoism, and their deliquescent escapades. This is why Bobby was so averse to sports, affirming that they were the most corrosive, demoralizing, and plebeian thing in this world. In the wee hours, when he carried his little moustache, glued above his lip like a bit of chlorotic brush, off to bed, he would run into troupes of hikers dressed in white – sometimes dirty white – desecrating the Rambla. Bobby was absolutely certain that the country had no chance of salvation. Sports had killed off slow-cooked and tenderly-seasoned love. Girls on the beach looked to him like androgynous animals.

The only thing that ever superficially modified Bobby's point of view was his brief relationship with Níobe Casas. When Níobe Casas moved to Paris, Bobby reverted even more to a mentality that could be captured in a meerschaum pipe with an amber stem.

At that point, it could be said that Bobby lived only for his mother. She was his only positive affection, the only person he admired a bit, and Bobby awakened every morning with fear in his heart, anticipating the catastrophe, sensing that at any moment her lungs could stop like a tired clock.

The widow Xuclà was just about to turn eighty, but her head was perfectly clear and she could still marshal some degree of energy. In those days of change and upheaval, Pilar was a grande dame who belonged more to an immovable ether than to the bubbling cauldron of the day-to-day. She managed not to take an interest in anything or to comment on any events. Her salons in the house on Carrer Ample, full of anachronisms, never breached by either the dust or the air of the street, were shining pendulums unvaryingly marking the seconds in a coffin of crystal and aromatic woods. Every morning, Pilar would have great sheaves of roses of every color delivered from the flower stands on the Rambles. The roses were the only thing that had not changed. They gave off the same perfume and the same grace that they had fifty years before. Pilar shared her life with the specters of her world, resting her arthritis on the pearl and garnet-colored sateen covering her intact sofas. Almost all the women of her time had disappeared. The Marquesa de Descatllar had been dead for three years. Lola Dussay, her sister-in-law, the Comtessa de Sallent – they were all inhabiting the land of ashes now. She almost never saw Leocàdia Lloberola, because both of them were pained by the present reality. As her forces waned, Pilar became more refined, more original, and more interesting. In Pilar's conversations, a good hunter of nuances could have found shades of green, blue, and rose that are no longer manufactured, and the formula for which has disappeared.

The person who visited Pilar most often was Hortènsia Portell. Hortènsia, much more refined than all the ladies who criticized her, recognized the worth of a true lady who had outlived an extinct fauna. Some evenings, Hortènsia would dine at the Widow Xuclà's house, and in that exceedingly severe dining room, painted the color of a Capuchin hood, with the precise accents of a silver service, Pilar and Hortènsia evoked a scenario without gas engines and polychrome bidets, smelling only of the natural fragrance of gardenias and the pomade of men's moustaches.

His eyes half-closed, affecting his usual air of ennui, Bobby let the ash of his cigar grow long, pretending not to be following the two ladies' conversation. In truth, though, he didn't miss so much as a syllable his mother uttered. He sensed that the music of Pilar's fatigued and rheumatic conversation was like a first-rate alcohol, of which extremely few drops remained, which had to be savored scrupulously and conscientiously.

One evening after dinner, Pilar felt a particular discomfort, as if someone were pressing delicately on her heart. The Widow Xuclà serenely caressed her son and gazed at him with eyes that betrayed the vicinity of death. Pilar was not mistaken; that was the annunciation of the angina pectoris that would carry her off definitively a few hours later.

Bobby acted as if it were nothing to be concerned about. The day had had to come, but he couldn't stand the thought. That night, Bobby was overcome with a weakness, an impotence, and an unhappiness that made him ashamed even to get up from his chair and look at himself in the mirror.

He escorted his mother to her bedchamber. She wanted especially to brace herself on Bobby's arm. Her memory, which was becoming cloudy, made an effort to sort out her sweetest images of herself and of that child who was now on the verge becoming an old man. Pilar held back her tears so as not to destroy a silence in which neither she nor Bobby had the stamina to say a single word. Bobby patted her twice on the cheek, and with a forced laugh advised her not to let herself be overcome by foolish apprehension.

Bobby went to his room full of dread. He wanted to believe it was for naught, that his mother was in no particular danger, and that perhaps she would still last a bit longer. Despite these reflections, Bobby sat glued to his armchair unable to open a book, waiting for he knew not what, as if he were on guard against the danger of some invisible thieves.

Bobby's skepticism and bitterness had reached a pathological moment. He would have liked for what he was sensing to make itself known all at once, because the doubts and threats seemed even worse to him. Through one of those peculiar associations that come in the night in situations of illness and enervation, as Bobby listened to the pendulums of the clocks in the hall giving off signs of life in the darkness, it seemed to him that that little ticking sound was the rhythm of his mother's pulse.

His mother's pulse! Facing the presentiment that her vital rhythms might be coming to an end forever, this man of glacial indifference and self-certainty discovered all his own insignificance. Perhaps it was then that Bobby realized he had always been tied to his mother by an invisible umbilical cord. He breathed with her lungs, and the perceptions of his retina were a reflection of the anachronic gaze and taste of that sensitive and original octogenarian. Bobby's Barcelonism, his way of living Barcelona, was nothing more than his shrouded veneration for everything that derived from Pilar. The premonition that he might lose his mother did not bring out in Bobby the natural fear and pain that in a similar situation might overwhelm a man who stands on his own two feet and has a free heart. Bobby's fear was of losing the light that gave color to his personality. With his mother's disappearance, Bobby would be nothing but a dying star, a silent lament amid a vulgar and uncomprehending hemisphere of flashing teeth and rosy cheeks.

Despite his brilliant position and his fortune, that night Bobby felt a true disgust with the very air that entered his lungs. Never before had Bobby considered worthless the vanities of the people he knew, and all the things he had seen or been informed of.

Bobby did not begrudge a dose of bitter pity to those who had ambitions or illusions of some kind, or who believed in their vocations, their work, or their creative faculties, but who, sooner or later, will have to face up to their impotence or their utter failure. He found desperately grotesque the attitude of those who think they are on the road to greatness by going into politics. Bobby took comfort in thinking that he had never done anything or even made an effort to take an interest in anything. He had invested a minimum of conflict and a minimum of criticism in things and people. He had suffered a minimum of disappointment. Never having given in to passion, never having got off the fence, he would go to the other world fairly free of resignation and regret.

Bobby didn't recall that just four or five months earlier he had practically been turned into a child by a girl who, from the outset, had set her sights upon him for purely utilitarian ends.

Bobby didn't realize that the bitterness of his thoughts simply obeyed his tainted temperament, that of a man who had always had what he wanted, and who couldn't countenance a natural misfortune such as the death of his mother.

Fatigued with dark ideas, Bobby fell asleep stretched out in his armchair and started to have a dream of the kind that appear when one's stomach is upset. He awakened with a start, wondering how long he had been sleeping. In truth, only ten minutes had gone by. Bobby made his way to his mother's room. Pilar was resting and her breathing was a bit slow. He wanted to put his hand on her forehead but he was afraid of waking her. Bobby didn't know what to do. He thought it would be too much to call for the doctor at that time of night. All in all, it was probably nothing. His mother didn't look better or worse than other nights, and Bobby began to have the feeling that both his and his mother's apprehension had been groundless. Bobby decided to go to bed, and after tossing and turning for a while, he fell asleep without a fuss. At five-thirty in the morning, his manservant rushed in to wake him. Despite his most recent reaction, Bobby was not surprised. He even had the impression that what his servant was saying was exactly what he had been dreaming at the precise moment he'd been awakened. When he entered his mother's bedroom, that thing he thought would not surprise him shocked him like an unforeseeable horror. His dead mother's skin was a color he would have been incapable of imagining. Her passing had probably taken place a couple of hours before, and it is very possible that not even she had had time to realize it, because the chambermaid who kept vigil every night outside her door hadn't heard any particular sound or a cry of any kind. Death had shown Pilar Romaní its kindest and least harrowing face.

The servants mobilized automobiles and telephones. The first to arrive was Hortènsia Portell. Hortènsia was truly moved, and it was she who dressed Pilar's cadaver with somewhat clumsy fingers. Inseparable from the yellow specter of his mother, Bobby didn't want to see anyone. Hortènsia took him by the arm to pull him away from that bleak spectacle.

Bobby kissed her hand with infinite gratitude. Only he and Hortènsia could comprehend the grace and beauty of an eighty year-old body that, as it grew colder bit by bit, was carrying with it the sublime air of a Barcelona that no longer existed.

"You are a good friend, Hortènsia, a very good friend…"

Pilar Romaní closed her eyes on a July morning. On the roof of the house on Carrer Ample the swifts and swallows screeched in pure indifference.

The stands on the Rambla were bursting with white and red roses, the very roses Pilar Romaní used to say were exactly the same as the roses of her day.

Over the Rambla hung a mingling of the odors of night dwellers, morning hikers, and democracy. The yellow taxis whisked the dregs of sadness and prostitution off to their beds.

Between the stands of red roses a gray man of indeterminate cheeks and age wobbled a bit as he walked, his stomach full of whiskey and his heart full of red roses...

July 1932

archipelago books

is a not-for-profit literary press devoted to
promoting cross-cultural exchange through innovative
classic and contemporary international literature
www.archipelagobooks.org